The Write Message

Presents

Author of Anonymous

JACKE*d*-Up

SISTAH

A NOVEL

THE WRITE MESSAGE

Karla Denise Baker

First Edition

This is a work of fiction. The characters and events in this book are fictitious. Any similarity to real persons, living or dead, is coincidental and not intended by the author.

ISBN-13: 978-0-692-83347-6
ISBN-10: 0-692-83347-1

E-mail: karlabakerd@gmail.com/karlabakerd@yahoo.com

Formatting/Editing/
Creative concept/Model: Karla Denise Baker
Photo: courtesy of Karla Denise Baker
Cover graphics: Toni: tirvolino@aol.com
Poems: 46 Knows and Jacked-Up Sistah written by Karla Denise Baker

Printed in the United States of America
10 9 8 7 6 5 4 3 2 1

Other books by Karla Denise Baker

Anonymous

Sleepin' Wit' the Virus

Kreepin' Wit' the Virus

Trickin' Wit' the Virus

Jacked-Up Sistah

Poppa

Ma'am

Ep (Epidemic)

Johnnie

Tyde aka Storyteller

Therron

Jewell

Antwone

Teka

Daisy

Xavier

Anonymous ...

This catches my attention. I turn to look their way. The darker-skinned woman wrinkles her upper lip pressing it against the bottom one.

"Positive. His results came back positive." She swallows hard.

I stare into space after hearing the woman speak. I feel sorrow and I wonder why because I don't know her, the other woman, or her son. While I am at the doctor's office I decide to have them test me for HIV/AIDS. I know there is nothing wrong with me. Yes, I have had men in my life, but the men I deal with are clean, polished, and successful. I don't mingle or socialize with deadbeats, drug-addicts or hoodlums. I have had relationships, not one-night stands. About a week and a half later I get my results back from Dr. Fulmore.

It's a Tuesday, in July. The sun shines brightly. The day is slightly humid. I receive a call from Dr. Fulmore's office at my place of employment, Bruman & Prescott Law firm in lower Manhattan. His nurse, Violet, states that the good ole' doctor needs to speak with me face-to-face. Violet's voice doesn't sound out of the ordinary, so I assume things are good.

Dr. Fulmore sits in his chocolate leather chair. His fingers are interlocked in a balled fist, and are folded on his mahogany desk. He leans forward, eyes overlooking his lenses with a blank look on his face. He seems lost... distant. I greet him with a nod and sit down sinking into the soft rust leather chair. He gives me half a smile which kinda makes his lips look like he once had a stroke. His eyes wander around the room. He extends his right hand up to his mouth and clears his throat a couple of times. I grow impatient, tapping my fingers on the arms of the chair, waiting. My eyes travel up to the off-white ceiling, and then lower to his camel colored walls with pictures of the anatomy. Slowly I move them across to his library of a thousand books, and then down to the mixed woven tweed wall-to-wall carpet of brown, beige, and rust, and then I end up at his mahogany desk.

"Avery," he pauses to scratch his throat. "Avery, I received...." He takes his gold-tone wire framed glasses off his face, pinches the inner corners of his eyes, and then places his glasses back on. He scratches his throat in between like he needs a lozenge. "...your blood work results came back." Dr. Fulmore stops speaking. There's deadness in his office, but I hear movement outside the door. He looks at me in a peculiar way that I will never forget. It's like he wants to spare my feelings and my life. I feel it. I see it in his crystal blue eyes. But I guess he realizes he can't, so he has to force the words out. His words spew out like blood from a slit wound.

"Avery, I regretfully have to advise you that you are HIV-positive." He slowly lowers his head as if I am a child who has been scolded by her mom.

I am stiff, silent, in disbelief. Then it transforms into anger. I want to walk outside of my body, leap over the desk, and strangle him until his eyes bulge out of their sockets. I am enraged and scared all at the same time. My eyes stretch wide in astonishment.

"What! Doc, there must be a mistake." In a crackling voice I say, "Dr. Fulmore, are you sure?" God I plead for him to have made a mistake.

"Yes." He dabs his taupe tanned forehead with a white handkerchief.

"How are you feeling, Avery?" he asks.

"I don't know how to feel, Doc. How am I supposed to feel?" I ask with a befuddled look on my face.

I shut my eyes tight. And in that moment of darkness I experience it again. I swallow the hard lump embedded in my throat. My skin is dank and cold. My eyes change to bloodshot red. They widen. "HE DID THIS TO ME!" My mind is full with rage. Figments of my imagination are kickboxing against him. I become numb, bewildered, and belligerent. I am like a volcano ready to erupt. Inside me combustive red-hot lava watercourses down the sides of my guts. I see bold letters highlighting "silence=death" in neon. I drop my face into the palms of my hands, and silently scream from within. Then stand, pace, and shout with my fists balled and my arms fighting the air, "the son-of-a bitch!" I massage my temples in a circular motion as tears swallow up my eyes. I sit back down astounded, hugging my skin, digging my fingernails into my upper arms cutting off my circulation. Dr. Fulmore is watching me with a teary eye. It's a preview of my HIV life unfolding.

I feel tainted blood running through my veins. Blunt forces stun me as I listen to Dr. Fulmore speak of a disease that kills the T-cells. Immune systems break down, while germs cling to invade. He explains "viral load" (how much HIV is in my bloodstream). The warmth of my blood runs cold and my faith evaporates. I'm HIV-positive. I am left speechless. I stare into space, until I realize that I am still sitting in Dr. Fulmore's office. I stand up, my body is sedated with pain, my feet are tingly and my toes crack with each step. I take baby steps to the door. I leave his office a changed woman. In my car I sob uncontrollably. I pound my hands against the steering wheel, wildly honking the horn. My hands tremble as I put the key into the ignition to travel a long, agonizing journey home.

"I write and sing about whatever I am able to understand and feel. I feel that it is healthier to look out at the world through a window than through a mirror. Otherwise, all you see is yourself and whatever is behind you."
—Bill Withers

"You can change the frame
but the picture remains the same."
—R. Kelly

"The finest teachers in the world are the Jacked-Up Sistahs in the 'hood."
—Karla Denise Baker

Author's Note: Real Talk

Ladies', the moment has come.

The moment for you to stop lying to yourselves. The moment to fess-up and see your reality. The moment to finally tell the truth. The moment to stop the pain that has been inflicted upon you. Eating at you. The moment is now.

Now is the time to remove your masks. Stop faking. Stop hiding. Stop hurting.

I'm going to share something with you all. And please do not take this out of context. By no means am I advocating violence. But what I am advocating is for you to rescue you.

It was back in the latter '80s. Before I reached my twenties. I think I was eighteen, nineteen. It happened so quickly, unexpectedly. The sensation throbbed against my face. It stung like a bee sting. It was the first time a man ever hit me. I was beyond shocked. I was bewildered as to what just happened.

By the time I reached my twenties I was a young battered woman. I had no idea of what I was enduring had a name: battered. I had no one to talk to. Turn to.

The hitting only progressed and the scenes got uglier and uglier and uglier. Then one day it got so bad that I felt paralyzed from the waist down. Still I never told.

By the time I reached my latter twenties it was imperative to be rescued. With no one to rescue me. I had to rescue myself.

I heard a noise at my bedroom door which broke me out of my light sleep. It was the jiggling of the door knob. The door was locked. Slowly I rose upright and slithered my quivering hand from under my pillow and pulled out a butcher knife that I had placed there, earlier. I knew that I had had enough. That particular morning I felt depleted. Defeated. Yet, I had made up my mind days, months prior that I wasn't going to take it anymore. I had two small children, one me. I needed them all.

Needless to say, I didn't have to use the knife. But by gripping the handle of that knife and gently running my forefinger across the sharp blade I realized how much damage had been done to me.

Avery

If I didn't know any better I'd say I am losing my "grown 'n sexy". I mean, based on society's standards I still got it. But I'm beginning to wonder if I do. Folks lie through their teeth. Women have no problem lying directly to my face.

I don't know why but when I am naked in front of my bathroom mirror "sexy" doesn't feel like the right choice of word to use.

Between the dimples in places that had no dimples. The cellulite that seemingly grew overnight. The rump that jiggles like jelly. Not to mention the midriff that obviously hasn't gotten my *drift*.

The thickness in my thighs I'd say my "grown 'n sexy" has left this here building. And it didn't even leave a forwarding address. The nerve of that heffa!

So here I am in my latter forties baffled by what or rather who stands before me. I mean, this chick is not hideous whereas I can stand the sight of her but those dark circles under her eyes isn't something I want to look at.

Looking at her in her present state makes me want to hop on my treadmill, do some bench presses, you know. Get back into kickboxing. Get my work-out on. Yes, I know I've been slacking.

No, no, no I'm not about to let myself go. And no, this has absolutely nothing to do with finding or getting a man. I know what I looked like before. Sho' life has done a number on me. But this is not "the end" result. At least not for me. I refuse to let myself go. I'm going to get my "grown 'n sexy" back.

I'll be the first to admit that I got caught-up in work. And I really wasn't paying much attention to the drastic transformation. But I'm paying close attention to it now.

All of this here woman is about to transition to not only be sexy but also a woman that ages gracefully. I don't want to look old before my time. And I definitely don't want this body all out of whack either. Which says to me that I have to make a vow to myself. Ok. Self, I vow to eat healthy, to exercise on a daily basis, to get proper sleep (while dreaming of that delicious man kissing my pinky toe), drink plenty of water (wine), and to be more positive (regardless if I do seldom get pissed off...as I know I will), to take moments out of my busy day and treat myself, and to appreciate the life that I am blessed to have, and to believe (and never stop believing) that dreams do come true. And when I'm feeling down and out to not pick up those scrumptious, moist brownies hidden in the microwave, or that jar of Cookie Butter in the cupboard or those three bags of Sriracha potato chips atop the fridge, eat an organic banana instead, then call it a night. Take my not-so-sexy-ass-but-will-be-sexy-again-self to bed.

After I accomplish my goals, then and only then will I get on that United Airlines flight to—

Oh well, why don't I stop myself right there. There is no need to talk about it. As my beloved, handsome nephew Antwone would say: "Single-Auntie, just do it!"

***

It was so long ago but a flashback of my parents having a mild discussion broke me out of my trance. It was early Sunday morning. I had to be about six or six and a half. Ma'am was standing by the sink in her faded lemon meringue housecoat with pink sponge rollers in her hair

12

towel drying the dishes from breakfast. The house lingered a scent of southern home cooking with slab bacon, cheese scrambled eggs, grits and fried potatoes.

Toast crumbs were sprawled on the center of kitchen table. An open jar of orange marmalade and a stick of melted butter drizzled along the sides of its chipped rectangular dish. Balled napkins set atop scraped and scratched-up ceramic plates stacked to be washed.

Ma'am was humming a song by Shirley Caesar. I can't recollect which one.

I was seated in the middle chair in my long nightgown Ma'am bought from the Red, White, & Blue. I was gnawing on the last strip of slab bacon wondering why Ma'am ain't make her fatback and homemade biscuits.

Poppa was seated at the far end of kitchen table dressed in his navy plaid flannel pajamas and shabby black terrycloth bathrobe, flat-foot and bare. His ashy feet were pressed in the tattered linoleum as he attentively polished his pair of dark brown church shoes.

I recall Ma'am talking in her child-like voice. She said something along the lines of: "Mista, if you expect to be heard you gotta raise your voice." It sound kind of strange hearing her say that because she was a quiet-kept woman. But on this particular Sunday, Ma'am looked tall, strong and fearless. That was the first and last time I ever saw her look so radiant.

I don't know why I'm thinking about this now but I sense it has some relevance to my own life and the choices that I'm currently making.

On this mission that I have tirelessly been journeying since my coming out gives me all the more reason to raise my voice.

Like Poppa often said: "Ain't nothin' promised. You can be here today, gone and forgotten about tomorrow."

Poppa was so right.

I don't know if I dreamt this or if God was speaking to me in my sleep. With so much to do and so very little time to do it, how can I kill two birds with one stone?

The first thing that comes to mind is social media. Folks utilize social media for dang near everything these days. I'm not looking to be a star or anyone famous. I'm looking to use social media as a microphone. A voice. As a way to raise women's voices and be heard. It feels like a win-win situation. Operative word: *feels*.

The only problem is, I don't have many women to join in this cause.

This was around the time I either dreamt or God was speaking to me in my sleep because He kept showing me images of women I've crossed paths with either in the hall or laundry room or lobby or downtown Paterson. Women living in this here building. Women outside of this city. Women I'd never think to invite into my sanctuary.

Well, it got me to thinking that if God is showing me the way who am I to go against His direction.

Johnnie? The image of him suddenly appears.

Still till this day I can vividly see him opening his arms and I walking right into love and resting my head on his chest as we slow danced to India Arie's "Ready for Love". That was such a memorable moment. Bowing my head, I miss my best friend.

***

As I stretch out on the chaise snuggled in Ma'am's old chiffon fuchsia throw many thoughts race through my head.

Leaping to my barefeet and rushing over to the kitchenette countertop I grab the personal-sized notepad and red ink pen and jot down: *Women???? What more can I do to help 'em?*

I let the thought roam around in my head. Marinade. Maybe something necessary will come to mind.

***

My neighbors: Wynona, Mama, Clarice, JoJo, Kellie-Wright, Gabriella, Glory-Bee, and this old lady on the fourth floor named Miss Murtha are some of the women I invite into my sanctuary to support the concept that I diligently brainstormed.

I am a bit skeptical in my choice of women but with limited time and a deadline of today, these ladies' will have to do.

Miss Murtha is particularly interesting to me. That old lady tries so hard to pretend to like minorities, but deep down we all know her true feelings of us. Her actions pretty much give her away.

No, I don't take too kindly to her or her way of thinking, but I figured by including her in this open forum might help her have a better understanding of black women, especially since she is *black* her damn self. Honestly, I don't know if it will change her perception, but I'm willing to at least give it a try.

I'll admit, killing Miss Murtha with kindness depletes one's energy. But for a couple of hours and two shots of Fireball Cinnamon Whisky, I think I can pull through.

Miss Murtha is very puzzling. If she has a problem with minorities (which *she* is), then why in God's name did she move in the friggin' ghetto in the first dang place? That is one question I am dying to ask her. Whether she answers the question or not is up to her.

Sometimes the issues you have with others can easily be fixed by removing yourself from the problems that one claims exist.

I personally think Miss Murtha needs to pack her bags and move to an all-white community. Since she thinks she's white. Maybe then she'll find some peace of mind and stop minding everyone else's business. Tend to her own backyard and weed out some of her black prejudice.

From the time that I have been living here I haven't heard one good thing about Miss Murtha. She has enemies upon enemies.

In this building there is a melting pot of folks and blacks do not outnumber any of 'em. But blacks do have a tendency to stand out because of the shades of their skin.

I can't say for sho' but I think Miss Murtha is still stuck back in the '50s and '60s and '70s—that Archie Bunker phase. I think she could be a nice lady, but it's just hard for her to overcome some hurtful times in her life. She got to be pushing her latter 70s. And if I'm not mistaken she never had any children. And she never remarried. She's practically alone. Well, not quite. She has cats. Like five cats living with her. Their like her babies.

You know, loneliness can make a bitter woman, especially if another woman was the cause. I think when Miss Murtha loses herself, she drinks heavily. Sloppily. That's when she acts out her pain. Start knocking on folks doors talking nonsense. Starting trouble. Making a mockery of herself. Wobbling like a drunk down the hall wishing she had someone to care, other than those damn cats of hers.

I also think another woman was Miss Murtha's cause for deep heartache. And if I'm guessing correctly, that woman must've been black. Could be the reason why she disassociates herself with black people, especially black women.

16

Miss Murtha sho' do have a filthy home along with a filthy mouth. The smell in her home alone will make you wanna vomit. I don't know why she doesn't change the cat litter on a regular basis. I had only had the displeasure of being in her apartment one time. It was during winter when she needed help taking out her air conditioner from her bedroom window. I don't know why she waited so long. I asked her why she didn't call maintenance. She gave me some lame excuse. I didn't bother to take the discussion any further. I helped her get the air conditioner out the window, and left.

Had I known how much trouble Miss Murtha causes, I probably wouldn't have helped her, but I was relatively new to the building. Hadn't even been here three months. I was raised to respect my elders. I figured she was just a sweet old lady. Boy, was I wrong. Not too many folks take to her. Actually, they can't stand her. And on certain days, when Miss Murtha reeks of booze and allows herself to be vulnerable to the outside world, I find that I can't stand her either. She puts herself in harm's way. I guess she hopes that someone will rescue her, but often no one does. We allow her to do as she damn well pleases. After all, it's her life.

When I say: "it's her life" that is when something triggers something inside me. If everyone carries that same attitude how will anything change? If women don't look out for women, how will women ever grow into helping each other in their darkest hour of need?

Something in me kept saying: "It only takes one, Avery." And that got me to thinking. Is that one, me?

Okay. Let me fess-up.

That was one of the reasons why I chose to invite her. The other reason was because I have a soft spot for Miss Murtha. Just like I do for my next-door neighbor, Mrs. Silva. Somebody gotta care for these old folks. Somebody.

Miss Murtha is getting older. She lives alone with her five cats. She doesn't have any family. And she

17

doesn't really have any friends. Just seems like a lonely life, you know. And plus, I wanted her to add some spice to our discussion. Her input could raise some brows. I figured it would be a good thing to help us get some followers. Maybe some seed money.

With the discussion being about "black women" and having a "black woman that's forgotten her blackness" expressing her views about us, (depending on what Miss Murtha says) could have some valid points that, we, as black women might not have thought of or considered or known.

Back in the day Miss Murtha used to be a schoolteacher. History, I think. That alone led me to believe that she could refresh our memory on the Jim Crow era. And maybe we could refresh her memory on the Rodney King era or seventeen year old Trayvon Martin era or twenty-five year old Freddie Gray in Baltimore with those cops era. Or, or, or... chile, there are so many I can't keep up.

But knowing Miss Murtha she'll try to talk over us. Make it seem as though what we experience as black folks has no relevance to what she'd experienced in her day. That "Black Lives Don't Matter". And that we are wasting our time trying to form unity in our own community because all blacks are doing is killing more and more black people. That lady don't have a caring bone in her body. I hope to God that that changes.

I'm more than sho' Miss Murtha's going to hit some nerves. She's not going to think before she speaks. Not Miss Murtha. She's going to blurt out whatever she wants to say. I just hope these ladies have thick skin and a conscience. 'Cause Miss Murtha has a tendency to get a bit shitty.

A little drama can't hurt but in Miss Murtha's case, it just might. Sometimes that old lady tends to go too far. She can be a bit disrespectful, too. Then she wanna call the police for every little thing she claims black folks have done to her.

Last time Miss Murtha called the police and claimed the tenant, Harold Jones on the first floor had told her that she was pregnant with a *black* baby. She liked to die. That is what Harold does to prank these old ladies. Miss Murtha was so drunk she actually believed Harold and told the police that Harold had gotten her pregnant and she wanted to press charges against his black ass and have him arrested.

We all knew Miss Murtha had some screws loose, but we didn't know to what extent. In other words, Miss Murtha, well, the old biddy is crazy as hell.

Harold told the police that he'd never touched Miss Murtha, and that he had no intensions of ever touching her. He told the police that his black dick couldn't possibly stretch from the first floor to the fourth floor. No way possible. Even though he was well-endowed he wasn't interested in boning Miss Murtha.

Harold said he'd rather go over to the Ho-Stroll (Van Houten) and buy some used coochie before he stuck his penis in her dry safari. Harold told the police that Miss Murtha was a scorned drunk mourning over the loss of her ex-husband. A man he once befriended years ago. Harold told the police that Miss Murtha was upset because he and her husband were friends. She was infuriated. She demanded her old man to respect her wishes by not mingling with black folks, but her husband disagreed. He wasn't a prejudice man and he wasn't about to become one to please Miss Murtha either. Yep. So, it's fair to assume that they had some issues in their marriage. Something till this day, Miss Murtha refuses to admit. Because if she admits it, then she has to admit that she was part of the problem.

Once Miss Murtha gets riled up ain't no stopping her. Forget about dropping F-bombs. Miss Murtha going to go for the jugular. Yep. The MFN word. Lord, I pray she doesn't do it today.

As I continue prepping in the kitchen, I ask everyone to have a seat in the living room and get reacquainted. Just because we all live in the same building does not make us friends. You know as well as I do that most women cannot get along. Especially black women. But black women are sho' good at putting up a good front, aren't they. As long as they put their best faces on and get along, honey, I'll be happy.

Wynona, Mama, Clarice and Gabriella are seated on the sectional, recliner, chaise longue just chit-chatting away.

JoJo, Kellie-Wright and Glory-Bee are seated on big, floor throw pillows I bought from Hobby Lobby the other day. They look comfy with their legs Indian-style snacking on almonds, salted shell peanuts, cashews, and pistachio nuts.

Miss Murtha is seated alone on the swivel chocolate leather chair being slightly anti-social as she nibbles on a plate of veggies with spinach dip. She's dressed in a pair of faded dungarees with an elastic waistband and a pink cotton T. She's wearing white ankle socks with sandals. Her wig looks frizzy like she stuck her finger in an electrical socket. Looks like she's having a bad hair day, even though it's not her real hair. That wig could use a washing.

Miss Murtha has the strangest look on her narrow face. I don't know if she feels uncomfortable being in a room full of black women or if she is plotting to stir-up some drama. Miss Murtha has been known to blurt out obscenities that nearly got her ass whooped.

Do you know it had to take three big, healthy women to get Tabitha John to not stomp Miss Murtha in the ground for calling her a crackhead hooker.

Just because Tabitha had on a tight-fitted mini-dress that put you in mind of the '60s and high-heeled patent leather thigh boots and sported a high afro did not make her a hooker. But Miss Murtha kept on insisting that she was.

It was later brought to my attention that Miss Murtha was once married to a police officer and her husband had cheated on her with some fine, brown-skinned chick that Tabitha happened to resemble in a cheap motel in Lodi, New Jersey.

Miss Murtha swore on everything that Tabitha was the hooker. That's one of the reasons why I didn't invite Tabitha. Plus, the fact that Miss Murtha said that all black women look alike. Hookers. I didn't want to have to call the police case Miss Murtha started running off at the mouth. You know, snapped. And Tabitha took it upon herself to whoop that old lady's ass in my living room in front of a bunch of black eyewitnesses. So I didn't invite her.

Miss Murtha is making me a bit nervous with her shifty eyes. Those black eyes of hers go from side to side as if she is thinking a little too hard, a little too much. I hope she doesn't do anything stupid when the video camera starts rolling. But knowing Miss Murtha, she just might can't help herself. She may look at this opportunity as her one moment of fame.

Kellie-Wright is introducing the ladies to her makeup line. That girl sho' knows how to boost a bootleg product.

Look at her. That caramel-coated skin of hers sho' looks like she's glowing. Gotta be that man of hers keeping her happy and satisfied.

That chile's makeup is flawless. And her hairpiece today is working for her. Normally Kellie-Wright wears her hair in a natural afro, but she has it pulled back with a colorful scarf wrapped around the front of her head looking like Savannah on the book cover of Terry McMillian's *Getting to Happy*. She has an afro-puff ponytail. Her eyebrows are arched so nicely. Shoot. I may have to have her do mine.

JoJo and Glory-Bee seem so engaged in what she's saying. Kellie-Wright is a natural when it comes to selling her "Gurrrrrrlllllllll! Git Yo' Own Cosmetics".

Kellie-Wright is good for getting pre-orders for Any Day. If you order the Any-Day package it includes: foundation, eyeliner, shadow, lip-gloss, and concealer. It's affordable for the low income woman.

I happen to be a hard sell for her because she knows how I love my Bobbi Brown. And she if can't come better than Bobbi, then we have nothing to talk about as far as makeup goes.

Faye called to let me know she is on her way. I called Blessive and invited her. She said she'd love to partake in an adult conversation about how black women treat one another. Just by the tone in her voice I can tell girlfriend is going to have a lot to say. Lord, Lord, Lord. Hopefully this cause to help women won't turn into a cat fight.

Narlena

My "bitch" status has skyrocketed.

I don't want to be labeled a bitch anymore. Especially from a man that I'm screwing.

There are certain things in my life that have to change. First, being me.

Being a desireable woman comes with a lot of setbacks. A lot of regrets. A lot of soul-searching. I really am taking inventory. My happiness will not come from a man.

Of course, I want a partner. Someone to love me through and through. Grow old with me too. But I know deep down I have to change some things about myself. I want to be a better person, better woman. Someday become wifey.

Who am I fooling? That's a bunch of bullshit I'm trying to spoon-feed myself.

Once a bitch. Always a conniving bitch.

I'm soooo *damn* angry!

Angry because I let him get through. I let him shatter my inner glass with his potency. I let him sweet-talk me right out of my panties. And we got downright nasty with it.

It took me a long, long time to build that glass wall up inside of me. A long time. But somehow he chiseled his way in. I was jonesing from first taste of him. Me. Craving him like sea salt dark chocolate. What's a woman to do with a man that has it going on, and knows it? Salivate.

Midnight.

I must have a good excuse as to why I am still wide awake. Actually, I do.

Think of my catastrophe as the: *EAT, PRAY, LOVE from a Hoodwinked Sistah.*

I'm a few days late. Could be stress throwing my cycle off. Could *be*—? I don't even know how I'm going to break the news to him...*if*— I don't even know how this happened. There must've been a hole in the latex or it must've been defective. How else can this be explained?

Stretching out my arms, I belt out a loud yawn.

This is not the first time he's been a no-show, no call. No. Try fifth. Each and everytime he has an explanation. A well thought out excuse. Nothing Oscar worthy, though.

Most of the time I have no response. It's easier that way. Keeps us from arguing over something that I feel probably won't make a difference to him anyway. He's a man that chooses to do as he damned well pleases. I don't even think he thinks about what he does to me. Probably never crosses his mind. I am human. Sometimes I wonder if he realizes that. I'm not just a fucking machine. I do have a heart.

It may or may not seem like it to him because of my hard exterior but I have to be hard to get ahead in life. With all this competition out in the world a girl has to play hard to get paid. I have expensive taste and that cannot be compromised. I will not lower my standards.

Hmm. Seems I already have with him. Had this been a couple of years ago, I would not be in this predicament. I don't know what is happening to me. There is something about him that makes me weak in the knees.

I'm too wrapped up to stop this thing we have. I don't even know what to call it anymore. Dating? Casual fling? Hooking up? It's complicated. If only—

If only I'd...stop. Truth be told, I'm too feeble for this man. Too feeble to turn my emotions off. Too feeble to walk away. Too feeble to block him out. Too feeble to stop putting up with his dumb shit. I let him have his way. Keeps the arguing to a minimum. Keeps him coming back for more—for me. With the exception of tonight, of course.

Sighing.

Dinner was supposed to be at 7:30 p.m. sharp. Sad. I'm not even worthy of a cancellation call.

Time and time again I tell myself. My *unprofessional* self, that is: "Narlena. Stupid-bitch, stop tripping over this brother. If he doesn't have the decency to call or show-up for a home cooked meal, don't sweat him. Bitch, you are too fine to be dwelling over one man. Move on. He's acting like one of 'em. One of 'em sheisty niggahs."

Agreeing with my inner *bitch* I decide to call it a night. I trash the food, place the dishes in the dishwasher, and then head up to the masterbedroom.

After undressing down to bareness, wary brown eyes gape at my reflection in the thirty width by forty height midnight mosaic design mirror mounted on the east wall.

I give my five-feet-ten-inches an once-over: soft, supple fair skin, well-endowed firm breasts, natural brunette hair, stomach flat as a pancake, ass for days on end, curves, curves, curves, in every direction. Long silky legs. Yes, I must say I have a physique similar to former runway model Tyra Banks and looks that resemble the likes of Tracey Edmonds—only prettier.

Doesn't he miss this and all that I have to offer?

I reside in the private community of Edgewater Colony. A beautiful contemporary home that has everything a girl like me could ever want. Three bedrooms, three bathrooms. Vaulted ceiling, large entry foyer, huge living room with fireplace, stunning view of the Hudson River and New York City Skyline.

I moved to Edgewater because of the community as well as the commute to New York City. It's literally a breeze for me to get to and from work.

I bought this home a year ago before meeting *DeVaughn*. That man knows how to make a woman come alive. With him I felt so young, free, and extremely sexy. Yep. It's fair to say that *DeVaughn* broke me out of my sexual shell. A freak was born!

I used to know how to keep *DeVaughn* coming back to eat dessert. But now I can't even get that man to come by and lick the batter from my cake bowl.

A part of me wants to call him. I told you I'm weak for this man, but that stubborn bitch in me won't hear of it. My shit is too good to be chasing after him. Hmm. Maybe I am getting to the point where I really don't give a damn. Please. Who am I kidding?

I sit on the plush bloody-red vanity chair and continue to gaze at myself in the mirror.

Sometimes I have to come unglued because—*DeVaughn* is driving me *fuckin'* crazy!!!! And *no*, I don't mean *DeVaughn* as in *his* name—I mean "*DeVaughn*" as in the proprietor (Blu McDowell's) piece. Must I shout it out? Okay. Blu's big black dick...*DeVaughn!*

DeVaughn and I have an amicable relationship. Blu? Well, not so much. *DeVaughn* and I are intuitive. We are sexually compatible. I enjoy *DeVaughn*. Obviously *DeVaughn* enjoys me. Do *I* overindulge in *DeVaughn*? Of course. What a dumb-ass question.

To have *DeVaughn* on a regular basis and then all of a sudden be without him really messes up my day. Toys with my mood. Plays on my emotions. Triggers withdrawals.

A-g-r-e-e-d.

It is sooooo true.

I can easily get *penis* from anyone, anywhere. But see, that is where the issue gets a bit *sticky*. I don't want just *any* stick poking around in my shit. I want *DeVaughn's*.

For the past two weeks I have been doing ridiculous things. Things I'd never think I'd do. Things like, like...embarrassing things. Things I would normally take to my grave but since I'm in the mood to share my dirty laundry I may as well come clean.

I'll get to it in a minute.

I rise to my feet and walk over to my wine fridge and pullout a bottle of Riesling and pour myself a glass. I take one sip, then return to the vanity chair.

Guess what?

A longtime girlfriend of mine from college invited me out to this popular lounge in Harlem, New York, *Dirty Treat*.

According to her, it's supposed to be the "happening" spot. Smokie said she wanted to see a friend of hers perform at the lounge tomorrow night. Said he played the sax. I'm all for a musician that can play the hell out of a saxophone.

Anyway, girlfriend even offered to pay should I not have the funds. After she said that I couldn't help it. I had to laugh out loud. I thought the gesture was nice coming from her ratchet ass. *Listen to her*, I thought, *thinking she's "Big" time.*

Hmm. I can't think of the last time a so-called friend of mine ever offered to pay for anything for me. Pay me no mind, yes, but come out of pocket...*c'mon*!

I am a bit reluctant to go because—

Well, for one I haven't seen Smokie Nicole in ages. Ugly bitches and I don't exactly see eye to eye.

Back in college, Smokie was always a good-hearted person. Not some whore trying to get her swerve on with every man that stepped her way. Not like...ah, *Avery*—.

Let me not even go there and stir that dirty piss pot. It's already all over BLAB.

People do change. But Smokie? I can't see her going out like that. She had too much emotional baggage. Low self-esteem too. First of all, Smokie was not every man's fantasy. Maybe she thought she was eye-candy. Singing boosted her confidence. And maybe her confidence was the reason as to why men were attracted to her.

Back in the day, Smokie managed to stop traffic a time or two. Smokie was not swayed. Not by a long shot. The chick was gifted. And she knew it. She always said that eventually she'd get picked up by a record label. Who knows? Maybe record producer Clive Davis would discover her.

It's not really about Smokie, though. Although, it would be nice to hear her sang. That's right...*sang*. Oh, the girl can blow. She has some pipes on her. I always said she'd be the next "Lady Tee," "Ivory Queen of Soul" ... Teena Marie. Just four shades darker. Size two frame. Small waist. Small breasts. Skinny long legs. She stood about five foot two inches tall. Built straight up and down with a little booty. Her butt was small enough to fit in the palm of my hands. That's how small it was. Although, men, they seemed to like her little ass and slim frame. She wore her hair nappy, said she was staying true to her roots. Men, they seemed to like her nappy head mainly because they accepted her and focused on her personality. Smokie had a great personality. She was down-to-earth. Sweet girl.

Personally, I didn't very much care for the ugly bitch. I don't think Smokie knew her full potential. If I had lungs like that—

Smokie always had that natural ability to make a brother stutter and sweat. Half the time all Smokie had to do was open her mouth and sang. And men, they would be drooling all over her. She had that natural look. You know, that Tracy Chapman rolled into Grace Jones rolled into Macy Gray...kind of sistah.

Back in the day, Smokie intimidated a lot of females. Not purposely. For her to be unattractive but gifted a lot of chicks disliked her. She could still pull men in and most of the girls on campus just couldn't compete with her because she was talented and just being herself.

I, on the other hand, was never intimidated by Smokie. I didn't give a shit about her growing up in east Brooklyn, Brownsville. She applied herself in school and managed to get a scholarship. Lucky her. The fact that all her mother could afford was the projects and how all she wanted to do was make her mother proud by getting a college degree and moving them to a safer neighborhood was sweet, but not my concern. With her mom working three jobs to provide for her and her oldest brother that suffered from Autism, she had a lot to overcome. Her dad was incarcentrated. Had been for some time. Regardless of her unfortunate upbringing I felt no empathy for her. Her sob story was nothing that I hadn't heard before.

Smokie often talked about music going to be her ticket out of that hellhole. That she was going to one day make it big and buy her mom a big house and car and they would travel to different countries and see the world. Smokie was a dreamer.

Dreamer or not. Smokie couldn't compete with all that I had to offer. I was beauty, brains, and yes, I was fortunate where I wasn't raised in the projects. I was blessed with more opportunities than her. I got a scholarship for college, too. I pretty much got whatever I wanted. Especially when it came to a man. I knew how to make grown men come back for more. My powerful punany was serious. And so was I. I was serious about making it to the big league, while Smokie was still dreaming. She was always a dreamer. Sangin' those bluesy songs with a nappy ass head.

I remember when she attempted to write this song. We were feeling good that night and just horse playing around. You know, laughing and joking about nothing, really.

But when I heard Smokie sangin' the song, I blurted out, "What the fuck was that?!" and you know that caused some bad vibes between us. E-x-a-c-t-l-y.

Women are sensitive. And maybe I did hit a soft spot when criticizing her song. Perhaps I should've encouraged her more. But I didn't. The song was that bad. So bad that I never forgot it. It's one of those things that kind of sticks in your head. That's when I knew Smokie probably wouldn't make it. Possibly she just wasn't good enough. She needed a hook and sangin' a song like that was not going to turn any heads. Not to sign a record deal. That was some (1926) Ma Rainey "Trust No Man" blues. Nobody wanted to hear that old shit.

It's been years since I've seen her but we recently communicated through Facebook, Twitter. That's when she invited me out. Said she was performing at *Dirty Treat*, too.

Next Sunday she said she's performing at The Village Underground, the following Saturday at Blues Lounge, and the following Saturday and Sunday's at Smoke Jazz & Supper, and Paris Blues Jazz Club and the Apollo.

According to Smokie, any exposure is better than no exposure. She also mentioned something about auditioning for *The Voice*.

Now, that would give me a reason to go out of my way to interview her for BLAB. Really give her some exposure. But...right now, Smokie is small time. And "Narlena Scott" does NOT do small time.

The thought of sitting in a smoke-free lounge filled with an assortment of men is NOT really what I had in mind for Friday evening.

Actually, I made no plans. I am hoping that plans will be made for me—for us to spend some quality time together but as I've said *he* has yet to call or show-up.

***

Just the other day I had gotten lost and found myself cruising through the streets of Paterson, New Jersey. I was heading back to New York and inadvertently made a wrong turn. I knew I should've used my GPS, but I didn't think I'd get lost.

The vibe of the streets seemed overwhelmingly low-spirited. A lot different from New York City. I thought to stop by my man's house but figured he'd call me later. Plus, I had a meeting. I had to get back to work.

It was midday Thursday, and to see so many black men just standing around—moping, smoking cigarettes and/or weed and drinking cheap wine and/or beer was somewhat of a turn-off for me. I understood that the job market was very challenging, but these brothers didn't seem too eager to find a job. There was nothing *sexy* about a man holding up a wall. Standing in front of a liquor store and/or Chinese takeout begging a *woman* for a quarter, fifty cents, or dollar.

The sistahs that stood on the corners looked as if they had lost their femininity. Most were in desperate need of a comb, some teeth, others a shower. Sistahs looked emaciated. Yes, they were looking hard, hungry, nappy, and very unhappy.

To distract myself from gawking at those dried-up wilting bitches, I turned up the volume to the radio. I motioned my body to Drake's (feat. Rihanna) new hook "Too Good" while I cruised up the street.

When I got to East Eightieth Street and looked toward my right. There was this young, (damned near butt ass naked, matted weave wearing) sistah showcasing all of her *bad* news—obviously trying to sell herself during the midday hour. I scrunched up my nose and put the stank-face on because she looked like she stunk. *Eew*!

As I got further up the street, I idled at a traffic light on Madison Ave. White BMW sparkling under the bright blue skies. I turned to my left and as I did I stopped dancing. Just paused. Face was flushed. My body heated up and my adrenaline was pumped. It was like I transformed into this "territorial" bitch. Me? What the fuck!

I ogled out the driver's side window. I could've sworn I saw *his* silver Mercedes. Or, shall I say, *a* silver Mercedes that surely looked identical to *his* parked in the McDonald's parking lot. I squinted my eyes and saw that someone was seated in the driver's seat.

As the traffic light turned green I swerved into oncoming traffic like some crazed chick only to see if it was indeed him behind the steering wheel. Only to find that it wasn't him. It was a fat Puerto Rican chick. That somewhat annoyed me. I wanted to catch him in the act. Give me a reason to act a damn fool. No. That wasn't it. I wanted it to be him. And I wanted us to get into an argument. And I wanted him to come over and *stroke* me. But—

From block to block I found myself eyeing every tall, dark, bald, black man that resembled *him*. Do you know how many tall, dark, bald, black men exist in this city, alone? A lot.

I saw someone that looked like him and I immediately slammed on the brakes, jumped out of my car like I was strung out on crack. I had to catch myself. Pull myself back. I had a "Jazmine Sullivan" moment. And yes, the thought of busting his window did cross my mind.

Having come to. I slowly eased my *fine* self back in my car and drove off as if it wasn't me. But it was me. I felt incredibly foolish. My need to get high was getting the best of me.

I have ~~never~~ gone out of my way to hunt down a man that I was grooving. Never. And to start on some dumb shit now is just not me. I don't do shit like that. What was I hoping to find? I wasn't hoping to find anything.

Okay. I'm lying.

I was hoping I *didn't* find anything that I wasn't prepared to handle. But then I came across yet another silver Mercedes that surely looked similar to his.

As I got closer to it I saw that the license plate read: 322BLU. Not 321BLU, which was a big relief. I mean, all I could think about was seeing his car parked on a side street, in someone's driveway, or worse, just leaving the scene of an unknown residence after sharing "*DeVaughn*" with an unknown woman. Just the thought had my stomach in a bundle of knots.

I need to take it down. Clear my head. Breathe. But my thoughts are all over the place. Wondering. Speculating. Hating on bitches.

With wine glass in hand I gulp down the last drop of white wine and stare in the vanity mirror with a grimace on my face.

The wine has taken effect because I wonder to myself, *when did this beautiful woman suddenly become so insecure?*

I am furious with myself. I let me down. And I have no problem admitting this behind closed doors, of course.

A part of me wants to climb in bed and bawl, but I'm too strong for that shit today. It's Wednesday. Hump Day. Normally I'd have my ass mid-air waiting for him to come *kiss* it. Pucker up.

I refuse to give him the satisfaction of knowing that *I* miss him deeply. I refuse to pick up the phone and call him. Bad enough *I* am thinking about him. Talking about him. Wishing, wanting him to be between my thighs, tasting my blues. *I* refuse to allow myself to become weaker because of his melodrama. *I* refuse.

I'll admit I've caved several times for this man. And each and every time he gives me nothing but a handful of unnecessary crap to deal with.

Sometimes my cookie does get hot. Hot and super-duper wet. And sometimes I do need a tune-up every now and again. He gives me exactly what the body needs.

Good dick. But what about the rest of me? My mind? My heart? My spirit? My ambitions. Why doesn't he feed 'em like he feeds my pussy? Blu sure knows how to disappoint.

Okay. I'm fine as wine, but there is more to me. More than he seems to *know* or want to *know* or care to *know*. This is where the problem lies. We are *not* on the same page.

You see, I have a major problem with a man that cannot be discreet. I don't want a man (I'm dealing with) to share intimate details about our sex life with other men. It's soooo disrespectful to me. Sooo grammar school.

Do men think that that's wrong? I mean, suppose they later develop feelings for the same woman they "slut shamed"? I guess men don't think about that, do they?

I was *never* the type of woman to allow her mind to be influenced by a man, other than by my dad. I was *never* the type of woman to lead with my heart. My Dad taught me that when I was a pre-teen. Dad said, *"Lena, allow the right man to earn you. Know your worth and eventually he will too."*

I can honestly say that I had a good upbringing. I never wanted for anything. And no, I was not born with a silver-spoon in my mouth. Mom was a unit clerk for University Hospital in Newark, New Jersey, up till her retirement. And dad worked as a property manager for a complex in Bayonne, New Jersey. He also sold affordable life insurance policies. He felt that Black people failed to acknowledge the importance of having life insurance to take the burden off of their loved one. Dad was dedicated to getting low-income families to purchase small policies. My parents were intelligent, hardworking people. Their smarts and work ethic was instilled in me to work hard too.

After college, after landing my dream job, after working my way up to where I am now, material things didn't seem as important simply because I bought myself pretty much everything I've ever wanted. Being single and available to any man that took an interest in me didn't seem as important either simply because every man I've ever wanted seemed to want me, but things never amounted to much. It was merely physical. Sex. But even the physical got challenging. After a while I just stopped searching and settled for what I could get, when I could get it.

Getting a man was sooooo easy. Keeping him, well, that was another story. I don't consider myself complex. But I am a serious individual. I don't take things too lightly. I'm very dedicated to my work. And anything other than that is a pastime for me. Being an independent, black woman on the rise is all I ever dreamed of becoming. *Men* or *a man* never seemed as important as my career.

If only I'd listened to Dad's advice. If only I'd protected my heart. No. It wasn't supposed to matter. It was just two grown adults having fun. Hooking up. I wasn't supposed to care. Catch feelings. But it happened. And here I sit bewildered, highly disappointed, feeling used.

No doubt I got comfortable having him around. He is the *only* man I am currently seeing on the regular. I stopped playing the field because it got boring. Redundant. Predictable.

Dating no longer excited me. But with him, he always excites me. He knows exactly what to do, what to say, how to say it, and how it will make me feel when he says it. He always knows like he is in my head. Reading my thoughts. I never utter a word. Not one solitary word.

When we first started hooking up there *was* never a day when he had me feeling less-than. He put me high on the pedestal. That crafty, confident bastard reeled me in. Oh, so cleverly too.

With my index finger and thumb I reach in the solid white box of Kleenex next to the array of fancy bottles of expensive perfumes and pullout a thin sheet.

I cover my nose with the tissue, inhale the faint fragrance of aloe, and then blow sounding like a bullhorn. Crumpling the tissue with my fingers, then discarding of it in the small waste basket alongside the glass vanity table.

Reaching for another sheet of tissue I gently dab about my teary eyes, damp cheeks, and chin as I think about him; and the way he talks at *me*, lies to *me*, and so unfeelingly too. Obviously he takes *me* for granted.

Tension. I feel a whole lot of tension building inside me. Migraine coming on, too.

I was never one to pop pills but lately that's all I seem to be doing. Excedrin. It does the trick. If I'd just let go. Move on. Find another playmate I wouldn't be dealing with this shit. But I am. Is he worth the constant headaches? Honestly, do I *really* need to answer that? If I want to keep it real with myself. Yes, I do need to answer that. Not now.

Sniffling. Dabbing the tissue about my eyes to catch the tears that fall.

Still gaping at myself in the mirror, parting my moist lips, I whisper under my breath, "Why am I so fuckin' needy? So unlucky?" while simultaneously hearing his week old words ring in my ears: *"I fucked YOU with that fuckin' condom!"*

Yeah, ok. You're absolutely right, *Mr. Blu McDowell*. You did more than just *fuck* me. You seduced my mind with your good dick. Okay. I'm not exactly putting the blame on me. Not exactly. If anything I'm pushing the blame every which way but where it needs to be. With me. He seduced me sooooooo well. This is the end result, huh? I'm home. *Where are you, Blu? Where the fuck are you? And who are you sticking "DeVaughn" in this time?*

Last week we had a heated, heated argument. I've never felt so down before. So low. That argument really took its toll on me. His tone was deep and strong, but unconvincing. I knew. I knew in the pit of my stomach that he had explored *other* pussies. I heard through the grapevine of how he passed himself around. Of how *available* he made himself. And I disregarded all the gossipy rumors. Yep. Even though I smelled it on his breath and tasted the fishy residue on his lips and tongue. I never uttered a word.

Many, many times I just ignored it because *in my mind* none of those skanks compared to me. Overconfident, I presume. I just couldn't see it. But then reality put me in check while I sat back in my office, square tips tapping the desk, mind deep in thought. Something came to me.

I couldn't consider it *cheating* if the discussion of us being "exclusive" had never been talked about. Blu was free. And so was I.

If he's not with me I knew without a shadow of doubt that he was with someone. Yep. A woman. And as much as it hurts to think about, to hear myself say, I know it's true. Yet, for some *pathetic* reason I still allow him entry into my *home*, my *bed*, and now my *heart*.

With the demands of my position as Editor-in-Chief of BLAB, Blu has no idea of my responsibilities. *I* am in charge of creating editoral boards and overseeing all department editors; I have *final* say on what gets published and also serves as the publications representative at social functions, which means there is some travel required; developing budgets for the departments; manage all the day-to-day operations; overseeing all of the assistant, or department, editors to ensure our issues are released on time; responsible for hiring, especially of the assistant editors; assistant editors and I create the editoral board for each of the publication's editions or issues; *I* review all articles and photographs for accuracy as well as potential vilification

37

or slander, and provide ideas, if needed, about any changes to make before the publication goes to print; layouts and designs are approved by me; *I* have the *final* word about which stories and photos get published; attend regular meetings with the publication board to discuss issues, plans, and other business relating to the publication; drawing up budgets proposals and other information requested; create ideas for new way of doing things, such as technology, executing ways to increase readership, utilize new media; tough problems are handled by me as well advice about editorial issues.

With all of this on my shoulders I'd say my time is *very* limited. And still I try to provide some time for him. And yes, quite often I have to pencil in *DeVaughn*, and remember that I had. But I always make up for it in some way.

In the beginning, Blu claimed he understood if a date slipped my mind. We happily made-up. And it was everything a busy professional woman would want from her man. No squabbles. No pressure. Everything seemed to work out. We made the best out of the time *I* made available.

It was mesmeric to meet a man that was okay with a woman in high demand. He seemed willing to appease. That only intrigued me. Plus, I was enticed by him and his good looks. And, of course, what he was packing down below sure did come in handy, especially on those days when I felt like pulling my own hair out during those long meetings. Instead, he did the pulling for me. And sucked on the toes, too. I have to admit, I l-o-v-e-d it! Absolutely loved every moment we shared together. Blu seemed to fit in my life. And *in my mind*, that alone meant so much to me because my ex Morgan couldn't handle me. Couldn't deal with my fast-paced lifestyle. And neither could Roger or Kendrick or Sean. Neither could Billy or Michael or Peter or John or David or Deron or Thomas or Charles. They all seemed to run in the same circles of: *"Narlena, I never see you. And when*

I do you seem preoccupied. Work is always on your mind. I don't fit in your life. I don't see how this can work."

Oh yeah, I remember those days. Those men. As fine as they were, they were needy. Needing me to stop what I was doing to do to meet their needs—satisfy their sexual appetites. If he wasn't willing to get it and go. That was not my problem. I just couldn't bend with synchronizing our time for "getting-to-know-you" purposes. I wasn't ready to give of myself, my heart, my soul, blah blah blah.

Eventually I understood where they were coming from. I don't think they understood me. Most of them were well-off. I guessed they just assumed that once they got me that I'd be willing to be at their beck and call. That I would be the *perfect* wife and bear their *perfect* children. Be a stay-at-home mom. *Me?* Not!

I have a career that depends on me. Men? They come in numbers. One walks out, another walks in. Simple.

That's how I use to feel. Actually, back then, I had no feelings. Nor did I show any feelings. I was a rock. Look at me now. I'm an utter mess. Things are not simple. It's not simple when you find yourself thinking and dreaming and wishing for that someone you never thought would be that someone you'd want. Someone you'd want to spend the rest of your waking days with.

Deep breath.

Warm fingertips massage in a circular motion about my eyes. I stare in the vanity mirror. Red puffy eyes stare back at me.

Have I confused lust with love? And if I have, how and exactly when did I do this to myself? Do I consider him my "everything"? Am I being foolish? Is he the "right" man for me? And, if so, what is it? What is it about him that makes me think he is so right for me? What the hell is it?

39

Freshly manicured fingers rake through my thick hair. The insatiable fragrance of rosemary shampoo lingers on my fingers, and in the air.

Sighing.

Who the hell am I? R-Really? Am I this woman so desperate for lust in her life? Have I conjured all of this love shit up in my head, my heart, because age is catching up with me? Forty-something is far from old.

Okay. OKAY. I am emotionally attached to someone that does not feel the same for me. He doesn't look at me as "marriage material" nor "girlfriend" for that matter. And when he does look at me, often I wonder what he sees. Most of the time we don't have eye to eye contact unless I am on my back staring up at him looking down at me with those empty eyes of his. Asking myself and him, do you love me?

How did I let things get this far? That's a good question. *Why did I allow things to get this far?* That's an even better question. But the most important question is: *Am I in love?*

Wow. I don't know. I think so. I-I really don't know simply because most of the time when we are together it doesn't feel like we're together. I mean, physically, yes, we are both *naked*. But often I feel *naked* even with clothes on around him. It's like, that's all he sees when looking at me. My ass mid-air. My mouth suckling on his long, hard dick. Cunt wet as tears. Nothing more. Nothing deeper than that.

I have strong feelings. Stronger for him than any other man I've ever screwed.

Believe you me, I tried to keep some balance, some space, that *"you-do-you"* and *"I-do-me"* between us. Not seeing him every day I thought would make both of our hearts grow fonder. I thought. But I find that some men know how to shut their emotions off. Women? We have a tendency to turn up the volume to a love ballad as if that '78 Bobby Caldwell blue-eyed soul-styled single "What You Won't Do For Love" was going to somehow change

40

how men feel for us. Somehow make him feel a need—a want for me.

I was too busy listening with a keen ear to the pitter-patter inside myself. Instead of listening to him, and his truth. It saddens me, just a little.

Evidently I got caught-up in that bad girl drawn to bad boy fixation. Shit happens. Women? I know they look at me as this wicked bitch that doesn't have a sensitive bone in her body. If only those bitches knew how sensitive I really am. I break just like anyone else. Bleed just like anyone else. Only I do it behind closed doors. Pick myself up and strut to Tiffany & Co., and treat myself to a diamond tennis bracelet and continue on with life as if nothing matters. No cares. No worries. Bullshit. Everything matters. Everything when it comes to matters of the heart.

I know what happened to me is that I let my pussy-slash-career consume me. Make me into who *I* am. But when the lights are turned off and I sit in the quiet of night, alone. I'm just an ordinary woman yearning for what any other woman yearns. A good man. A worthy man. And lots of foreplay and phenomenal sex.

Sometimes I shock myself by being so damn blunt. No need to lie to myself anymore. No need to pretend behind closed doors of what my heart truly desires. Marriage? Children? Old age with my soul mate? Yep. Those thoughts do travel strongly through my mind, but then reality sets in and they derail leaving me back where I started. Waiting and wanting for that someone that doesn't want me to be lying beside me. Filling this empty space of coldness.

Country

One day something hit me hard. Hit me wayyyy below my understanding.

Peoples.

Peoples disguise 'emselves every day. Hmm. It's funny now that I think back. Funny, um, 'cause I never saw myself as someone who hid behind walls, windows, and locked doors. It never occurred to me that I was disguising the truth with fake smiles, fake laughter, and fake happiness.

Honeychile...I realized mo' about myself than I cared to really knows.

Me. Country Billow-Martinez.

Standing at five feet four inches tall, cashew-colored complexion, brown eyes, and gray roots of thick brown hair plaited under an Aunt Jemima scarf for practically a decade or mo'—sounds like a homely sistah, don't it? That's 'cause I is.

This homely sistah... fooled... me. And I was so good at it, too. Uh-huh. Until one day—

One day the *truth* knocked me down to my knees. Chile, that *pain* was so severe. Truth hurt mo'.

That wintry December mornin' I sat down at the wooden kitchen table with my diary my mother had given me. Herberto had drank himself to sleep.

In the silence I wrote down my thoughts as best I could. Misery sho' was speakin' that mornin'.

My words spit out. Like they's was waitin' for that moment. That moment to just free themselves.

I took several breathes. Feeling the words as if they was "his hands" and I shook with each word I wrote, 'cause the thinking was so intense in my head. So actual on my woman.

I wasn't foolin' nobody, but me. Every day. Others probably saw but no one said nothin'. They let me play possum.

I was soooo deeply in love with a man that I assumed loved me just the same. I was a joke. But nothin' was funny. Nobody was laughin', but me.

I traded so many times. Agreed on things I never wanted to do, but did. I smiled on cue. Gave mo' than I got.

Ursula

The silence is just as bad as telling him a lie to his face. At least *I* think so.

Torrid.

The store has been buzzing since the time I opened till noon. Big women want to look trendy, sophiscated and sexy too. Once I get the line down to one customer I have Gigi, the salesassociate take over while I go on my lunch break.

While nooking my Weight-Watchers cheesy meat lasagna in the RCA microwave my mind drifts to a conversation I once had with my best friend in the whole wide world. Country.

Country said, "*Ursula, honest peoples lie.*" I don't know why she said it, but she did. And I-I pondered over it for weeks.

You know, huh, I'd realized that Country's wisdom held some truth. *Honest people do lie.* Honestly, I feel that *I* am one of those peoples she was talkin' about. No, I haven't been lying to myself. Or *maybe* I have. I know I've been lying to my man by not saying what is truly on my heart.

Woolridge stature is solidness. I love a man with some meat on his bones. A meaty woman like myself. You betcha. Woolridge is not sloppy flabby fat. He just solid and soft. Feel like cushion when I snuggle up with him and all of his manhood.

Woolridge is a good, good man. We have great communication. Talk about just about anything. That man works himself sick to give me the finer things in life. Great big home, nice and roomy two car garage, finest furniture money can buy, hot tub, patio deck, masterbedroom and masterbathroom, and gazebo, and expensive African art, 2015 Jaguar XJ. He gives me the world. The world. And I'm so thankful for him. I am blessed to have him. Blessed. Truly blessed.

Just recently, maybe three weeks ago, Woolridge took me to this fancy restaurant here in Charlotte called Swanky-Dankly. The place was gorgeous. Elegant. A lot of the uppity black folks tend to go there. The ambiance was very romantic. It was the perfect setting for couples madly in love.

We sat across from each other. I was dressed in a white spaghetti strapped dress with a plunging neckline showing off my big girls. Oh, they were perky in that sexy dress. Woolridge, he loved it. Couldn't take his eyes off of me. I felt so sexy in my skin, you know. Big and Black and Beautiful and Sexy.

Woolridge had on a nice white suit. Oh, he was looking debonair, if I must say so. My man was looking good!

For him to be a big-boned man, that suit was tailored cut to fit him to the tee. We looked like the perfect, loving couple dressed to kill.

It was a beautiful, sunny June day. Woolridge did the unexpected on that day. My man, in front of everyone in that restaurant got on one knee—as big as he is. His six foot self was on one knee. I couldn't believe it. I even got teary-eyed.

I was so moved by his courage. Even more so, when I had to look into his dark brown eyes as he'd said, "Ursula, baby, it took me a long time to find a woman like you. Long time." Then he asked with tear-filled eyes, "Would you do me the honor of marrying me?"

With everything in me, I so wanted to say yes. But there was no way that I could. And yes, I looked at what was before me. This man was heaven-sent. So I-I took my time, found my words, and shook my head from side to side and simply said, "No. No, Woolridge. I *won't* marry you."

Chapter
One

Avery

Sometimes I feel like I haven't moved any mountains. Folks say, nothing worth having comes easy.

I do respect and appreciate the patience and understanding along with the encouragement and kind words from Dr. Cristal during my sessions. It means a great deal coming from her—a psychologist and all.

I walk into the office for what feels like my hundredth time. Gretchen, the administrative assistant, is seated at her desk on the telephone. I wave to say hi. She nods her head in acknowledgement as I have a seat.

Gretchen changed her hairstyle from Halle to Marley. I can't tell if they are real dreads or extensions but it suits her.

Today is supposed to be an important day for me. A breakthrough as Dr. Cristal says. We'll see.

After ten minutes of waiting Dr. Cristal's door opens.

"Avery," she calls out.

I stand and greet her with a smile, then step into her office.

She doesn't give me much time to get comfortable. Immediately she starts to grill me. "Did you remember to bring them as I had asked?" Dr. Christine Cristal says as she stands tall behind the onyx desk and gazes at me with those gumball eyes of hers.

I wonder, is she any kin to Tracee Ellis Ross? What big eyes *they* have.

I nod my head as my deep-set brown eyes shift. Already I feel on edge. Disinclined. What does she expect me to say, exactly? Just the thought disturbs me tremendously.

Setting my attention toward the fresh paint of pale green walls. The color is inviting. Soothing.

Alongside the entrance is a tripod plant stand with two spider plants in it. To the left of it is the plush red sofa with new velour multi-colored stripe and pattern throw pillows.

Reclining back on the sofa. I adjust my white denim capris in the crotch area and straighten out my white tank top so that my midriff is not exposed. A few pounds can make a once sexy woman feel a bit self-conscious.

A headful of nappy natural coils of more salt than pepper sink into one of the velour throw pillows. Last week I was thinking of letting it grow out for the summer. Rock a new look. Maybe a kinky 'fro. Or, just shave it bald like an African beauty.

Dr. Cristal ambles over to where I am and sits on the buttercream leather loveseat directly across from me with notepad, felt-tip black pen, and manila folder with an affix white label that reads in bold capital letters: AVERY LOVE in hand.

I must say, Dr. Cristal looks spiffy dressed in a navy and optic white dress that fits her curves very nicely and embroidered pointed toe navy and white pumps.

The dress really complements her dark skin tone. And with her hair now shoulder-length with loose curls— she looks years younger. I see she hasn't changed her taste in lipstick, though—still blackberry.

Dr. Cristal opens the manila folder, studies a few lines, then closes it and sets it on the cherrywood endtable.

I stare up at the ceiling counting every second of this session. Praying for it to hurry up and be over with.

To break my train of thought, Dr. Cristal says, "I see major improvements and growth in you, Avery." Her words sound so exuberant. She continues, "I still remember the first time you stepped foot in my office. You've blossomed into this confident woman. A woman you used to say you lost touch with. You've come so far. Are you ready to begin?"

I swallow the glob of spit that has formed in my mouth. Beads of sweat have already multiplied on my forehead. Nervous? A bit.

In my hand I unfold the first piece of handwritten lined paper and smooth it out. Reaching in my black Manhattan Portage backpack for my reading glasses. I place 'em on, then swallow hard.

The thought of me doing this seems rather useless but Dr. Cristal assured me that it would benefit my recovery. I am still a bit reluctant. Not sho' if I'm setting myself up for failure. I mean, how can this really benefit me, huh? I guess she knows best.

"Anytime you're ready," she says.

My body is a sweltering hotbox. I feel lightheaded too. Jitters. That is all it is. Just my nerves.

"Remember I'm here, but don't rely on me. I want you to relax and think of a tranquil place you'd be reading this letter aloud. A place that gives you comfort. Freedom. Take your time."

I nod.

Within seconds the tranquil place appears in my head. There I am standing on the stage of Anonymous. I feel so free, so capable, and so fearless. The place is empty. The ambiance, the lives that used to reside on this stage bring forth a feeling—I feel at home.

I get tongue-tied saying the first words, *"D-De R-Ra..."* Taking a deep breath I slowly sound the words out, *"D-De-Dear R-Ra-Rapist,"* and as I do something takes ahold of me. Something calming. It let's me know that my words won't harm me, hurt me. That my words will reinforce me. Free me.

I sit upright on the sofa and stare at the words as if it is the first time I laid eyes on 'em. As if I didn't author 'em.

Exhale. Inhale. Exhale.

"Dear Rapist,

"I know this letter must come as a surprise. Well, this is the very day, eight years ago that I read a letter from my dearest friend expressing his love for me. And on this very day I am going to express my feelings toward you.

"Today I feel empowered. Inspired. Strong in my pursuit. Strong enough to write this long awaited letter to you. I'm kind of disappointed that this letter will never be mailed, and the thought of writing it to you really pisses me the fuck off, but I have to find closure any way I can. Right now, I really don't care how much I hurt or how much energy it takes out of me or how much time it takes to put my pain on paper because I'm not writing this letter just for you.

"I'm writing this letter to all women who have been raped and cannot find the will to address their rapist through a letter such as this.

"I'm sho' you haven't forgotten about me. Seeing how you abruptly entered my life. Lord knows I haven't forgotten about you. Or, what you've done to me. It takes time to accept, to deal with and heal from the pain that you inflicted upon me. Motherfucker you changed my life.

"Please. Please. Don't insult my intelligence by claiming that it wasn't YOU! Be the bigger asshole and

admit what you did. Own it. Don't coward out now. I mean, after all these years it seems rather absurd, don't you think?

"*If my memory serves me correctly it was a nippy evening in January. The 9th of 2000, to be exact. That ill-fated day...you turned my whole world completely upside down.*

"*I remember it as if it were yesterday. Can't get it out of my mind if I tried. Can't get you out of my system. I've cried a thousand tears and nothing anyone says or does can change the life that you chose for me. I don't know why you did what you did to me. I don't understand why you chose me. I don't know what occurred in your life to make you just take it upon yourself to force yourself on a total stranger. I don't know how many times you've done this to some innocent girl or woman, but I do know that you need to get some serious help.*

"*Do you remember the day? I do.*

"*There I was strutting, dressed in a pinstriped navy skirt suit, heather-gray silk blouse, and four inch Stuart Weitzman high-heeled pumps with briefcase in tow.*

"*Turning the volume of the city down, I can literally hear the clicking of my high-heeled shoes on the hard concrete. Click. Clank. Click. I remember feeling a bit lethargic. I had had a long day at work. That day I was inundated with case after case after case. I loved my job! My career, I should say.*

"*I was heading toward the parking lot on West Broadway to get my car. Black. Ford Five Hundred. Then head over to Montclair (Villa of Locks) to my hairstylist Aja. She was awaiting my arrival. That day I was so looking forward to getting pampered. Get my hair washed, conditioned, trimmed and styled. Yep. Maybe grab a bite to eat at Crockett's Fish Fry. Maybe treat myself to fresh fried whiting, macaroni and cheese with a side order of collard greens. Or, possibly grab a bottle*

of Beringer 2000 Chardonnay and walk down
Bloomfield Ave to Indigo Smoke unwind and listen to
the jazz band they have featured, then head home to my
quiet apartment. Soak that mental tiredness in a
soothing bath of Calgon milk while de-stressing to the
melody of James Blunt's "Goodbye My Lover" sweeping
me away as I sip off a stem glass of crisp white wine.
Then slip into a sexy, silk purple nightie, and engross in
a good read. Retire to bed. Awaken to a brand new day.
But all of that was a thought. Because the reality of my
fate didn't go as planned. You raped me.

"I remember the feel of you. Your stench. Your
raspy husky voice, but nothing connects me to who you
are.

"Is it possible that we met, prior? Had we crossed
paths? Regret? Oh, I have a lot of regret. Remorse. Anger,
too.

"Why didn't I listen to the Rape/HIV Counselor?
Why didn't I do the rape test kit? Why did I shower away
the evidence? STUPID!!!!!! No. I wasn't stupid. I was
RAPED!

"I was dragged like a Persian rug and RAPED.

"You! A total stranger put your nasty stuff in me!
You put your dirty dick in me and screwed my life up!
And it numbed me. It hurt so much that I couldn't stand
the sight of my own self. Yes. I loathed me. I can finally
admit that I hated me. Me. Because of what you did to
me.

"Today, I don't want to keep harboring over
something that can't be changed for the rest of my life.
But being raped is not like a common cold. It is not
something that just goes away.

"A woman who has been sexually assaulted
always remembers: the month, the day, the year, as if
she'd just gotten married. Wedding anniversary.
Birthday. Death of a loved one. The date is embedded in
her head and pussy, forever. Like giving birth to a
firstborn. It takes an overwhelming amount of: patience,

51

understanding and acceptance to come to terms with what happened to her, me. It takes strength and courage to speak about it in front of a group of folks, strangers. It even takes a woman who has been raped years of therapy, especially when the weight of it is too heavy to deal with alone.

"With you not captured, with no news footage, no article in the local newspaper, no trial, no name, no face, with NOTHING!—my attack is pretty much still an open book. There is still no closure. I have to somehow try—try to find closure within myself. And still till this very day I have yet to find that closure. So without closure I have to learn how to live with the possibility of never finding it. I have to tell myself that. I have to listen to my voice say those very words. And believe you me, it upsets me like hell swallowing my own words back down my throat.

"You don't understand how much you ruined my life. But know this, you no longer own my mind, my body, my spirit. I'm taking it all back!

"Oh, and by the way, tell your Momma I said it's not her fault that you grew up to become such a grimy muthafucker.

"Sincerely,

"Anonymous"

I take one deep breath, then unfold the other letter with a slight sense of solace. I think of others in my same predicament. And as I do, warm tears leak from my eyes and stream down my face and plop one by one onto the letter.

"Dear Avery,

"After my traumatic ordeal I it took upon myself to start writing in my journal, Sis, because I was too embarrassed to talk to someone, anyone on the outside. I

had to find an outlet. So I expressed my intimate thoughts, my anguish and my resentment on paper. Often times, I cried it out. Other times, I relived it. I felt the anger. I embraced my vulnerability. Eventually I sought help by going to see psychologist, Dr. Christine Cristal.

"From there, I committed myself to the sessions, and really got in touch with self, and confessed and talked about things I hadn't talked about in years.

"In her subtle, but effective way, Dr. Cristal really made me acknowledge my fears, revert back to past and present pains, and even, if I had to, cry in front of her.

"Plenty of times I had meltdowns, which wasn't a bad thing. It meant I was opening up, instead of hibernating within. Other times, I merely shutdown. Faded.

"In time, with Dr. Cristal's help I was able to admit outwardly that I was afraid. I was afraid of living and dying. I was afraid of liking and loving. I was afraid of losing and gaining. I was simply afraid to be me, because deep down I didn't know who I was anymore. I changed from this 'overconfident woman' to becoming this 'unknown woman'. And it scared the shit out of me.

"It was like he stripped away my identity. But slowly I began to come to—come to grips with what happened to me. I regained consciousness. And every day it was a process of looking myself in the mirror, and asking myself: who are you? What is your name? What is your purpose? Girl, look at me. Answer me. I was mute. I didn't know how to answer those questions. So day by day, I asked myself. Then one day, I finally answered myself. And no, I wasn't going crazy. I was trying to find me again.

"I bawled because it was just too much to handle. I bawled because I felt my spirit slightly come alive. In that moment, I felt God too. I kid you not! I felt His powerful presence. I bawled some more because I had

53

someone. I had the Almighty in my corner rooting for me. Day and night I prayed for a healthy recovery. I asked God to give me strength because I felt as if I had lost it all.

"In the beginning, oh, I was livid with God. It took me awhile to talk to Him. I blamed Him for this happening to me. I yelled at Him. I screamed at the top of my lungs at Him because in my mind I felt He could've prevented it. He could've forewarned me. But He didn't. And I couldn't comprehend why. Why did He allow this horrific act to happen to me? I thought I was special. And deserved special treatment. What did I do to Him? Well, I shut Him out of my life. And then when things got rough I called upon Him expecting Him to be at my mercy. And God stood still. Still as a rock. He wouldn't move one muscle for me. I had to learn how to take that leap of faith. I had to learn how to crawl, then walk. Move one foot and then the other. No. God never left my side, but He sho' taught me a valuable lesson. Lord knows, it took time and whole lot of determination.

"When I reentered Temple Cross Baptist Church I didn't feel a healing come over me. I didn't feel cured. All I knew was that I was surrounded by folks who knew me and folks who didn't, yet welcomed me back in their home. A home I had distanced myself from. I can't say at that very moment that I connected with God because my heart was still closed. I was still bitterly angry. But what I can say was that I felt God's presence along with Reverend Giltroy's (God rest his soul).

"So yes, woman, I was afraid. I was so scared that I was going to die by the hands of my rapist. Those grimy hands of his were strong hands. His hands felt like an octopus all over me! Forcefully, he manhandled me. His jagged nails, they cut into my flesh like a box cutter. Slitting into me. I felt the sting when his saliva splattered onto the slits of my scratched-up skin.

"He terrorized me. He wouldn't stop. I pleaded. I begged. I tried to fight back and he still wouldn't let up.

Wouldn't stop to see that he was ripping into me. He wouldn't stop stroking his filthy dick inside of me. Whispering his perverse dirty talk in my ears as if to arouse me. He fucked me! Fucked my body! Fucked my mind! Fucked my life up! And he took pleasure in fucking me too. Hurt? Hurt is too mild of a word. Sometimes I wish he would've killed me. Just fuckin' killed me!

"I don't think 'men' understand the trauma of a woman who has been raped. I think they just assumed that 'it happened' and that we are supposed to just get over it. And get on with it. Just function with normalcy. Be our normal selves.

"Note to men: once a woman has been raped there is no more 'normal self'. Half the time she doesn't even know who she is anymore. And to expect her to act as she once did, man, you are asking for a lot. The fact that she is able to get in bed with you or any man after an experience such as rape, says more than you know. And if you don't know what it says, well, I'll tell you.

"It says that she is trying to overcome what happened to her. It says that she is trusting you to protect her so that it never happens again. It says that she is trying to express a deeper love for you, for even staying with her. She doesn't have the confidence she once had. But knowing that you are there, showing that you care, man, it says more than words could ever express. But remember you have to handle her with tender loving care because she is not the same woman, but that is not to say that this 'new' woman can't be the love of your life. Men have to remember that women are fragile beings. I don't care how strong she claims or appears to be—once violated the thought, the experience… never goes away.

"If men could imagine someone coming out of nowhere and strapping 'em down like a dog, touching 'em, kissing 'em, groping and grinding 'em, then forcefully climbing on top of 'em and sticking his dick in

*their ass, then I think men will have a better
understanding of how a woman that was raped feels.*

*"That day I had no one. That day— that day was
the very day that I lost faith in God. That day was the
day that I lost love for Him too. That day was the day
that I stopped believing in the power of love.*

"But—

*"I learned that nothing remains the same. Not
days or nights or circumstances. Everything changes
with time. Even raped victims.*

"Love,

"Avery"

***

Arriving home at 3:15 p.m., I have this urgency to talk. Unfortunately there is no one here to talk to. I don't want to have a longwinded conversation over the phone. I'd rather face-to-face with someone I trust. Someone whose eyes I can look into as I bare my soul.

I head up to my bedroom and reach out to the only thing that gives me the freedom to speak freely. Sis.

I get comfy on my bed, and pour out what is still hurting me. My past. I need to remember, rethink. Did I play a role in this, somehow? There still lingers some self-blame.

I think to myself, *retrace your steps, Avery.* I've gone over the story in my head what feels like a hundred times. It becomes redundant trying to fill the gaps. That split second gap that could've prevented it all.

I think and overthink. The agony I put myself through. Constant agony.

"Give it one more go," I hear Avona say with such empathy in her voice.

"Yeah, Avery, give it one more go." Karma insists. "We got you."

I nod my head.

July 29, 2016

Dear Sis,

Broadway. Yes, I was walking along Broadway. It was quiet that nippy evening.

I was heading toward West Broadway. That is where I daily parked my car in the lot. I was on the opposite side of the street, passing the Municipal Complex. That is when—

I felt someone come up from behind me. He wrapped his arm around my neck and dragged me through a dark alley into the back of an Electronics store.

Whoever raped me? Left me for dead.

Somehow I managed to get up on my feet and stagger to the front of the Electronics store.

As I attempted to cross the street an on-coming car nearly hit me. I fell, and the driver jumped out of his car and ran to my side.

I remember hearing him vaguely call 911, he then fled the scene. I remember hearing sirens. Two men hovering over me. And me being lifted and put on a gurney.

I remember being rushed by paramedics to Hopkins Hospital and Medical Center by way of ambulance. I also remember a woman, ah, ah, what was her name? Mrs. Margaret McCarter. She was the Rape/HIV counselor. She was trying to convince me to let the hospital staff do a rape test kit on me. But I refused. I just wanted to be discharged so that I could go home and wash his filth off of me, out of me.

Sometime later, maybe a year or so after, I had an appointment with my primary doctor for a routine check-up. Dr. Fulmore.

As I recall, it was a Tuesday in July. That day, Dr. Fulmore changed my life by his unwelcoming news. Not only was I now a raped victim, but I was also diagnosed with contracting HIV.

Wow. Yep. Wow is right.

It was a difficult time. Poppa had passed on and so had Ma'am. I had no immediate family to turn to in my time of crisis.

Life after rape and HIV? Hmm.

I suffered from anxiety, paranoia. I was afraid of my own shadow. Which led to me eventually resigning from my career. I went into seclusion. Dropped off the face of the earth. I was so alone, lonely. That was, until I reached out and called my very best friend...Johnnie.

Johnnie Rivera unknowingly took me under his wing and brought me back to life. But unfortunately, Johnnie divulged to me that he had AIDS. Yep. My flamboyantly gay, Latino, best friend was dying.

After Johnnie's death, I received an unexpected visit from a man—a lawyer named Byren Clausen. Byren was representing Johnnie and had come to inform me that I was Johnnie's primary beneficiary. I was overwhelmed with grief, pain. How? Well, it was brought to my attention that Johnnie had purchased life insurance way before he contracted the virus. I couldn't believe my best friend was dead. Yet, he thought of me. Surreal.

With a letter from Johnnie as well as a check in the amount of one-hundred thousand dollars, I was beside myself. Completely incoherent, in disbelief, as well as fortunate.

Day after day, night after night, I'd have memories of conversations Johnnie and I had. It got me to thinking about my future goals. But I was also thinking about men. Having a man in my life. Indulging in sex again. So, gradually I began to come out of hibernation for the second time and I ventured off into the dating world.

Back in the day I was partial to dating only white men. Brothers really didn't do much for me. I had a lot of animosity toward my dad so I chose to date men that were the opposite of him. I was content. Not happy.

Still grieving over Johnnie, I decided to get out of the house. I went to Garrett Mountain. There I met a gorgeous black man named Blu McDowell. Everything was good between us. It was so unexpected. We had great conversation. Chemistry. Lots of laughs. All the things I had missed, we shared. We had fun just sitting on a blanket talking. I took my time in telling him my status. I mean, I didn't know him and he didn't know me. I didn't see any reason to share. Honestly I didn't think he would be interested in me. I really didn't. My confidence had diminished some. But when he handed me his business card that pretty much summed it up. The ball was in my court.

When I finally did get the courage to share my status with Blu I chose for us to drive up to the Great Falls. That was a complete and utter disaster. Blu went ballistic. He threw me out of his moving car. I can't tell you how humiliated he made me feel. It was a pretty ugly scene.

Sometime later, I met a man at His and Her Boutique in Montclair, named Travar Atkin. Oh, talk 'bout finne! Travar was irresistible. Long dreadlocks, honey-toned skin, tall and lickable. We exchanged numbers. I finally had gotten my nerve up and called him. He had a great sense of humor, which I liked. We made plans to have dinner but Travar chose to cook me a home cooked meal. I was flattered.

When I arrived at his home in Montclair, man, he looked delectable. I wanted to eat him up. Fuck dinner. I wanted to fuck him. He rubbed my feet. It put me in mind of when Jason was massaging Lyric's feet in Jason's Lyric. I was in heaven. Travar made me feel so sexy, so beautiful, so wanted. That was, up until I disclosed my status, which was far from being easy. I mean, I was horny for that man. But I had to keep it real.

When I told Travar, the place grew silent. He shut down. He was distraught. It really took him by surprise.

When I saw one tear scroll down his cheek I felt horrible. Like the worst person in the world. I didn't intend to hurt him, but I did. And in turn it hurt me too.

I had to keep reminding myself that it was the right thing to do. To not be selfish and indulge in this attractive man, knowingly. I wanted to have protected sex with him but not like that. He needed to know. So I stopped him as hard as it was to do. I did. My body was afire for that man.

All I could do was gather my shoes and purse and keys and get the hell out of there. So I did. I never regretted my decision. All I ever regretted was allowing him to touch me, feel me up, taste my skin, only to have to stop. God, it felt soooo good to be touched by a man again. So good.

I had to live by Johnnie's words. And that was to always make sho' I told the truth. I had another regret. Johnnie didn't know about me being HIV-positive.

In the letter, though, Johnnie did admit that he knew about me being raped. I don't know why I didn't tell him when he told me about him having AIDS. I guess it just didn't feel like the right time, you know?

After Travar, I didn't think dating was for me anymore. But—

One night I was dwelling over my life, so I hopped in my car and took a drive to Pathmark for comfort food. That was when I met Zaelyn Homes, owner of Homes Improvements. He was southern chocolate and simply delicious to look at. Tall, dark, and oh so, fuckin' handsome. That southern charm was a delight in my book. He knew how to treat a woman. Or, so I thought.

Painting the town red with Zaelyn really opened me up to the possibility of loving and being in love, but I was skeptical in telling him about me. Look at what *happened with Blu and Travar. Yeah. They both handled it differently.*

Date after date I was being swept off my pretty little feet by Zaelyn. Dinner. Dancing. Just enjoying myself. I found myself having wet dreams of him, too. I wanted him in the worst way but I also wanted him to know the truth.

Finally, I had built up the courage to tell him when he came over for dinner. God, I was petrified. I didn't want to lose another man because of—

It was a risk I was willing to take. Not knowing what the outcome would be, I was hopeful.

Well, that evening Zaelyn shocked the hell outta me. He undressed me, then gently took my hand into his, and led me to my bedroom. OMG! That man, made sweet, sweet love to me. It was everything I'd imagine and more. So much more. I guess too much more because neither one of us knew that the condom had come off. I panicked. Rushed into the bathroom and did all kinds of stupid things. I was sooooooooooooo afraid.

Zaelyn took it hard. Yeah. He freaked. But tried to keep his composure in front of me. I could tell. The silence pretty much told all. I wanted to be there for him for moral support but he didn't want me around. I respected his wishes.

Later that evening or sometime after, I always get my days mixed up, he called, then hung up. I had a gut feeling it was him, so I called him back. I had to call his niece, Danell to get his home address, then I rushed over to his house. I'd never been to his house before. Nope.

He answered the door, drunk. He could barely hold himself up. I helped him into his bedroom, not knowing where his bedroom was, so I had to rely on him to help show me drunk as hell. I felt responsible. I mean, maybe he didn't really understand or educate himself on the virus. Obviously he panicked and thought the alcohol would numb him.

I wanted to care for Zaelyn. Love and care for my man. Funny. I'd soon discovered that Zaelyn wasn't unspoken for. He was married. He never told me but I found out the hard way. By helping him, helped me see that Zaelyn was nothing more than a player, a liar, a cheater—the proof was setting on the mantel—his wedding picture, along with a family photo with his wife and two children looking so dang happy. I wanted to breakdown right then and there but I didn't. I simply handed him a cup of black coffee and left with the thought of never seeing him ever again.

Writing Zaelyn a letter ended the "oblivious" affair. Heartbreak led me to redefining my life and reevaluating my purpose on this earth. God works in mysterious ways.

There I was at Villa of Locks, a young chocolate girl walked in with flyers in hand asking for donations for Red Alert Hotline Service. Red Alert was looking to hire folks for their Call Center. It was a 24-hour hotline service for people with HIV/AIDS. People who had no one to talk to. It was an outlet for folks like me.

I called Red Alert and explained my interests. Set up a date for an interview. The founder, Mr. Xavier Combs III met with me, and he hired me to work in the Call Center. Simultaneously, I was already inquiring about a building I had seen on Bloomfield Ave in Montclair, through Tribe Realtor, realtor, Mrs. Charla Jenkins-Rollin.

Since Johnnie's death I found myself envisioning opening a business which involved: poetry. But then the idea expanded into a performance arts gallery. The name Anonymous came out of nowhere, but I loved it. I loved it because it made me think of me as well as Johnnie. It seemed to fit. Between working and dreaming I was a pretty busy woman.

But then, I met a photographer. Oh, let me backtrack.

I still owned Anonymous but I was looking to venture off into other things. So I took some pictures and sent them to this modeling agency in New York, and they signed me.

I met Hellman Middleton at one of the photo shoots. We spent a lot of time together and eventually we fell in love. Hellman proposed. I was elated to accept. I thought we would be happy, you know. Unhappy was I.

Hellman was not what I expected. He was abusive, belligerent, selfish, and I was heartbroken. But I was in love. I thought over time things would change. How stupid was I? Very.

Things only got worse. The fights only got worse. The verbal abuse only got worse. And the last straw was when Hellman dragged me out of his home, which was supposed to be "our" home. I found myself sitting on the gravel in the driveway, face streaming with tears, embarrassed, alone, just a complete mess. And to add insult to injury Hellman's lover, (which I didn't know at first), but when they meaning: "him and him" tongued each other down, that sho' was a dead giveaway. I felt duped. Played. More so because I had already given up Anonymous. Why? I did it for him.

Hellman had an issue with me working long hours, devoting to my passion. It is fair to say that Hellman was jealous of my business. With me helping folks cope and deal and heal through the arts, through poetry, music...Hellman felt I was committed more to my business than him. I had given up my baby, Anonymous for love. And I felt so empty. There I was a battered woman. Me? Avery.

Feeling foolish, yet still in love, I had to find a way to move past my pain. But with the everyday reminder of what flowed through my veins, HIV, I felt like I was hitting dead-ends. Until—

Working for IMG Modeling Agency, I regained my confidence. I then met a man named Stacy Blazman. A no-good hustler-slash-womanizer-slash-thief that claimed to be wealthy and able to take me places in my modeling career. Don't believe the hype!

See, Stacy was nothing more than a crook. He was the one to introduce me to cocaine too. He physically abused me. Then got me high as a kite and kidnapped me, coerced us in marriage. Yep. It's true.

Being high off of cocaine, chile, I did some unethical things. Dark shit. I was completely bound to cocaine. And I really saw no way of stopping my addiction. It had a strong hold on me.

Being homeless and a junky, I was out of control. That wasn't the Avery I knew. That junky was losing it, fo' real. I was barely holding on to life, shit, I was already doomed with this shit inside of me. Then to get hooked on cocaine. Not good.

God is good. Yep.

I entered a rehab program. Did the 12-Steps, and filed for an annulment from that bastard Stacy. After which I began to work on me. It was indeed a process.

Knowingly Sleepin' Wit' the Virus, I had to accept my fate. Regardless of the rumors that festered of me Kreepin' Wit' the Virus. Regardless of being put out there by my ex-lover Zaelyn. With him collaborating with Editor-in-Chief, Narlena Scott of BLAB magazine, and divulging my HIV status without my consent. NOT to mention, Zaelyn implications that stated that he was not informed of my health status and that I had purposely tried to infect him with HIV, NOT to mention the fact that Zaelyn also implied that I contracted HIV from Trickin' Wit' the Virus, so basically he was saying that he had slept with a prostitute or whore or ho, however you choose to word it. Of course I know that all of his accusations were false. He had no premise.

For me to say, it didn't bother me would be a complete lie. It infuriated me. I loved him. And to be in love with someone that would backstab you was so disconcerting.

I put in blood, sweat, tears, and what I got out of it all was …Anonymous. But stupid me, let it go.

Eventually something good came into my life. A man that accepted me and all of my flaws. Yep. Xavier. And no, we had never been intimate as in having sex.

Only kissed. Hugged. Held hands. Cuddled. I guess it wasn't enough. Because as you know, he stepped out on me and had meaningless and unemotional sex with JaVonna Banks. Yep. The same bitch that shot me.

The same chick that attempted to kill me because of her anger over her break-up with lesbian wife-to-be Danell Owen.

Danell tossed that vindictive bitch to the curb and that bitch tried to do away with me. Ain't that a blip? The bullet is still lodged in me.

While I was in a coma JaVonna seduced my man. Xavier found out through my books that I had several encounters in my past and assumed that that was how I contracted the virus. He leaned on JaVonna for support instead of being by my side—in my time of need. He got her pregnant. We tried to reconcile our relationship once he found out the truth about me and JaVonna. But once JaVonna exposed being pregnant to Xavier and me, I wasn't quite sho' which way things would go. I wanted to trust him and his word and his heart, but—

Well, unbeknownst to me Xavier ended up marrying JaVonna in prison. Only to later die. He suffered from— well, you know, he suffered.

I liked to die! Literally.

It was like one thing after another and another and another. C'mon! Life was doing me in. I was beginning to throw in the towel. But my Messengers in heaven had a different plan for me.

Talks to you later, Sis,

Avery

***

Jordan Seymour?

How did he come up? Anndddd? What about him? Is it too late, Avery? Too late? He's married. Hopefully happily. There's not much else to say about Jordan. Other than to say, I wish him well.

I can be the bigger person. I'm not a grudge-holding woman. Jordan never did anything to me but— well, there is no need for me to hate the man. What was then, was then. He deserves to be happy. And plus, I refuse to harbor anymore ill-feelings towards Jordan. Yes, he hurt me deeply, but he has a right to love and be in love with whomever he chooses. I was just disappointed that he didn't choose me. I was mostly disappointed in the fact that he didn't invite me to the wedding. I thought I meant more to him as a friend.

Jordan is the least of my worries. If you must know, Hella (my vajayjay) and I have been bickering. Yesssss, again.

Every year since the rape we go through this six month phase.

For the past couple of weeks we have been going at it. Fussin' up a storm. Hella's on that vegan bullshit. I keep tellin' her that I need the protein.

Okay. I get the whole "meat" thing. But of all people Hella knows that I loves me a good rib-bye steak. I can't just give up meat with a snap of a finger. Hella wants me to go cold turkey. Not gonna happen.

I understand where she's coming from. Says if I stop indulging in meat that I'll live longer. Really? Just because I stop eating meat doesn't mean that I'll live longer. Hell, I could walk out the door and get killed just as easily as one, two, three.

Lately Hella has been in stank mode. She's bitchy and cranky and anal about every friggin' thing. I know why. She has to put more faith in me and trust that I won't put us both in jeopardy.

Celibacy is a great thing. It's a beautiful thing to do for self. You really have to be strong minded, though. Disciplined. It's the mind that fucks with you. It's the mind that teases you and persuades you and manipulates you. The mind.

Sometimes I tell my mind to shut the hell up because my body needs a fix of some hard stroking penis. But Hella fucks that shit up realllll quick. That hellacious bitch. Hella is a bitch. A stubborn bitch. But she looks out for me like a true sistah should.

Hella's not trying to open her door just for anyone to come waltzing in. She has standards. Limits. Purpose. And she ain't bending for noooooobody.

I, on the other hand, can't take it anymore. Doing it her way is most definitely the right way, but I have needs, wants, desires that overwhelm me. Hella doesn't know how to compromise. She's gotten worse after the rape, after the HIV, after the many failed relationships, after rejection, rejection, rejection, she's tired. I completely understand.

What about me? I can't function like this. Being man-less is one thing. But being man-less and dick-less. She gotta be kiddin' me!

It hasn't been easy coping. Coping with being raped. Coping with living with HIV. Coping with loss. Coping with being hopelessly *not* in love. Plenty of times I feel like giving up. But this little voice deep inside me keeps tellin' me not to.

Forgiveness. The road to forgiveness is a winding road. A dirt road that sooner or later I must travel. A part of me wants to forgive Hella for putting me through this shit. Yet, the other half of me can't seem to because she is being very selfish.

Funny. But after so many years, I have forgiven Poppa. It took time, though. And a lot, a lot of tears. I guess it'll take time with Hella too.

Currently I'm in a world of my own. No matter how hard I try my pain still runs deep. Deeper than I ever thought it would. These days I'm trying to overcome so many things that I can't seem to breathe. Sigh of relief. Yet, my feet are moving in the right direction, but my heart hasn't fully healed. And my pussy is wailing for some companionship. I'm still hurting. Still burdened. Still traumatized. Still wounded. Still unlucky when it comes to love. Shit. I'm miserable. Fuckin' miserable.

First Love. It's one of my Daddy*s Figurines & Keepsakes. Often I stare at the young black girl and young black boy so smitten that it makes me still believe that there is such a thing as true love. Where? I don't quite know as to where. But I do know that it's not here. This place, this town of Paterson is a hard lovin' city. Which currently makes me a hard lovin' sistah.

The sistahs here look sick and tired. You can tell that they've been through something in their lives. You can see it plain as day. It's a scary thing to witness.

The other day, I was walking down Ellison Street. It was eighty-something degrees out. Beautiful summery day. I had on my spaghetti-strap Guess jean dress and camel-colored sandals. And, of course, I was rockin' my signature cut.

There was this deep dark plum-complexioned man walking up the street with a backpack on his back and three bags in his hands. He was dressed in a jersey and cargo shorts. Stoutly built with a huge potbelly and a low-cut. He looked like he ain't miss any meals.

Well, anyway, the man took one look at me and said, "That's what summer used to look like." Then he smiled so wide, so big as if seeing me brought back some good memories of summertime.

When I got home I looked myself in the full-length mirror in my living room, and I, too, smiled. I knew exactly what that man was talkin' about. I was plain Jane, yet, he saw something beautiful in my plainness.

When I walk through the streets of Paterson, especially downtown, boy, I see more than I care to. Women have forgotten how to carry themselves like ladies. Look presentable. Feel sexy without undressing themselves down to translucent spandex, booty shorts and belly shirts with no bras. Skin is in. Leaving something to the imagination must be ancient history.

***

Quivering fingers press *his* area code (917), then the remaining 7 digits on my cell phone as I contemplate exactly what to say, where to start the conversation off.

Dang, this puts me in mind of Blu McDowell. The Great Falls. The hand sanitizer. Just the unforgettable scene of me jumping out of his silver Mercedes before he pulled off—leaving me stranded, face full of streaming tears, heart full of heartache. Every time I get to this place in my life, he's the first person that comes to mind and it makes me feel sick to my stomach.

I know.

Every man is different. And every man's reaction is going to be different. But I'm not concerned with "every" man at the moment. I'm concerned with the one I'm currently calling.

Out of nowhere, my *okay* mood shifts to my *fucked-up* mood. I find myself getting pretty damn angry. I guess I'm tired of reaching this destination, you know. I'm tired of feeling like I have to constantly explain myself. Put my shit out there like …BAM! I feel trapped. Like a nun in a dirty ass whorehouse.

In order for me to get un-trapped I have to reveal some personal shit. If I had my way, I'd just say what was truly on my heart. And leave it be, but—

What I'd say? Hmm. Well, I'd say:

Hello, this is Avery. Avery Love. Yes, that black chick with that "shit". You know, that "shit". HIV. Yeah, her. Me.

Well, I'm not going to take up much of your time seeing how I have many calls to make this evening. I just called to tell you—to tell you this...

Every man that has ever dreamt to fuck my brains out, I'm sorry I'm no longer good enough to stick your mediocre dick in. No longer am I fuckable. I get it. I'm sorry that when you look at me all you see is those three letters: HIV. I'm sorry that you feel I'm undesirable. That my chocolate pussy is so unappetizing. That the woman I am now has no feeling or yearn to be touched and loved by you. I'm sorry that my life partner puts a wedge between you and me. I'm sorry! Sorry that I can't change the unchangeable. Sorry I can't fix the unfixable. Sorry I can't make you want me. Or persuade. Or seduce. Sorry that I can't peel back this skin of mine, take what is inside these veins and flush it out. Or pretend that everything is okay. Sorry that I don't have all the answers to solve all the humiliation and emotional distress and embarrassment that you claimed I caused you. Sorry I can't do a damn thang about what has happened to me, about what has come of me. I'm sorry, so very, very sorry to come to know—

Pressing my ear against the phone the ringtone of Fetty-Wap's "Trap Queen" blares loudly as my thoughts continue to wander: *God, I hope he'll be in a relatively good mood. And not try to bum rush me off the phone pretending to be soooo busy that he can't talk like he did last time. I don't care who you are nobody's that busy.*

Normally it takes three to four rings before he picks up. Last time I got his voicemail so I hung up. Didn't want to talk to a machine. If that were the case I would have texted instead, but— finally, he picks up. Five rings in.

"Hello?" His voice is deep. Strong like a cup of brewed black coffee.

I hear loud music in the background. Muffling voices too. Club? Perhaps. He loves to dance. Entertain. Be in the limelight. The center of attention.

"Hi. It's me. Avery." *Why do I always identify myself?* I don't know. Force of habit. Just want to make sho' he knows whom he's talking to. But yeah, he should know my voice by now. "Um," I stammer. Cell phone clench between my neck and shoulder blade. Adjust my neck for comfort. Ask the question. Get the answer. Hang-up. Simple. Not really.

"Ah, are you available later this evening? I really need to talk to you. Um, it's really important." I emphasize "really" and "important" to see if it will pique his interests.

With my arms behind my back I struggle to unfasten this sexy midnight push-up bra.

He merely breathes into the receiver. "You women kill me with that 'important' shit. Everything is of importance with y'all. Why y'all always sweating a brother?"

Rolling of my eyes. "Quote *'sweating a brother'* unquote." I say to myself. Then sigh. "No. It *really* is important." I insist, while inching the low-rise stretch bikini down my long sheer legs.

I sigh again full of frustration.

Stepping out of the midnight panty I pick it up by the keyhole back detail and fling it in the wicker hamper alongside the commode.

With a crumple forehead I say, "Can you readjust your schedule. I'd only need about an hour of your time. It's just I need to speak with you face-to-face. And yes, it is important."

He breathes out heavy into the receiver as if annoyed. He then says, "I bet. Well, I *can't* make it, Avery. Next time."

I think to myself. *Next time. Hmm. It seems I hear that a lot.*

"Well. I kind of figured that, but was hoping you'd have a little time to squeeze me in. It's not like I call you. I can count on one hand how many times I've called you. You rarely hear from me." I grimace. "Wow. I see I'm only good when you feel you have nothing else better to do, huh? I get it. But dang. Couldn't you have been a little bit more discreet?! I mean, the last time I saw you—you know what—forget it."

"That's true, Avery. My bad. Well, Avery, I-have-have to go. Can't keep my *bitch* waiting. Talk-Talk soon."

"Wow! Just like that, huh? It's that easy to jump from woman to woman to woman without as much as a second thought as to how the *first* woman feels. Never mind the second." Twisting of my lips, I say, "No problem. Enjoy *your* evening. Goodbye."

After I hang up, I stare blankly at the African leather mask of a dark complexioned woman with dreadlocks feeling totally dismissed. Dissed.

I think to myself, *No need to share the unwelcoming news with him. He pretty much said all that I needed to hear. How does the sistah version of that book read: Chile, he's just not that into you, soooooo fuck 'im!*

Chapter
Two

Making my way into the living room I turn on the television to catch the eleven o'clock news.

"This is Traci Stretch with Breaking News. Actor Charlie Sheen talks with Matt Lauer about being HIV-positive. The actor revealed that he is currently taking the antiviral drug Triple Cocktail four times a day."

I flip OFF the television.

HIV-positive? Charlie Sheen? Hmm.

Leaning back on the sofa I revisit Dr. Fulmore and my conversation: *"Avery, I regretfully have to advise you that you are HIV-positive."* I wanted to blackout. Go ballistic in his office. But thought against it. I pleaded for him to have made a mistake. Shit! I thought. Timing is a *mutha-you-know-what.* This can't be happening to me.

It seems every time I get a break something weasels itself in and blows everything that I have accomplished up in my face. Or, at least tries to. Like, for real? Why does this keep happening to me? Jump out of one hot pot without getting burned, jump into another. Dang. I don't understand.

My inner woman interjects to explain. *Yes, you do.* It's frustrating. *Not really. Be honest with yourself, Avery.*

It was two consensual adults that got a little twisted off of that bottle of New Amsterdam Peach Vodka and one thing led to another. Precautionary measures were taken, but shit happens.

Now that I can finally see the light at the end of the tunnel I don't need anything blocking my view. At least not right now. Not like this. With this whole HIV thing.

That "thing" you're referring to is called your life, Avery. Not a …thing.

This is definitely bad timing.

Then you should've practiced better restraint. But it's too late to think about that now. You have other things that are far more important to concern yourself with, don't you think?

I drop my head and make my way up to my bedroom hoping to turn my mind off. Climbing between the cool, disheveled cotton sheets, I elbow Connie May Fowler's book *Before Women Had Wings* that is flipped open to page sixty-five, exactly where I last left it. Not in the mood for reading I remove the book from the bed and place it on the nightstand.

Balling myself up in the sheets and plaid comforter, eyelids fold me into a deep sleep.

Chapter
Three

I think every woman goes through a cycle of change at some point and time in their life. I'm not talkin' about *menopause*, either. I'm talkin' about *men*.

Just like women change their panties on a daily basis. There are some women that change their men on a daily basis. Those women are seeking something and they won't stop until they find it. Other women take their time and get to know someone before moving into a new relationship. Me? Well, I give myself a certain amount of weeks before I cut a man loose. But that is only if I'm not really feeling him.

I've come to realize just like women want to *feel* needed so do men.

Have you ever found yourself wanting a man, getting the man, but after getting him and keeping him, months to years later, he leaves a bad taste in your mouth.

It's when you go through this phase of having shitty breath, day after day after day. Your taste buds for that particular man goes bad like spoiled meat. It's as if you have a rotten tooth that needs to be pulled. And what do you do with spoiled meat or a rotten tooth? Well—

Some women throw the spoiled meat out and go back to the store for a fresh pack of meat. Some women go to the dentist and get that rotten tooth pulled out. But then you have some women that'll rather walk around with shitty breath just to keep that *same* shitty man.

For you down-to-earth 'hood sistahs. You know who you *is*. I'm just gonna keep it real.

I can't *shit*. As in *doo-doo*. As in *defecate*. As in take *a dump*. There. I said it!

I don't want you to get too caught-up in my choice of words. If anything, I want you to broaden your mind to see my vulnerability. Sometimes things don't always have to be spelled out and expressed in politeness, refine words. Sometimes it becomes more understandable when you think outside the box and just put all the niceness aside and come from the gut of all the bullshit that you truly feel. I'm not coming at you as a dainty flower all dressed up strutting in her stilettos. Not today. I'm coming at you hard, raw, rough, ill-mannered and unrefined. It is necessary for you to see the differences in my character traits. For you to understand where the hell I'm coming from. I'm from the 'hood. Born and raised in Paterson, New Jersey.

It's been nearly *two weeks*!

I got shit atop of shit inside me. I mean, I feel like I have to go to the bathroom. I got cramps galore. I'm bloated. Every time I get up to go to the bathroom, nothing happens.

I can't shit!

I mean, I got poison all up in me and I can't shit it out. What am I supposed to do? Of course I'm worried. This is a serious matter.

It's been nearly two weeks of not shitting. Not even a stool softener will do me any good right about now. No prune juice either. I have tried practically everything I can possibly think of, and nothing works.

It was then that I came to the final conclusion that the only time I can't shit is when I am constipated from men.

Hear me out?

Last year I was allergic to 'em. Men. Yep. Broke out in hives and everything. Benadryl didn't even work for me. Had to be rushed by ambulance to the emergency room because my throat felt like it was closing up. Uh-huh.

Of course I was advised by the attending physician to follow-up with my primary doctor and to see my psychologist.

Dr. Fulmore gave me a prescription and I had to carry around one of 'em EpiPens, just in case I had another allergic reaction. It was terrible, you know. Every time I think I'm about to have a bowel movement, nothing happens. It feels like it wants to come out. Be right at the opening but then it sucks itself backup. It doesn't matter how hard I strain either. I mean sometimes I strain so hard it hurts. It's just an uncomfortable feeling.

Dr. Cristal advised me that I may have to remove *men* from my diet. At least until one found me that I could stomach. She said I was indulging in men like appetizers. When I'd stress I'd find myself engaging in conversation with a man and as soon as things didn't work out—the *very* day things didn't work out my body would react to the emotional distress. Next thing you know…I'm constipated. I thought cheese was the only thing that had this effect on me. But no. Just like I had to change my eating habits. I had to do the same with men. I mean, thank goodness I'm not *dependent* on men because lately men have not been likeminded with my lifestyle. And I guess that led to the cramps and constipation.

Changing the subject for a brief moment.

Danell called.

She called while I was in the middle of trying to handle my business, so I asked her if I could call her back.

77

Before rushing her off the phone I distinctly heard her say something about doing lunch at the delicatessen across the street from her gallery *Virtue*. Honestly, food is the last thing on my mind. And no. No, I didn't inadvertently tell her that I am sitting on the commode trying to shit. I just didn't. It didn't seem like appropriate talk between girlfriends. Women are supposed to be discreet, dainty, show etiquette. But let me tell you something about *some* women. Some women are the nastiest heffas ever born!

Well, since the door is open I might as well step in by saying this...

You ever have to go to a public bathroom at a restaurant or library or movie theater or bus terminal or department store or supermarket. The smell alone will turn you off but you really have to go, so you hold your breath thinking that you can handle your business without passing out.

You push open the door to the stall and feel like you're about to throw up. Women don't flush the toilets behind themselves. They throw used, bloody tampons or sanitary napkins in the garbage unwrapped. Yuck! They take a dump and don't flush the toilet. They pee all over the toilet seat and don't wipe it clean. And some women, (I have witnessed this firsthand) take a dump and don't even wash their hands. That is why I make it a habit of not shaking hands with women 'cause they nasty as aw hell.

Ok. Back to the subject of men and my constipation.

What I am looking for in a man is a man that can accept me as a woman infected with HIV. Communication is definitely key. I don't want a man that can't let simple mistakes go. A man that holds grudges and believes in retaliation based on hurt, pain, disloyalty. I need and want a man that will respect me and not punish me for mistakes that I know I'll make. Don't punish me or ridicule because I may or may not be on his level intellectually. I may not see things from his perspective. I may have my own perspective, own way of doing and seeing and handling things. Respect me for that. And know that it's okay that he doesn't always like me and my ways. As long as he never stops loving me. And know that I'm not always going to share what I want in a man. I prefer that he just shows me who he is. And if it is someone that I'm meant to have in my life, then it shall be. Hopefully we'll become one. Let it happen naturally. Purposefully. A man that can and will carry my five feet eleven inch self over the threshold after marrying me. A man that can stomach the stench of my doo-doo. A man that will do his research and homework to be with me. A man that will go the distance and show me that he truly cares about me. Show me by his words and actions and attitude. Show me that he is sincere and ready and willing to embark on something challenging. I know I can be a handful. I also know that not every man can handle a woman like me. But if it were possible I would love to meet this man. Thus far, I have yet to encounter anyone remotely close to him. I guess that explains why he only exists in my head.

To some men: Avery + HIV= AIDS. That is simply untrue. I'm nowhere's near my deathbed. They should know this by now. I mean, who doesn't with my life story in the pages of BLAB as well as on their website.

My mind shifts gears.

Forgive me, but I got caught up in reminiscing about what *used* to be with men. Back then I was having the time of my life. Those men I indulged in were *real* men. They knew how to cater to a woman like me. Woo me. Feed me. Fuck me. And woo and feed and fuck me some more. There were no conditions, no rules, no expectations, and no complications. It was just about me and him having our moment. But now that I think about it. Hmm. It should've been about us communicating, asking questions, and getting to know each other's medical history. Not just about having sex.

Anyway, being constipated takes me out of my creative element. I'm cranky. Irritable about every little thing. And the slightest sound of a man's voice nauseates me. I'm so done that I can't even put into words how done I am. I mean, there are only so many woosas I can say. Instead of driving myself mentally insane and before I take another teaspoon of Castrol oil hoping it relieves me of this constipation, I've decided to step back into my celibate heels and just starve myself. Eventually the taste for men will dissipate.

Chapter
Four

On the jitney heading back from my second opinion I observe how young mothers handle their children. I notice a disturbing pattern of young mothers fussin' and cussin' their children out. None have any patience. And they are very short fused. They don't want to hear what their child have to say but they are quick to listen to some joker on their cell phone. Oh, they got all the time in the world for *him*. I don't understand why some teen mothers or women, in general, put the "boyfriend" or "shared man" or "potential" before the child. It really baffles me as to why *they* do that.

This young, coffee-colored girl and her son get on the jitney. She is an average-looking girl with bone-straight hair weave, but it actually enhances her oval face. She wears gray sweatpants and a white wifebeater T (with the bra straps exposed…tacky) and Nike Air Max sneakers.

The little dark-skinned boy is so cute with his plump cheeks. He looks to be no more than five years old. Kindergarten age. He has a fresh haircut and his jeans and T-shirt and camel-colored Timberlands are clean. He tickles me because he talks and talks and talks his mother's ears off but she doesn't get upset or yell or cuss the child out. She listens. And acknowledges him and answers any and all questions he asks.

Inwardly, I smile.

When they get off the bus on the corner of East 25th Street, I watch her make sho' he is in arms reach. Not walking ahead of her or too far behind. Side by side. I watch them until they cross the street and are completely out of my eyes view.

Where is his daddy? I wonder.

As the jitney makes its way toward downtown Paterson I continue to observe the streets. Most of the mothers pushing strollers are alone. Not a daddy or man in sight. Of course that doesn't mean that a man is not in their life. He could be at: work, in prison, or perhaps he moved to another state and only sees his child during spring or summer break. Having a man in a child's life is very, very important. Being a single mother, in this day and age, is a difficult job. Single mothers are overworked and still underpaid. And *men*, well, you already know if you're a single father.

I grimace.

I think about when Stacy waltzed into my life. That sorry man put me through hell. Pure and simple hell. Hellman, too. Zaelyn, too. Although, Zaelyn took me by complete surprise. I never thought he'd be so vicious.

My thoughts revert back to Dr. Fulmore.

I didn't want to second-guess him. I value Dr. Fulmore's opinion. Have for so many years. But I felt with him being overworked, traveling to and from Detroit to cater to his other office, under staffed that maybe, just maybe he'd made an error of some sort. Okay. I was hoping he had. But to no avail, I got my second opinion and the outcome is no better than the first. Seems Dr. Fulmore suspensions were right.

I can't even picture it. Me? Avery.

It's scary. Especially with no one in my life. I've managed to get by. Don't know how half the time, but I do. Take one day at a time.

This is not how I pictured it. Of course I have options. I'm just not sho' which one to choose. But I know I better choose wisely with Trump as our 45th President. Change gon' come.

Dr. Fulmore feels I can do this. I'm not convince that I can. Not sold as of yet.

Hmm. Sighing. I cannot think clearly.

As we stroll down the block I turn and stare out the window, sightsee Broadway which has a mass of brown faces. From the BP gas station to Midtown Liquors to the Chinese Take-Out, everybody seems to be chillin' as if they haven't a care or responsibility in the world. I don't know how black folks do nothing all day and *expect* to get ahead.

Annoyed by the mural of "Black Poverty" I pullout my composition notebook from my duffel bag. Open it up mid-section to where I had jotted down outlines for my next book.

Dang! I can't concentrate. It's too noisy on this bus. Papi has his Hispanic music blasting like he's deaf. This loud-mouth light-skinned chick seated in the back of the bus is talking loud as hell. She even has the nerve to have the caller on speaker. Straight-up ghetto. Not to mention this Jamaican guy seated next to me. He's dressed in a pair of ripped up Levi's and a dingy wife-beater T. His disheveled dreadlocks look dirty as hell. And his armpits are *seriously* humming. His musky stench is so potent that it makes my eyes tear-up. I swear you'd think he was chopping onions or something. I cut my eyes over at him. He looks straight ahead as if nothing is wrong. I grimace. Obviously he is immune to his body odor. It don't make no dang sense.

When he lifts up his arm I try to hold my breath. The stench sweeps across my nostrils. I grimace. It ain't no reason for this grown-ass man to be smelling like this. No reason whatsoever.

Not able to stomach the funk of this man I belt out, "NEXT STOP!" before I puke all over myself.

Papi quickly swerves the jitney and pulls over onto the corner of Straight Street. I get off across from White Castle and walk my way down Broadway. The fresh air will do me good.

I feel a headache coming on as I get closer to the Electronics store. Keep going, I tell myself. Face your fears and keep on going. So I do.

By the time I get home, the sick feeling still lingers. I walk into the kitchenette. Open the fridge and pullout the half a gallon of almond milk. Open the cupboard for an eight-ounce glass and pour myself three quarters of a glass. I take a sip. Then another. Then gulp the rest of it down. Turn on the faucet and rinse the glass out and place it in the sink.

Looking at the wall-mounted clock. It is three forty-five. Kicking off my (Guess) high-heels, I leave them lent over by one of the barstools. Make my way into the living room and reach for the lighter and light two sage and lemongrass candles set on the saffron coffee table.

Inhaling the inviting scent, I think to myself, *is this my breakthrough?*

Chapter
Five

Seems I'm having a moment. Find myself on the Obituaries-YESSSSS JESUS LOVES ME FUNERAL HOME website.
As I go to SEARCH OBITUARIES, I fill in:

> First Name:
> Last Name:
> Service Date:
> Date of Death:
> Date of Birth:
> City:
> State:

After filling in all the pertinent information. I then it hit (Search) and suddenly Magnolia "Daisy" Wily's photo and history appears. I just stare at her photo for what seems like twenty minutes, wondering, wishing, dreading, remembering, thanking, and appreciating.

The first-print of *Ev'ry Ho Gotta Daddy* is doing tremendously well. Rocka-Bye Bitch is a spokeswoman for prostitutes around the world. Word-of-mouth has played a major role in getting the book out. A testament that speaks to young girls and women living the life.Working the corners, filthy motels, alleys, backseats, basements, doing all the dirty work to please their pimps.

The book is more than words on paper. So much more. I think it is everything and more of what Daisy wanted. Everything and more of what I worked so hard to achieve. I can almost see myself stepping in those shoes I've always saw myself wearing. Fulfilling the void will close the door of doubt. Open more doors of opportunity.

Trepidation comes over me. Instantaneously I turn into this mess of a woman.

Honestly, I never saw myself as this scaredy-cat running in the opposite direction from success. What is so wrong with making it to the top? There will be so many benefits to it. I'll be in a position to do more. Help women across the world. Travel. Experience new things and meet new people. Use my wealth to do some good in this broke down city. So why am I so shaky about it? It feels attainable, yet, I won't allow myself to embrace it. What's holding me back?

It's is relatively quiet this evening. Eight o'clock. Cars screech through the block like they're drag racing...again. Muffling voices echo through the thin walls...again. That old biddy, Mrs. Silva's music lightly plays: Lena Horne "The Man I Love," Dinah Washington "September In The Rain," Bessie Smith "Nobody Knows You When You're Down and Out," and Nina Simone "Isn't it a Pity." The music sho' fit the mood.

Nina's song. It resonates. Makes me think of how "we" as *black* women break each other down instead of build one another up. How "we" flock with our cliques. Switch our asses, twist our lips, and scrunch up our noses, thinking we are "the shit." But not giving a *shit* about anyone else. It is a pity. A daggone shame to be so self-important. Yeah. Nina gives me plenty to think about. Her words permeate through to the depth of me. The soul and meat of me. It makes me look outside of myself. My actions. My mirror. And-And not exclude myself from the problem, but include myself as part of the problem, not the solution.

As I think back, huh, I was reaching out to others but not fully extending my full potential. Not extending my arms to catch that failing and falling sistah. I felt as if there wasn't much that I could do if the sistah wasn't willing to help herself. I couldn't make her. She had to want the help. Feel that she needed the help. I devoted time to the tricks. But that was only because of Daisy. The book and Daisy. Had Daisy not forwarded me the manuscript, none of this would be as it is?

I was teaching from experience not certification, but I wasn't breaking it all down in a way that that uneducated underprivileged sistah could grasp because of her drug usage. I left her dangling on false hope. I saw her as a space cadet trying to be down with her clique. But deep down, she ain't know shit. And I knew she didn't know shit. But I allowed her to pretend to know, because I didn't want to deal with the aftermath. Her finally coming to and remembering all the bullshit that she so tried to forget once she sobered up. I didn't want to be that shoulder to lean on. And I knew. I knew she wasn't strong, okay. I knew. And I knew. I knew deep down I couldn't be strong for her. I couldn't fight her demons for her. I wanted to be able to go in and get out unscathed. Unmarked. With very little clips of memory. I didn't want her burdens toppling over my burdens. Adding to. Making more for me to bear. Instead of taking her under my wing and explaining this and that I left her hanging on words she didn't even know how to pronounce or enunciate or lookup in a dictionary but thought she knew. I didn't feel the need to critique her. She couldn't even sound certain words out. She tried. Tried to impress, but she failed miserably. And I said nothing. Who was I to correct her when she'd been talking that way much of her life? Her Ebonics seemed fine with her. So I let it be fine with me. Indeed it was/is a pity. I feel so small.

I was no scholar. I didn't have a high IQ. I wasn't an avid reader either. Or bookworm. But I knew from being raised by an illiterate father that reading was fundamental. So I engrossed myself in books that appealed to me. Books that reminded me of me. Written by folks that looked like me. Yep. Black folks. I dug into Richard Wright, James Baldwin, and Alice Walker. I had a difficult time trying to grasp Toni Morrison. She was a little too *deep* for me. I considered her a hard read. Very hard. I think the only book I got that she wrote was *The Bluest Eye*.

Slowly I developed an interest in other writers. Not all black writers either. My passion for books grew. But it took me wanting to learn, self-teaching, and not focusing on what I didn't know. Words I didn't know I simply looked them up in the dictionary, which broadened my vocabulary. Sometimes what you know can lead you down other paths that you never thought you'd go. My goal was to not be that: stupid, illiterate, black nigger. My goal was to rise above the stereotype and become somebody influential.

Chapter

Six

D ressed in black slacks, black blouse, bejeweled with black feathery earrings, beaded crimson necklace and matching bracelet, I sit on the saffron sofa. Don't read. Don't write. Don't watch television or a DVD movie. I just sit.

I just sit and listen to the music—to the footsteps that walk across the floor—to the doors that slam—to the elevator that dings—music, footsteps, doors, elevator...the orchestra of movement throughout the building. And I wonder, where are folks going? And have *they* mistakenly forgotten to slip an invite under my door?

My eyes skyward the ceiling. I breathe out, then in. Then I begin to speak, softly. Gently. Calmly. Just speak in a mellow tone of voice as if I am talking on the phone to a family member, girlfriend. I haven't called anyone. No one has called me. Although, my mouth and lips are moving. And my inner thoughts are being spoken. But there is no one here, seated here, but me. Yet, I don't feel completely alone. I feel as if I have company. So I keep talking to this invisible company. Don't think that I am going crazy or anything like that. I just keep talking. Freeing my mind, my spirit. Uncluttering myself. I have packed a lot of boxes with stuff that I could've given away a long time ago. But I didn't. I hoarded a lot of things. A lot of emotional baggage, you know. I complicated my life by doing so. So here I sit unpacking these cardboard boxes, break each box down, then discard of them, along with the pain.

This goes on for a couple of weeks. About two. And in these two weeks I find myself chatting. Just chitchatting away. Finally, it dawns on me that I am chatting away with God.

There feels like an energy surrounding me. I can't really explain it other than to call it an energy. It's warm. Body heating warm. I feel wetness on my chest area. That is how warm it is. As if the sun in beaming down on me.

I rise to me feet. Walk over to my vintage bookshelf and randomly pullout a soft paperback *Does God Have Toys in Heaven*.

I open the book and my fingers seem to have a mind of their own as they flip from page to page. Stopping at page 127 that quotes the author Karla Denise Baker:

"How did my life get so mangled? I fell in love with someone who didn't love me back. Someone who only chose to control me because he knew I had no one. He manipulated me. He belittled me. He dissected me down to a small person and I crawled in this hole and devoured his every thought of me. I ate it up, gobbled it down like it was the best meal I had ever eaten. I had lost my identity. And I became submissive to him. Loving him. Caring for him. Giving my all to my children and him and neglecting myself."

Her words speak so candidly. So fearlessly. So identifiably. So relatable that I walk back to the sofa and sit down and lay the book flat on my lap between pages 127 and 128.

I lean back on the sofa and sigh. Taking a brief moment to think. I then ask myself that same question: "Avery, how did your life get so mangled?"

Chapter

Seven

Weeks go by.

After my discovery I get all emotional and start bawling like a big ass baby to God. I express some concerns hoping He'd be able to point me in the right direction. Because I haven't a clue as to which way to go. Left or right, north or south, east or west.

Since my last visit to Dr. Fulmore, I divulge a great deal with God. More than I thought I would considering the topics weren't things one would think to discuss with Him. I felt no reason to hold back. The guilt was killing me. There was no need for me to play shy. Innocent. The damsel in distress. May as well confess. I mean, it isn't like He doesn't already know. But by me speaking it makes all the more difference. At least to me it does.

I screwed up big time. And every time I reach out to *him*, (*you-know-who*) he never has time to talk. What am I supposed to do? It's not a subject that I can just blurt out over the phone and expect him to understand. No. I have to talk to him face-to-face but he never seems to have or make the time. So where does it leave me? Where I am.

I thought of writing him a letter but thought against it. He needs to see me in person. We need to have eye to eye contact. That's the only way for this to be handled.

Texting. Leaving a voicemail. Emailing. None are options. I have to tell him face-to-face.

God and I talk about many things after my mishap. From the men in my life, my past, my present, Poppa, Ma'am, Johnnie, Antwone, Jewell, Therron, Storyteller, Teka, Ep, Daisy and Xavier. We talk about any and everything under the sun. Well, *I* talk. He listens.

I will admit, sometimes—sometimes I get beside myself. Wear these breeches tight. Yep. Get carried away and fuss God out something terrible. You know raise my voice and fuss Him out. I'm not making any excuses for my actions *but* it usually be on those anxious days when things aren't quite going my way. Those on edge days. Each and every time I get out of character with God, best believe He has one of his servants tap me on the shoulder and remind me who *is* boss. And I don't get loud and/or obnoxious with His servant or mad or start yelling like a raving lunatic. No. I simply shut my mouth, listen, and relate to the message that He so generously delivers. I believe He knows I am overwhelmed. And He also knows that it is only spoken out of anger, disappointment and pain. So much pain. So much pain.

After acting like a brat I put myself in check. Caution. Uh-huh. Yep. Sho' do. I mean, who the heck am *I* to be snapping back at God? After I am through acting a damn fool I need to rest this worriation off by laying my simple-minded-self down and go to sleep.

Chapter
Eight

I *had* the best intentions after hearing the unwelcoming news from Dr. Fulmore several weeks, prior. I took heed to his suggestion to get my house in order. Took into consideration his role in my life, too. His commitment to me. Dr. Fulmore is like a guardian. Father-figure. I really trust him with every fiber of my being. And yes, it hit me like a ton of bricks when he delivered the news. A slap of obliviousness made me come to. Mentally I had drifted to this other place that rejoiced and laughed and smiled and made goofy faces. It was not a time to be adult-like and serious. Mature. It was time to be child-like and fun and silly and giggly. The news took me by the throat and tried to choke me to death. I gasped so full of turmoil and astonishment. Ideally I wanted to leap up and run but time would not allow me the effort. I had no choice but to stay and listen and feel the words that caused me so much grief.

After many, many afterthoughts. And after repeating Dr. Fulmore's words, and after tasting the aftertaste from each syllable I had to accept. Regain a sense of self. Understand the magnitude of the situation.

From there, ah, my mind was set to get closer to God. I know we had a rocky relationship, but I was to make amends. Just last week I started reading scriptures, studying the bible, even looked into joining another church. Either St. Luke Baptist Church or Gilmore Memorial Tabernacle or Christ Temple Baptist Church or Calvary Baptist Church or Agape Christian Center Word Faith or St. Agnes Church or First AME Zion Church or New Shiloh Missionary Full or Upper Room Church of Christ. Honestly I got a headache trying to decide which one to step foot in. I narrowed it down to rotating Sundays which would allow me to visit each one, then decide which was best suited for me. That way I could get a feel of each without excluding any of them. I truly want to find another church but I just need to take my time in doing so.

Chapter
Nine

There is so much going on right now that I need the empowerment from God to get me through. I will admit it is pretty scary walking into God's home, but knowing that He knows me, my heart, that is, I don't foresee Him shunning me away. He hasn't before. So, I'm not too worried about Him, per se. However, I am kind of skeptical of folks. Things are so *different* now. Folks that know of my predicament. Yes, HIV. I wonder, will they be as accepting as God? I can't say for sho' because now that more know, more are aware, more seem to judge without asking or at least getting to know me as a person, a human being; a sistah from their stomping grounds. I think that is what scares me the most. No one likes to be the black sheep, especially in front of a bunch of nosey strangers. But I know it has been known to happen. And quite frankly I don't know if I have the tolerance to let someone try to tear me down in a crowded room of strangers. Me being me I'll more than likely give 'em a piece of my mind. Tell all those ignorant muthafuckers to kiss my black ass in God's house, under God's roof, then storm out with a knowing that I'll be going straight to hell. Really? Will it come to this? Lord, I hope not.

Something is happening. Something or someone is breaking. Brittle. Weakened by circumstance. I feel so much distress. I feel this strong compulsion compelling me, pushing me to get a stronger hold on me. Of who I truly am inside. My soul often feels weary. My heart is still warm. I still have a caring, nurturing spirit, but my faith is slowly weakening. I don't know why but I feel like my destiny is coming to an end. That soon I'll be six feet under buried in a cardboard box with heavy rocks in it to sink me under the Passaic River instead of casket. To some, I'm not even worthy of a proper burial. Just plastic wrap my infected body and call it a day. Honestly, the thought scares me tremendously.

Every night I keep seeing myself falling and the only one that catches me is God. I need to give Him more credit than I do. All the praise. And I do. In my way of doing.

Every night before bed I get down on my knees with tears rolling down my face thanking Him for *never* giving up on me. I thank Him for allowing me the ability to reach out to others. To not be selfish by thinking of *only* myself. I thank Him for giving me strength and courage and wisdom to know the difference of things I cannot change. I want to make amends with Him. To build a spiritual relationship with Him. To commit, you know, but—

At the current moment, there are a few things putting a wedge between God and me. I have to get some things out of my system, off of my chest, first, before I go on this: Bucket List journey. Because I know if I don't God won't be pleased with me. So I ask in prayer that He give me a little mo' time to get my act together. I don't feel as though I'm asking for too much. I-I just want to be right within myself before I—

I want to be completely free. Make Him proud. I want Him to see that I ain't going off the deep end. That I actually have taken my time to really appreciate Him. And I do appreciate all that He has done for me. It's just that I have many, many regrets. And yeah, I know He is a forgiving God, but—

See, I don't want to be wishy-washy with Him. But at this moment, I feel like that is exactly what I will be doing because I still have some unresolved issues that still linger about. I have a lot of shit on my mind. Things that I feel He won't approve of, you know. Um, at least I don't think He will.

God. He already knows my fate but the shame of me knowing that He knows is why I am so reluctant to face Him. And-And I shouldn't be. But my love for Him is so strong that it's (putting it bluntly) its effin' with my conscience. I-I just gotta get my shit right before I lay my burdens down asking for forgiveness. That's just how *I* feel.

I want Him to understand my plight. But I feel like I might be asking for too much. That He may think that I am making excuses again. And I can honestly see how He'd see it that way, but it's not. I am being as sincere as I can be. There's just some things that are bothersome to me. And-And I need to address them before things get quiet. Before the sounds of living become soundless.

Lately a lot has been irking my nerves. So I'm trying to diffuse the situation by asking God to understand and have a little mo' patience with me. I never claimed to be perfect. And no, I am not putting a man before Him. But I am putting what is significant in proper perspective. Hopefully He'll understand.

Chapter
Ten

He took it there!

And I went in for the kill. Not with God. But this jackass that thought he was God's gift to *every* woman. Me being me I put him and his bullshit on pause without any hesitation. I was tired and I felt from past experiences that I didn't have to take the shit that he was dishing out. Had I been the chick from back in the day, huh, he wouldn't have been able to handle me. He'd walk through my front door with his pants on and his dick swinging. But after I'd gotten through with him, chile, he'd walk out that same door with an apron wrapped around his waist, a big spoon and bake book in his hand telling me dessert is ready. I'll be the one wearing *his* pants.

For real, though. That's not the image I would want in a man of mine. Of course, I want a man that can burn in the kitchen as well as the bedroom, but I also want a man that shows that he is the man in the relationship. I know I have a strong untearable disposition. Kind of a fucked-up disposition at times, I'll admit. 'Ey it is what it is. But it is not meant to scare men off. Although it has been known to happen. I guess I hadn't yet met my match. Someone that can have a strong hold on me and still have love for me, too. A man that will allow himself to be free and willingly fall in love with me. Want to make love to me. I miss the connection. And yes, my body has been deprived. But I use mind over matter and deal. Well, that was before I goofed up with *Mr. You-know-who.*

This is what *I* don't get.

Men claim to want a sistah that is strong in her position as the woman of the house. But as soon as she is not willing to put up with their bullshit and she voices her opinion on the situation then she's considered hard and unreasonable. To me it's like a contradiction, you know. Which one do men want: strong, intelligent woman? Or a weak, *yesssssssss* chick that responds to "C'mere, bitch," "Get your dumb-ass over here, bitch," "Shut the fuck up, bitch," and "Do as I say, bitch!"

I'm not quite understanding how men pick and choose women anymore. I used to think that men saw something they liked and went for it. Usually that was how it worked. But sometimes women meet men and they tend to play head games. Men say just about anything to get in some drawers. I'm not one to play games of any sort, so therefore, I know I wouldn't last a week with a joker like that. My mind is too sharp and my tongue too salty.

Back in the day I saw myself as an explorer. I enjoyed the company of a man, especially one that showed great interest in me. The softness that I had did show, but not often. I had to keep that soft chick hidden because I knew once men saw *her* they'd play me like a violin.

Hell, after Poppa had kicked me out I had no alternative but to grow strong. From that day going forward that became a part of my makeup. Had it not been for my dad I probably would've had a different life. Possibly would have met the man that deserved me. I never considered myself *not* marriage material. After Hellman the thought of marriage became just a thought.

But when Xavier proposed I felt like I was really ready to commit. It hurt me to my heart to love that man only to lose him *twice* in the end.

Back to what I was saying. *Him.* Yep.

First of all, I took the initiative to express my displeasure. I thought it best that we stop before anything escalated and feelings developed. Or before things got ugly and we ended up being enemies. I tried to handle things in a diplomatic fashion but I guess he got his feelings hurt. So he decided to not only throw stones at me but went a bit further by making it seem like he was never interested in the first place. Like I put a gun to his head and made him come out. As if to say I made the whole story up and I was sweating him. I didn't even know this man on a personal level. I had seen him in passing. Spoke by just saying hello. So where was he going with all this nonsense.

First of all, he approached me. Talked about how good I'm looking. How sexy he thinks I am. What a great body I have. What he failed to realize was that I was not moved by compliments. Don't get me wrong, compliments are nice and everything but it is not a requirement for me. I'm not one who is easily influenced by sweet-talk. Never was. And probably *never* will be.

Anyway, I never saw him coming. He never entered my mind as far as someone I'd go to third base with. Some men I just look at as men. Nothing more. Nothing less. Figured we could be friends and leave it at that. But I find that men will play that "friend" game just to see how far you'll let the so-called friendship go.

Next thing you know you find yourself on top of him riding that thing called a *dick* like your life dependent on it. Not today. I'd rather self-pleasure and scream out my *own* fuckin' name. Shit.

For some strange reason *men* got shit twisted. I don't know who in their right mind told *men* that they were the rulers of a woman's pussy and mind. Men got another thing coming if they think I'm going to lie on my back and comply with whatever *they* say. Hell, no!

Last time I checked I was in control. Even without a car at the present moment I'm still the driver of my *destiny* and moist *cookie*.

Chapter
Eleven

S eated on the commode, plaid burgundy and navy boy-shorts scrunch down around my ankles. I adjust my reading glasses about my ears and reach in the wicker basket filled with reading material as well as notebook and blue ink pen. You never know when a thought might hit you so I make it a habit of always being prepared.

Opening the fresh notebook I draw my attention back to the issue at hand. Him.

Aug 4, 2016

Dear Sis,

The guy I was tellin' you about the other day. I know. He must've really gotten under my skin to still be talking him up. Yesterday I was venting. Today, well, I guess I'm still venting. That's right! I can't believe he had the audacity to go there by sending me this unsettling text. Talk about too through. Chile, you haven't even begun to see "too through" with me.

This is the very reason why I stopped dating. It's just a waste of precious hours of me getting dazzling for some nitwit with no substance. What the hell happened to chivalry? Has he really died? You know what? I'm beginning to think so.

ME

Today 7:00 AM

"Goodbye. I was hoping that I was wrong about you, but you're no different from the men I meet. I won't text after today. Delete my number, please."

C'MERE

Today 1:23 PM

"I'm glad you said that because I was going to say goodbye last night. My reason? I think something is seriously wrong with you, and I do not want any parts of it. I did have a condom last night, but I responded like that because it was my way of saying, no, I'm not ready for that. I'm glad you sent me this text before I sent it to you, and whatever you think about me doesn't matter. Putting it nicely you are very strange. Good luck with everything in your life, because whatever happens it's everyone else, and not you. Your number has now been deleted out of my phone, my mind. No need to respond— just get lost #aweirdo."

His words don't bring me down because I've been called worse names than weirdo, but it sho' got me feelin' a tidbit annoyed.
    The next to the last man that called me unflattering names was a man Akil had introduced me to. I didn't want to meet this fellah named Laurent Lee, but Akil spoke so highly of him it kind of had me curious. And with Akil being so insistent and persistent I should've taken that as a red flag that something

might've been wrong with this fellah. But I didn't. Big mistake.

Akil said he was an Executive Chef for a restaurant in Harlem. They went way back as far as childhood and have been pretty close ever since. He also said that Laurent had been married twice and divorced twice. No children from either marriage. Currently Laurent Lee was married to his work. But was looking to jump back into the dating world. So Akil asked if he could give Laurent my number. I said okay. Big mistake.

Over the phone, Laurent had insisted that he pick me up. But I suggested we meet at the restaurant instead. I don't know it was just something I heard in his voice that made me feel that way.

Upon my arrival to TABLE-4-2 on Route 4 Paramus, New Jersey, I must admit I was a bit nervous. I mean I hadn't had a blind date before and I wasn't exactly sho' what to expect. But I was open-minded. Optimistic.

Upon entry of the dim-lit restaurant I was greeted by a hostess named BeBe. A skinny red-headed white woman with well-endowed breasts dressed in plain emerald green dress with sexy Jessica Simpson gold pumps. I had given her my name because I had made reservations, prior. She checked her listing and asked me to follow her into the well-lit room of modern furniture, plants, and in the center of the space was a black tinted glass and marble bar that seated twenty or more.

While thanking BeBe for her hospitality, I noticed this gentleman seated at the bar dressed in a dark-gray suit. Based on the photo Laurent sent me through text, from his side profile he fit the description of Laurent but I wasn't one hundred percent sho'.

As I was making my way toward the gentleman, he turned in my direction, stood, and greeted me with a dazzling smile, then introduced himself as Laurent Lee.

How did he know it was me? I wondered. But figured Akil must have shown him a picture of me, because I sho' as hell didn't. That snake.

Within seconds this caramel-colored, dark curly-haired man dressed in black slacks and matching vest with a white collar shirt approached us and escorted us to a table meant for two. It was cozy, quaint. The red lighting set a mood of mystery, which I thought was appropriate since this was our first meeting.

Laurent was tall like NBA basketball star Lamar Odom, but lankier. He put me in mind of Michael Baisden because he did resemble him, but he wore a bald head. He was fair-skinned and a fairly decent looking man. Not eye-candy. But not unattractive. Average. However, Laurent had the sexiest hazel eyes I'd ever looked into.

Quickly I'd come to find out that Akil's boy was a complete dickhead. A compulsive liar, a pit-bull, and a womanizer. I wasn't feeling him. Obviously the feeling was mutual because Laurent was showing his black ass. And I didn't like it. I didn't like it one bit. But for some reason I figured since we were both adults we could end the date amicably. You know, in a civilized manner. Unfortunately, it didn't go down like that.

For one, I could instantaneously see that Laurent was used to having his way. I heard it in his deep voice. And dealing with a woman with backbone was not his normal cup of tea. He wasn't satisfied until he had the last word. He most definitely had a hot temper.

Laurent ranted on calling me names like: bar whore, leach, beggar...what? I was completely puzzled. We hadn't even ordered dinner yet. I was still nibbling on the warm basket of bread. Where is this coming from? I wondered. Had he drank before I arrived? I couldn't say. He did have a glass setting in front of him with clear liquid in it when I arrived. It could've been vodka or water with a wedge of lemon. It didn't matter. I didn't even know that man. That nut. And he didn't know me. I had never asked him for anything. Had never known he existed if it weren't for Akil. That bastard! Laurent was brash. Belligerent. Vulgar. Crass. He had no clue as to who I was or how I was. I had just met that fool and already he was trying to control my mind. A woman he had just met not even an hour ago. I was like...whoa, what's up with this fool? Obviously he'd been hurt before. Was insanely miserable with himself. Having a mid-life crisis? Which? Chile, I couldn't say for sho'.

According to Laurent he was given opportunities to get out of the 'hood when he was in his latter teens. But ole boy got sidetracked when his girlfriend got pregnant. I'd say, Laurent was still bitter.

Next thing you knew he was back where he'd started. Back in Paterson. Working a backbreaking job, while taking night classes at Passaic County Community College-PCCC, and supporting his baby, so that he wouldn't have to deal with his nagging girlfriend threatening him every day. He was mad at the world because he had not fulfilled his dream of becoming a professional football player. But he had no one to blame but himself, and fear. I was nowhere in the picture. So therefore there was no reason why he should've been taking his anger out on me. I didn't do it. I didn't fuck him. Nor did I fuck his dream up. I wasn't that little voice in his head telling him to come back to these mean streets. That was some chick named Trinity Griffin. His ghetto-ass so-called girlfriend that he'd only known for two weeks. Yep. Two! She threatened to take him down to child support if he didn't come back and help raise their daughter. Not me.

If Victor Cruz had the God-given talent and he went for his dream. Then Laurent should've done the same. But no, he didn't. He allowed his girlfriend to dictate his future. A girl, mind you, he barely knew. He chose what he chose. He chose to live in a box of an apartment, cook all day, scheme and lie and cheat himself out of having a comfortable life, to play on women's emotions, then complain and blame, and think, actually think that he was going to meet a woman that actually wanted to be with him after he treated her so unkindly, badly, and spoke so ugly of her.

It was apparent to me that Laurent needed to lay off the bottle. Stop smoking weed and deal with the hand he dealt himself.

I sat across from him and gave him a piece of my mind. "Laurent, you might wanna stop dating those crackerjack tricks, find yourself a wholesome woman, and, dude, grow some damn balls. And learn, really learn how to appreciate a beautiful, black woman." He just looked at me as if I was speaking in Greek.

I could not believe this guy was in his mid-fifties and was acting like a spoiled child. I was sooooo turned off.

I didn't know what the hell he was talking about. And I didn't care for him to explain. I just wanted to go home and watch a DVD movie. Wished I had Netflix. I'm more than sho' it would've been far more interesting than Laurent Lee.

I'm sho' there are some desperate women out there, but he had the wrong one that day. I was not going to sit there and take it. I kindly got my five-foot-eleven inch ass of woman up in my multi Bonita Maxi dress that fell past my ankles and exposed my shoulders and V-neck line. Yep. The one I ordered from the ASHRO.com catalog. That dress was bursting with colors of: green, black, and ruby, pink, yellow, olive, which, might I add, enhanced my complexion. I wore my black, three-inch back tie heels, which made my French pedicure toes look sexy. Keeping it real, honey, I was looking fierce! I scrunched up my nose and gave Laurent an once-over.

I then looked around at the lovely crowd and I spoke in the loudest tone I could muster up. Loud enough for everyone in that restaurant to hear. "Oh, by the way," I said, "...here's a tip..."

All heads turned in our direction.

107

I had six twenty-dollar bills dangling from my fingertips. I released them as they fell to the table to give that nitwit a hint. With a straightness of face, I said, "Here's one hundred and twenty dollars' worth of real woman, bitch-ass! Women rule! Bitches fuck-up the groove!" I then walked away with a sway in my hips.

As I was making my way to the exit, my girl, BeBe slapped me five, and out the door I went.

Once outside in the humid air, my initial thought was to call Akil and let him have it over the phone, but then I thought against it. This was waaaayyyy before the "CHURCH" incident at the strip club. I believe that was the last time we spoke. No. The last time we spoke was when he called me asking me questions about Zaelyn. Since that day I hadn't spoken to him and I wanted to keep it that way. Family or not.

I was so angry with Akil. But mostly angry with myself for even considering. From that day I vowed to never go on another blind date again.

Don't get me wrong, I loved me some black men, but it's no wonder why I preferred white men.

Huh, men?

You can't live with or without 'em, but sometimes you got to, especially when they act like ghetto bitches.

Talks to you later, Sis,

Avery

After handling my business, washing my hands and towel drying 'em, I exit the bathroom. Body is gradually feeling relaxed but my mind—my *mind* is still overthinking.

I reenter the bathroom and grab the notebook and pen and head into the living room. Seems I got more to say.

Aug 4, 2016

Dear Sis,

I'm not quite understanding some things between men and women. And I am not the type of chick to just let things be. No. That frustrates the hell outta me. Lettin' things be...especially when someone else causes the chaos. They cause it, then dismiss themselves as if they had nothing to do with it. Man up, shit! Why can't men just man the hellllllllll up?!

Frustration messes with my creativity. And right now, I don't need to be messed with. I have more important things to devote to. A ~~man~~ is not top priority.

Inundated with manuscripts up to my eyeballs I don't have the time nor the patience to deal with meaningless gibberish. But for some reason I can't let this one slide. I don't know why.

Could be I'm just fatigued. Fed-up with meeting morons. Could be relationships are becoming a nuisance. Could be the thought of meeting someone worth engaging in has become less important. No wonder why I bury myself in stories. At least they pique my interest.

When things tend to tick me off I have to express myself. No need to stress myself. I've done that too many times. All it's done is decease my appetite. I end up with a pimple on my forehead, the tip of my nose, and under my chin. My stomach gets unsettled. Alka-Seltzer and ginger beer can only do so much. My nerves get shaky. Then the nail biting starts. I become unbalanced. It's nerve-wracking to go through the mixed emotions, you know. Even more so when you're trying to understand, as I have done, exactly, what the hell do men want?

Do men only think with the head below their belt? And I know you can't judge all men based off of one man. But dang, they all seem to act the same in one way or another.

I know. I know what you're going to say. Men are as complicated as women. You'll never figure 'em out.

Believe it or not, I can deal with complicated. I'm complicated. But I can't deal with disrespect or insensitivity or misrepresentation. And a lot of men misrepresent themselves.

Is it just me? Am I being irrational? Am I internalizing too much into this? Do I have my wires crossed? No. I don't.

I'm more than sho' that there are women out in the world that will appreciate where I'm coming from. Do they (women) notice that as soon as we (women) stand our ground and show that we are not airheads, show that we actually have a mind and use it, show that we are now taking moments to think before we react, before we bed or kneel on our knees and give a man head we-we actually ask questions that make him stammer. Men don't like when a woman asks questions. I think it makes them nervous. Like she actually took time to stop, think, and then request. Yes, request. Some women are so desperate that they only see dollar signs, not the signs of a cheating, unfaithful, selfish man. Men want to be in charge, but when a strong sistah who knows what she wants and verbalizes what she won't tolerate, oh, it's a problem. Most of the time women just go with the flow because they don't want to be alone or lonely. BITCH-UP, GIRL!!!!!! Not anymore. Not on my watch!

What really gets my panties in a wad is when a man who claims he's a man doesn't get his way...lo and behold women become every nasty name a man can conjure up. I mean, fo' real. Men have resulted to name-calling to get their point across. Ridiculous!

I guessed it was supposed to bruise my ego. You know, make me cry like some little girl. I'm a grown ass woman! You betta' recognize!

Just because I don't choose to entertain him—he takes offense and without even as much as a second thought whips out his measly three inches and pisses right in front of me. Scrunching up my nose. Who does that? So disrespectful!

110

Half the time I have tunnel vision. I don't know whose winking, whistling, or beeping as I sashay down a street. I am in my zone. These days a man is the furthest thing on my mind. I'm too busy, too deep in thought to really see a man checking me out. But it has been known to happen. And it did happen. Just the other day, C'Mere Cedric approached me.

I had seen C'Mere more than a few times walking the beat and nothing was ever said about being interested in me. Not until a couple of days ago when he was directing traffic because a NJ Transit bus had hit a traffic light pole and it uprooted from the ground and had fallen in the middle of Main Street, right across from Bank of America.

I was standing on the corner waiting to cross while eyeing him in his navy-blue uniform. We caught eyes. It kind of took me back, you know. I never looked at him as someone I would date. Get to know as a friend, yeah, but not date.

The way C'Mere looked at me, mouthwatering. Those dark brown eyes of his were sinking deep into me. It kind of made me feel like he was only interested in one thing. And I had no problem asking the question.

I said, "C'Mere, do you want to fuck me?"

Of course, he denied it and pretended to want to get to know me and my interests.

Whatever. I wasn't fully convinced.

C'Mere volunteered his number, but I was reluctant to take it. Past experiences, let's just say. He asked for mine and I saw no harm in giving it to him. Mainly because I didn't think he'd use it. He seemed like an okay dude. Operative word: seemed.

Hadn't he read my book, Anonymous? I wondered. But was reluctant to ask because I really didn't want to know.

I didn't want to feel like being grilled with question after question. And I'm pretty sho' if he did read my book he wouldn't have wanted my cell phone number.

I don't know why but I felt strongly that he'd go berserk if I'd told him right then and there. Oh, I do believe the truth would've came out in due time. But that day, no. I wasn't quite prepared to deal with him ranting and snarling and bitching about me and my circumstance. I just couldn't see him being a stand-by-his-woman-kind-of-guy. Nope.

He'd seemed shallow, but I recall a time when I was shallow too. Give the brother a chance that inner voice in me spoke. As reluctant as I was, I said okay.

Honestly, I wasn't fully convinced that he was interested in getting to know me, but I tried to give the brother the benefit of the doubt. Sometimes you just gotta go with your gut instincts. Read the eyes, they say soooooooooooooooooo much.

His eyes scrolled me from flip-flops to my trendy jeans to my white T-shirt to my big hooped earrings. To him, my aura was sounding off some serious signals that I was oblivious of. That day I put no effort in the way I looked. I didn't care. I was in "writer's mode." And "writer's mode" is simple comfort.

To the outside world I was probably looking plain compared to my usual attire. Dress to impress for no one, but me. That particular day, I was as natural as can be. I had on minimal makeup. I hadn't brushed my hair. I let it air-dry because I had recently gotten a fresh cut. But according to C'Mere's eyes, I unknowingly was making his nature rise. Yep. He had a hard-on.

During those few days of us communicating either by phone or text I was everything from: sexy, attractive, interesting, smart, but then something shifted when I got a call from him stating he was outside my building.

Outside my building uninvited, mind you.

I do remember expressing a need to release my frustrations from a long day of working and reading manuscripts. And I do recall him volunteering to help me out, but—

It kind of through me for a loop as to why he would just assume I wanted him to come over, uninvited. Or had I unknowingly, unintentionally invited him? Hmm.

Sho' we'd engaged in texts. And sometimes we would use our writing talent to communicate. Sometimes it got steamy, but it was all in good fun. It never went as far as that. But as he once stated in his text: we are both aware that words are powerful. And I agreed.

I might've had a slip of the tongue depending on what we shared. He might've too. Again, I saw no harm in two grown folks tickling their fancy. Well, not then, but I do now.

Huh. I saw The Perfect Guy and that movie woke me the hell up. It changed how I view dating, men, even me.

Sometimes you have to be very careful what you reveal, how you reveal it, even in having fun. We were just passing the time with innocent dialogue. But sometimes even innocent or sexual words are taken to heart. Out of context. Words may imply one thing when all you mean is another.

As C'Mere had so eloquently stated in his text, his reasoning was to come by and say, goodbye, because he no longer had an interest in me or in seeing me. Kind of makes me wonder if I had allowed him up, and if I had allowed him to sex me till my pussy ached, what would he have done then? Would it have still been goodbye? I'd have to say, yes. Considering.

Without him knowing or asking the question that needed to be asked. Me being me, I wonder if I would've openly shared. Would it have mattered to him after the fact? Probably. Most definitely.

Not knowing is easy. Knowing is what kills the mood, the groove. Kills you or gets you killed.

In my case, it'll kill me for having HIV.

Sex. That was his intensions all along, but I saw through his bull and I stood my ground by saying, no, thank you.

Of all the years I've looked at myself in the mirror, never had I seen what he implied: weirdo. Strange, yes, but weirdo, no.

Enough about C'Mere. He's yet another history lesson. Another bruised apple added to my bunch.

Talks to you later, Sis,

Avery

Chapter
Twelve

Aug 7, 2016

D*ear Sis,*

Girl, just bear with me. Seems I'm going through something and just need to vent.

I had a REALLY bad day yesterday.
WOMEN!!!!!!

Some women can be real heffas. And yesterday I encountered one. One real fat chick with a jacked-up weave and a fucked-up attitude that needed to be put in check.

It kind of through me off because I'm not use to folks being so indirect when speaking directly about me to my face. You know my motto: "Keep it real, bitch."

I've come to realize that when you're in a position of authority folks tend to want to shine in front of an audience oppose to one on one behind closed doors. I mean, do what you feel makes you feel grown and brand new 'cause I'm going to do what makes Avery feel grown, new and improved.

One thing I can't stand is an insecure, jealous heffa. What really annoys me most is a woman that has a man and don't know how to keep him.

Let me say this, Sis.

In this instance of what I'm about to tell yah, I had to piss in her cup that was already overflowing with her bullshit. Yep. In other words, we had to go there.

Yesterday I was not in the mood to debate over something that occurred dayyyyys ago. My issue: (Disgruntled, Manager at I-HOP).

Obviously I struck a nerve in her by my presence and she couldn't handle it, you know what I'm sayin', girl. So she decided to try me. And I gave her the unexpected because most black women would fly off the handle and lose their damn mind, especially if they feel singled out. Not me. At least, not yesterday.

First of all, I'm not a thief. I don't steal spotlights. I give spotlights.

If I see your error, and I inquire, does that make me wrong, especially when it applies to me? No. It makes it known that some clarity needs to be addressed. But if you're too headstrong and can no longer see beneath you, you'll never see the mistakes that you've made. The errors and unnecessary bullshit that you've caused all because your man gave me a compliment. Tell me something. How did it go from compliment to creeping with the virus?

As I've always said, I gotta image to uphold. I kept my cool and simply walked out the door before I found myself in handcuffs being hauled off to the County jail. I didn't feel the cause was worth the punishment, so I handled the situation by not making it a big deal. Of course, I was heated because I get tired of being judged based off of looks, body, and status. This is how God made me. Black and beautiful. What happened happened. I can't change it. Women need to get over it. And get on with their own lives. And leave me the hell alone.

Understand. God gave men eyes for a reason. And if you're not doing the pleasing, best believe someone else is. But that "someone" doesn't mean ME!!!!

I wasn't trying to do the pleasing. I respected her in the utmost way. I had never been formally introduced to her. But knowing, knowing that she was a sistah. No, I wasn't about to do her dirty. I was trying to change the mindset of black women by not reducing down to the level that [some] black women stoop.

I wanted to uplift ole girl. But see, that-that heffa (notice I didn't say...bitch) never gave me the opportunity to tell her that. She jumped to conclusions after seeing me. That dirty bitch lucky (ok, one slipped through the cracks) I removed myself from the scene. Because had I not. Oh trust, we would've been tussling in that place. But since I can't do jail, I felt it best to step away and think before (Sistah-girl in me) cracked that jaw. Bitch must've misunderstood. I'm from the 'hood!

Understand. When I get in that mindset of "Sistah-girl" there ain't no holding me back. I don't care if you go get: May-May and Peaches and Pookie and Snooky and Shortie and/or Rah-Rah, bitch, it's on and poppin'. You could go get your aunt your momma and even your grandma and we'd have to battle that shit out.

Now, I'm not advocating violence, I'm just sayin'.

I try to the best of my abilities to act like a lady, but sometimes, sometimes you gotta act a fool to get these jealous bitches to leave you the fuck alone.

Sometimes you have to see things for what they truly are. People too. Even if that "thing" is you. 'What happens it's everyone else [fault], and not you.' Those were C'Mere's words. And I'm only referring back to 'em because they apply to this other jackass named Haswell Emmons. How the hell would he know? That was my initial thought, too. Huh.

Let me backtrack.

Haswell had been inside my "sanctuary" one time. Meaning: my home. Once. And I'll admit, brotha was looking something sexy. He was. He sho' was. Just thinking about him now. Even chocolate skin, deep-set milk-chocolate colored eyes, curly jet-black hair, muscular built, and height of a tall tree. Oh yeah, he was downright finnee! But—

Haswell sat on the sofa. I sat on the chaise longue. We talked about back in the day. High school. Life. Things that we'd endured. And I guess he went home and confided in his girl (Manager at I-HOP) about me, but obviously the story got twisted. Can't say I'm surprised.

Okay.

I took the conversation there because I felt like getting it out the way. He can't see it just by looking at me, I thought. So, I put myself out there. Bam! There. I gave him an option to deal with me and my "package deal" on a platonic level, since he, too, had made it known that he was interested in being my friend.

How quickly did that change? How quickly do you think?

No, Haswell didn't make it known that evening, but I could see something within his eyes. That look that folks like me get. I mean, has he walked in my shoes. No, I doubt that he has. But see, this is the very reason why I take my time when meeting men. I don't leap, jump, do backflips, cartwheels because I know as soon as I say what needs to be said, here comes the bullshit. It never fails. And I take the brunt of verbal abuse through technology because men are not bold enough to come tell me to my face. Cowards.

Respect. Love. Trust. It all has to be earned as far as I'm concerned. Folks just expect me to disregard their actions. Let bygones be bygones. Nah. I can't. I'm too upset to let the insensitive things that others have done to me go. I'm not holding a grudge. But I'm tired of always being the one who always tries to find a resolution to the problems that they cause. I'm tired of being the peacemaker. The one that shoves their crap under a doormat and act as if it never happened. I'm simply tired. And you know what. I ain't taking it anymore!

Men. It all boils down to the men in my life. Every man that has ever fucked me consider yourself lucky. I'd say you dodged this bullet and was able to live a happy and fulfilling life. At least I hope you have. Regardless of my situation I'd never throw salt on the memorable times we'd shared. I was way ahead of my prime. So glad I didn't wait for age to catch-up and ruin my fun.

Sometimes you have to go for yours 'cause if you don't, you never know what may happen. Life flies by and next thing you know you find yourself by yourself.

Talks to you later, Sis,

Avery

Chapter
Thirteen

These days my favorite words are: "*I am not interested.*" But saying those very words doesn't seem to sink in the head of a twenty to twenty-eight year old. I don't know why but all of a sudden their eyes is fixated on me. It's not like anything is different about me. OK. I've gained a few pounds. So! I'm the same old Avery Love. Still sporting my signature cut. Look the same. Talk the same. Walk the same. Sassy as I wanna be. Maybe that's the attraction.

Yes, I'm a bit frustrated at the moment. But I have good reason to be. Yep, yet another jackass.

I hate to call a brother out his name but this *nincompoop* was trippin'! I'm pretty damn upset because it could've so easily have been me.

I've been a faithful customer to my stylist Aja's salon, *Villa of Locks* for umpteen years, okay. Aja's my girllllll.

Feeling the urge to walk down memory lane I get comfy on the saffron sofa and reach for my journal off the coffee table.

Aug 10, 2016

Dear Sis,

I met this guy.

And yes, you are soooo right. I meet guys all the time, but this one. Honeychile, this one takes the cake.

I'ma let the story tell itself. 'Cause this one is a trip.

Sis, as always, take heed. Every experience is an Avery "REALITY" episode. You might need a drink before you get into this one.

You know what???

Why waste precious time dwelling on him. It can wait until tomorrow.

I popped the cork to this bottle of Middle Sister Drama Queen Pinot Grigio I had set in the wine rack.

Cheers!

Talks to you later, Sis,

Avery

Chapter

Fourteen

Aug 11, 2016

*D*ear Sis,

4:53 PM

Last Thursday

"So, Avery, how was the Dom Pérignon last night? It must've tapped you out because you never returned my call." Swett (Need-2-Cut-It-Out) Coy says, in his deep husky voice.

First of all, I don't know where he got off calling me. I mean the bottle of Dom Pérignon was a nice gesture, but I don't think Aja would appreciate him calling her clients, especially her frequent clients. The big tippers.

Okay. I'll give it to Swett—the brother can cut. And he is very thorough, very detailed, which I like. But if it weren't for Aja, brother-man wouldn't even have a job. He'd still be on the cross-streets of Broke and Ass trying to make a hustle.

122

Listen. I ain't kickin' dirt in nobody's face. I ain't mad at Aja for giving him a shot. You know, see if he's made to be molded into an honest-wage-working-black man.

Coming from the streets to working in a salon setting ain't exactly quick money. But if he got skills, the know-how to communicate with people, anything is possible. The fact that she took a chance on a joker with a rap sheet as long as my right leg, said A LOT. Whether Swett knew it or not. I sho' did.

I mean, he stepped in the door fresh to impress (gators, Gucci, diamond stud in his ear, money-clip of 50s and 100s, you get my drift) but the 'hood in him was still evident.

Aja was the one recruiting for a male barber for Villa of Locks. Some of her female clients had suggested the idea because they were tired of going to the barbershops—only to sit and listen to men gossip like little bitches, listen to hip-hop music with profanity degrading women as chickenheads and inhaling what smelled like skunk, but what was obviously weed. So Aja decided to add another chair and find a reliable barber with: license, skill, swag, looks, smile and style. To her, Swett fit the bill.

Don't get me wrong. Swett was a handsome devil. His thick jet-black kinky afro did complement him. Dark, flawless, luscious skin. Body scent of Sean John cologne. Thick lashes and dark doe eyes. He stood about six-foot-one. Physique was not bad for a man that claimed he didn't work out at the gym. What Planet Fitness was beneath him? He claimed he had a home gym in his townhouse basement in Burlington County, somewhere in Delran, New Jersey, which he wanted me to come and check out, possibly workout with him. He claimed he was going to teach me how to shoot some hoops in his spacious backyard and martial arts. Of course, I declined. What kind of chick do you think I am? Don't answer that.

As you probably figured out. Swett claimed a lot of things.

First of all, I have nothing against change. I'm all for change. Pan-handler asks for a couple quarters, I'll help the needy out. But don't make it a habit. And don't think just 'cause you fine as chocolate wine that you're gonna pull a wool over my eyes.

First, I knew Swett used to be a drug-dealer. Now reformed drug-dealer, so he said. Second, Swett had a shitload of babies that came with a package full of baby mommas. That ain't nothing but a restraining order. Third, Swett didn't have a townhouse, he lived in his momma's attic. Fourth, Swett was a compulsive liar. Moocher. Fifth, I knew that that Dom Pérignon set him back a few...dollars. Sixth, the reason why I knew was because his momma came into the salon asking for her RENT money. Yep. She put him on blast! I laughed my ass off. Seventh, obviously Swett was irresponsible. Eighth, why would I want a man that took money from his momma? Ninth, the fact that Swett still lived in his mother's house and was pushing forty-two said a lot about what type of man he was. Tenth, I WAS not about to set myself up and have a man like Swett trying to shack up with me and pull me down. Hello! Eleventh, I was not interested in Swett. He was not ready for the real world. And the real world was all... I...knew. Twelfth, I wanted a man that was capable of keeping a job, paying his own bills, giving his momma respect and helping her out from time to time, catering to his woman—basically standing on his own two feet. Thirtieth, Swett had a lot of work to do to ever get a taste of this red-velvet cake.

Talks to you later, Sis,

Avery

Chapter
Fifteen

Aug 12, 2016

D*ear Sis,*

"Swett, the champagne was delicious. I was busy with work so I didn't have time to call you back. Plus, it was in the wee hours by the time I was through, and I didn't want to disturb you."

"Cool. You preparing for work?" Swett asked.

"No. I'm reading over some paperwork from the New York State Department of Taxation and Finance."

"What time do you have to go in to work? I've been up a little from last night, wonder if you'd let me hide out by your place for like two hours?"

I thought to myself. Hide out??? Oh, hell no! What...? He running from the cops! My mouth dangled open. Is he for real? No, he can't be. Only one way to find out.

Before I got a chance to ask a simple question, Swett said, "Don't think you can tuck me away for a few hours?"

Oh, he is for real.

"I'm not alone. I recently started seeing someone and he is here with me."

"Hold up!" Swett snapped. "You gonna give him some or shuffle him for our moment?"

I remained silent. What the fuck is this dude's problem?!

"Damn. I wanted a little of that you got." He said.

Oh, he is really feeling himself.

"Sorry, Swett, but— Are you listening to yourself? I thought we were building a barber-slash-client rapport, but I see your mind has gone somewhere else. I'm not understanding you right now. I mean, where you get off—get the impression that you could call me and talk to me in this disrespectful manner and think—actually have the audacity to think that I would be willing to let you come over and tap this ass! C'mon. What you think your dick is that skillful that you can get the coochie wet with this weak come-on?"

"Oh, pardon. I thought I was speaking with my Dominican mami. I truly apologize, sincerely....ah, who is this again?"

I pursed my lips. Temples throbbed. "Listen here, Swett, I don't think you made a mistake in calling me. But since you have let me school you on something. For future reference I'm a lady. I'm too much of a lady to just have a revolving door of men come over and hide out for a few hours. That is NOT my style. And if you do happen to have a Dominican mami, I truly hope you show her some respect, if she does allow you entry into her paradise. And if you know that you won't respect her, leave her alone, and let another man treat her in a manner that is respectful."

At the end of my little speech, Sis, all I heard was...Click!!!

Shit! Now I gotta find another barber. But that's okay. At least Swett knows not to play little boy games with me. I'm NOT the one.

Sis, the best way to get rid of a headache, is not to take Bayer aspirin. Just use that mouthpiece that we all have and let a joker know from the door that you ain't some chick that don't have standards. You gotta speak up, set a brotha straight. 'Cause if you don't, the next chick that he meets gonna have to deal with that foolishness.

I know that that is her business for even entertaining him, but c'mon, it's time to stop being so damn petty and selfish and help a sistah out. That's right! I said it. Get out of bitch mode and gain control. Don't let a chump soup you up to the point where you don't care about anybody or anything. He ain't worth all that you got to give. Believe that.

Sis, do you believe that?

Listen girl, first, block his number. Don't give it a second thought. See, by blocking his number you won't have to worry about ever hearing his voice. Well, not ever because he can always call from a different number and still get in contact with you, but only if you pick up. You can even go as far as deleting his number, but let's keep it real. More often than not, women have a tendency to renege on their words. Women, often find themselves retracing their steps when they feel that itch tempting 'em to call his number. Hell, I'm guilty of it. That is why I am saying what I am saying.

You know how it is. It is so easy to reconnect with him by texting. Then calling. Then you are back to square one again. Save yourself the heartache, and pickup one of my books and read till your heart's content. In due time, you'll find another brother. Hopefully he won't be a replica of... Swett Coy.

See, what you don't know is...yep, Swett was running from the cops. Come to find out, through the gossip mill Swett had been a naughty little boy. Yep. Brother was on the run for raping this sistah he met on Tinder. Dang!

The day he had hit me up to come over, huh, was the very day she allowed him over to her crib. Seemed they had got their wires crossed and Swett just assumed that he had it like that to go over and feast off of her. But she wasn't that type of chick, you know. She actually just wanted to get to know him. But Swett had other things in mind. One thing led to another by a simple kiss, and the sistah found herself under attack. He forced himself on her, then in her. She fought back but after the fact of him reaching his climax. Anyway. She managed to escape and ran down the hall naked as a jaybird to a next-store neighbor, and called the police.

Two days later, Swett was arrested. Where? At another sistah's house. What had happened was. The woman's daughter was on this blogging website and saw Swett's profile. Under his profile was comments. Anyway, apparently the woman he raped put her story out there for all to read. Alarmed, the daughter immediately called the police, gave them her address, and listened from her bedroom of Swett and her mother in the living room engaged in conversation. Her daughter was twelve.

It hurt his momma's heart when she was notified of what her only son had done. To know that her son was a repeat offender of rape, oh, she was beside herself. Where had she gone wrong? She wondered.

In my open opinion, after reading the article in the local newspaper the only thing that I saw that she'd done wrong was, she never encouraged him to seek a life of his own. She allowed him to remain under her motherly wing. Swett didn't know what it took to be a man. Witnessing what his mom had experienced as a wife. Oh, yeah, she was in a dysfunctional marriage. He used to watch her get hit by his dad like it was normal behavior. For one, his mom never called the police. Of course, his dad groomed him into disrespecting women, and getting away with it too. Eventually, his dad left his mom and moved in with some other chick named Slut

Bucket. She lived right across the hall. He left Swett too. Left him in the hands of an abused wife, mother, woman that treated Swett more like a friend, than a son.

Some brothers don't know how to take "no" for an answer. In Swett's case, his mom, she never told him "no" because she was too afraid to.

So I say that to say this, some sistahs are stronger than others. Even at twelve years old.

Talks to you later, Sis,

Avery

Chapter

Sixteen

Country

I loves my man sooooo much. Can't see myself living without him. If I can't have him, I feels like I'll die. Funny. I feels like I'll die *with* or *without* him.

I should've known betta' but I didn't. I don't knows how to separate myself. How to escape from his way of lovin' me. If he don't hit me I feels unloved.

A *slap* for me is as if he'd given me a passionate kiss.

A *punch* for me is as if he'd given me a quickie from behind.

A *closed fist* knockout for me is as if he'd fucked me good and hard.

And a *chokehold* for me is as if we were on the living room floor making love.

Like I says 'fore if he don't hit me that means he don't love me. I need my man to *love* me. So to me, his form of affection is like-like...*love taps*. His way of saying, "..., I love you..." Hearing these words in my head and taking the blows on this here body of mine is something I am *willing* to take—to *keep* him. To keep him from leaving me and to continue to hard love me.

All these years I didn't realize how broken I am. It sounds so not like me. If that makes any sense. I seem to have lost myself in this marriage.

Nothin' clicks. NOT even the sound of his fists crackin' into me. Breaking me. Breaking bones in me. Love taps. I still call 'em "Love taps."

I don't knows. O-kay. I do. But I don't. It's hard to explain why. But every day I ax me: *"Country, why you stays with this man?"* I guess I'm not tired of axin' the question. 'C-'Cause I'm only axin' me. It's not like someone else is axin' me. And if someone should I often wonder what my reply will be. Knowing me as I do, I probably shrug my shoulders with a blank look on my face as if to say I don't knows. It's like my feet is cemented to his heart. I can't seem to part ways to save my life.

Believe it or not, once upon a time things was magical between us. Herberto and me. Special. But those days is long behind me. Those days vanished in the night. Ain't no mo' bright in my sight. All's we has is now. *Now.* It frightens the hell outta me.

Hmm. Every day is a day of unknown for me. An unknown *day* of death. An unknown *time* of death. An unknown *place* of death. No. There is no mo' good times. All's I see before me is bouquets Black roses, pallbearers and a pine box.

What happened? Hmm. I don't knows, exactly. But what I do knows is, I wish I could do away with my mind and heart. Between the two: *mind* and *heart*, they keeps me motionless. Herberto knows. Yup. That Puerto Ric husband of mine knows that I love him mo' than I love air to breathe.

"Now I lay me down to sleep, I pray the Lord my soul to keep, if I should die before I wake, I pray the Lord my soul to take."

Every night before I crawl, literally crawl into bed, I says my prayers.

Every day is a blessed day—a God-given day when I rise and has sight and the privilege to sees peoples I knows. Peoples who sees me. Peoples who think they knows me. But don't knows me at all. Don't knows my situation, my circumstance as complicated as it is. They hasn't a clue. Not one daggone clue.

When I sees theirs faces, something deep inside me wants to say—says so many things my troubled mind and heart yearns to says, but the words—these feeling words just won't climb outta me, crawl outta me, leap outta me, and talk. Naw. Instead, they lie dormant in me. Lie still in me. Just lie in me. Die in me.

I gather my laundry and shove it in the cobalt blue laundry bag that is set in the laundry cart and will my way to the Laundromat. Herberto is sound asleep, as usual, with a bottle of Fifth clenched in his hand. He holds it mo' than he holds me. He holds it like it's his kept woman. Every day that man of mine cheats on me. And every day I let him.

***

"Dirty bitch! If you caught fire right now I wouldn't even spit on you! I'd let yo' bitch-ass burn da fuck up! Fuckin' slut ass bitch!" The young, deep charcoal-colored boy says with such belligerence in his croaky voice.

Immediately his violent words pinch a nerve in me. My neck nearly snaps back when I hears him say that to this young, pretty black gal. It really tees me off! Makes me grit and grind down hard on my teeth. Makes me hurt. So much so that my hundred and eighty-seven pounds of woman is ready to cut loose. "Oh, I's gives you a dirty bitch, aiight," I scream in my head. "C'mon on the dark side you li'l punk. You big. You bad. C'mon over here

132

and show me whatchu workin' wit'!" I has to catch myself 'fore I storm outta this Laundromat and give him a piece of my dang mind.

Before my feet exit the door, something snatches me back and reminds me that-that this ain't back in the day where you can interfere like Mrs. Jane, our next-store neighbor used to do. These young peoples is hard talkin' and walkin' and livin'. Ain't no mo' in between seems like. Ain't no mo' gettin' through to that thickness in their hard heads anymore.

I takes a deep breath to shake my nerves. I think it is so insensitive and cruel to say things like that to a gal, especially with so much conviction and strength and power raging in his voice. It's the power that's threatenin'. Yup. The power.

I stand before the Laundromat window in my floral housedress, Easy Spirit casual shoes, and colorful headscarf wrapped around my head, deeply disturbed by what I am witnessin'.

Chilllle, back in the day peoples didn't argue in the streets. They had too much pride to do such a thing as this. But nowadays, peoples just don't care no mo'. They don't care 'bout 'emselves, let 'lone nobody else.

I gets a sick feeling in my chest every time I witness something like this. The world is so ugly. Infested with corruption and drugs. These kids be high every day of the dang week. High off that crack, heroin, and that K2 (synthetic marijuana) too. Use it to float in their minds to forget certain things that happened in their lives. There is still so much peer pressure for 'em younglings. They don't knows how to handle it, so they get high, rob, murder, and eventually die. Either by spirit or conscience.

It really gets me upset when I sees 'em grown black men's act hard. They lost in 'em streets, too. Uh-huh. With 'em fatherless homes, these young boys act like wild children. And the way they act in front of they own mothers, such disrespect. They talk to their own mothers like she some two-dollar-whore. It just breaks my heart to sees how they put fear in their own mother. Don't even 'preciate hasin' a mother—the woman that birthed 'im into this world. Such a daggone shame.

Just watchin' these teens bicker back and forth gets tiresome. They so young minded—too young to be lettin' that young puppy love gets the best of 'em. Too young to even see that that is exactly what is happenin'. Naw. Naw. Naw. They can't be no older than seventeen, eighteen, but right now their actin' like spoiled children, bratty babies.

The girl crosses her arms about her busty bosom and stare blankly in the boy's face. Her dark brown eyes is watery, wary. I wish I could tell her. I knows, honey, I knows. A part of you just wanna burst and knock that *motherfucker* out. But you ain't got that "tired heifer" in you yet. Give it some time. I betcha she gon' come out swingin'. And when she comes out swingin' ain't a dang thang you gonna be able to do with that scorned sistah.

The boy, well, his face is all tight and his eyes is dark. I knows that look very well. I think I met that look waaayy back.

My eyes heavenward as I mumble under my breath, "Lord, what is dis world comin's tuh?"

Then I turn around away from the window 'cause I feels myself gettin' highly upset. I then walk away. And as I do, I think to myself, *how many peoples just walk away?*

I stand before the washer and gaze at it spinning 'round and 'round thinkin' 'bout how peoples' lives is spinning out of control.

For the most part, it's pretty quiet this mornin'. It's about 7:45 a.m. Peoples don't normally start rising from their dead sleep till 'bout noon on this side of town. That's on account of 'em partying so hard throughout the week.

134

Police comes to Eavesdrop Avenue every other night to ambush their house parties. You'd think peoples would get the hint and just stop, but naw, they gotta get their party on.

For it to be Tuesday I pleasantly surprised of how quiet it is. Don't gets me wrong, it's refreshing to be able to hear myself think. Most of the time I can't 'cause of the loud Puerto Rics or that nerve-wracking hip-hop music all times of night and day. Whatever happened to being courteous of others? Hell, whatever happened to a man gettin' up outta his seat on the bus and lettin' a women's take a load off? Whatever happened to men's openin' the door for a gal? Carryin' her bags of groceries? Or, or a man walking away during a heated argument instead of smacking the hella outta his old lady out in public? Tells me that. I done seen it all. Things sho' has changed with these generation of peoples. Sho' has changed.

"Hello, Mr. Sonny, how you?" I yells across the way and wave my hand. Mr. Sonny waves back.

Mr. Sonny is an early riser likes me. He always on his front porch watering his plants or sittin' down on that tree stump reading the newspaper. He's in his early eighties. Handsome as he wanna be. Gray woolly hair coiled around the sides and nape of his pea-sized head. His copper-colored skin reminds me of a penny. He's tall. Well, he used to be taller. Looks like he might've a shrunk a bit. Stand 'bout...ol' six feet opposed to six one. Maybe 'cause age done caught up with him. He looks pretty frail to me. Might has to bring him over a pot of hot grits and buttermilk biscuit to fatten him up. I think he got that cataract too 'cause his eyes look mo' gray than brown. He's a nice elder fellah. Pleasant man to talk to. He's a widower, too. Has been for quite some years now. His beloved wife, Terry-Ann, her gone to be with the Lord.

Ringggg, Ringgggg, Ringgggggg.

I feels my hip vibrating and hears my cell phone ranging.

Oh, my Lawd! My eyes liked to dance. "Whatchu knows," I say to myself with a huge grin on my face, "Whatchu knows!"

The most likeable name miraculously appears on my cell phone. A name I often think of, wondered 'bout how she is doin', and hope to hear from her soon. And look-a-here: Ursula Lofton.

There is so much I wanna tells her. So much I have bottled up inside me. Lord knows I need my best friend. But I don't wanna use her up. I try to deal with my own problems, my own way. Not to say that I gotta handle on 'em. 'Cause I don't thinks I do. But I tries to do what I can on my own. Things is so distressing, depressing, and I don't wanna bring anyone from the outside in my confusion. 'Specially the police. I just-just wanna be freed. Can't be freed if I'm too afraid to leave. Amen to that.

So much has occurred in my life. Nothing that a woman with pride would wanna share. Not even to God himself.

I turn my head distracted by the noise. Must be a tornado or hurricane comin' 'cause folks actin' strange. Devilish. Tempers is in the highs. It's lotta attitude floating round in the air. Bad energy. Lotta bad talk, too. Rowdiness. Lots of fightin' with couples out in the streets. Just airing out all their business for everyone to listen. They sho' knows how to capture a crowd of peoples.

The man all up in the women's face, spittin' and everything. It's just awful.

Lawd, I pray he don't hit her. Lawd, I pray, I pray. Don't do's it! Don't you dear, dear do's it! Gal, just-just walk away. Walk the hell away! But naw. She can't find the will. Why can't her find that damn will?!

I hears the sirens bellowing and sees the red lights swirling from the window. Police is on their way.

Police arrive and breaks up one of the couples that steady flapping their gums.

The crazy part is, I knows this one couple. They my next-store neighbors. Allison and her old man, Frankie. Those two carry on like they teenagers. Squabbling over nothin'. It once was cute. *Once* was. But now, chile, it makes you wonder why they even together. I don't knows how they last as long as they has with all the fights and arguing they do's on a day-to-day basis.

With the thin walls in my apartment I hears 'em making up. Her be howling at the top of her young lungs and he be grunting like the old fart he is. I guess that's their way of showing affection to one another. Lawd knows I knows something 'bout that too.

There is some commotion going's on between the laundry attendant Nilla—a slender, dang near anorexic Puerto Ric gal and a young thug I hasn't seen before. He might be new to the neighborhood or just passing through. He looks to be in his early twenties. Stands about 6'7". Kinda big-boned. Rough-around-the-edges type. I can easily detect that he has very little home schoolin' and most definitely shows bitter hatred towards women of any race. A rough lookin' boy. One of 'em hardcore thug's with a potty mouth. No respect whatsoever. Ruthless. Just plain ole ruthless.

Nilla is a gal I has seen many times in passing. Like I says, she is extremely boney. Looks to be in her mid-twenties, shoulder-length brown hair with cashew-complexion and big brown bright eyes. A hard working, kinda weird looking gal. Friendly, though.

One day I seen her and she had blue hair, then the other day I seen her and she had pink hair, then the next day I seen her and she had strawberry-colored hair. I ain't one to judge 'cause she kinda puts me in frame of mind of me. Back in the day, huh, I loved being different.

Nilla is the same gal I had generously given one of my too young to be sashaying down the ghetto streets in sexy dresses. Twenty, huh, even thirty has long left this forty-something year old body of mine. I figured why give that beautiful, colorful designer party dress to the

Salvation Army or thrift shop when all's they gonna do is sells it. And plus, I seen Nilla pushing that double stroller so I knows her plate is plenty full. Three babies. Two little big headed boys still in Pampers. And the li'l girl who looks to be 'bout four or five years old, walking with her mother's hand in tow.

Being a mother (don't knows if Nilla is a single mother) but she working a job that deals with ghetto peoples. Huh, chile needs a sexy dress to strut her stuff in. Don't matter if it's a little bit of stuff. It's her little stuff.

Good night Irene! I can't believe my eyes when I see Ursula's name. I smile from ear to ear. Seems like I hasn't hears from her in umpteen years. Sho' does seem like.

When we were kids, we used to wallow in fantasy. Dream about who'd we marry. How many children we'd have. Type of jobs we'd be working. I wanted to be a flight attendant 'cause I wanted to travel and see the world. Ursula wanted to be a famous gospel singer. Those dreams were sweet. I've come to knows that sweet dreams often disappear.

When I was ten. Ursula was nine. That spring of '78 we vowed that when we experienced our "first kiss" we'd tells one another. Gal gossip. But we never got a chance to on account Ursula was shipped down south to live with her grandma in Charlotte, North Carolina. Her mom had suddenly tooken ill so we kind of stayed in touch through lettas (letters), but we never really talked 'bout boys on account her grandma was very, very strict. Any lettas Ursula received from me, her grandma opened and read first. I was very careful in what I says in 'em lettas. Very careful. I never wanted to gets my best friend in a heap of trouble.

"Hello."

"Hi, Country!" Ursula says in a chipper southern tone of voice. "How is you, Country?"

"Ohhhhh chile, its soooo good to hears your voice!" I says bursting through the seams of my housedress.

Funny how Ursula the one living in the country and I end up with an accent too. I'd only visited South Carolina as a chile, but that southern twang ain't left me yet.

"I'm hanging in there, Ursula. Tryna go back to work, somewhere. I'd gotten sick with some wicked cough, so I been home for 'bout six months or so collecting SSI. The older you seems the harder it gets. These young folks got it good and don't 'preciate nothin'. Once you hit your forties don't nobody wanna take a chance and hire you. But I gotta believe that something will come through. 'Cause you knows good and well I ain't one to stay home and twiddle my thumbs. All in all, I's good, Miss Lady. Keepin' my spirits up."

"Yeah. I know this must be a difficult time for you, Country, wit' your mother and all."

Mama. My mama, Mrs. Kenzie was killed by the hands of her, my fa—her husband. I don't much talk about it. Too painful to recall. I haven't forgotten. It's just I try to think of the mo' pleasant times with her.

My Dad shot her in a jealous rage. Never told anyone where he left her body. God only knows.

I miss Mama. Miss the way she used to prank. We used play hide-n-seek. Fun things we done together. Sho' saddens me not having her in my life. I'm grown but I still need her. Doggone shame my own dad took her life. He long died. Probably from guilt.

Mama was young 64. Still can't believe she gone but then again I can. Upcoming Wednesday is her anniversary.

Ursula breaks me out of my trance. "Well, I'll be there for a funeral. My great uncle, Wolf died. He always told me that when he go to Glory he wants me to sing at his Home-going Celebration. I can't let Unc down"

"Oh, I'm sorry to hear that 'bout your uncle. And naw, you can't let 'im down. He was the funny one. The one who told funny jokes. Used to have us crackin' up."

"When God calls you you answer the phone, honey. Ain't no such thang as Call Waiting with God? God called. And Uncle Wolf picked up the phone. God said, 'Grayson...Wolf c'mon, man. It's time to come home.' Great Unc was good man. Good to me that is."

I smile.

"Well, Country, I want to take you out to dinner while I'm in town. We ain't seen each other in ages. Heck, none of us have. Last I heard, Betty-Joe, Tommie-Ann, Selma, Rose and Verne were doing okay." Ursula pauses, "Lemme ax you somethin'. Has you heard from or seen Avery? I knows she lives somewhere in Paterson. Gal, heard through the grapevine that she-she wrote a book. One of 'em urban fiction books. I think that's what these younglings call it. Don't matter much what they call it 'cause these grown women's is engrossed in that book. Even churchgoers. They jaws justa drop!"

My eyes widen, surprised. "Churchgoers? Whattt?! Who, Avery?" I take a split second to think about it. A brow raises. "Wait a cotton pickin' minute, Ursula, you talkin' 'bout that tall, bony chile? That gal that wassa tomboy?"

"Uh-huh. That was Avery. And she wrote a book. I has a copy of it rights here. *Ev'ry Ho Gotta Daddy.*"

I twist up my lips unenthused. "Hmm. It sound like smut to me."

"Don't matter much here, chile, these sistahs, they raving and carryin' on 'bout this book. Say they ain't read nuthin' quite like it. Heck, they even started their own book club, 'Church Sluts'. I know it sounds crazy but these ladies is changing by the day, honey. Ain't no mo' shame. No mo'. They steppin' out on faith. No mo' shame."

"You read it? Wow. Avery wrote a book! Well good for her!" I murmur. "Good for her."

"I just started it. I'm on, um, page one hundred."

"You on page one hundred! And you just started reading it?!"

"It's over five hundred-something pages, Country."

"Five hundred-something pages! Sweet Juju Beans. Guessed that chile had a lot to write about, huh?"

"It's two women stories, Country. That's why it's so thick. Chile, once I dug into it, I just couldn't stop. If it wasn't on account of me having to go to choir rehearsal the next day I woulda stayed up and read it all night."

"Is it that good of a book for you to wanna stay up allllll nighttttt longgggggggg?"

"Well, I can't speak for others, but something about the way it is written that captures you 'cause it's so raw. Um, it's written with grime and grit and pain and sufferin' and love. You know, stuff women like. I feel like she covered every emotion."

"Well good for her." I says. "Folks sho' do's surprise you, huh, Ursula?"

"They sho' do. 'Cause I also found out through the pages of Avery's first book, *Anonymous*, that that chile had been through some serious traumatic stuff."

"How many books her wrote?"

"Well, I think about four, if I'm not mistaken. But that *Anonymous* book, gurrrrl, that book is something else. You gotta read it. It's so personal and honest. Avery draws you in and makes you feel like you could see it actually happening. She really opened up about what happened to her. I don't think I would've done it. But she did. And Country, it's a true story, too."

"Whatchu mean...what happened to her?"

"You ain't *heard*?"

"Heard...what?"

"Avery writes 'bout coping with being raped."

I sang out a, "Whatttttttt?! RAPED!"

"Uh-huh. And gurrrrl, that ain't the whole story. She later finds out that she is HIV-positive."

"Oh, my goodness!"

"Country, she's having a book signing that Saturday, at ah, Silly Chicks Banquet Hall. This fashion designer I knew from back in the day is hasin' another fashion show there too. Maybe we can go and show some support to our black folks. You know, support our sista and brotha. It'll be nice if we can all get together. Country, I don't wanna forget what you look like. It'll give us time to catch-up on thangs. What'll say? What *is* your plans on Saturday?"

Saturday is the 15th. Mrs. Kenzie was *killed* on the 13th.

Saturday? I take a moment to think. *What do I has to do on Saturday?*

"Well, I'm just waitin' to sees if this lady is goin' to call me in referral to a job. But other than that, I don't think I has any other plans. Matter-of-fact, I don't. Gal, just call me. You knows I loves to see yah. I miss you soooo much."

"I mis— "

"Excuse me, Ursula. Hold on for a sec," I interrupt Ursula midsentence in order to listen in to the loud voice in the background.

"Ok."

The voices between the thug and Nilla take my focus off of the phone with Ursula and on to 'em. Especially when the thug is verbally threatenin' to do the chile harm? I don't take too kindly to that. Right then and there, chilllleeee, something inside me locks. What could've happened to set this thug into a bitter rage? I don't knows. Could've been her opened one of his dryers. Or she might've bumped into him by mistake. Or she might've mistakenly stepped on his big toe. Who knows? It don't take much to set one of these young peoples' off. They seem so angry all the time. Frustrated by this or that. And they use others: family, friends, even strangers as an outlet.

I wasn't paying much attention 'cause I was yappin' on the phone. All's I can tells is whatever it was that that chile done, it sho' piqued my curious, especially when he voiced out in public that he'd kill her. My ears is just'a ranging. I blink twice, heart thumpin' still hasin' Ursula on hold.

I narrow-eye him and says, "Ursula, lemme call you back."

After ending my brief conversation with my had-not-heard-or-seen-in-umpteen-years-best friend. I study this thug. My eyes peer down and I slip my hand in my housedress and pull out my bifocals and place 'em over my eyes and I scroll my eyes down to his black Timberland boots up to his boyish round face. I notice he has two teardrops near the corner of one of his eyes. I've seen that on some young peoples before. I figured it was some type of tattoo. But my daughter, Honesty hipped mother to the deal that it was a sign of the devil. Satan was a very, very busy man. I give him an once-over 'cause I need a good description just in case this fool does try to kill her. He is still mouthing off 'bout beaten that bitch down. Saying that he don't give an effin' thang 'bout peoples'. And that prison don't mean nothin' to him. He'd do's it once, he'd do's it again.

Well, I think that that is just plain stupid. Who'd wanna intentionally be locked up like a jailbird? Lawd knows I knows how that feels too. I'd never gone to prison per se, but I've been confined behind locked doors a time or two.

I press my full thick lips together and simply shake my head from side to side, quite bothered by this young thug.

My heart is deeply hurt, especially when he looks over at me with a scrunch up nose and crumpled forehead and 'em dark eyes. He says with the straightness of face. "I'll murda everyone in this muthafucka washerette! Catchin' a body don't mean nuthin' tah me! One body, two

143

bodies! That shit don't mean nuthin'. I ain't scared of no muthafuckin' body."

I says to me, "I betcha scared of God. I betcha that."

On that note I gets my old tail outta here 'fore this young thug snaps and executes his plan and shoots the whole dang place up.

I hurries and fold up my clothes, bedding, and towels with a scowl on my face. I put five quarters in three dryers and my stuff is still damp! I has the gumption to go over and tells Nilla off but with all the commotion I says the hells with it. I'll let 'em air dry at home.

Once I finish folding, I put everything in my laundry cart, and as I is walking pass the young thug, I cut my eyes at him reallll sharp and I part my lips to says reallll clear, "Be safe, black man." He just looks at me with that brown face of his, then says, "O-kay." Kinda dumb-lookin'.

As I is exiting out the Laundromat, I and Nilla's eyes meet. She has such sadness in 'em big baby browns.

One thing I wills say is that Nilla keeps her narrow hinny in that crawl space of an office. At least the chile has good, commonsense.

On my walk home, I says to God: "Lord, I hope she lives to see another day. Can You be gracious 'nough to help a chile out?" Hmm. I ain't talkin' 'bout Nilla neither.

I'm referring to myself.

Chapter
Seventeen

Narlena

Deep sigh.

I rise my nude body from the vanity chair and make my way to the king-sized bed, fling back the rich embroidered gold diamond-patterned quilted bedspread and slip myself between the 800-thread count Egyptian cotton sheets.

I lay on the right side. Stretch my curvaceous body out and rest my head upon the fluffy down pillow. Close my eyes dreading the fact that the left side feels colder than my disappointment.

Somehow I manage to slip into yet another wet dream of Idris Elba. That man sure knows how to make a grown woman drool.

With Idris caressing my well-endowed breasts the wireless video doorbell chimes me out of my erotic reverie. Damn. Idris was teasing me with his bulge. That man looks tasty. He'd be the only man I'd cheat on my lover with.

On the oyster-colored marble nightstand, next to the crystal lamp, I gape at the still photo of a man on the monitor. Indecisive. Should I or shouldn't I let him in? Heart races.

Climbing out of bed, I amble over to the sage wingback recliner and reach for my navy-night silk kimono on the arm as I cover my bareness, then exit the lavish masterbedroom.

Bare feet hastily make their way down the winding limestone staircase.

Cautiously opening the door. Scowl.

"Blu?"

He is standing tall at my front door. Overoptimistic.

Instantaneously fury burns in my throat, chest, and then shoots up to my eyes as they scroll him dressed in a pair of Scotch & Soda white cigarette jeans, white polo shirt, and Salvatore Ferragamo white leather loafers. Clean-shaven baldhead, flawless deep dark complexion, winning smile, not to mention a powerful attitude, overinflated ego, Blu is not making my pulse rise or my pussy moist. I'm bone dry. And my attitude and body are as cold... as...ice.

"What, Blu? What? Why are you here?" I ask standing in the vestibule. Tightening the belt to my robe—hazel eyes pierce walnut black. I inhibit my fire that is burning on all highs.

Undressing me with his seductive look. Blu says, "May I come in?"

Contemplate. I step aside and invite him in. We make our way into the immaculate, eclectic living room. Index finger flicks the light switch up, crystal chandelier illuminates above our heads.

I stand at one arm of the Hoffman Koo sea-green leather sectional. Blu stands at the other.

The distance within us is evident.

Crossing my arms about my chest.

Blu slips his hands in his front pants pockets.

Our eyes connect, then shift.

My eyes yearn for truth.

His eyes remain still, unmoved.

146

Facing me, Blu says, "What? I can't come see my lady?"

I smirk, then reply. "I'm not your lady."

Blu takes two steps back as the hardwood floor creaks.

His left pants leg nearly touches the thick arm of the sectional as well as the smooth edge of the triangular aqua-glass coffee table. "Oh, it's like that, huh?"

"Like what, Blu? You no longer have a hold of this here A-list pussy. You don't own me!"

My thoughts revert back to when I first met Blu.

I saw him across the room at Mary J. Blige's: "Thick Of It" soon-to-be-divorce from Kendu Issac party. It was a huge crowd. Massive. Celebs wall-to-wall. Blu was alone. Looking available. I was famished. Half-starved for the likes of a man. Our eyes locked. He approached. I didn't shun him away. I entertained. Let my hair down and got more than my feet wet.

"You know how much I like that buttermilk, L. Can a brother get some love up in this muthafucker? I had a long day. I just want to relax under my woman."

"At two-thirty in the morning, Blu? That's what this is about. Some booty call, huh?" I purse my natural lips. "Ah, excuse me, but, ah, you don't have it like that, anymore."

"Why you actin' shady on me? So fuckin' uptight lately." Blu asks.

"'Cause you're shady, that's way."

"So what are you trying to say, L? That you're *over me*. That I'm *history*. That you *never want to see me again*. Which one is it *this* time? Because I think I've heard 'em *all*, yet, I'm *still* standing here."

I roll my eyes. Knowing he's right. Yes, he is still here. Still fine as ever. Still cocky too.

I press my lips together, nod my head. "You had a good thing with me, Blu. We had a sweet thing going but you had to go and mess it up. Not me. *You.*"

"I'm just being me. Brother not gonna change. Either you deal or you don't. Make up your mind."

I think to myself, *Is it really that simple to cut me out of your life? Why didn't I see this coming? Because I was too busy...coming, screaming, panting, cursing, begging, pleading for more and more and more, harder, stronger, longer.*

Narrow-eyeing him I say, "You're really smellin' yourself right now, huh?"

Raising my right arm. I scratch the crown of my scalp with my index finger. Then stare into his vacant eyes.

Feeling exhausted from this getting-me-nowhere conversation, I say, "Listen, Blu. All you have to do is tell the truth. But no. You wanna come over and tease all of this—then lie to my face as if I'm some damn fool. Some *stupid needy bimbo!*"

"Well, if the shoe fits." Blu smugly says, then smirks. "C'mon now, L, give a brother a break, shit! I ain't come over here to hear your muthafuckin' mouth. Shut the fuck up, damn!"

"This is my house! You don't wanna hear my mouth, then LEAVE! All I ask is where the damn condom is. Three come in a box, not two, Blu. Three."

Blu sighs. "That's how I bought 'em from the store."

Instantly my brows knit. "Oh, sooooo now you trying tell me that the store sells condoms like looseys. What you think I'm stupid? You—"

Blu looks at me with that come-fuck-pimp-daddy look in his eyes.

I remain firm. "I don't wanna hear shit you gotta say, unless you're going to tell me the truth. All I want is the truth, Blu."

"For the last week or so you've been acting funny toward me, L. Getting new and shit." Blu gives me a piercing look with those dreamy eyes of his, "What's

148

really going on, huh? What...you seeing someone or at least considering it? C'mon. Tell me what's up?"

"No, no, no. Don't even try to turn this on me. You're the one out doing dirt, not me. Hear me out. YOU!" I lower my tone of voice. "You come over here with a box of open Trogans. I look inside the box only to pullout two condoms instead of three. What did you do with the missing one, huh? What happened to the missing one? That's all I want to know."

Silence.

Simultaneously my right and left temple throb. "So, like I said the other night, if you didn't fuck me with the condom. *Who the fuck did YOU fuck, Blu*?!"

With such superciliousness Blu says. "Woman, how could you forget all of this big dick, huh? For the last time I *fucked* YOU with that *fuckin'* condom, L!"

My head snaps back as my eyes roll. "Oh, now I got amnesia?! That's your comeback? That-that, um, obviously I was under the influence of a fuckin' twelve ounce can of Boxer Ice beer and, and, and fuckin' forgot that you *fucked me* the last time you were here with the missing condom. Black man... please! Please."

"You're wrong, L. Dead wrong."

I raise my voice two octaves. "I'm *wrong*! No." Vigorously shaking my head from side to side. "Uh-huh. No. Blu, you're wrong! Just tell the *truth*. Who'd you *fuck*? Because you damn sure didn't *fuck* me. You're killing me right now. You're like friggin' Houdini, you know that. You come around when you fuckin' want to, then disappear for two to three months, then you have the audacity to text me stating that you want some pussy. And me being me I let you come over. I welcome you into my *home*, into my *bed*, between my *legs*. You pullout an open—hear me out! Open, not NEW box, but OPEN box of Trogans and YOU expect ME to believe that you FUCKED me with the missing condom! You're telling me that I was soooooooooo drunk off of fuckin' beer that I fuckin' forgot. Bullshit! That's some bullshit, Blu! First of all, the last time we *fucked* we used condoms from my stash, Blu. My *stash*. So, I am going to ask you again, Blu, who'd you *fuck*?!"

Blu stammers. "I might've..."

I bark. "YOU MIGHT'VE...WHAT???"

"What difference it make?"

My hands rise and glue to my waist. "It makes a world of *difference* to me!"

Blu looks at me dumbfounded. He opens his mouth but no words, no truth escapes.

"Oh, soooo NOW you're not sure if you had sex with someone else or not? Either you did or you didn't, Blu."

Blu remains quiet, removes his hands from his pants pockets, and admires "Shame Face" an African-American woman with natural hair by black artist C'Babi Bayoc on the living room wall.

I shake my head in disbelief. Then gape to my left at the vibrancy of "The Songstress" by Maurice Evans and "Summertime" by Andrew Nichols.

I blink for what feels like eternity. Wishing, wanting, but knowing. Fully knowing that this is our goodbye. Like Blu said he isn't going to change. He is who he is. And I'm not willing to put in work, time, and energy, not anymore to try and mold him into a man for me. I just won't commit to that. And I won't condone this treatment toward me either. It came out of the horse's mouth: *"either you deal or you don't."*

Slowly opening my eyes, still hoping, hopeful that he'll realize what we shared. How beautiful a time we used to have. But when I look at him, into him, I know. And it makes my heart ache. A painful ache. I sigh, soften my voice to a whisper. Try my best not to reflect pain in the words I speak, but it is evident in my eyes. I am deeply hurt. "Just tell me the truth."

Again, Blu has no words. Just a blank look in his *baby-please-come-take-this-dick eyes.*

And I want to. I want to take his dick and play with it, tease, squeeze, suck, fuck, but I can't. I just can't. Not with knowing that someone else has been licking and kissing my tennis balls. And slobbering all over what used to be my joystick.

I swallow. Unloosen the belt to my robe and expose my bareness.

A crackling in my voice emerges. "You see this…" Big beautiful bountiful breasts. Chocolate-covered areola and nipples. Hairless vagina. Silky, soft buttermilk skin. Long sheer legs. "…all of this *I* cherish. Got to protect it. I don't know who you *fucked* but I know you *fucked* somebody. Guilt is written all over your face."

Blu remains quiet.

I nod my head. Then shake it from side to side. "I am not trying to *die*, Blu. Not for you. Not for anybody. And with you out here sticking your dick in every skank bitch with dirty pussy! Obviously I don't mean shit to you. *I don't mean shit.* If all of this is not to your satisfaction, then—"

Blu breathes out. "We were *never* in a committed relationship. It was just *sex*, L."

I smirk, then nod. "Yes, it was. Indeed it was. But—I didn't sign-up for the extras in our fun. You never consulted me. Included me. How do you think that makes me *feel*?"

Silence.

Feel? Feelings, what the fuck! Blu thinks. *You women kill me with this feeling shit. All you need to feel is this grown man's dick. Other than that, what the fuck is there to feel? And please, please don't say it. Don't come with the L word or the M word 'cause I ain't trying to hear it. We started off as a fuck, which is all you'll ever be to me. A one-nightstand fuck. Bitch, I got you wrapped around my finger. I got your mind wrapped along with the other bitches. Black man like me will never, ever get trapped. You ain't nothing but a fuck. An uptight piece of side pussy.*

151

I look Blu in his eyes. Wondering what he's thinking. What he thinks of me. Study his body language. "You're just going to stand there and pretend that you haven't done shit. That I'm making shit up. Hmm. Niccccceeee."

Silence.

Blu walks toward me. My body stiffens up. He leans in and pecks me on the forehead with his warm, tempting lips, then shows himself out.

With hot tears rain storming down my cheeks, and lead in my feet I slowly walk to the door and shut it behind him.

As I turn to head back to the masterbedroom I feel cramps and stickiness between my legs.

Climbing the stairs I bow my head and whisper under my breath. "Thank God, I'm not pregnant."

Chapter
Eighteen

Ursula

Talk about quiet. Everything stops in the restaurant. Folks stare. Some have their mouth hanging open, shocked. I guess they don't know how Woolridge will react and neither do I.

I've never seen him get angry. He's never raised his voice at me. Nor has he ever hit me. He's a very respectable country man.

The look on his rotund face says I've broken his heart. He's the most wounded man that ever lived. His eyes are engulfed with tears that he lets roll down his plump cheeks. Everyone in the restaurant witnesses it. All these black folks whisper about us like we are Stedman and Oprah. A couple of men shake their heads, as if to say, "Dang, man." Some of the women kind of snarl and scrunch their nose up at me. Some purse their thick lips, while others roll their big eyes. This one chick, white chick at that, with long wavy blonde hair and layers of makeup on her scrawny face, and a smart behind mouth, says to her man, who mind you is fine as he wanna be... that black man is something sweet to look at. Woo!

Anyway, that broke down biddy has the audacity to say to her handsome man, "Why did she say no, especially in here of all places? Couldn't she have waited until they got home? She should've played it off and said yes. Everyone in here is staring at 'em. She should've lied to save him the embarrassment. What a stupid *bitch*. Look at her. She ought to feel lucky that someone asked her fat-ass to *marry* him. Looks like she weighs over two-hundred pounds."

I start to get up and walk over to their table and sock it to her for minding our business, but I don't want to draw any more attention to us. I have to pray at this very moment because the devil is working on me. He is working on my last nerve. Blondie was about to catch a case of whoop ass. But the Lord saved her. She ought to feel blessed.

As Woolridge is getting up on his feet, the maître d takes the liberty of laying the check on the table and quickly walks away. Woolridge reaches his big hand in his suit jacket pocket and pulls out his American Express credit card. He even lays some cash on the table. Leaves the white, blonde-haired maître d a hefty tip. Woolridge flags the maître d down with a wave of his hand. The maître d rushes over and Woolridge hands him the check with credit card. The guy smiles as he sees the tip waiting for him on the table. He walks away and rushes back and hands Woolridge his credit card.

While Woolridge stands in place. The maître d is clearing the table. He slips the tip in his back pants pocket and as he does, he says in a thick southern voice, "For what it's worth, man, you tried. Don't beat yourself up. Sometimes things are just not meant to be. Keep your head up." Woolridge nods his head, then sighs. "Thanks man."

Woolridge heads for the exit of the restaurant with his head hanging low and I follow suit switching everything the Lord blessed me with.

On our drive home, it is silent. Not even the radio is playing. Woolridge loves to listen to music. Me, too. But all I hear is Woolridge's heavy breathing. I keep replaying in my head Woolridge proposing and me saying no. I just couldn't say yes. Even though he's a good man there are some things that I don't think I can live without.

I simply love my dark-skinned black brothers. I'm not particularly fond of arrogant men who overcompensate themselves. It's a turn-off for me. But I do like a confident, strong, even sensitive man. Woolridge is that type of man.

What Woolridge and I share is a home. Not a house. I'm a childless woman, at least for now. And that is by choice. Woolridge wants a shitload of babies. I'm independent. I like to have my own money, even though he takes very good care of me. I like to work for mine. And I absolutely love God. And I love singing too. Actually singing is how Woolridge and I met.

Woolridge was working his *fourth* job as a stocker-slash-cashier at Walgreens. His *first* job was as a forklift driver (at some company in downtown Charlotte), *second* job was as a crew member at Trader Joe's on E. Arbors Dr., and his *third* job was as a plumber.

I walked into Walgreens to get a few things and as I was browsing the store, I was humming a gospel song. When I got up to the check-out counter Woolridge heard me. He said, "Sing me a tune, sweet lady?" So I did. He said, "Woman, you have a voice of an angel." I smiled. He smiled. And he asked me for my number. He was such a teddy bear, I couldn't resist.

We've been a couple for nearly five years now. And I know. I know Woolridge wants me to be his wife. But there is this thing that I must have that Woolridge doesn't have. He wasn't blessed with it, you see. And the older he gets, the smaller it'll get.

See, I'm a romantic. Woolridge romances me somethin' good. Flowers, chocolate, bubble bath, expensive trips to: Cancun, Las Vegas, Miami, Florida, Bahamas, Dominican Republic, so many places we've traveled. Like I said Woolridge is good to me. And he is marriage material. Any woman would be lucky to have him as her man. But currently I'm that woman.

The problem is, Woolridge doesn't have the right equipment to satisfy me. Actually, to keep me. I mean, we've tried everything, but nuthin' seems to work. So I asked myself time and time again, how can I marry a man that penis does nuthin' for me? I'd be lying to myself if I said that size doesn't matter. Because it really, really does. At least to me.

Honestly is this the real issue? No. That's not the problem. The problem is... I have *never* stepped out on Woolridge, but I'll admit I've been tempted. I don't know how much longer I can put up with him and these feelings I'm having. Lord knows I'm trying. And I don't know how to tell my man that he just doesn't do it for me. That no matter his length or width or how much he eats my chocolaty stuff—that he just doesn't tickle my fancy anymore. Every time we have sex, I don't feel a damn thang. And he be inside me. What am I supposed to do with—?

If I ride him, I don't feel nuthin'. If we do it doggy-style, I don't feel nuthin'. If I give him head, I swallow the whole thang in my mouth. The *whole thang*. It's just disappointing. Even more so, because all he can do is lick my chocolaty stuff. After a while that gets old. Because I need more than licking. My big and beautiful body needs to be caressed by the softness of a *woman*. I wanna feel her tongue all up in me. I'd like to think that a woman knows how to pleasure a woman.

I don't wanna hurt him anymore than I already have. So I try to think of ways for us to pleasure one another. He's content. Says he's happy. But me. No. Not by a long shot.

Often I wonder if I do leave him will God be disappointed in me. Women would love to have a man like Woolridge. The man still works *four* jobs to keep me happy. But that's all material things. A woman wants to feel loved, not only told it. I know he loves me. Am I wrong for putting my wants and needs first? I prayed on it. Many nights. And I asked God to guide me—to help me decide what is best for me. If it's all about the physical, which it's not, does it make it wrong to want a woman to make love to me? Woolridge tries. But he is always unsuccessful. Marriage? Sex is a part of a healthy and happy marriage. So what am I to do? Keep a good man and be content? Or, leave him and let some other little lady snatch him up? Hmm.

Chapter
Nineteen

Narlena

I am over Blu. Really. I am. Blu and *"DeVaughn"* is dead to me. At least that's what my mind seems to think. My body? Well, it seems hooked on *"DeVaughn"*. I just can't seem to get enough of the big black dick.

My knees sink into the soft, firm mattress, hands lay flat, fingers spread wide upon the magenta satin sheets as my ass is mid-air, forehead snuggles in the down pillow as he thrusts me from behind.

"Mmmmmmmmmmmmm it feels sooooo good!" I bellow.

"You keep me hard, L," he grits through his teeth.

I love when he calls me... L.

"Yesssssssssssssss!" I moan.

Breathless. My forehead sinks deeper in the pillow. Eyes squeeze tighter as I feel the exhilarating eruption burst inside me. God. He leaves me completely breathless.

After Blu showers and gets dressed, he kisses me between my wet and sticky legs. His damp bald head brushes against my inner thighs as he slurps and teethes my clitoris. Sticking his long tongue inside me, he licks the fleshy folds so insatiably. He kisses me wildly as I taste my juice. Then he lets himself out.

I lie back against the pillows finally catching my breath. The feel of his well-endowed penis still throbbing inside me so dreamily. Instantaneously I become teary-eyed.

Honestly, I can't remember the first and/or last time a man made me feel so damn luscious. It's like everything I imagined, but fifty times better with Blu. Each thrust his eight-inches delivers makes me beg for more. More and more.

The sensation—the feel of his hard member—the feel of my glistening body shuddering, convulsing the sweetness of coming multiple times. Oh, he took me—took me farther than any man as ever taken me. Unequivocally, I've fallen.

To say that what we share is meaningless sex is such an insult. It is an inaccurate depiction of our relationship. What we share is indescribable. It is not magical, whimsical, but it is explicitly sexy. Oh, he invigorates me in such a way that I become voiceless. Me? I have never been sooooo enthralled in a man as much as I am with him. Sucking *"DeVaughn"* gives me such a *pussy rush*. Blu isn't just any man. Shared or not, I have the pleasure of fucking him. It's no wonder why *Thursday's* are now my favorite day of the week.

The point *is...what's wrong with me? Narlena.* That's what you jealous bitches are thinking. I mean a woman who settles for a man with no love for her, what's up with that shit? Either she's stupid, pathetic and desperate or suffers from low self-esteem, or is needy or just plain greedy or just plain horny as hell. But could it be that she is possibly head-over-heels in love? It could. It very well could.

See, I'm well aware of my actions. I know if I play with fire I will get burned. Blu? Oh yes, he is fire. But it's something about that fire that turns me the fuck on.

I may not need Blu for his money, but I sure want him and *"DeVaughn"*. How ugly does that make me sound? Shit. I tell you this, at least I know what I want. And yes, I am willing to suffer the consequences of my actions. Blu is not the last man on this earth but I've invested time. Too much time to be wasting away on getting to know another man. A man that might not have the right tools to make me tremble between the sheets. I need that tremble every now and again. Sue me for being free and allowing what he has between his legs to compromise my happiness.

"You sound real stupid!" I hear my inner voice say. *"You are a leader and yet you allow this man to cloud your judgment. You're not in-charge of your own life. Constantly in need of "DeVaughn" is really taking its toll on you. Look at you! Nar, you need professional help. Maybe a Sex Therapist is worth investing in. Of course, you would think seeing a Sex Therapist is ludicrous, but ask yourself: "If Blu wasn't laying down the pipe as good as he is, would you still be interested in him? And is it fair to say that Blu is not the main attraction, "DeVaughn" is. You really have no use for Blu, do you? But since Blu holds the goods you have no choice but to put up with him. You don't want that man. You just want his penis."*

Chapter
Twenty

Avery

"Good morning, my sista." A tall, dark-skinned dreadlocked-haired man greets me while I am walking 125th Street with a lovely smile on his face. I see this brother often, dressed in his Kenta cloth dashiki and stretchable hand-knitted kufi. I have yet to catch his name because most of the time when I'm walking through there is usually a cluster of folks surrounding him as he vendors. Sells his paraphernalia, plays his CDs of African music to give a listening sample, and showcases his many assorted bottles of fragrant body and home incense oils.

Last time I saw him, two NYPD officers were walking the beat and stopped to harass him about his permit. I don't think it was displayed where they could see it, so they kind of gave him a hard time. But he kept composed. He didn't allow them to take him to that place of anger. Hmm. I was impressed because I kind of took him as a man with a level head. A *think* first, *react* second, *run* third kind of guy.

"Mornin'." I reply back to him as I make my way through the crowded street of mix culture folks. Diligently I stand at the corner and wait for the traffic light to turn red and the cars to slow down. This is a busy

161

city. Everyone seems in a rush to either get to work or school or wherever they go in the early part of the morning. It's pretty lively.

My eyes skyward this tall building across the street as the sun peeks out from the hazy gray sky. Looks like rain. *Good thing I brought my umbrella with me,* I think to myself.

Mmmmmmmmmm. I inhale the fresh aroma of hot brewing coffee. The scent lightly lingers in the air. I'm tempted to stop at Starbucks to grab me a large cup of Chi tea but I'm too close to the office, and I really don't feel like walking further down the street. I'll wait till lunchtime. I'm sho' I have some tea upstairs. Either orange passionfruit jasmine or Blackberry pomegranate—one of the two.

I try to avoid drinking a lot of coffee because it stains your teeth. Lord knows I despise the dentist so I try very hard to take care of my teeth. Floss, twice a day. Brush, twice a day. And rinse with mouthwash to keep my mouth smelling minty fresh.

Which reminds me. I do have a dentist appointment coming up. I dread the thought. But I have to go because sometime last week while on my way home from New York to Paterson, I stopped at a local restaurant and I ordered a cheeseburger. As I was eating the cheeseburger I felt something hard like a pebble in my mouth. I chipped a piece of enamel from my front tooth. Talk about self-conscious. I was too embarrassed to open my mouth. End result was to call the dentist and schedule an appointment. Problem is, without any dental coverage I will have to pay one hundred and fifty bucks out-of-pocket. Dang, is right!

In my Lenox Ave office, I sit at my desk sifting through a pile of bills that have to get paid. I place the envelopes down near the side of my Toshiba laptop and set one of my many Annie Lee (God rest her soul) paperweights "Holy Ghost" and place it on top of 'em. Then straighten up the mess I left from the other day when I was inundated with phone calls and emails and texts and what have you. It was one of those crazy Monday's. Good day, but crazy.

In the middle of me tidying up, I hear a ding from my iPhone which alerts me that I received an email.

I stop what I am doing and check the latest email on my computer.

Spam! I delete it. Then lean my back against the black leather swivel chair deep in thought of why Narlena contacted me. I wonder, what her motive is.

Of course, she stated she heard the buzz about *Ev'ry Ho Gotta Daddy*. Said she even read it.

I press my lips together and let out ah, hmm. For some reason, I'm not sold. When does she have time to read when all she does is destroy peoples' lives? The sad part is, she enjoys doing it.

Narlena is shrewd. She's not the giving type. More of a taker. She likes to get her way, however she sees fit. I observed her very carefully that day we had our interview. Business minded, yes, she is. But Narlena is like poison too. Any and everything she touches either withers a slow demise or dies at the scene. So what is her scheme? What is this wicked bitch up to? Hasn't she had enough of fucking with me? Obviously not. I think she's just getting started.

I crack my knuckles still trying to figure this cunning bitch out. What do I have that she wants? Good question.

I sigh. What will she ask me? And what will I say. Narlena is a hardball. Hardball knows hardball.

I look at the time at the lower right corner of my laptop. I better get a move on as to not be late for my appointment with Miss Blabbermouth.

I stand, stretch, and grab my purse, lock the door and make my way down the steps.

Once I get outside I hail a cab to West 27th Street (across from Fashion Institute of Technology-FIT).

As the Peruvian driver pulls up to the building I reach in my handbag and pullout the fare. The greasy-haired cabdriver stretches his long arm back with his palm facing upward and I place the money in his calloused hand.

After he hands me my change, I exit the cab and make my way to the tinted black double glass doors of BLAB.

Chapter
Twenty-One

The array of folks is interesting because everyone has their own style, own swag. I see a lot of uniqueness in the young ladies and men that work here. Nobody looks dull or boring. Everyone appears to be in good spirits. Alive. Vibrant. Colorful.

Funny, I didn't notice this when I was here before. Oh, yeah. That's right. Before? Narlena seemed so secretive. Said something about our meeting should not be divulged to anyone. And that she didn't want anyone to know of her secret location for us to meet for the interview. Funny. I never questioned why. It never occurred to me to probe. I mean, I was merely there to tell my side of the story. Where she held the interview didn't matter to me. And plus, my mind was focused on protecting my name from the bastard that was trying his best to ruin me. Yep. It was a tense moment.

But now, seeing what I'm seeing my hope is that some of this good energy rubs off on her. I don't want today to be a reenactment of our last encounter. I mean, I feel that I kept my composure. But girlfriend was most definitely pushing some buttons in me. Hopefully today she'll a bit more pleasant.

Don't get me wrong, Narlena I'm assuming means well. She's a shark, but I think it comes with the position that she holds. No. By no means am I making excuses for her. I'm just saying that women, especially black women in positions such as Narlena seem to have something to prove. I don't know if it is for self or someone else.

The gold-chrome elevator doors open. I step on along with a slew of folks and press 11. Excusing myself as I am exiting off, I nearly rub against a rather obese black woman rocking a mini-dress, and might I add, she knows she looks good. Honey, if you can see what I see you'd be thanking your lucky stars you're a size 2. She looks like she stuffed every bit of herself in it. It does not look flattering. But I think she knew that when she squeezed her big ass in it.

Making my way off the elevator I proceed to sashay down the colorful corridor that leads to the double clear glass doors of BLAB. With one gentle pull of the gold-chrome door handle, I enter.

My shimmery, glossy lips part, eyes wander from the eggplant-colored marble floor. The ceiling is mural of musicians, poets, singers, writers, and the walls are a soft lavender with inspirational plagues that hang horizontal and vertical. It looks very eclectic and posh. From the looks of this place I'd say Narlena is doing her thang. I mean, the sistah has issues but she is most definitely paving a way for other black women to aspire to her success in journalism.

I walk up to the receptionist who sports a big fluffy 'fro. The gold-plated nameplate on her desk reads: Blessive Night. With her sitting down behind the black glass desk I can't really tell how tall she is. But if I had to guesstimate I'd say probably between 5'6" or 5'8". Her bright eyes do put me in mind of Wendy Williams. They are so big and beautiful. She is dark-skinned with thin heart-shaped shimmering lips. High cheekbones accentuated with amber tone blush. The glittery gold eye shadow makes her eyes pop and really defines her long, thick jet-black lashes and perfectly shaped arch eyebrows. To say that she is pretty is an understatement. The woman is well put together and incredibly gorgeous.

As I walk up toward the desk, I greet the young woman with a smile. "Hello."

"Hi."

"I love your blouse." I say.

Blessive tilts her head to the side, bats her jet-black lashes and says, "Oh, this ol' thang," in a screechy soft voice. She then giggles.

"It's a lovely color. Amber brings out your skin tone."

"Thank you," she replies.

I kind of stare at her for a brief second. "Do you sing?" I ask. "I really don't know why I just ask you that."

She nods her head and as she does her 'fro nods too.

"Yep. Started in the church. Currently working on my demo. I just work here to makes ends meet until I get that break, you know?"

I chuckle, then nod. "Yes ma'am, I do."

"Are you here to see someone?" she asks.

I chuckle. "Oh, yes, sorry. I'm here to see Ms. Scott."

"Is she expecting you?"

I nod.

"Ok. Well, have a seat, and I'll ring her and let her know that you're here."

"Thanks."

As she picks up the phone, her bangles jiggle. She uses one finger with a long acrylic nail extended from it and daintily presses three numbers on the phone. Then she diligently waits for someone to pick up. She places the phone back in its cradle. "I'm sorry, ma'am, but what is your name?" she asks a little embarrassed.

"Avery Love." I say as I sit down on the eggplant-colored leather couch and help myself to a BLAB magazine featuring an article with Viola Davis hugged up with her hubby sporting her natural hair. Viola looks sensational.

"Ms. Love, she's not picking up. She might be on another call. I'll try her back in a few seconds."

"Okay. No problem. I'm in no rush."

As I indulge in the article of the two lovebirds I hear the sound of heels click-clacking against the marble floor. I raise my head and look in the direction of the sound. I see Narlena through the double glass doors. She enters wearing a tight form-fitting tangerine floral print dress. She doesn't stop at the receptionist. Nor does she greet me. She walks past us both in her spikey six-inch heels with a distress look upon her face. A face, might I add, that is red-looking with a matching pair of eyes.

Narlena Scott…crying? Whoa. I guess she is human after all, I think.

I don't bother to stand to greet her. I wait for her to come to me, but she doesn't. She walks past me and rushes into the guests' ladies' room. I hear the door lock.

Blessive and I lock eyes as if to say: "What's up with her?" Blessive shrugs her shoulders and resumes back to her duties. I resume back to reading the article.

A few minutes into the second paragraph someone walks through the double glass doors and stops at Blessive's desk.

I don't bother to look up.

"Excuse me, Blessive, have you seen—?"

The voice sounds too familiar. I can't help but look. I'd know the back of that head anywhere. It's Blu McDowell.

"How are you, Mr. McDowell?"

"Just great." Blu says dryly.

Small world, I think to myself. *Of all the people to see it just had to be him. And how? And when? And what? And why? He makes me want to retch.*

Blessive's exuberant demeanor is not swayed by him. She smiles when she says. "Yes, ah, she's in the ladies' room at the moment."

"I see." Blu turns his head as his walnut black eyes pierce the door to the ladies' room as if he is contemplating whether to knock or just barge in.

He sighs a bit impatient. I bury my face in the magazine. Blu takes a seat. This is when he notices me. "Avery?"

I smile, and give him a wave. "Hi."

The entrance double glass doors swing open and someone walks in. I can't see who it is because my back is toward the door. Blu seems startled. Whomever it is, she is an *unexpected* guest.

I don't know why I think it's a *she*, but my intuition tells me it is.

In quick motion, Blu rises to his feet.

I'd never seen someone so tall jump so high.

Blu has a look of surprise on his handsome face. "Smokie! What the hell are you doing here?!"

Oh sugar! I think. *Something crazy is about to unfold. I can't help but think that Blu is about to get busted. I just hope this isn't what I think it is. Because if it is, all hell is about to break loose.*

As soon as Blessive sees this person, she immediately opens her desk drawer and pulls out a book.

This whole scene feels odd to me. And it is only going to get worse once Narlena walks out of the ladies' room and sees this woman.

Dang. Is Blu and Narlena now an item? Lucky bitch.

A part of me wants to get up and leave, but then the other part of me is curious to know what the hell is going on. For Narlena to be up in everyone else's business, huh, it seems she has some business to tend to of her own. Business that I know she won't advertise in BLAB that's for sho'.

Everyone hears the door unlock. The door opens and Narlena steps out with her head dangling downward. I guess she must've forgotten where and whom she is, but so quickly she resumes back and lifts her head up and straightens her posture. And as she do, her eyes like to pop outta her head.

The look of surprise on her face is a moment to capture. Dang! I wish I could take a snapshot, but I won't do the sistah dirty. Me sitting here, witnessing it, is probably more humiliating anyway.

Once she sees Smokie, Narlena slightly staggers in her heels. Had she been drinking? I wonder.

Narlena looks from Smokie to Blu. Blu to Smokie. "What's going on?" she asks a bit puzzled. She then quickly switches to her throaty professional voice. "Smokie Nicole, what brings you here? It's been a long time, hasn't it, *girlfriend?*"

Apparently these two know each other. Well, three, I should say.

There is silence between the three of them.

Finally, Smokie comes from around the couch and stands a few feet from where I am seated.

I eye her from head to toe. Dang, she is *fly*! Her long blonde weave dangles to the small of her back. Not a strand out of place. Long lashes curled to perfection. Flawless chocolate skin with a minimum of makeup. She dresses in a Lil' Kim red number. Tight and skimpy. Her posture is erect. And her stance in them red thigh-boots states that she is bad. A bad bitch in red.

Oh, this is awkward. I think.

"What's going on is...." Smokie begins to say in an assertive, yet proper tone of voice, but is interrupted by Blu. "Ladies, why don't we discuss this in Narlena's office?"

The edges of Smokie's Botox lips curl upward in a vindictive smile.

Narlena seems a bit speechless. Her eyes cut in at me, but I don't let her intimidate me. I look her dead on reminding myself of how she tried to destroy me. And took great pleasure in doing it. I narrow eye her then hardline my lips letting her know that I hadn't forgotten.

170

Narlena looks Blu in his eyes hoping he'd rescue her from this ugly scene.

"Here," Smokie says, "...seems befitting to me. Blu, this won't take but a minute of *her* time."

"Blu? Whoa," I say to myself. She's on first name basis. This is more than meets the eye.

"Smokie, don't make a mockery of yourself. We don't need to make a scene. Let's just go in the office and talk like respectable people."

Smokie cackles loudly. "Respectable people! Nonsense, darling." Her cat eyes scroll Narlena and as they do, her lips purse, then twist.

"Darling..." Blu tries to reason by walking over to Smokie and stroking his hand up and down her bare arm. Smokie is not moved.

Smokie turns and smiles at him. She caresses his face with the back of her soft hand. "Trust me, honey...this won't take but a minute." Smokie takes a few steps toward Narlena and looks her piercingly in her eyes. Narlena doesn't appear to be moved. She stares back. Smokie smirks, then says, "Have you had *fun*? You were always a sore loser at NYU. But I do, I really, really do appreciate you *fucking* my man while I was away singing my little heart out. Now that I'm back, we won't be needing your services any longer. I'll forward you a check in the mail. And please, don't ever contact my man again. You know, in college I always looked up to you. And *I* suddenly don't know why. You know what, *dirty old whores* need to stay in their lane. Wouldn't you agree? Just remember, he's mine and so is '*DeVaughn*'. Don't you think it's time for you to get a man of your own? Not all woman like myself believe in sharing."

On that note, Blu and Smokie exit leaving Narlena in a state of embarrassment.

Oh, shit! That bitch just got dissed! I think to myself.

I sit in disbelief as to what has just taken place.

Narlena stands still. The look on her face stresses mortified.

Dang! That was worse than my interview. What in the hell has Narlena gotten herself into? Of course, I'm laughing inwardly, but I won't show it on the outside.

Blessive keeps her eyes buried in whatever book she is reading and I-I try to find the words to say something comforting but nothing comes to me, so I stand and take Narlena or whomever this *dirty old whore* is by the forearm and slowly walk her to her office.

Blessive lifts her head up and says, "Ms. Love, once you go through the double doors, it's the third door on your right."

I nod.

Narlena and I enter her office and I shut the door behind us.

In her office, Narlena plops down on the white leather couch, and places her hands up to her mouth, and sobs hysterically in her palms.

Dang. No this bitch ain't crying. What happened to the strong, black woman who interrogates sistahs? The shark with sharp fangs that sinks her teeth into your flesh and bites down hard until you bleed to death. Where'd she run off to?

My eyes skyward the ceiling, scroll across and down at the wide window with a magnificent view of New York City.

I stand quiet trying to figure out exactly what to do to comfort her. But I swear, nothing comes to mind.

Without thought, my feet begin to move closer to the couch. I sit down and find my hand on her back stroking it gently. What else can I possibly do? Honestly, I don't want to do shit. But leave. Let her feel her pain. Let her know what it feels like to be humiliated. Why do I even care? Why am I still here? *"Good question."* Avona *says in a harsh, hard tone of voice, which is unlike her.* "I *would've left da bitch right where she stood. Avery, leave.*

172

Just walk out the door, shut it, and leave. Leave her trifling ass here on this nice ass couch, and fuckin' leave."

Why can't I be like Smokie for a day? That chick put her foot down, and said, "You low-class bitch, this is my man. Get your paws off before I stomp your bougie ass in the ground." Well, she didn't exactly say it like that but that is my interpretation. Look, those were fighting words Smokie threw out there. I gotta give it to her. Smokie did it with *style* and *class*.

Deep down I want to leave her sobbing on the couch. But-But a part of me, dang, hates to see any sistah down in the dumps. I'm mo' than sho' Narlena played a major part in this craziness.

I take it our interview is cancelled, so I say, "Um, it's been a day. Maybe I should go. I'm sho' you would rather be alone right now. Um, you can call if you'd like to talk. I'll be home. Or you can call me on my cell, wherever you feel the urge. You'll be fine, Narlena, just fine."

The sound of her bawling is killing my mood. I just want to walk out of this office, find me a bar, and drink until my heart is content. This is just a little too much for me to handle.

As I stand, Narlena wipes her tears with her fingers leaving streaks of black mascara on her aggrieved face.

"Are you leaving?" she asks in a delicate tone of voice.

I am a little apprehensive in answering for fear she may ask me to stay. I'm feeling reallll uncomfortable right now. "Yes."

Almost near the door, about to open it and exit, I feel her presence on my back, the heat of her body permeating through my sheer turquoise blouse makes me immediately swing around not sho' of what she is about to do. I don't trust this heffa.

Narlena stands still with her head dangling low. She then leans in and places her head on my left

173

shoulder. I gently pat her head, then upper back. Whisper in her ear, "You're gonna be fine."

I've never seen her so vulnerable, so feeble, unenergetic. I must tell you, it is not attractive at all. And no, I don't feel happy that I witnessed it. If anything, I am very empathic toward how she feels. Yeah. I actually care even though a part of me wishes not to.

This whole display lets me know that Narlena is no different from myself. She just pretends to be as most women in high positions do. But now that the curtains have been drawn, and the truth has been exposed, Narlena Scott, can finally be herself. A *woman*.

I exit Narlena's office with a heaviness on both of my shoulders. Even though her problems are not my problems I feel a sense of empathy for her. I've been in uncomfortable situations numerous times in my life, and going through the emotional process, alone, might I add, really gave me a window to look through. All I seemed to see was a reflection of myself. And that allowed me to ask myself questions of why I chose to entertain the folks I chose. The only answer I seemed to come up with was: *I refused to be lonely*.

When I met Blu McDowell I was physically attracted to him. His tall stature, handsomeness, the sound of his deep voice, him being a manly man, not to mention his other attributes. I was lusting him on first sight.

Deep down I knew I wanted to have my way with him but I also knew that there was this barricade between us— stopping me from throwing myself at him— and us indulging in each other. If not for this barricade, I would've feast off of him like a hungry wild cat.

Despite his reaction when I confessed of what I housed inside of me, it only slightly changed my perceptions of him. Slightly. I still get that tingly feeling whenever I see him, which tells me that the attraction is still there. Still strong. But the thought of us ever crossing that barricade I don't foresee it ever happening.

Travar Atkin. That drop-dead gorgeous man was some eye-candy, if you ask me. Very generous, sensitive, and loving man. God. If only I didn't have this shit running through my veins I do believe Travar might've been my knight in shining armor. The way he made me feel the night he cooked for me, catered to me, I hadn't felt so alive and sexy and freaky in a while. He really put forth effort to impress me. And I must say, he did. He went beyond my expectations. Wayyyyyy beyond.

Zaelyn Homes. Even though we are no longer on speaking terms. And even though things are pretty shaky between us. Believe it or not, I still have *love* for him. Sometimes I can still feel him inside me. Loving me. Making love to me. Often I find myself thinking about where we were and where we are now, and it saddens me. I never thought things would get so crazy. Just as I never thought he'd be bitter as I see he is, so angry, so hurt, and so deceitful. You just don't know a person, you know. Folks wear many faces that disguise who they really are. Had I known, Zaelyn would've never gotten to first base—let alone third? But I didn't know. I allowed his charm, his southern mannerism, his drive, as well as his hunger for me—I allowed myself to be taken in by him because I truly desired him. *I* wanted him. A part me even felt a need for him. The *need* to make me feel like a *desirable* woman again.

***

Aug 18, 2016

Dear Sis,

I never shared this before but since I'm on the topic of my disastrous relationships I may as well add another to my roster.
Mr. Hunt Treasure.

I met him, fifteen or possibly nineteen years ago. It's really hard to say with time flying by these days. At the time I didn't have my car. Actually, I did have my car, but my car was in the repair shop, so my only transportation was the bus.

So here I am at City Hall in Paterson, waiting for the New Jersey Transit 712. It arrived. I got on. Sat down. Got to my destination, which was to Willowbrook Mall, in Wayne, New Jersey, to return a dress I had bought for a job interview that was cancelled. Back then I was struggling to make ends meet, so every little bit of money I had I had to stretch. Returning the dress was no big deal to me. Sistah had to find means anyway she could. At least until I found a job.

Well, this man happened to see me walking as he exited out of his burgundy Volvo.

Before I entered Lord & Taylor, he approached me.

The handsome man said, "Hi. You sure are beautiful."

I blushed because it had been awhile since a man had complimented me. "Hello."

"My name is, is. Oh, damn, gazing in your eyes, I nearly forgot my name. I'm Hunt Treasure." He extended out his hand to shake.

I reached out and shook his hand. "Avery Love."

"Nice meet you, Avery." He said in this deep, deep voice and his full thick lips expanded into this sexy smile. Man, that smile was unforgettable.

"Same here." I said, not sho' of what to say next because I was sort of caught off guard.

"Um, may I ask," he said, "Are you involved?"

I slowly shook my head from side to side, then replied, "No."

He smiled again.

I just stood there wondering, what's up with this dude?

"Well, Avery, since you're not involved, and since I'm not involved, do you think we can exchange numbers, possibly meet for coffee, lunch, dinner?"

"That sounds fine with me." I said.

So we exchanged numbers. Hunt called me the next day. We talked for about an hour getting inside each other's head. We decided to meet for dinner the following evening.

It was a beautiful summery day in August. I wore a J. Crew hot pink halter dress. A gold vintage necklace. And these pink and gold flowery earrings I found at a boutique in Montclair. A pair of wedge open-toe sandals that accentuated my legs. It was my first time wearing those shoes. I was breaking 'em in.

Hunt called and I met him downstairs in front of my building.

He was across the street leaning against his Volvo with tinted black windows. I was never one who cared for tinted windows on a car. Especially on a car with a man in his early fifties.

As I got closer to Hunt he stood before me with open arms and greeted me with a warm hug. A tall, possibly six-foot-six, bow-legged, salt-and-pepper haired man with flawless caramel-colored skin, and really big feet. The sexiest eyes any man could have, nice teeth, and a sexy beard and goatee. He was the total package, if I must say so. A treasure. No pun intended.

Hunt took me to this quaint restaurant in Hoboken, New Jersey. Said he knew the owner, a man he'd worked for when he used to cook. Said he went to school at Johnson & Wales in Rhode Island a ways back. Said it was a very demanding field, and he loved it. He tried opening up his own restaurant a couple of times but he said it was a lot of work, long hours, under staffed, not finding folks with strong work ethic, money, money, money issues, so he finally called it quits, and decided to become a truck driver where he still got to travel, didn't *feel confined behind closed doors. He had his freedom. Plus, he was making good money.*

At the time of meeting him, I was fresh out of college. Unemployed. But I never misrepresented myself. Never claimed to be someone I wasn't. No. I didn't play head games.

The date went very well. The food was out of this world. I met the owner, Balsa—a well distinguished Italian man that had impeccable taste in quality ingredients. You could literally taste the freshness. The authenticity in each and every bite of his lasagna. The feast of fresh warm bread, salad, great wine, the whole evening was just spectacular.

On our second meeting, Hunt seemed a bit different. I didn't know exactly what was wrong with him but I knew something was. He still was a pleasant man. And that smile hadn't dimmed, but something definitely was different. I think it was him.

It had been nearly four months since I had seen Hunt. That was pretty much on me because I didn't want to see him on a constant basis. I wanted to test the waters with other men, meet other options, so to speak. Play, but not dirty, you know. Do Avery.

November came.

Hunt and I met at this sports bar called The Dive Sports Bar in Clifton, New Jersey.

It was a little dive where mostly white folks went to have a drink or two. But, at the sports bar, they made you feel welcomed regardless of the color of your skin. So we met up there.

Hunt was dressed in sneakers, jeans, a Jersey, and a fitted. I was dressed in jeans, T-shirt with a denim blazer, dangling earrings, and black ankle boots with my black and silver studded clutch bag. We weren't dressed to the nines, and that was fine with me.

We sat at the bar.

The bartender, a medium-framed, dirty-blonde haired, blue-eyed, scruffy in the face looking mid-thirty year old white man who smoked Newport 100s greeted us with a pleasant smile and nicotine breath. He introduced himself as Mack.

"Hi," Mack said, "What can I get you folks?"

"What kind of wine do you have?" I asked.

"Well, Miss Lady, I have pinot grigio, chardonnay, cabernet, ahhhh, I think those at the moment."

"I'll have the pinot grigio." I told him.

Hunt said, "Chardonnay."

Mack said, "Do you wanna start a tab?"

Hunt replied, "Nah. How much?"

Mack smiled at me and then said, "Oh, just give me ten bucks."

Hunt reached in his front side pocket and pulled out a twenty dollar bill and placed it on the counter.

To make a long story short.

Hunt had two glasses of chardonnay. I had two glasses of pinot grigio. Hunt also ordered ten spicy buffalo wings, which came to nine dollars and fifty cents. And the total for our date came to a whopping, twenty-nine dollars and fifty cents...$29.50.

From the moment of us getting reacquainted, and having met this man many years ago, there we were seated side by side, engaging in meaningless conversation, sipping on wine and eating spicy buffalo wings, watching the news, and sports, and listening to Bluegrass music.

Before our meeting, Hunt had let it be known over our phone conversation that he had an abscess on the top crack of his ass. I don't mean to be so vulgar but if I'm going to tell you the story I have to tell it as it was.

The evening of our date, that is all Hunt talked about. The top crack of his ass was not appropriate conversation sitting at a bar having drinks. But I rolled with the punches because obviously it was a concern of his. It happened to be a turn-off for me. Especially when you are trying to get reacquainted, whether to establish a relationship, casual dating, or quarterly dating, I found the conversation…gross. The wine had more robustness than Hunt and his abscess.

Listening to him babble on and on about his ass and how he thinks he got the abscess: sitting on a public toilet at the gym without placing toilet tissue on the seat: sitting for long hours while driving the freight truck; or because he is a hairy man might've resulted in the abscess on the top part of his crack. Plus, the fact that he doesn't shower every day because he felt the chemicals in the water would damage his skin, could be another contributor, especially while driving and sweating and not getting any air, which cause bacteria, and not walking because of being stuck in traffic because of construction and constantly sitting in the heat, could have been another reason. Who knows?

In spite of all of that, and in spite of his original plan for us to go see a movie, where he only bought tickets, might I add, no condiments? You know, overpriced buttered popcorn that got stuck in-between your teeth or flat root beer that taste like flavored water. I'd rather be entertained by the music the white bartender, Mack was playing than him.

To me, I'd say the date was about a four on a scale of one to ten. But I think Hunt would beg to differ. Anyway, the date seemed to take a turn for the worst.

After we left The Dive Sports Bar, Hunt didn't really have any other plans for our evening, which was kind of disappointing to me. But I didn't complain. I was ready to go home anyway.

Hunt got me home safely, and as I was getting out of his car, he said, "Thanks for wasting my time. I could've gone to the movies instead of wasting my damn time on your broke-ass!"

I didn't respond back. But I was taken aback because I didn't know where that was coming from.

Once I entered my apartment, I replayed the evening with him in my head. Did I say something that *might've disturbed him? I didn't think so, other than when I asked him, "Are you involved?" he seemed a little agitated but he played it cool. "Are you?" he asked. I said, "Hmm." And he said, "Are you involved? How many...men are you currently seeing?" I smiled because I was feeling devilish, so I said, "Hmm. Let me think. Five." Yep. I blurted out five with a straightness of face. When actually he was currently the only one. But I didn't want him to know this because men have a tendency to treat you differently once they know that you are taking your time.*

All of sudden I felt a shift in Hunt's energy. He seemed cold. What happened? That's what I wondered.

At first I thought possibly I hurt his feelings by saying what I'd said. Or possibly he felt stupid for spending his money on me after I openly admitted that I was seeing other men besides him. I guessed he thought he had it like that. That he could just do me any ole kind of way and I wasn't supposed to have a comeback. Well, I guessed I surprised his sorry ass.

Before I had even gotten in the apartment good, my house phone ranged. Dang! Where did this chick live? I mean, was she across the street or around the corner from me. I hadn't gotten in the house good and this asshole was calling me, mind you, from his bitch's phone. Can you believe it? The audacity of him.

Anyway, all I heard was him yapping about this and that and stating that I used men for money. Money and drinks. Me? How? And what money was he talking about? His measly twenty-nine dollars and fifty cents...$29.50. Was he kidding me? I laughed in his ear. I mean, it was ridiculous and hysterically funny. I mean, that was the most entertainment I'd gotten that evening. And he wanted to waste his money on going to the Fabian Theater. Kevin Hart had nothing on him. Hunt Treasure was on a roll!

Maybe he thought he was a big baller with fat pockets of money. And he could've been. But just didn't splurge with me. And I didn't question it because it didn't matter to me. I honestly didn't care. Because Avery did for Avery.

I mean, I dated men who didn't have and I have wined and dined them for more than twenty-nine dollars and fifty cents. I didn't male bash them for not having, because I understood that sometimes you hit a rough patch in life. Sometimes you only have just enough to put food in the fridge and on the table and keep a roof over your head. I didn't question their mental state and call them names like: bipolar. Or insinuate that they had a mental problem and needed to get help because they were different, unique or eccentric. Or because their view on certain topics of discussion did not meet how I saw things. We were different for a reason. That is what made me attracted to them.

But with Hunt, I immediately got bashed. I felt it was juvenile and unfair because he didn't have the balls to say it to my face. No. That coward called me ranting and raving like a spoiled little kid.

Well, first of all, Hunt called to say that he was involved, which I had long suspected. And that I was merely a piece on the side. Correction: we had been sexual, twice. I mean, c'mon. Whether he stayed the night or not didn't faze me. Always checking his beeper. Pretending that he was trying to shut it off instead of being honest and saying that he was expecting a beep from one of his bitches that he more than likely was possibly meeting after he dropped me off.

The other thing was, in conversation at The Dive Sports Bar he mentioned that he'd thought that I thought that he was a player. Why would you even divulge that to someone you claim you are trying to get to know? Because, he was a player, and Hunt wanted it to be known. I don't know if it was to boost his ego even more than it already was, or, for other purposes that I was oblivious of.

182

That evening Hunt was lusting for me something terrible. Wetting his big, juicy lips as his sultry eyes glanced down at my apple-shaped ass overlapping the barstool. Yep. My butt was spreading in those jeans. Hunt thought he was being slick by tucking in my blouse so that he could feel my soft smooth skin. Yep. I let him have his little thrill. It seemed harmless.

Because contrary to what Hunt knew, that would be all the ass he'd be feeling on me. I had no intentions on sleeping with him. None. Having drinks was one thing, fucking was another. And-and truthfully, I was not sexually attracted to him. But I did once or twice have sex with him, protected, of course. And I think that was another reason why nineteen years ago, I never gave him the time of day. The sex was whack! Or, it could've been the conversation about the abscess, or the non-conversation because he was so in his own head, that might've turned me off, too. I enjoyed his company, thought he was an attractive man but I knew that he was preoccupied in thought. Possibly eager to get the date over with me, so that he could go out and play Mr. Game with the ladies. You know, play his player games.

Having sex with Hunt was not a memorable moment. Indeed it was whack. As quickly as it happened it was a forgotten thought. If anything I remember of him, was that he'd bought me some washcloths from Marshalls. Yep. Marshalls on Route 46 in Wayne, New Jersey. And as I recall, those washcloths were two dollars and ninety-nine cents apiece...$2.99. That day, Hunt bought me either seven or eight washcloths.

Now possibly in his mind, he thought he was shopping at Bloomingdale's or Neiman Marcus showering me with lavish gifts. But no, it was Marshalls and the washcloths were two dollars and ninety-nine cents apiece. He didn't break the bank. That's all I'm saying.

Regardless of the cost of the washcloths, I thought it was the thought that mattered most to me. Possibly he was thinking something else.

Since I'd known Hunt he didn't appear to be a big spender. If splitting a meatball (foot long) from Subway which equated to five dollars was a big spender, then all women need to BEWARE of a frugal spender. Women clench your purses because Hunt is on the hunt. And he will bash you if you don't make him feel like a man should feel. You'll get bashed for merely being a woman who doesn't mind having a man spend on her. I never belittled him. Never showed dissatisfaction with him and/or his way of living. I simply accepted him, and his flaws. Because in spite of what he thought, that joker did have flaws.

It seemed funny how he'd praise God. Never wanted to be around someone negative. It was always about being positive. And if a woman happened to have issues, unresolved issues, okay, he felt she wasn't the woman for him. Said he'd never marry such a woman with so many problems, because to him, he had that choice. Okay. I agreed with it being his choice, but I didn't agree with his way of thinking when it came to the other shit he was talking. Because life comes with hurts, wounds, unresolved issues. Nobodies' life is positive every day. People do fall short of themselves, a time or two.

To me, Hunt was full of himself and full of shit. And wanting a woman with money to lavish him with, or make him feel appreciated, I see nothing wrong with that as long as your intentions are good. I could not for the life of me see Hunt as a man with good intentions. I saw him as a man who used women, bed women, then dismissed himself from their lives, because of his own selfish reasons.

The other thing I thought was most comical was when Hunt stated that us Paterson women use men for drinks and then talk shit to them. He reasoned, that that

184

was the reason why he dated out-of-town women because they had the funds, and they weren't frugal. That they enjoyed spending their money on their men. Okay.

I don't know where that bullshit came from. There are a lot of successful professional black women who live in Paterson, work in New York City that would be able to accommodate his needs. But the fact that he bashed Paterson women because he felt we lacked certain things that he could find in out-of-town women was a slip of the tongue on his part.

In my opinion, Hunt should've kept that to himself. Because, first of all, he didn't know what that out-of-town woman was doing in his absence. And if he was with her, the way he was with me, then trust and believe, she was being entertained by another man in his absence. Just like a woman wants to be wooed, so do men. I get that. I'm all for that. But never underestimate a person, male or female. Sometimes we as people get so caught up in ourselves thinking that we are the "shit" only to find out later that your shit may not be the "best" grade of shit. You can be replaced.

If your focus is only on getting laid and pampered, then maybe you need to use your finances and buy your pussy from a prostitute. And if she's not good enough, then maybe you need to take your tired, abscess ass home and play with your penis until you fall asleep.

You see, years ago I had already met Hunt in other men. Men, might I add, worse and better than him. The brother was exactly what I suspected. It was not a total disappointment because I had no expectations. I was actually impressed with his consistency and persistence to get my attention. All those years was a long time to still be attracted to someone. I'm not knocking him for wanting what he wants. But what discourages me about the aftermath of that evening was how me not inviting him up to have a nightcap, him feeling as if I wasted his precious time, him feeling the need to confess that he had a woman, and that I was merely his side piece, that I used men for money...all a bunch of teenage bullshit is the very reason why, Avery Love, does for her damn self. I don't beg, I don't ask a man for a monetary thing. All I ask is to be respected, treat me like the black queen that I am, and conduct yourself with respect. It doesn't hurt to show a woman a little chivalry. But nowadays, women, especially minority women are doing it for themselves. They are lacing themselves in diamond and pearls. They are driving the Bentley. They are feasting off of duck and splurging on a pair of Christian Louboutin's—just because they can. They are traveling across country: Italy, Europe, and Trinidad...solo. They are so confident and powerful in their position that they don't need any man on their arm. They prefer the right man on their arm. Or at least a decent man. They are no longer just housewives and babysitters and free pussy waiting for their hubby to come walking in the door and place his (one) pack of bacon on the kitchen table. Honey, they are ordering slabs of bacon with their hard-earned money and freezing their shit for that rainy day when his jealous ass decides to leave, and they call their man over and serve him breakfast in bed. You ask, why? Because of tacky men like Hunt who brainwashed himself to think that he was/is God's gift to women. Not! Women are sick and tired of these trifling ass cut-rate men. Sick and tired!

Talks to you later, Sis,

Avery

***

In the wee hours I get up because I can't sleep. I reach for Sis on the nightstand, then I place the journal back. I have no energy to write.

186

Tossing and turning about the bed, restless. A brother named Prinze Charming invades my mind.

My hands have a mind of their own and pickup Sis from off the nightstand.

Aug 19, 2016

Dear Sis,

Prinze Charming was one of those "refine" men. Well, he portrayed that role out in public but behind my closed doors, Prinze was a weakling and a cheapstake. I could have had that man any way I wanted. And I did. But one thing about Prinze was that he boosted his ego up so high that his penis and his ego weren't on the same page. It was like his ego was on page 200, but his penis was still on page 54—trying to catch-up.

I never tried to crush his inflated ego but Prinze was not all he thought he was. Maybe to his options, but not to me. And he sho' couldn't perform as he claimed he could. At least not with me.

I was a run for his money. Money, might I add, I never asked for. I was merely intrigued by Prinze's confidence, and his shortcomings, but to Prinze, he had none. Of course, I begged to differ.

One thing I couldn't/can't stand was/is a cheap man. If you added: cheap + self-absorbed + selfish that =Prinze Charming.

In all of my years of dealing with an assortment of men I had never met a man quite like Prinze.

I was a great hostess. I enjoyed catering to my part-time man. There was nothing better than coming to a woman—a sexy sexy sexy woman in her negligee, piping hot food on the table, and an ice bucket filled with ice chilling in it, as she awaited her man and his generous bottle of wine.

Dessert, of course, was a slice of cake made from scratch, along with a taste of me as a nightcap. Well, that's how it played in my head the last time I saw Prinze.

It was about 9:00 PM. Prinze arrived looking dashing in his navy-blue business suit. The alluring scent of men's Chanel cascading in the air. Dang! That man smelled sooooo good. And he looked even better.

"For you," Prinze said.

For me... what? I wondered. I could only assume he was talking about himself, because Prinze came empty-handed. I let it go. Because that man was looking so yummy. I was already drizzling in my thong.

I smiled one of those "I-can't-wait-till-dessert," smiles. Letting him know I was gonna eat him up. Just devour him with my sensual loving.

Prinze walked in. He noticed the ice bucket on the kitchen table. He looked in it and saw that it was filled with ice but no bottle of wine. He had this perplexed look upon his face.

I, too, was a bit baffled. So I watched him, observed his usual behavior.

Prinze opened the fridge and checked each compartment as if he was looking for a missing person or something. Then he opened the freezer. Looked inside. All that was in there was frozen meats, ice cubes, ice cream, and frozen vegetables.

What's up with him? I thought.

He turned and looked at me, and said, "Babe, where's the wine I bought/brought here?"

"Wine you brought here?" I said to myself. I just know this nitwit ain't talkin' about that bottle of wine he brought here like three weeks' ago.

Just for clarification, I asked, "What wine?"

"What wine?" he retorted. "That big bottle of Chardonnay I bought/brought here. That's what wine."

"Oh, well, Prinze, that was like three weeks ago. You couldn't possibly expect that same bottle of wine to be here, could you?"

I needed to know, if he could or couldn't.

"You know," Prinze exclaimed as he looked at me intently, with those light-brown eyes of his, "I'm beginning to feel a certain type of way."

"What way is that?" I asked, with a hint of frustration in my tone, and on my face.

"I bought/brought that big bottle of wine, and it isn't here. So—"

"Soooo," I stressed with emphasis.

"All I'm saying is that I'm feeling a certain type of way, that's all."

That's all? Oh, you buggin' for real. What did he expect? He was gone for THREE weeks! Oh, so if I have company I'm not supposed to offer them a glass of wine if I happened to have one myself? See, this is what I mean by: cheap, self-absorbed and selfish.

In Prinze's mind, he figured: Oh, Avery, I bought/brought you this wine, but this big bottle of wine is for me, not you. So when I stop through I expect you to still have that same bottle of wine because I bought/brought it.

Hold up! Does he expect me to hit him up to see if I may have a glass of his wine, too? HELL, NO! That sounds sooooo stupid!

Whatever one brings to one's house as a gift offering, a kind gesture of generosity, one should never expect one to just savor it and wait for him or her to come back after THREE weeks and expect it to still be there, chilling cold, awaiting his or her grand entrance. That was absurd to me.

I have never gone to someone's place, bought/brought them a bottle of wine and expected them to have the same bottle of wine there when I returned— three weeks later.

I've never experienced something so bizarre in my life.

Anyway, since Prinze felt, a certain type of way, I said, "How much was the bottle of wine that you purchased, Prinze?"

He didn't hesitate to answer. "Thirteen dollars and ninety-nine cents ...$13.99."

"Thirteen dollars and ninety-nine cents." I repeated.

I climbed the stairs up to my bedroom, opened my purse, pulled out a twenty dollar bill, walked back downstairs, handed Prinze the twenty dollar bill in the palm of his hand, and said, "Baby, come eat."

No, I didn't throw his ass out. Not after I'd slaved over the stove cooking us a hot meal and baking a cake from scratch. I fed him. Fed him good, too.

Yeah, I wanted to make sho' his belly was full. Once I knew he was good and full I said, "Well, I had a lovely, lovely evening, but it's getting late." And as I said those words I undressed in front of him, stood before him butt ass naked.

He looked at me with this gleam in his eyes, mouth dripping with drool and said, "Damn, baby, you look good enough to eat."

I said, "Do I?"

As he began to unloosen his expensive necktie and slip off his expensive suit jacket, I stopped him.

"No, baby, no. You see, I gave you that twenty dollar bill for a reason. Won't you go and buy yourself a clue as to how to treat a woman, especially this black woman. I am not some floozy that you just treat any ole kind of way. You come in my house looking for some wine that you bought/brought here THREE weeks ago, and you expect me to give you some 'Black Luxury Pussy'! You must've lost you goddamn mind. If you want all of this here, it's gonna cost you!"

He looked at me flustered. "Are you for real?"

"OH, yes, I'm for real. See, sweetie, I know what you like, and I know how you like it, soooo, what's it gonna be?" I turned around and spread my ass cheeks, jiggled 'em too.

Something must've registered between (his inflated ego and his horny dick) because Prinze handed me back my twenty dollar bill and let himself out the door.

It had to be about twenty minutes later, when I heard my buzzer go off.

"Hello."

"It's me, Prinze. Let me up, baby."

I contemplated for a minute or two, should I or shouldn't I, but then I was curious as to what Prinze wanted. I didn't see any of his belongings left behind so what was up? I wondered.

To be entertained, I buzzed him in.

Seconds later, I heard a light tap at my door. I peeked through the peep-hole and saw Prinze standing there.

I casually opened the door with a straight face. Prinze eyes scrolled me up and down, down and up as he massaged his bottom lip with a swipe of his moist tongue. I was not turned on, and I assumed he realized that by the pokerfaced look I gave.

"Can we start the evening over?" he asked.

I nodded my head, and stepped aside to let him in.

"Avery," Prinze said. "I'm sorry." And as he said those very words he extended out a bigger bottle of wine than the one he'd left three weeks ago. "Do whatever you please with it." He said, then smiled as if he knew all had been forgiven.

I smiled with my eyes, then replied in a rather seductive tone, "Oh, baby, I intend to."

Prinze smiled.

Needless to say, the evening wasn't a total disaster. Well, that depends on how you look at it.

Since Prinze killed the mood, he left out with a hard-on. I, on the other hand, sat back on the saffron sofa butt naked sipping on a chilled glass of Red Chocolate wine.

Talks to you later, Sis, -Avery

191

Chapter
Twenty-Two

Country

It's not every day a woman meets the man of her dreams. Or shall I says, a man she dreamt and met in her dreams. It's easier with a dreamt man compared to a real one, you knows.

These days it's difficult to tell what is real or what is fake. Woman have a tendency to make things up in us head. Embellish. Recreate what is bad. Dress bad up to fit our fancy. Over-exaggerate what is good to make others envious. Jealous.

In other words, women's lie through us teeth. For what? All for the sake of hasin' a man. All for the sake of being in love—wanting love. Wanting someone to love us back.

Sometimes I has to catch my breath a couple of times. Thank my lucky stars that I live to see another day. Sometimes I has to tug on my love handles, believe that it really is me, me standing 'fore this cracked mirror, eyeing this *cracked woman*—checking every inch of my body, while wondering what happened to my mind.

Sometimes I find myself drifting axin' myself many questions, and *not* coming up with any answers as to where *I* went. When did *I* lose? Lose...me? It's hard to pinpoint. Decades. Perhaps?

A sigh used to help. But nowadays even a sigh gives too much of myself away. It explains a lot. Then nothin'. Makes me tremble. *Why do it take this, Country, for me to get that?* Hmm. I don't knows.

I guess I has to go through something horrific to find that mustard seed of hope, courage. I guess I has to take off these bifocals and face my fears. Acknowledge that sound that rangs, wails, and begs—screams so sincerely, so boisterously in my ears. It's deafening. Hearing the acquainted sound. My *own* sound trying to save my life.

***

Fussin' led to baby making. At least that was what Mama said. One slap torched a flame and the next thing you knew Mrs. Kenzie's belly was swollen. Her ain't much care for the slaps from his lily white ass, but her sho' ain't mind the makeup sex.

My daddy, Big Wheel was an undesirable man. I don't fully 'member how he was when I was a little gal. Some pieces of my life has been blocked. Don't knows why there blocked. Just knows that they is.

I do 'member livin' in Puttin'-A-Hurtin', a small town of about ten thousand folks. Not too far from Beat Dat Biddy, South Carolina. Yep. There was a lotta blood in us home. Yes siree.

See, I come from a home of bloody nose, face, arms, legs—justa lotta blood and whole lotta blame. I knows my mother went through a lot with her dad. The stories she used to tell me, quite unbearable to listen to. Bringing a white man home to meet her daddy musta been the hardest thing to do. Especially when she had to admit that her had fallen deeply in love with what my granddaddy would consider the "enemy."

Making it through slavery, segregation left a bitter taste in granddaddy's mouth for white people. It took time. Dang near a lifetime for granddaddy to come to grips with hissa daughter wanting this white man.

Granddad kept an evil on him. Best believe. Big Wheel stayed on his best behavior when granddaddy was alive. 'Cause he knew, without a shadow of a doubt, he knew that if he even dared to cross him and touch his little gal, he'd never wake to see the sun rise again.

It was no deep secret to Big Wheel, 'cause granddaddy looked him straight in the eye with his silver hair tightly coiled on top of his head and told him to his face, time and time again.

Unfortunately granddaddy didn't live long enough. He died in the early '70s. Eighty-eight years old. And just as he was being lain to rest, Big Wheel had put a hurtin' on Mrs. Kenzie. He beat her for all the years he had to put up with her mean-spirited, prejudice father. He beat her ferociously. And dared her to tell a soul. He put so much fear in her that her mind blanked out on her. Her wasn't the same women's, let 'lone mother.

It was hard upbringing for me. I watched with these old soul eyes of mine, my mother gets treated like dirt. I must admit I didn't recognize it at the time. I was such a gal. My eyes seen what my mouth wouldn't say. Agony. Death was perched on us front porch. Seem like a thousand black crows circled us home. Squatted like wanderers. Huh. Big Wheel might as well had put a white sheet over his head, the way he treated my mama.

Time and time again she'd take it. Made up many excuses as to why and what led to him blowing up and raging out on her. Then on me.

I'd never forget, Mama sang in weak voice, she said, *"Country, your daddy loves you and me sooooo much!"* Yep. That's what she said. And I-I never doubted her words. Mama said, *"Chile, dat man loves you to death."* I believed her. Till this very day, I still believe her. Believe that my husband loves me to death, too.

When my second boyfriend, which was my husband, Herberto. When he put his Puerto Ric hands on me it wasn't to hug me tenderly. That boy tried to choke me to death. Yep. I thought of Mama's words. I also thought I'd never see the light of day after that. Pity the fool. Somehow those chokeholds turned into a marriage proposal, engagement, and then us getting married at City Hall. I was already knocked up at eighteen. Belly full of baby. That was supposed to be a happy time in my life. But—

I didn't think she'd survive. So many hours in labor. Not to mention the hurt I felt from Herberto's fistful of punches: face, stomach, face, stomach. He literally tried to beat my baby outta me. "Die, puta (whore)!" He repeated with each hard forceful kick and rib crushing blow. But by the grace of God...Honesty was born.

The first time I laid eyes on Honesty I was a bucket of tears. First thing I thinkin' was, *my goodness! Look-a-here!* She was so fragile, so tiny and puny. Smelled like life. Sweet and pure. She ain't weigh much, though. Probably four or five pounds, two or three ounces, at best. But she was mine. My bundle of love and happiness. But not my peace.

I had long left Puttin'-A-Hurtin'. Long left. At the time we lived in Camden, New Jersey. I worked a little while when Honesty turned about four. Put her in daycare.

This old burly woman named Mildred Coon used to babysit the neighborhood kids out of her home. Mildred was a blessing for me. Without her I wouldn't has been able to take on any job. Not too long after I took on a motel cleaning job at the Coo-Coo Train to make ends meet. Herberto worked as a mechanic, working on automobiles. He was a good provider. Good lovin' man for me. I thought I'd made the right choice by marrying that son-of-a-gun.

But then—

As Honesty grew in her teens, our mother-daughter relationship suffered. Herberto was a menace and Honesty got tired of coming home from school

195

listening to him bicker about nothin' really. He'd agitate her to the point where Honesty purposely got pregnant just to have her seventeen year old boyfriend, People propose. People never came to ax us for us blessing. To me, there was no need anyhow. Honesty was growing up. I had no control over the young chile's mind. If she wanted to get knocked up and married to some young boy that was on her. I would never stand in her way. And I didn't. That chile had wings and I wanted her to fly as far away as 'em wings would take her.

One day Honesty come in in a bitter rage stating that she was leaving this house that was not a home. She told me I was a fool to stay here with Herberto. A *damn fool*. That's what she said. Said it with such judgment to my face. Knocked me hard, you knows.

Honesty didn't understand being so young and all. But I knew me leaving Herberto would be the worst thing to do. He was my husband. He took care of me. Honesty couldn't and wouldn't try to understand my way of thinking.

I 'member Honesty said, "Ma, if you stay you will *never* know what it feels like to be free. Living here with that man ain't gonna get you nowhere but dead. You hear me, Mommy. Dead!"

Honesty's words went in one ear and out the other. Herberto was my man. Honesty had her man, so why couldn't *she* be happy and leave me be?

Honesty was young, feisty, vibrant, and smart. If things didn't work out with her and People, she'd easily find another man. One that would care for her and her baby. Probably marry her too.

Needless to say, Honesty ended up leaving. After her and People graduated high school. People's uncle hooked him up with a good job. They moved to Georgia. I has yet to see my grandbaby. Don't knows if I *ever* will.

Honesty sent me a few pictures of the little precious joy. Granddaughter's picture hanging on the living room wall in a cracked picture frame. She the spitting image of Honesty. My grandbaby's name is Darling. Honesty and I seldom talked. And when she was calling Herberto wouldn't even tell me she called. Only way I'd find out was after a heated argument. An argument he'd instigate. Herberto would get pretty fired up about Honesty. Just the sound of her voice pissed him off. He'd called her an ingrate. Selfish bitch. Whore. Trifling tramp. Ghetto slut. Said she wasn't nothin' but a low-class piece of smelly ass and stank pussy. He pretty much called her all kinds of names. He was pretty angry with her, especially when she told him that she disowned him as her father. Honesty said, *"What kind of man beats on his wife, every single day of the fuckin' week?"* Honesty said, *"As a little girl I used to look up to you. But now that I'm a young woman I see you for who you really are. You ain't nothing but a bum. An alcoholic bum. You ain't doing nothing but wasting away. Won't you just die and do us all a favor. Mom could do so much better, but since you got her trained like a dog she'll never know it. Don't you feel like a man? You sorry bastard!"* That was the last time I saw her. Sho' do's miss her. Sho' do's.

My chile, oh, she hated her father. Hated him with a passion.

I never tried to come between 'em two. Honesty had her way of seeing things. And I had mine. I loved my daughter mo' than she'd ever know. But she had her life, and I had mine.

My daughter was a beautiful, beautiful young lady. Lord, she was growing so fast. She was tall, slim, barely had any bosom. Long pretty black hair that fell to her shoulders. The prettiest cocoa-butter skin. And those eyes of hers. Chile, they'd melt you with one look. Hazel eyes. She sho' turned out to be such a lady. And I was so proud. So proud that she didn't turn out to be like me. I never set an example, I'll admit. But I'm glad that she stood her ground, while she watched me fall.

I never intervened with her and People. So I felt like she shouldn't have intervened with my marriage to her dad. Whatever we had going on was between us. All she had to do was close her eyes and keep her mouth shut. And she did. That chile of mine sho' did.

But then I guessed as Honesty grew into her own person. A young woman. She began to change. Things began to affect her. And I-I didn't feels strong enough to try to help her. Hell, I could barely help myself.

My love for my husband is serious. Call me naïve. Call me whatever. I sho' was wasted on that man. Couldn't get away if I tried. My love for him is solid. Solid as a rock.

***

It all started off as a gut feelin'. Instinct. Then it progressed into a knowin'. Each time that man would come home I sensed death on my heels. Smelled it so ripe in the air like fresh cut grass. I swear, each day I didn't knows. I just didn't knows.

There was always something troubling me. Something sparked a knowin'. A knowin' that my husband would take great pleasure in killing me.

My dad, Big Wheel was a firm believer that you stuck with your own kind. White with white. Black with black. Brown with brown. You didn't mix gravy with no chink, spick, or nigger. It went against everything he stood for. He'd go ballistic if I ever brought anything other than my culture (black) home. He'd probably kill me and him if he'd ever found out that I'd been with outsiders. I wanted to experience the difference in man. I needed to— just to curve the curiosity.

I think daddy must've forgotten that I was mixed. Black and white like a zebra print. Possibly he let it slide on account of me hasin his white blood running through my veins. Mama was full breed Black. And there was no denying that. I don't care how much she permed her kinky hair—she was Black.

Black and beautiful. Solid and curvy. A beautiful South Carolina women's. Skin the complexion of creamy fudge. And she was stacked in all the right places. I think that was what caught my dad's attention. Caught his eyes. Not to mention her could fry the best fried chicken and fried okra, collards, and macaroni and cheese, kidney beans and neck bones and cornbread like nobody's business. A good-looking women's, with no kids, could clean house and cook, and tend to her man, huh? That was all daddy needed. At least, that's all it seemed he needed.

I drift deeper and deeper.

"Country, where the fuck you been!" Herberto's words slur and his crimson dark eyes look deep into me while sittin' upright on the sofa. He still has on the dingy, holey T-shirt and boxer briefs from this mornin'. Five o'clock shadow, uncombed thick brunette hair, and he reeks of cheap wine. The apartment is in shambles. It don't matter how much I clean house that man purposely dirties it up.

Herberto cut his eyes down and glances at his hairy forearm, then wristwatch, purses his lips, tilts his head slightly back and takes a swig of his cheap wine.

With his free hand, he slides out from under his left thigh his evidence—a Polaroid he'd taken of me this mornin'. He looks at the picture, then me, me, then the picture. His eyes scroll every inch of me, staring and studying me as if a Forensic examiner. He is hoping— hoping to find an unloosened or missing button, a rip in my pantyhose, my collar undone, a disheveled strain of hair, makeup smeared, a speck of dirt on my shoe, or a distinguishing mark on my face. He never finds anything to make him think that I am cheating on him, but he always speculates.

"*Country, you're late again!*" *His eyes squints real low as he says,* "*You fuckin' 'round on me?! YOU fuckin' the mailman, ain'tcha?! Or, or, the handyman...I know you fuckin' somebody! Woman I gotta take what is rightfully mine, huh? You usedta throw the pussy at me like a wife should, what the fuck happened to you, girl?! 'Say here, Herberto, fuck me hard and good.' And I usedta tear that juicy pussy up.*" *He stares out in outer space for a brief second as I stands still. I don't know if I am excused or not, so I don't bother to make a move. I just ain't sho' where his head is. Is it here? Or is it back then and there?*

How could I not be late when he sabotages our only car? Every day I try to startup that Impala and it won't catch. I get up an hour earlier just to check. He never moves a muscle. And he's the mechanic. Mechanically he put the thoughts of infidelity in his own head. As unhappy as I is, the thought of cheating never crosses my mind. I am faithful to this man. Love him mo' than he'd ever knows. Yet he do everything in his power to shrink me down to nothin'. Maybe he feel if I has nothin' left to offer a man, then he'll be willing to leave me to fend for myself.

I come to.

Back then, huh, I was the one providing for the household. The breadwinner. Running myself ragged. Cooking, cleaning, and caring for our only daughter. Herberto. He would be too drunk to move. Half the time his boss would be calling axin' of his whereabouts. And I'd lie to cover up for him. After a while the phone stopped ranging. And Herberto stopped caring. And I kept on hurtin' because he kept on hurtin' me.

Living with this man has mo' setbacks, booby-traps, grenades, any and every type of firearm money can buy. I'm trapped. And as far as I am concerned the only way out is by the hands of my man, my husband.

I remain silent.

So many thoughts race through my head as to how my mother handled her situations. I used to watch her with careful eyes. She never showed any signs or indications that she was a "ruined" women's. She ran her house as if she was the happiest women's with that fuck-up of a man. She knew how to make it work. The dysfunction. She knew how to make him feel *whole* no matter how much he belittled her. She knew how to take it, wear it well, and sew it up when any loose threads began to fray. She knew how to pretty it up with rouge and dust powder and fake lashes. She knew how camouflage its bloody stench with the fragrance of sweet cake baking in the oven. But the one that stuck out the most for me learning from her was that she knew not to entertain him or sass talk him. And I knows from watching her not to give an explanation as to where I been. Herberto will turn anything I says into a lie. He is such a devilish man.

I stand a few feet away. Keys still clench in my hands—just in case I has to run out the front door and run frantic down the street. Herberto has a habit of keeping his sawed-off shotgun to his side. At any given time he can put me out of my misery, but instead he chooses to continue to beat me. And I *choose* to keep on lettin' 'im.

I just keep on dumbing down. And lovin' him up.

Chapter
Twenty-Three

Narlena

The pained filled vocals of Phyllis Hyman's "Living All Alone" streams from the stereo system into my ears, slithering up and down my spine as if a snake. I gaze out of the high-rise window, contemplating. I've come to the realization that *my work has become my worst enemy*. Invading peoples' lives is what I'm paid to do. Is it fair? It's what I do. It's what I was hired to do. And over the years it has gained me wealth as well as a name that enables me to live a lifestyle of comfort.

But what I know to be true is that my life is not as comfortable as it may seem. As beautiful as men may find me, I'm a very, very lonely woman. I attract people because they are looking for something from me. To them without what I do, I'm a ghost. My worth would have no price tag. I'd just be an ordinary, everyday woman. Working an ordinary, everyday job.

I used to shake that lonely feeling off by showing my face at many, many celeb parties—parties that they had personally invited me to. It was a way for them to stay in the public's eye. An article in BLAB heightened a lot of their careers. Bad publicity seem to outweigh the good publicity. All in all they benefitted. I never once heard a complaint, which told me that I was phenomenal at my job.

I think, or, rather, I know, I *love* what I do. But now I'm beginning to wonder, who *I* am? I've asked myself this question before now, and I never really answered it for fear of not knowing if I'd like the response. So I brushed it off. Carried on with life as if I was living in bliss.

Bliss. Yeah, right. That is some bullshit. I'm living in a thick fog of bliss. Nothing is as it seems in my life. Nothing. I'm no different than Phyllis Hyman. "I Refused To Be Lonely" paints a self-portrait of how I truly feel about myself. If I didn't have this status, drive a fancy car, live in a beautiful house, look the way I do, I often wonder would anyone see me. Notice me. Honestly, no.

As Editor-in-Chief, I am a magnet for successful people. I thrive on being the best in the magazine business. If it means cutting someone's throat, stabbing someone in the back, stepping on someone's toes, destroying someone's reputation, life, airing out someone's dirty laundry, sabotaging to make sells, I am that faithful, manipulative bitch. That dependable bitch. That conniving bitch to call upon and get the job done. That is me. Me. That trifling bitch. Narlena Scott.

I sigh, feeling this tight knot in my neck. I twirl it in a winding motion trying to get the kinks out. It has tightened up even more.

I walk back to the couch, kick off my heels, and recline my body. I position my head on two of the throw pillows, and stare blankly at the ceiling. A thrashing sound echoes in my ears as if someone is knocking me on the side of my head with hard knuckles. Thump. Thump. Thump.

The phone rings. And keeps ringing, but I don't answer. I don't move one inch of my body off the couch. I remain still as corpse.

Ringgggggg. Ringgggggg. Ringgggggg.

I don't answer. I don't move. For once, I don't answer the beckoning caller.

Call someone else! I scream in my head. Leave me the fuck alone! I got my own headache—my own problems—my own misery. I think my conscience is fucking with me. It says, *"Shame on you."* And I retort back, *"Fuck you! And your conscience. I did what was required, needed."*

In this business you have to be a snake in the grass. Keep both eyes open, ears included. When those big breaking stories come shining through, baby, you best go out and get it! Get it before the next magazine does, and wipes your ass with the article you should've gotten. Conscience? In this business you have no conscience.

A smirk outlines my face. A tear rolls down simultaneously. I sit upright on the couch and stare at the shaggy cream throw rug.

I think to myself, *if you really want to know the truth, yes, I asked Avery to come and speak about her book, Ev'ry Ho Gotta Daddy because I had a motive. I wasn't interested in that trashy shit. But the fact that she wrote it, the fact that her name was printed on the front cover of it, it gave me an idea to use it to my advantage. To peel back those wounds of Zaelyn Homes and create more rivalry between the two of them. She had a juicy story and I wanted to reap the reward of telling it and destroying her.*

But why?

What has Avery done to me? Lived. She lives. In spite of everything that that woman has stomached, she lives. She's an inspiration for women across the world. Fuckin' inspiration! And that shit is what pisses me off most.

Do you know how hard it is to find a man like Zaelyn? It's pretty damn hard. Day after day I spend an enormous amount of time in the confinements of my home, *alone.* I don't own a dog, cat, fish, reptile...nothing. It's just me. And here this bitch finds a man. A tall, dark, handsome man who sweeps her off her pretty little feet. And she—she goes and ruins it by confessing that she's infected with the fuckin' HIV virus! Dumb ass.

If it were me I would've kept my mouth shut. I would've played along until I couldn't play anymore. Did he really need to know? Was it that important to tell? No. He never asked and I wouldn't have said a damn thing. She made it harder for herself by playing that Goody-Two-shoes role. It was a stupid move, for a stupid chick. But you know what, I ain't surprised. That's right the Editor-in-Chief used the word: *ain't*. So fuckin' what!

Soooooo, HELL, NO! I don't feel for her. Sorry. No empathy here. I'm not sad for her. If anything, I *envy* her. Because even with HIV she still managed to catch a man, while I sit at home playing footsy with my damn self.

'Ey, sells went through roof with the two of them exposing themselves in BLAB. And the fact that Zaelyn put her on blast in *my* magazine, ohhhh that was gold! Exposing her HIV status to the public like he did really created a frenzy with the men that had previously dated her. Once they saw her picture in the magazine (I assumed) it was over for her ass.

The phone was ringing off the hook. I paid Blessive overtime to stay and take each and every one of those calls. My emails were by the hundreds, thousands within a weeks' time. And within a few days I replied to all of 'em. People were constantly texting me about the articles. It was a slam dunk.

All I saw were dollar signs. So I had it in my mind—I-I said to myself, "I'm gonna milk this pretty HIV bitch." Yep. That's what I said.

I received letter after letter in reference to if I knew exactly how Avery contracted the disease. The year. The month. Where did she reside? Did she go by an anonymous name? How long did she know she had it? When did she first find out? A slew of questions mounted in reference to this...Ms. Avery Love.

Some men wanted to know if she ever traveled to Africa. Was she an intravenous drug user? Was she a prostitute? I loved it! Because the more I milked the story the more money was to be made. And I-I wanted to shine. I wanted to bling-bling, okay. I felt I deserved it because I worked the hell out of my brain. Pushed myself day in and day out trying to prove to myself that I had what it took to make this industry grow into something bigger, better, stronger, more profitable than when I first walked through those double doors, at the age of 22.

Zaelyn Homes was no longer the topic of discussion. People, readers, were curious about this black chick from their 'hood named Avery Love.

With me in my position, I wanted to appease the readers, so I contacted Avery. Sprinkled some sugar on our conversation. Told her I read the book and how much I loved it. Blah blah blah. Of course, I lied. I wouldn't be me, if I didn't.

First of all, not to downgrade the book being self-published, but the book was self-published. Written about a white *trick* named Daisy aka Rocka-Bye Bitch. Excuse me, but where the hell was the inspiration? And tell me. Please. Tell me. How is that book supposed to help young girls and women find themselves?

A crackhead trick with full-blown AIDS.

Oh yeah. That's a *REAL* role model for young girls and women to look up to.

Come on!!!!!!!!!!!!

Chapter
Twenty-Four

Country

The mo' I try. The mo' Herberto expects from me. What is a women's to do with a man like mine? Herberto transformed. It's like living with a psychotic monster. I-I believe in my heart that he loves me. I do's. But sometimes—sometimes he makes me work for his love. I work hard for it too.

Other times I think, *Country, why he doesn't just up and leave. Leave. Walk out the door, and leave. Pack up all of his shit and leave.* But then I question how I'll react once he do's. I don't trust me. I knows once his feet hit the door I'll be begging him not to go. I'm not strong as some woman is. Not strong at all. My strength left me a long time ago. Packed its shit and said the hell with you stupid bitch, I'm out. And it (my strength) never looked back. Never came back.

I can't go a day without seeing my husband. Hearing him yell and cuss me out on a daily basis. It's like music to my ears. Feelin' his hard fists pounce into me. Those love taps mean so much to me. Tells me so much too. It tells me that Herberto can't live without me either. It's how he expresses himself. How he talks. I knows. I knows my man.

A small part, very small part of me feels so blessed. But then the other part of me feels so stupid. I knows the difference. But I still accept what he brings to the table.

Tells me. Where am I gonna find another man at my age that will provide, keep a roof over my head, food in the fridge, hand-me-down clothes on my back, and sleep next to me, whether he's mad at me or not. Whose gonna love me like him? Tells me, who?

I watch these men's in these here streets, and it's all 'bout catering to 'em. Uh-huh. They won't be bold 'nough to come out and say it, but deep down they knows it. They play these roles as if they is so into the woman that they is pursuing, when all along 'em is merely toying with her and her emotions. These days it don't matter if a women's holds out anymore. It could be fifteen years when this man tried to pursue her and her didn't respond, react. Then one day they happen to bump into each other and he gives it one last try.

In her mind, she's thinkin', *he's still tryna get me.* I mean, she's flattered. Stunned. She don't put out right away. She takes her time, tries to get a feels for 'im.

Two months' time it takes.

He plays along. She's thinkin' this guy must really like me. But all along he's scheming with some other gal on the side. Still in pursuit of her, though. He just makes it seem as if he is waiting, patiently waiting for her to feel comfortable with him. Comfortable 'nough to let her panties drop and invite him in. And when I says "in". I mean "in" her. In her living space, in her world, inside of her pain. That seems like lotta wasted time, wasted energy, wasted love.

With Herberto there is no pretending. The man knows what he wants, and he simply takes it without axin'. He demands. Commands.

Over the years, I've come to 'preciate him 'cause of that. 'Cause I don't ever have to wonder if what he is sayin' is true, 'cause Herberto is cut and dry. There is no in between with my husband.

Herberto is just goin' through something that-that I can't seem to help him with. That he won't ax for my help with. At least not right now. I can't seem to connect with whatever he is goin' through. I is his wife, yes, but I'm not a shrink. Am I sayin' that my husband needs professional help? Maybe. But I would never say it to his face 'cause I knows how he'll react. Let's just says, it won't be pretty.

Ursula texted me today. Says her be in town. Her uncle's wake is this evening. Tomorrow is the funeral. I wish I could go to pay my respects to her uncle but I knows not to ax. Herberto will have a fit. And plus, I really don't have anything 'propriate to wear. Nothin' fancy, you knows. 1 dress rather homely. That's how Herberto wants me to dress. I guess so I won't be noticed. He don't want another man gawking at his goods. I understand. I do's. Just wish sometimes he'd lighten up. I'm not gonna cheat. That's the furthest thing from my mind. One men's is 'nough. I don't need two men's beaten my brains in.

I enter the bedroom. It's so in disarray with beer cans, wine bottles, a large, half eaten pizza settin' on the nightstand, Herberto's dirty cloths sprawled all over the floor, stinky sweat socks, and smelly work boots smellin' up the room—the whole house. I shake my head. I just cleaned this room up no mo' than twenty minutes ago and this man comes and dirty it up all over again.

I wish he'd stop drankin'. Stop cold turkey. His temper is gettin' worse. And my body is soooo sore, soooo bruised with black and blues. No matter what, though, I won't leave 'im. Naw. I won't leave my man.

Am I hooked on the abuse? Like a heroin addict.

Chile, when I looks at myself in the mirror: face swollen, eyes barely able to see outta, nose bloody, scratches 'bout my face and neck, truthfully, I has to say...yep.

An empty bottle of Chablis crashes to the floor.

"Snap out of it, bitch!" Herberto snaps, his hot, stinky breath blowing in my face.

I blink once. And 'fore I knows it, he steps a few feet back and raises his leg as his boot comes ferociously forward and karate kicks me hard in the stomach.

I doubled-over spitting up bile.

"You ain't hears me calling you! Get in that kitchen and make me something to eat, *whore*!"

Still doubled-over, I slide my bare feet across the floor. Hands strap around my belly, wincing with every step I take.

Entering the kitchen, hot tears trickle down my face as I slowly kneel, grab the cabinet knob and pull it open. I stretch my quivering arm and hand inside as I pullout the only large cast-iron skillet I has.

As I grab ahold of the handle, my watery eyes darken, forehead crumples, lips tighten. Shifty eyes go from left to right, right to left. All of a sudden I feels this-this other women's inside me. I see her. But her don't look like me. She look strong and tired.

She boldly sits in Herberto's favorite recliner with a sharp-edged butcher's knife settin' on her lap. Fresh ripe blood stained on the blade. She just sittin' there with a Cheshire cat grin plastered on her streaked-teared face.

Chapter
Twenty-Five

Avery

Climbing out of bed I pull open my drawer and pullout some undergarments, a pair of tattered blue jeans, a black T-shirt that reads: 2-ThrU in bold red letters and head downstairs to take a quick shower.

It's already 8:15 a.m.

As I enter the bathroom, undress out of my nightshirt and turn the nozzle for the shower on, I immediately step in. I lean back and let the warm water drench my body, as I think about things I have to get done.

Saturday will be here before I know it. There is so much I gotta do as far as promotional material for this upcoming book signing at Silly Chicks Banquet Hall. I have to call the photo shop to see if the poster I ordered is ready. Then call the caterer to see if the menu is still as I had asked, don't want any last minute hiccups that I don't know about. Then call this new photographer I met in Harlem named Entice to see if he is still available for Saturday. He does magnificent work. But today I'll go ahead and order copies of the book and have them come Rush delivery.

I'm pretty psyched about this book signing. *Silly Chicks* is a unique hall owned by African twins named Sippa and Shy. Their concept stemming from when they were little girls playing pretend in West Africa led to them opening up such a place where you could have an empty room and dress it up however you'd like. It gave you the freedom to do your own theme, create a story for which you wanted to share with others. Using the imagination was such a beautiful thing to them as children that it sparked this incredible idea as grown women. I'm not quite sho' why they named it *Silly Chicks*, though. But I'm sho' they have a story behind it. It's a cool place to have this next signing at. Cool place. I feel really good about it because this particular signing is for a good cause. Domestic violence and sex trafficking.

I know of two women who had been victims of domestic violence and unfortunately both died at young ages. One was, I think 26 or 27. The other was in her latter thirties. They were young, much too young to be dying. Yes, I consider beating a woman a disease of the mind and heart...anger, jealously is a terrible, terrible monster.

I decided to do something I call a *fifty-fifty*, whereas fifty percent of the proceeds will be given to: SISTERS, MOTHERS, and DAUGHTERS, GRANDMOTHERS and GRANDMOTHERS-TO-BE FOUNDATION in helping to save our women and children. It's the least I can do. The very least.

***

"Avery!" I hear a male voice calling out for me, but I don't bother to stop and see who it is. My head is pounding from this splitting headache. Too much work not enough relaxation time.

"Avery!" the male voice calls out for me again. As look toward the street I see a striking face driving a brand new black Volvo staring back at me.

I nonchantlantly say, "Hello, Hunt."

"Hi. You need a lift anywhere?" he asks.

"No, I'm good. Plus, I could use the exercise."

"Looks to me like you've been working out."

I don't bother to comment.

Hunt pulls his car over and parks on a side street. He then gets out and leans against his shiny car. I stop to see what he wants, not that I really care but I'm not going to be mean to the man.

"Avery, I can't stay mad with you. I got too much love for you. Have for a long time. And besides, the sex was awesome."

I breathe in slowly, then exhale. "Really? Is this the reason why he stopped me?" I say to myself.

Hunt continues. "We just have to learn to watch our mouth with each other. I miss you."

"Look, I'm having a day. I dropped my phone and cracked the screen. I'm hungry. I'm on edge. And I want a seltzer water."

"Seltzer water? What's wrong with you?" he looks at me strangely.

"Nothing. I just like seltzer water. But you wouldn't know this..."

Hunt chuckles.

I am not smiling one bit. Since I am in the presence of this still good-looking man I take it upon myself to not waste this opportunity.

"Hunt, you're always claiming to miss me, but you didn't know how to treat me. You said some pretty hurtful things to me. And now you claiming that the sex was awesome. We haven't had a good time with one another because as you stated you considered me your side piece, which was even more hurtful to hear. How can two people reconcile if one feels so ugly about the other? How can one trust someone that speaks so ugly of her?"

"Avery, please…"

"Let me finish. It's not that cut and dry with me. Watching how we communicate is wise but it takes more than just that. If you wanted twenty women that was on you. But don't think that I was going to be okay with being a part of those twenty. I knew how to be alone but not lonely. Still do. Then you said that something was wrong with me."

"Wow. You still going back, please, don't do it. Twenty ladies, where you get that from, and if I said things that hurt you in the past, I'm very sorry, okay. But if you still feeling some kind of way, I hope one day, month, and year that you can find it within to forgive me."

I remain silent. Look deeply into his eyes.

Hunt continues. "You still turn my head when you pass through, okay. Can't resist the look of you. I can just taste that thing on my tongue. What do you say we hook up at one o'clock? I'll bring a bottle of wine."

I cannot believe my ears.

"I'm not mad at you, but you can't just expect me to be open to you. I tried to give you the benefit of the doubt. I waited sooooo long to allow you entry in my home, my body, my head, but you made me feel like I was some *whore*. Like all I do is wait for a man. You had me all wrong. And now you expect me to invite you into my home. The forgiving part I've done years ago. That was never an issue. This issue was you. You never stepped up to the plate and apologized directly to my face. You don't want me. You want something to play with. You just want sex. But you know what I want? I want to be treated with respect. I want a man interested in me to show me, not only tell me. I want a man to pamper me and appreciate me. I want a man to love me and make love to my body and mind. Leave the kids play for the kids. I'm a grown-ass woman. And you're a grown-ass man."

"Yep. But it's not only about sex, Avery. And good luck finding that perfect man. I'm not perfect and neither are you. Love the one you're with. There is a song called that."

I look Hunt from his leather shoes up to his button down dress shirt. "See, that is exactly what I am talking about with you. I'm with me. And you're with whomever you're with."

"I have not given up on you. I'm just hearing you out and respecting what you want out of a man. You seem to think I'm not him, so I salute you're future choice, that's all. I'm crazy about you, but you don't believe me. I've always been regardless of what we've been through. We all go through some changes in our life."

I nod in agreement. "Yes, we sho' do. See, Hunt, I knew you were a hardworking man. And yes, I was very attracted to you. And if I allowed myself back then I probably could have developed feelings for you, but see, all that you are saying now you should've been saying then. Life changes people."

On that note I say, "Well, it was good seeing you again. You take care of yourself. Have a blessed day."

"You, too." Hunt gets back in his car and watches me stroll down the street.

Chapter
Twenty-Six

Narlena

I've been locked behind this office door for a day now. Why am I afraid to walk out the door? So *many* reasons. Blessive has been checking in on me as I told her I was working. Of course, she didn't question *me*. She knows better than to do something like that. Question *me*? Oh no, *never* that.

My stomach growls rather loudly. I massage it in a circular motion with my hand. I'm famished but I feel unsettled in my stomach, so instead of eating something light I get up and walk over to my small fridge, pull open the door handle and grab a small bottle of club soda.

Twisting the cap I wish it was Smokie's neck. I'd snap it off. And leave her ass for dead.

Have mercy? The inner woman in me says. Please. Me? Have mercy for someone? I don't think that's in my DNA. I don't think that's possible.

Getting my first whiff of the magazine industry, I started off as a writer, then worked my way up to assistant. No. I was not like I am now. I was eager, thirsty, hungry, charged to show my potential. And I-I accomplished my goals. I worked hard. Harder. The hardest of most of my colleagues. Pushed and pushed and pushed. I was determined to be the best. And I advanced rather quickly. I never wanted to become soft putty in anyone's hands. I'd kiss enough asses. Licked enough balls. Had 'em smack my juicy ass too many times. I was done. *Done*! So I molded myself. Branded myself into this egregious woman I am.

In a sense, I, too, became the man. A man in a woman's body. The ballbuster. The shot caller.

My lips outline into a devious smile.

Knock. Knock.

"Ms. Scott, are you all right in there?" Blessive asks with concern in her voice. "Um, I took it upon myself to get you some lunch. Maybe you should eat something, okay. I'm leaving it by the door. Please eat. You need to eat to keep up your strength. You're a power-suit. A power-suit woman, like yourself, has to eat."

I smirk, deviously.

Power-suit. Hmm. Blessive has a point. Power-suit. That *I* am.

"One man walks out, another walks in" those were my words. And sure enough my words came back to bite me once again.

***

I never intended to fall in love with a married man. I was merely hired because his wife wanted to keep him happy while she underwent radiation and chemotherapy, while she battled cervical cancer.

The odds were against her. So she put an ad in BLAB wanting to recruit a woman who'd match her criteria as a mate for her husband.

Young, energetic, intelligent, flexible woman interested in accompanying handsome, wealthy, distinguished white gentleman to charity function. Great sense of humor, extremely attractive, poise, model potential, enjoys the nightlife.

Our first encounter seemed amicable. Queene wasn't in the best of shape but she had her chauffer bring her here for us to meet in person.

My first impression of Queene was that she was courageous, an upstanding black woman going to great lengths to appease her white husband. I found it profoundly moving. Yes, it touched me, unexpectedly.

I had never met a woman quite like her. Strong in her weakest moment. Generous with her man. An unselfish woman who really loved her husband and didn't want him sexually deprived. I thought it was admirable, but precarious.

I ran the ad in BLAB, and received several responses. I can't say that I was shocked because Underwood was a catch. Queene was not impressed with the women who responded. She felt as though they were money hungry. Too eager. Too young and too inexperienced to handle her man with a high sex drive.

By the following week, I received a call from Queene asking that I accompany her husband to the charity event to raise money for children of West Africa.

With short notice, I declined. Queene wouldn't hear of it, so she sent her driver here to pick me up. And he followed her precise instructions.

First, we stopped at Saks Fifth Avenue where this stylist, P.G. Cummings was awaiting my arrival. She transformed me from business to ballroom. This was a black tie event and she wanted me to look fabulous on her husband's arm. Neither had ever gone in person to any of these events, so they didn't know if I was his wife or not. They mostly donated by check giving a substantial amount of money.

It seemed like the perfect plan.

Neither Underwood nor I ever thought things would progress. All we were trying to do was oblige Queene's wishes.

But now this bitch done flipped the script on me. Making it seem as though I hunted her man. No, she came to me. Now that she is in, I assume remission, what, she thinks she's running things. Think again.

I'm not bailing out so easily. Underwood may be her husband, but my imprint is all over his dick. She can't compete with me, because he knows that what she has to offer is nothing compared to what I have.

There is no doubt in my mind that Underwood will be back. I'll give him another day, and best believe sugar bear will be coming to lick his sweet honey.

Chapter
Twenty-Seven

Avery

Exiting out of the taxi, I stand across the street from Port Authority and hop on a jitney bus heading back to Paterson. My feet hurt. I have a pounding headache, and for some odd reason I can't seem to get the image of Narlena bawling in front of me out of my head.

At first, it did feel humorous to watch. But then a part of me felt sadness for her. I know if that had happened to me she'd be full of glee. Telling everybody without a care in the world for my feelings. Deep down I know she'd be the ultimate bitch.

I pull my cell phone out of my purse, go to my Contacts to find her name, and call.

I press the phone to my ear because it is so noisy I can barely hear it ring.

"BLAB, Blessive speaking, to whom may I, direct your call?" she asks in her professional telephone voice.

"Hi, Blessive, this is Avery, um, I was wondering if Narlena is available to speak with?"

"Oh hi, Avery, let me transfer you to her. Hold, please."

"Sho'."

"Narlena Scott, speaking."

Wow. She sho' bounces back quickly. I think to myself.

"Hi, Narlena, this is Avery. I was just calling to see how you're doing. I figured I'd give you a couple of days to yourself before I called."

"I'm great!" Narlena exclaims. "I appreciate you calling but I'm not one who stays down for long. My skin is too thick to be wallowing, having a pity-party."

Hmm. "I see. Well, like I said, I-I was just checking on you, you know. I won't hold you up, I'm sho' you have a lot of work to do."

"Swamped. These articles don't write themselves."

"Ok. I'll let you go. Have a great day."

"You too. Bye."

"Bye."

After we hang up, I feel like kicking myself in the shins. Why did I even entertain that bitch? Knowing. Fully knowing that she is enjoying my feeling sorry for her. I don't feel sorry for her. I don't even envy her. Shit. I don't even like her. Her life must be miserable. Yes, fuckin' miserable. As much dirt that she digs on others, there is no way dirt hasn't step foot on her doorstep and slapped her in the face.

My thoughts of Ms. Narlena Scott quickly faddddeeee away.

I arrive home safe and sound. Dang! Left hand smacks my forehead. I forgot to check my mailbox. With my keys still in hand, I drop my purse on the kitchenette granite counter, and walk back out the door, down the hall, and press "Down" for the elevator.

I lean my back against the wall, hearing my next-store neighbor, Felix snoring up a storm. Next thing I know, tenants, Lysa Hardy (her cougar self) and her Adonis, Floyd (looking like he is still in junior high) come storming out of her apartment only to argue out in the hall.

"Take that shit back inside," I say to myself.

I shake my head and whisper under my breath, "So ghetto." Every time Lysa kick him out, she take him back. I don't know who she thinks she's fooling. Maybe herself.

The young, white gay boy named Sued with his flamboyant self makes a whole lot of ruckus as him and his Gotham-looking friends take the stairway down. That boy have company over all times of the wee hours as if nobody in this building has a job.

The elevator door opens, and I step on with another tenant from the fourth floor named Wynona Shepard. Her and her companion, Buster make a rather cute couple.

Wynona has a scowl on her honeyed-tone rotund face. Her hefty body is shaking all that flab under that pastel pink bathrobe she's wearing. And that floral head scarf is squeezing her brain tight covering all those naps on her big head. Chile, her big forehead is crumpled and those beautiful greenish-gray eyes of hers is bloodshot red. She looks like she is about to blow the hell up. *Oh dang, what has Buster done now?*

I keep my eyes focus toward the elevator door. Don't want to make her think that I'm studying her. I don't even bother to say hi. That might stir-up some conversation that I don't want to hear.

Wynona sucks her snaggletooth and stares at her reflection on the shiny stainless steel elevator door. And as she do, something triggers inside of her and then suddenly she lets loose.

"Oh, that motherfucker makes me sick!" She snaps. "He such a mean, son-of-a-bitch! I can't stand him! Always calling me: 'Wynona do this and Wynona do that.' Waking me up at goddamn one in the morning to help him turn on TV. Turn off the damn TV. Get up to make him a pot of coffee or clip his toenails or scratch his back!

Or fix him something 'good' to eat as if to say what I do cook ain't good! The man ain't paralyzed just 'cause he in that motherfuckin' wheelchair. I told him just the other day," she breathes out, "I looked him in his cold, grayish eyes and I said with so much pain in my heart and hurt in my voice, I said, 'You-You Cuban sucka, as soon as you get that surgery done on yo' eyes and can see betta', baby, I'm gone. I'm hightailing it outta here! I can't take being screamed at, yelled at, or cussed at like I'm some child of yours. I'm a big and beautiful black woman. Huh. You betta' recognize all this *voluptuousness* before someone else do! I don't know why I moved in with your dirty ass in the first damn place. OK. So what, we used to court. That was way back then! Way before you got sick. I'm sayin' if I could date you when you was up on your feet, then I could be a decent friend and help take care of you, while you're down on your luck. But baby, I didn't ask for all of this bullshit that you're giving me! I try my best to do right by you. But doing right by you, Buster, don't seem good enough. Buster, you sure don't make it easy on me. Especially with that mouth of yours. That whiplashing tongue, I can't take no more of your slick ass comments. You wasn't like this before—before you got sick. You used to be a-a nice, good-looking man that held a job! Now you this mean and nasty and disrespectful...piece of smelly shit!' Woo! Honeychile, that man just makes my stomach bunch up in knots! Ooh, he makes me so fuckin' mad! I just..."

The elevator doors opens on the ground floor, and I step the hell off. Wynona steps off too, then makes a left and heads in the direction of the Laundry Room.

Wynona says a mouthful, and I understand where she is coming from. I do.

A woman can give heart and soul, cook, clean, fuck the shit out of her man, and he still ain't satisfied. What more is a woman to give? Blood, sweat, and tears. Hell, women give that too. After she gives that, what's left of her? Nothin'.

I make my way toward the lobby, to my mailbox. I insert my key. Pull the little silver handle open, and pullout a stack of mail, then insert the key to lock it back.

As I am about to turn to head back to take the elevator, Mama and her old man, Omar come out of their apartment. *Those two chain-smokers gonna catch cancer together*, I think to myself. That's all they do is smoke and talk shit to one another. And stare at folks.

Omar is a bit of a peeping Tom. Omar is tall and lanky. Ain't much more to tell about him. Mama, she just looks spacey in those beady brown eyes of hers. She's a petite woman, but stoutly framed. Light-skinned with thin strains of short, mousey brown hair, that's never combed. Her bottom lip droops. Soon it'll be hanging down to her flappy breasts looking like she got three titties instead of two. She walks so damn slow and drags her feet when she do that it literally takes her twenty-five minutes to walk from her door to the lobby door, and she lives on the ground floor. It's gotta to be old age. Or maybe whatever she's smoking, if you get my drift.

I step on the elevator and head back upstairs. The elevator door opens and I exit and make my way back to my apartment. Once inside I enter the kitchenette, place my mail on the counter, and open the fridge for a bottle of seltzer water. Twisting the cap off, tilting my head back, and taking a long swig of water. It's refreshing. I then pick up the mail and make my way into the living room and take a seat on the sofa as I sift through what is junk and what is important.

While opening my mail, I think to track my order. My books have yet to arrive. Saturday will be here in two more days. I don't need any mishaps.

I place the mail on the coffee table and stand to walk over to the kitchenette counter where my purse is. I slip my hand in it to pull out my cell phone.

I go online to the website and track my packages. Dang. My books have already arrived. The office signed for them.

I exit the door, and make my way to the elevator, down to the lobby, and knock on the office door.

Someone buzzes me in.

I open the door and greet the property manager, Ira Grey. God. That man sho' is something to ogle at. Sexy. Tall. Bald. Muscular. All the makings of a well put together man.

"Hi, Ira. I just came down to see if you received any packages for me?"

Ira smiles. And when he does, I swear the world seems brighter. I can marvel this man all day long. Look at 'im in them heather-gray trousers. Mmmm. *Fifty Shades* in the remaking. His suit jacket hangs on the back of the navy leather chair. Heather-gray accentuates the color of his baby-blue eyes. And the pink collar shirt makes his outfit come alive. I love of man who can rock the color pink with confidence. His lips are thin, but I betcha last dollar he's a wild, passionate kisser. And look at the baldhead just a shining.

"Hey, Avery, how've you been?"

His mellow voice breaks me out of my trance.

"Oh, can't complain. I'm great!" That "great" comes out a little too over-exaggerated.

"Good to hear. Good to hear." He says, then nods his head with a smile on his face.

I just want to touch that head, massage it, and lick it.

Ira walks over to a large wooden table stacked with packages. *Look at that tight ass.* I think to myself, while biting down on my bottom lip.

Ira lifts one box and places it gently on the floor. Then places two more boxes on top of it. "Looks like you have three boxes here, Avery. Do you need help taking these up?" he turns and his eyes pierce mine.

Suddenly my mouth gets dry. *"Say something stupid! Don't get quiet now. The man is looking directly at you, Avery! Open your dang mouth! Talk woman, speak!"* Karma bellows in my head.

"I-I-I can go and get my cart. It'll be easier than carrying 'em. I'll be right back." As I turn to face the door, Ira says, "Nonsense. I don't mind helping you that way you won't have to make another trip down."

"Oh, this handsome man is a keeper." I say to myself. Is he married? My eyes scan his ring finger. Bingo! Wedding ban. Dang! Another cutie taken.

"Ok. If you don't mind. I appreciate it, Ira."

"No problem." He replies.

Ira stacks two boxes atop each other and lifts them as if they were light as feathers. I carry one.

We head toward the elevator. I press the "Up" button, and we patiently wait.

While waiting we engage in small talk.

"So, how does it feel being an author?" Ira asks.

"Strange." I reply. "Folks have a tendency to look at you differently. They place you in this category that puts you in a status of unique, or different, or even, if you will, famous because you've done something out of the ordinary, you know? You're from the same place as him or her, but because you stepped out of the box and stand out in a crowd of people—the fact that you stand out separates you from the rest. Being different either intimidates folks or interests them."

"I bet. It must feel rewarding, though. I mean, all the attention and all."

I shrug my shoulders. "It can be a bit too much, at times. Constantly having folks keeping tabs on you is not necessarily the life I want. Believe it or not, I don't like being the center of attention. Keep me behind the scenes and I'm good. I'm content. I just wanted to do something that I never thought I could, you know? Something that inspired others, carried a strong message, and have meaning and purpose."

"I understand perfectly. I play in this rock band and when I'm beating those drums, man, I feel this rush run through me. And then, then I fade. Fade far away from the here and now."

"I know exactly what you mean, Ira. I used to feel like that when I'd get onstage and recite poetry. It was like I walked outside of myself. I felt free."

"Exactly." Ira says, then tilts his head to the side, "Wait a minute! Didn't you used to perform at this spot, ah, ah, Anonymous. I swear I recall seeing you there. Matter-of- fact, if I'm not mistaken, you owned it, didn't you? When I first saw you here I said to myself, she looks so familiar but I couldn't place it. It was you, right?"

All of sudden the feel in the air changes from mild to bone chilling cold. Oh God, I hope. I pray. I hope and pray he wasn't there on opening night when I divulged to everyone out in the crowd my story of how I contracted the virus. Oh, God. Please. Please. Pleassssseee, tell me he wasn't there.

The expressionless look upon my face, says it all. I'm busted. I remain quiet.

Avona places her hand on her right hip, then says, "Own it, girl, don't clam up now."

Ira breaks the silence. "I know it was *you*. I remember that day so vividly. You spoke of how you were, you know, *raped*. You spoke so candidly of how you didn't know who raped you—that the man might still be on the loose. I thought about you all that evening when I got settled in at home. I thought about my life partner, and how I would feel if that ever happened to *him* or *me*. You really gave me something to think about. Insight. You gave me as a man something to take in, especially when you spoke on how difficult it was to look yourself in the mirror; how you wanted to peel off your skin; rinse your (*worthless*: as you put it) body in bleach to rid of his grimy hands all over you; how you wanted to cut the most sensitive part of your body off to not feel the sensation of a man's penis rubbing against your clitoris ever again…that part really got to me because I never realized how horrible a woman could feel after being raped. You wanting to emasculate your body affected me as a man. And even though I'm gay, the thought, the image that you painted left me speechless. It left me wondering, does *other* women feel as you, women that were raped? Actually the thought never crossed my mind until *you*. I guess because all of my friends, the women, that is, have never confessed to something as awful as that happening to them. But you made me wonder, if it *had* would they be as forthright, as candid, as explicit as you were? Honestly, I can't say. But if it were to happen to me, I'll tell you the truth, *no*, I wouldn't want anyone to know, especially my partner, Lamb. The *fear* of him or anyone close to me: family, friends, co-workers knowing would destroy everything. My life, for me, would be over. I wouldn't be the same man that he met. And I'd question why he'd still want to be with me. Why anyone would want to be with me. Sex would no longer be fulfilling or pleasurable. Just the thought of Lamb wanting to touch me, I'd probably lose it and snap. Have a nervous breakdown or something worse. We'd breakup for sure because I'd be no better—not to him, not to me. He wouldn't know how to reconnect with me. I'd find myself alone, afraid and alone. Lamb means the world to me. Avery, I had you on my mind since that day, and I never stopped wondering how you were. How you coped, how you were holding up, you know? I felt like I wished there was something I could do, or say, or show you to make you feel valued, because I felt like a part, a *huge* part of you was missing. I felt your energy. It's good to see that you've held up pretty damn well." He smiles, "You're a very strong woman, Ms. Avery Love. Very strong."

I stare into his eyes, speechless. Such gentle, beautiful eyes he has. "I-I don't know what to say, Ira. Um, that really touches me. Um, you're— you're kinda putting me on the spot. Remembering my words *verbatim*. I must say I'm a little taken aback. Embarrassed. Not because you were there. Well, a little. But because you took the time to sit in your quiet moments and think of me. Me? A total stranger. That really means a lot to me."

The elevator door opens, and we step on.

Ira and I step off the elevator, and head for my door. There is a FedEx man dressed in navy shorts and navy and yellow polo shirt that is standing in the hall with a perplex look upon his square face. He holds a small package in his hands. The short, bald, white man approaches us and asks. "Do you happen to know, ah, ah, if a Marlene Fisher lives here?"

I shake my head no.

The man says. "Nobody knows their neighbors anymore."

Ira interjects, as he places the boxes in front of my door. "I can sign for her, sir. She's a tenant here."

"Thanks, pal." The man extends his notepad and Ira signs. "You can leave the package with me. I'll make sure she gets it." Ira says.

"Thanks, again." The man says, and takes the stairs down.

I open my door, Ira lifts up the boxes and steps inside.

"Wow," he says as if amazed. "This place looks incredible. Very eclectic."

I shrug my shoulders. "Thanks. You can put those boxes here on the floor." I point my index finger towards the floor by the door. This way I won't trip over them.

Ira places the boxes down exactly where I point. Then he continues to look around at my apartment. "I see you're into African masks, figurines. I see you like plants too. Is that a 'money tree plant'?"

I nod.

"It's a beautiful houseplant." He says.

"Thanks." I say as I place the large box on the countertop.

"This place has a neo-soul type of feel to it." Ira says, "I like it! I really, really like it." He makes his way over to the bookshelf. "Whose you're favorite author, Avery?" he asks with his back facing me. Distracted by his backside I break my train of thought by looking in one of the drawers for my box cutter. Finding it, I place it alongside the box. I then make my way over to Ira. We are face-to-face giving each other direct eye contact. "Hmm. Well, I'm currently reading Courtney Summers' novel, *Fall for Anything*. I really enjoyed Bernice L. McFadden's book, *The Warmest December*. Cupcake Brown's memoir, *A Piece of Cake* and Terry McMillan's *The Interruption of Everything and Nappily Ever After* by Trisha R. Thomas were good reads, too. *Ordinary Beauty* by Laura Wiess was an awesome read! I started reading *Paint it Black* by Janet Fitch but I never finished it because I caught up in work. I did see the movie, *White Oleander* based off the novel she wrote. That was a good movie. J.D. Mason's book, *And on the Eighth Day She Rested*, that was another awesome read. Oh! And so was Pearl Cleage's book, *What Looks Like Crazy on an Ordinary Day. Butterscotch Blues* by Margaret Johnson-Hodge, *Brown Girl, Brownstones* by Paule Marshall, *Breathing Room* by Patricia Elam, and *32 Candles* by Ernessa T. Carter and *Queen Sugar* by Natalie Baszile. I've also read two of E L. James's books: *Fifty Shades of Grey* and *Fifty Shades Darker*. I was in the midst of reading the third, *Fifty Shades Freed* but then the movie came out. I was so anticipating to see it, and when I did I couldn't even get into it. Talk about highly disappointed. It wasn't as I would've thought it was going to be. Now they have the movie, *Fifty Shades Darker* premiering but I don't know if I'm going to go see it."

"Yeah, I know what you mean. Lamb was all into *Fifty Shades* trilogy, too. He couldn't put the books down. I must admit I started to get a little jealous because E L. James was taking time away from me. Stealing my man with her nasty talk. We went to see the movie. Lamb was highly disappointed too. He said the book was much better."

I smile.

"Well, I best be going back down to the office. It was good talking to you, Avery."

"You too, Ira."

I walk Ira to the door, he leaves out with the package in his hands.

I reenter the kitchenette and use the box cutter to open the box. I pull one book out, and sigh. I swear it feels like I'm holding a newborn baby.

With the tips of my fingers I gently caress the matte cover. "Look at me," I say to myself. "Posing like I'm in one of those fashion magazines." It sho' puts me in mind of IMG Modeling Agency. Had I not gotten caught up in drugs (cocaine), who knows where I would've been by now? Milan, Italy, Aruba, Hawaii. Just the thought kind of saddens me.

"No need to live in the past." I say to myself. "Look toward the future. Look at what you've accomplished. You're holding a part of your future in your hands." A wide smile extends on my face.

Ev'ry Ho Gotta Daddy may not be for everyone, but I know that someone out there can relate to this story. I am proud that I took the initiative to help Daisy out because in the end Daisy really changed my life. She gave me a brand new start. And this time I am not going to blow it.

I sit on one of the barstools at the kitchenette counter and I contemplate what I want my next book to be about. Of course, something dealing with women, but I want it to dig a little deeper, pull back some layers of discomfort, despair, something that will hit home, hit that sensitive spot in a woman.

Extending my arm out I reach for the mini-size notepad and blue ink pen set next to the can opener. Then I close my eyes and release all tension that has invaded my mind space. I just sit here until I feel completely relaxed. Suddenly my heart speaks for me as I write down these words.

Am I just something to do
On a Monday afternoon

Why am I feelin' all this Monday Blues?
Are you kin to Annie Lee?
Or,
Am I just something to do
On any given day—

Slowly I relinquish my pen, place it down on the counter. "Where did that come from?" I ask myself baffled. Hmm. Subconsciously I must've been thinking about something from my past. A person, perhaps. But who?

I ponder, nothing and no one comes to mind.

I get-up from the barstool and walk into the bathroom, pull down my pants, panties, sit on the toilet, and think.

My eyes well up. And this rush of heat brushes against my skin. And then, then I see his face. *Jordan Seymour.*

Why can't I seem to let him go? He's happily married now. He's taken. Spoken for. Move on, Avery, move on.

I hear the warm water run out of me, and then I sigh full of relief. I wipe myself, pull up my panties, pants, flush the toilet, wash my hands, and towel dry them, then exit the bathroom with a nagging headache.

I reenter the bathroom and open the medicine cabinet and pullout a prescription bottle of Ibuprofen 800 milligrams. I twist the cap and take one pill out, then twist it back, and place it back in the medicine cabinet and shut it.

I enter the kitchenette and open the fridge and reach for a bottle of Alkaline Water + Electrolytes, slip the pill in my mouth, then twist the bottle open and take a generous swig.

Chapter
Twenty-Eight

Country

Herberto hit me. This time harder than the last time. So hard a vein bursts in both of my eyes. They fill with blood. Herberto won't call 911, and he won't let me either. He shows no fear but I knows deep down he's shittin' bricks. Fearful of the police ever finding out.

S'pose I call. S'pose I file a restraining order against him. Just run to the kitchen, pick up the phone, and call. I don't think I'll make it. Herberto would beat me senseless. But just the thought of the Paterson police grilling him and me—axin' *him* a million and one questions: *what happened? What happened to her eyes? Ma'am, who did this to you? How long has this been happening to you? How often?* Those questions will result in an interrogation that he won't be prepared for. Me, well, I'll see it as a rescue. A relief. But then I'd probably feel that flutter in my heart and lie for my man. I'd want to protect him. Save him. Keep on lovin' 'im with these bruises on my skin. Bruises that he put on me.

I blink. Wince.

What have I done this time?

According to Herberto, he says I stared him down and he didn't like the look in my eyes. He says they were fuckin' wit' him. Talkin' to him. So in order to get 'em to shut the fuck up he jumped up out of the recliner and with a forceful swing of his right hand he backslapped me. All I felt was hard knuckles crashing into my face as my body swung round and then somehow lifted off the floor. It feels as if a tennis racket has hit me with full force. One of 'em Serena Williams's two-hand back swings.

I land on my back, but not before banging my head on the pointy edge of the coffee table.

Dazed, dizzy, disoriented.

Herberto barks with spit flying out of his mouth, "Bitch, I'll kill you *next* time. Stare me down like that again. I'll *kill* you."

I lie on the floor, whimpering. Wanting to stop breathing—wanting to provoke him, say, "Kill me, then. Get it over with 'cause I can't take this *shitty marriage* no mo'. Kill me, and make it quick, and as *painful* as you possibly can. Get your satisfaction. Then kill yourself. Save these woman's from the miserable person that you is!"

Instead, I says nothin'.

Herberto walks toward me, then steps over me, and enters the kitchen. I hear the fridge open, and something clanks. Like glass bottles toasting. He then returns back into the living room and sits in his recliner with a Presidente beer in hand, while I lie sprawled on the floor like a raggedy, shaggy brown rug.

Head is spinning, throbbing, thumping. A soreness pounds from the back of my head.

With my fingertips, I very gently press to feel the back of my head. I locate the slit. It feels long and gooey. Stings from the perspiration on my fingertips. I wince. Grimace inwardly, as I see thick blood on the smooth skin of my middle finger. Eyes stretch wide.

I want to raise up but I'm afraid he'll knock me back down. Slowly and cautiously I raise my body, sit upright, and reach out for the leg of the coffee table for support, as I pull myself up and slowly stand. Herberto entertains himself by reading the local newspaper.

The headline reads: "Paterson Man Gets Life for Fatally Stabbing Woman as Spectators Helplessly Watched."

I hope he doesn't get any ideas. I don't want to be dead like her. God, help me?

"Flip the page," I want to say, but I dare not to. It will only anger him and God only knows what he'll do to me, then.

Herberto's dark eyes shift in my direction as he takes a swig of his beer. He then places the newspaper on the coffee table. "C'mere! Get your ass up and c'mere."

My heart is pounding in my chest. My body stiffens up on me. I dread, pray, dread and pray. Oh Lord, what is he going to do next?

"Strip!" he says with lust-filled eyes.

I blink.

Slowly I unbutton my blood splattered housedress and remove it from my person. I then nervously unfasten my support bra. Pinching the strap with my index finger and thumb I drop it to the floor. Standing 'fore him in my granny underwear, I inch 'em down to my thighs and let 'em fall to my bare feet, I step out of 'em and leave 'em on the floor where I stand.

I raise my head, and stare at the wall, not my husband. The wall. Stand staring at the wall completely naked, *vulnerable*. A rush of cold draft passes me and my nipples harden. The coldness from his frigid stare, it also makes me cold and sick to my stomach. *What's coming next? What?*

With the Presidente beer in one hand, Herberto sets it on the end table. He then slips his hand in the slit of his plaid boxers and pulls out his limp penis—eyes glazed over with filth on his mind.

"Come closer, *fat ass*. C'mere, Country. Stand right here." He points his index finger to a spot right in front of him. Knee touches knee. "Herberto, won't bite you." He says, "If you be a good *wife* and give me what I like. You know what I like, don't you?"

I nod. Moving one foot, hesitate to move the other.

"C'mere."

Inwardly, I feel like a sleaze.

This is my husband and I find myself utterly repulsed by him, yet still madly in love with this handsomely, handsome attractive man he used to be with that dark disheveled hair of his, strong manly features. He used to make me *feel*. Now I don't feel at all. He literally beat the feeling out of me.

Chapter
Twenty-Nine

Ursula

The sky is smoky gray. Melancholy. A chill runs up my spine as if a spirit just ran through me. I shiver.

When I was a little girl whenever I had a shiver such as this it either meant something bad was going to happen to someone close to me or something has already happened to someone close to me.

Immediately I pullout my cell phone from my handbag and I call Woolridge to make sure he's okay.

"Hi, honey. Just called to make sure you're all right."

"Oh, okay. It's raining there. Muggy, too. Huh, you don't say."

"Well, Uncle Virgil and Aunt Maggie just walked into Kentucky Fried Chicken. No. The one on Broadway. By the railroad tracks. Uh-huh. Yep. We arrived in Paterson a half hour ago."

"The weather is humid. Gray skies, though."

"Huh?"

"Well, baby, Uncle Virgil and Aunt Maggie are coming out of the store now. We gonna head over to Beverly's house. I'll call you back once I get settled in. Eat some supper and wind down a bit, okay."

"Love you, too."

"Talk to you later tonight. Bye."

Carroll Street is jam packed. As I make my way inside As God Is My Witness Baptist Church a gush of hot air caresses my face. I see a cluster of folks seated, fanning themselves with programs and bare hands.

Walking up the aisle I see a slew of folks I knew from back in the day. High school days. I get a little misty-eyed when I see Uncle Wolf lying in the cherrywood casket dressed so dapper in his white suit. It complements his dark complexion. Whoever shaved and cut his hair did a magnificent job. He looks like himself. I can't believe he's gone. But I know he's been sick off and on for quite some time. Well, he ain't suffering no mo'. Thank God.

"Ursula," I hear someone behind me call out my name. I turn around only to be greeted by Wolf's *only* daughter Kali.

We embrace in a sisterly hug.

"How are you, Ursula?" she asks in her squeaky voice.

"I should be asking you that, baby. How you holdin' up?"

"Oh, I'm okay. Daddy is in heaven with the Lord. What better place to be, you know?"

"Let me look at you, chile. You are growing up so fast. Give me a spin, honey."

Kali gives a slow spin dressed in her basic black dress with black pumps. Her hair is in what looks like a hundred twists that really complements her big eyes and pudgy nose and full thick lips glossed in a natural, yet shimmering gloss, enhancing her deep dark skin. Wrapped around her slender neck is a pearl necklace with matching earrings. She looks so sophisticated for her mid-twenty year old self. Very lovely.

238

"Chile, a couple mo' inches you'll be taller than me."

Kali smiles. I do too.

"You look great, Ursula! Where's your man?"

"Thanks, baby. And as far as my man goes, he's doing just fine. Woolridge couldn't make it because he had to work."

I look around at the church. "Everything looks so lovely, dear. So what have you been doing with yourself?" I ask her.

"College. Tryna get through school and then find a 'real' job, you know. I'm currently working for a shelter for domestic violence victims. I enjoy my job, but the pay sucks. But hey, it's a job. I'm getting the experience while in school. Other than that I don't have time for much else. I *had* a boyfriend but that didn't work out. Men? It's difficult to understand what they really want, you know, Ursula?"

I nod my head up and down. "I sho' do. But you have your head on straight. For as long as I've known yah you've been very intelligent. A man can wait. Just focus on your goals, chile, if you're meant to meet someone, you will."

"That is what I said to myself. I can't devote my every existence to a man. Daddy told me that. And it made a lot of sense to me. Relationships are about compromise, but it feels like us sistahs only see it that way."

Someone in the distance, near the far back entrance of the church calls out for Kali.

She turns around and waves at a young girl dressed in a white usher uniform with white gloves on her hands, who looks to be in her latter teens. "Ursula, I'll be back."

"I'll be here," I say to her.

I make my way down the aisle. Lord I need to go to the bathroom and adjust this girdle I have on. I didn't want my panty line to show in this black dress I'm

239

wearing. It's not snug, or hip hugging, it kinda drapes over me, but as big as I am every big thing stands out.

I can't believe all these folks showed up for Uncle Wolf's funeral. That man sho' must've left a lasting impression on these souls.

There are so many teenage boys here. Well, he did used to coach a little league team. And I do remember him being a mentor for the My Name Is as well as Brick City Afterschool Program in Newark, New Jersey. And he used to be a Big Broh for some of the youth in poverty-stricken communities and fatherless households. Not only was he spreading himself thin to help disadvantage children, he was also a father, husband to his lovely wife, Penny. Maybe by giving of himself, he gave a little too much.

My thoughts revert back to Woolridge, and how much of himself he gives to me. I bow my head, feeling my emotions building, climbing up to my throat. I must be the worst girlfriend in the world.

How can I sit here pretending that our relationship is everything I've ever wanted? Having everything I've ever wanted includes my man making sweet, passionate love to me. Be truthful in the house of God now. Okay. My eyes begin to well-up.

God. Almighty God I have sinned. Sinned by thinking about being with a woman. Please forgive me. Forget my sinful thoughts. I don't want to disrespect my happy home, but I don't want to deprive myself either. And no, sex is not everything. But without it, without feeling wanted and needed, it is the first thing that will make a person stray. Amen.

I don't know how to convey this to Woolridge. I don't know how to say these very words and hope he understands where I'm coming from. I don't know where to begin the conversation. But I know that it has to be said. I can't live like this much longer. My body needs to feel the earth rumble inside of me.

Country? She quickly creeps in my thoughts. I'm so very lucky to be friends with such a warm and loving person. Ever since I met Country she has always been a good ear, shoulder, tree for me. That woman is something special. Friends like her, you don't find all the time.

I have some friends back home, but every time you want to just sit and find out what's up with 'em, they never seem to have a moment of time. Everything is of haste.

I called my friend Jolene and she said, "Oh, my son's birthday is today."

I called my friend Eva and she said, "Oh, I have a wake to attend after work."

I reached out to my girlfriend Sandra, "Oh, I made plans with my husband tonight. Maybe tomorrow."

Then I reached out to my other girlfriend Louise, "Oh, girl, not tonight I got my boo coming over. Call me next week."

But then the "one" that always comes through for me, the one that will set everything aside just to please me...is Woolridge. That man is soooo wonderful, soooo giving of himself that it really makes me weep inside. I love 'im. And I am in love with 'im but I just can't be with 'im. And it is killin' me inside.

No. I don't have a potential mate as of yet. It's just the feelings that I do feel in the presence of a woman I may be attracted to. I haven't reacted to the feelings, is what I'm sayin' but I know that they're there. They exist. And it becomes a lot to bear when you have acknowledged it. I don't want to feel like I'm living a double life. You know, sleeping next to Woolridge, thinking of someone I never even met, but can see myself with. It's not the same as having a dirty fantasy about getting down and dirty with a chick. Nowhere the same. My dreams are intimate, soft and endearing.

I lift my head up, and as I do, I say to myself as I view Uncle Wolf in his casket, "Life is too short. You have to live your life as you see fit. Telling Woolridge will free me from the burden. Tell the man, don't waste another day, Urs. Tell 'im. Tell that good man the truth."

Chapter
Thirty

Country

"Hello."

"Hey, gal."

"No, I hasn't forgotten about the book signing today."

"I was going to call you."

"What time?"

"Oh, um..."

"Yeah, dinner after, okay."

"I'll see you at one o'clock, Ursula."

Hanging up the phone, I think, *what am I gonna do?* Ursula is coming to pick me up at one o'clock for Avery's book signing. Herberto is sitting in his favorite chair engrossed in television.

"Okay, okay," I say to myself, "You want out, figure it out. How are you going to get him to let you out of this cage, chile? How?"

I don't knows, but I gotta think of something. I need an escape.

Staggering to the bathroom, bloody hands and fingers quiver as I lock the warp bathroom door.

I turn and press my bloody back against the inside door. Standing still I feel every inch of my body breaking down.

As I walk out of the bathroom, Herberto is standing in the kitchen, gulping down another beer.

He narrow-eyes me. "Where the *fuck* you think you going, black puta (whore)? Pinche idiota (fuckin' idiot)!" Herberto snaps while using his middle finger to scratch under his hairy balls.

I swallow what tastes like blood down my throat, then say in a crackling voice, "'Member. Um, you said I could go out with Ursula."

"Well, don't stand there looking stupid, go get dress. Put something decent on, too. Don't want nobody thinking I ain't taken care of my wife. Clean yourself up woman, shit!" he snaps again as his dark eyes grow darker. "You betta' not be going to no...casa de putas (whore house)."

I remain quiet. Bite my tongue as hard as I can and remove myself from his sight.

In my bedroom I scramble to find something nice to wear. Herberto threw all of my nice clothes out the window the same day he tried to throw me out with 'em.

The Lord saved me that day. I don't knows what happened to make Herberto change his mind, but he did. Whatever I did that day I vowed to never do it again. Only problem was I couldn't 'member what I did. Seemed that man knocked the sense outta me.

I settle on a plain black sleeveless dress with plunging neckline. Seem like the only color I has hanging in my closet. Wonder if Herberto is trying tell me something. Could be. Ain't no tellin' with that man? Ain't no tellin'.

I wait on the front porch for Ursula to arrive. Herberto is sitting in the window with another beer in his hand watching as the cars pass by. Watching me. Any shift in my eyes. My body language.

I feel jittery. Nervous. I wonder what she gonna say about how I look. Ax me a million questions about what I've been doing with myself. Jobless. Collecting a monthly SSI check. Food stamps. Check and food stamps that I don't see. Herberto controls the income. Yet I'm the one with the disability. How many lies am I willin' to tell? Ursula is no stranger. I'm sho' she'll see that something is wrong with me.

Under these dark shades I can feels the swelling of my eyes. Why didn't I just tell her no? Why am I taking this chance? 'Cause. If I don't do something I'll forever live in captivity with a man who do nothin' but beats me. Beats me repeatedly.

I look at him and think to myself, *Country, is this the life you really want?*

An unfamiliar red Jaguar pulls up in front of the house. Herberto is still in the window sipping on his beer. I can sees that the driver is a female but I can't make out if it's Ursula or not.

The female adjusts the rearview mirror and glides what looks like lipstick on. The driver's side door opens and the woman slowly stands to her feet. From the side profile it looks like Ursula. Lawd, if it is her, she sho' put on some pounds.

The woman walks to the front of the car dressed in a chiffon accordion pleat halter dress looking like a glow of sunshine. Her auburn-colored hair is pulled back in a slick ponytail. Ursula was never one to wear lotta makeup. She keeps it at a minimal with a light shade of eye shadow and a natural lip-gloss. Her looks at me and I look at her through the lenses of my knockoff Coach shades but neither reacts. But as soon as Ursula reaches the steps and looks at me, her says, "Country, is that you?"

Herberto remains in the window staring at the both of us. I nod my head. Ursula rushes up the steps in a pair of Enzo off-white patent leather high-heel mules and gives me a much needed hug.

Immediately my body flinches from her large arms and heavy hands touching me but I try to play it off. My body is so sore with purple bruises.

"Gal, look at you! Just as thin as you wanna be. That husband taken good care of you, huh?"

If only she knew how well he takes care of me she'd probably black the hell out.

My eyes are welling under these shades, but I don't let one tear fall. Not here. Not now.

"Well, ain'tcha gonna introduce me to your husband?" Ursula asks with a smile on her pretty round face.

As soon as Herberto hears her say that he sticks his head back in the window and pulls it down.

I wave my hand at the air. "Chile, don't mind him. He's hasin'a day today. You'll have plenty of time to get acquainted with Herberto tomorrow, okay."

"Sho'. Gal I know how men can be. Them and their mood swings."

"Yep."

"Well," Ursula says, "I guess we best get going."

We both make our way down the six steps. Ursula clicks the car remote and I pull open the passenger side door and get in. Ursula gets in on the driver's side, adjusts her seatbelt to fit around her rotund frame.

I struggle a little with the seatbelt too on account of the soreness in my arm but finally manage to strap myself in.

Ursula starts the car engine and pulls off with Billie Holiday's, "Ain't Nobody's Business" playing from the CD player.

Chapter
Thirty-One

Avery

Slipping on my *Velvet* square cat style shades, I hightail it out the door with my portable luggage bag filled with three boxes of my books, one oversized poster of the book cover in a cardboard container, business cards, pens with my logo and email, book holders and a table cloth.

Exiting off the elevator I rush out before anyone sees me and stops me in my tracks. I don't want to be late for my own book signing.

As I walk out the lobby door, the Uber is sitting in front honking its horn so impatiently. I wave my hand to let the driver know that it is me who called and hand signal with two thumbs pointing upward indicating for him to pop the trunk, so that I can put my stuff in.

Once I stack everything in the side corner of the trunk, I shut it, and hop in the backseat of the cab.

"Where you headed?" The young male Jamaican driver asks while gnawing on a peppermint chew stick. *He must be a smoker*, I think. He has thick dreadlocks but they are well-groomed. His skin of flawless milk chocolate looks good enough to lick. And he has the cab smelling like black butter body oil.

From the backseat he looks like he has a muscular physique but that is only from the neck down. I can't say about from the waist down.

Anyway, it doesn't matter because I am not looking for anyone at this point and time in my life. It's about work, getting ahead, staying focus, making a difference.

"Silly Chicks Banquet Hall on 672 Belmont Ave, in Haledon."

I scoot back in the seat and take a deep breath. I have been up since four this morning and I feel like I haven't gotten a thing done. It's just my nerves. I go through this every time I have to interact with folks. Butterflies. It ain't nothing but butterflies.

I take a breath, but deeper, and rest my head back on the warm pleather.

The iPhone is jamming with Anita Baker, "Close Your Eyes." I take in Anita's words, *"Your dreams become reality/ if you close your eyes and see/come and fall through clouds of doubt/ fall through clouds of fear, clouds of fear…"*

The driver presses something on his iPhone and instantly we hear, "Like You Used to Do" then he looks back at me with my eyes close. "Whatchu you know 'bout dhat, mizz? This wuz 'fore yo time." *Tell me he is not flirting with old me.* I smirk inwardly. I don't bother to open my eyes because I'm feeling so relaxed at this moment and I don't want to lose this feeling. I smile, then say, "A lot. I know a lot about this, sir. Just haven't experienced it lately." Without opening up my eyes I can *feel* him smiling back at me.

I listen attentively trying to pinpoint the guy singing duet with Anita. He kinda sounds like Babyface, but I'm not certain. This song gets me in the groove. Today is going to be awesome day! 'Ey if I don't boost myself up, who will?

It takes ten minutes to get to *Silly Chicks*. I slip the driver his fare and he pops the trunk for me. But this time he gets out and tries to be a gentleman. We reload everything in my portable luggage bag and I say, "Thank you."

"If you need a taxi to go back here's my business card." He says, as he extends his hand with the card between his forefinger and thumb. I reach for the card.

"Oh, by the way my name is Desyre Cerulean."

"Avery. Nice to meet you, Desyre."

"Avery," he repeats and nods his head.

Desyre stands still and I take a scroll up his tall frame until my eyes meet his dark brown eyes. He smiles one of those seductive Taye Diggs smiles. *Man, he is simply gorgeous*, I think.

Woman, stay focus, I scream in my head. But honestly how can I? I mean, with this fine sculpture of man standing before me. As much as I don't want to sink my teeth into him, a big big big part of me does. He's sexy. And he knows how to relax my mind without even knowing me. 'Ey that's a plus in my book.

Trying to control my hormones, the best thing for me to do is walk away, so I do. And as I do I don't bother to turn around because I can feel Desyre watching me head inside.

I open the door and roll my luggage bag in, then turn slightly around as I see him get back in his car.

There is a crowd of cars in the parking lot. As I walk inside the lobby I can see a mob of folks scattered about enjoying the ambiance. As soon as you walk into the lobby you are greeted by a beautiful water fountain. It's a sculpture of an African man and woman engaged in a French kiss. *Something I haven't seen before*, I think.

I enter the hall. The runway stage is in the center of the room. Rows of chairs are on both sides like you see on Fashion Week. I feel like I'm in New York City right now.

Various vendors are unloading their goods and setting up. I locate where I'll be stationed and start setting up too.

I unzip my luggage bag and pull out the books wrapped in bubble wrap. I set them on the table. Pullout the table cloth and arrange it over the table.

I take one step back and try to figure out how I want to display the portable easel that I brought. Finally, I decide to put it next to the table where it is not blocking my view of patrons coming and going.

I unwrap the books and stack them five at a time with five rows going across the table. I place the book holders: one to the right, one in the middle, one to the left and place three books on them. I pullout the book marks and unwrap them and place them on the table like a Chinese fan. The pens which are an advertising tool with my business name and email and logo on them, I set them on the table for patrons to take as a token of my appreciation.

To my left I see that Sippa placed the mike to the side of me for my introduction, Q&A, and an excerpt reading from the book. Everything looks in place.

Ring...Ring...Ring.

I reach my hand in my handbag and answer my cell phone.

"Hello?"

"I'm here already." I hear Faye say sounding like she's out of breath.

"Okay. Do you need me to come out and help you bring the food in?"

"That would be nice," she says.

"Coming now."

I hang up with Faye.

Faye from the Pynk-Ghetto Book Club. She started catering as a side hobby and I jumped on the opportunity of being her first client. I ordered: fried chicken, potato salad, pasta salad, toss salad with balsamic vinaigrette, dinner rolls, and since *Silly Chicks* is a BYO (bring your own) I included three bottles of wine: Chardonnay, Cabernet, and Pinot Grigio. For dessert I ordered banana pudding, peach cobbler, and carrot cake.

Silly Chicks supplies the plates and utensils and napkins, which was part of the package that I paid for. They also arranged the tables and chairs and setup the decorum for the room since they knew they'd be having a fashion show with vendors selling different products. I don't know if I'm the only author here, but if I'm not mistaken I believe I am because Shy doesn't like too many of the same genre at their events. She said it's less competition and plus, it gives newcomers a starting point to get their works out to the public. I thought that was a very clever idea. Great business sense.

I reach in my luggage bag and pull out my Client list. It's a list of all the women and men I've met at different venues since the book was released. I kept a list of names and emails, so that I could reach out to them and tell them of my next event. Majority of them reached back to say that they'd be coming. Hopefully everyone does. I even suggested that they bring a friend. The more the merrier. Plus, my old school chum Chicago is the one doing the fashion show. For as long as I can remember he has always been into fashion. I can't wait to see his latest designs. I've been to two of his fashions shows. One was at the Robert Treat Hotel and the other was at NJPAC in Newark, New Jersey. Both of his shows were incredible.

After I finish setting everything up, and run out to help Faye bring the food in.

By the time I make it to the door, Faye is coming dressed in a white halter dress and Michael Kor white flip-flops on accompanied by the Uber driver Desyre.

I walk up to them with a stump look upon my face.

"Hi. Wow. Faye, you cut your hair. You remind me of Ellen DeGeneres. It looks great!"

"Hi, Avery, can you grab this for me. I can handle the rest." Faye says, exasperated, as she hands me a large silver tray filled what smells like potato salad and opens her purse to put her cell phone in it. She reaches back for the tray, I hand it to her.

I give Desyre a funny look.

"Who's your friend?" I ask Faye.

"Oh, I don't know him. He was dropping someone off in his Uber and asked if I needed any help. Such a gentleman. Avery, you better snatch him up while you can. He's a keeper."

Both Desyre and I remain quiet, while Faye walks off.

To break the ice I yell back to Faye, "Is there anything else I need to get out of the car?"

Faye yells back, "Just two more things. I have a van. He knows which one."

Both Desyre and I head outside. He points to the white van with FAYE'S CATERING on the side. *Boy, when she puts her mind to something, she doesn't play,* I think to myself.

"So," Desyre says, "What kind of event are they having in there?"

"Fashion show. I'm vending a table to promote my book."

Desyre's eyes light up. "So you're a writer, author, *and* artist?"

"Yes, I am."

"Interesting." He says as his hand rises and gently massages his chin with his meaty thumb.

I give him a perplex look. "Why is it interesting?"

"Because with all the passengers I have picked up and dropped off I have never met a real author that sat in my taxi before."

"Well, I'm not big time yet."

"You will be. And when you do, please don't do like some of the rich folk and forget 'bout where you come from. I can't stand that. This is why I stay single. Single, black man in America, ain't that some shit. I'm scared to get involved with American women. Petrified." He says with a grimace outlining his chiseled face.

"You're serious, huh?"

"Yes. It's like okay, you made it, but come back and use your talent to help the community. A lot of people come but they don't come back to help. They come to either do a show or promote or whatever, but they don't come to give back. Paterson is a city that desperately needs love. Paterson's heart has been broken. Shattered. Junkies run amuck. Mothers prostituting. Children out of control. Black men jobless. Drunks, pedophiles, thugs, hustlers, rapists, murderers. People here are struggling to make ends meet and they are angry. Anger only encourages violence among each other. Black killing black. Young dying young. Do you know how many times I come so close to being robbed at gun point? Too many. How many times a trick has approached me wanting to give me a lap dance. Too many. Or a man pretending to be a woman, dressed like a woman, but fully man tries to convince me that I need to let him/her suck my cock. C'mon! Do I have stupid written on my forehead? The money I make from this side job I send back home to Jamaica to my mother. She is my prize possession. I'd do anything for mother. So, Miss Lady, Avery, when you make it, just remember what I've shared. It is a gift to write in story. To be able to express your point-of-view in art form. Truly a blessing."

On that note, Desyre and I reach for the last two trays, and head inside.

Desyre says, "By the way, what is the name of your book?"

I bite down on my bottom lip and unintentionally twist my face up like I'm constipated. I'm a little embarrassed to say.

"Why are you making that face?" he asks.

"Because."

"Because, what?"

"Um, I really don't know what you're gonna think. Ah, man, you putting me on the spot."

"How so? Aren't you here to promote the book? Won't you have to say the name of the book, so why are you actin' shy wit' me?"

I shrug my shoulders.

"C'mon, tell me?" He smiles showing nothing but big, pretty, white teeth.

I blush, then say, *"Ev'ry Ho Gotta Daddy."*

Desyre tilts his head back and burst out in thunderous laugh. I never heard a laugh so beautiful before. Hmm. This man is certainly different than any man I've ever encountered. I cut my eyes at him, wondering, what gives? Can he really be this charming, a great conversationalist, not to mention attractive to marvel at, but is... he... real? *Is he a real somebody? Karma snaps in my ears? Girl, isn't he standing in front of you? Reach out and touch him then ask yourself if he's real or not.*

Of course I'm skeptical. I mean it's like some women say, he's too good to be true. What am I talkin' about? I'm not on the market anymore, remember? I'm not looking or expecting or fantasying or— it's about work, nothing but work. Work work work.

Avona slips in. But truthfully, if it were about playtime he'd be the first to consider, right?

I don't know. There is something about him that makes me want to be whisked away in a dream. Yep. Dream. Drench my thoughts in a romantic dream.

"Where did you go, Avery? I hope you're on an island drenching in sapphire blue waters wearing a white string bikini that accentuates your curves as the sun beams on your silky brown skin, as your mind drifts from the here and now sipping on a cool pineapple martini and enjoying God's ambiance."

I stare into his eyes as his lips move so very slowly. This man has me in a daze, trance. I can't think. Even his words captivate me. I feel butterflies. Beautiful yellow butterflies.

I smile. Can't help but smile. He makes me feel. That's it! He makes me *feel.* This is scary.

I mean, suppose he's married. Suppose he's seriously involved with a woman outside of Paterson. Suppose he's on the verge of getting engaged. Or divorced. Suppose he's one of those guy's where he can come to me but I can't go to wherever he lives to see him. Suppose he's concerned about us being seen together. Yep. One of *those* men. I mean I would have no choice but to understand. It's just that I've been down that memorable road a ways back. It's not a good feeling when you're trying to get to know someone. It kind of makes you feel like you're dealing with a married man or a man that is not being totally honest about his living arrangements or status.

Look at me. Speculating. The man is standing right in front of me, but I can't find the nerve to ask that one simple question: *are you involved?* I guess because if he says, yes, I don't want the disappointment to show on my face. And if he says, no, I don't want to be doubting his word. Either way you look at it, he doesn't really stand a chance with me.

No, it doesn't sound fair. But people are people. Some will be forthright and tell the truth. And some won't. I am only looking out for myself. I have to.

Honestly, I can take him home, sex him up and down, and not give it a second thought. No strings, no ties, no commitment, nobody all up in our business, you know. But is that truly what I want? Hmm. Yes and no.

I ask myself time and time again how many damn bubbles baths are you going to take? Chile, you liable to shrivel up. Call yourself taking the edge off. Girl, I know you get tired of "dating yourself". And I know you miss the feeling that a man gives.

Of course someday I want a meaningful relationship with a decent man. But for now, I'll take what I can get. A breathing one will suffice for now. Really.

Well, okay.

Yes, I miss the feeling of having a man in my presence, and in my bed. And yes, I meet men here and there but I haven't met anyone that piques my interests. A brother with some substance, charisma, swag, intellect, common sense, etiquette. A man that knows how to treat a lady like a lady. And no, he doesn't have to be black. And no, he doesn't have to be rich. But he does have to be into me. And I do pray that he doesn't come with a small package. Don't get me wrong, I love men but I also *love* to feel what he's holding. And when I can't feel what he's holding I'ma tell you right now...it's a huge disappointment.

When you don't know if he's inside you or not and you have to *ask*...girlllll, go pop that cork and drink your disappointment away. Get smashed. Fuck it! Now if you're a recovering alcoholic I wouldn't advise you dealing with someone with a small package. I'm saying this as a disclaimer so that you can't come back at me and say, 'Avery, it's your fault that I got drunk." No, honey, that's your fault! You better take accountability for your actions. I warned you.

Anyway, I don't want to take up all of his time, but it would be nice to have someone want to spend some quality time with me. Gaze into my eyes and express with sincerity, "*Avery, this is your time*." It would be nice to hear those words come out of a man's mouth about me, and actually mean it.

A girl can dream, right?

Desyre scratches his throat to grasp my attention. I lift my head up and gaze into his eyes. "Well, I want to know, *if*...," Desyre pauses, then sticks his rough and dry hands in his front pants pockets of his denim Abercrombie & Fitch jeans, "...*if* you'd like to go see a movie with me?"

"What's playing?"

"Nina Simone's documentary. It's playing at The IFC Center in New York."

My eyes light up. "When?" I ask excitedly.

"Friday. You can Google it, but the documentary is called, "What Happened, Miss Simone?"

I don't hesitate to respond, "Sho'. I love Nina Simone's music. The chick is deep. Deep sister."

Desyre nods his head in agreement.

"Well," he says, "I guess it's a date."

I blush. "Yeah. A date."

"Well, let me get back to work," Desyre says, "Can't take a woman out on a date with no funds. What would she think of me if I did something like that?" He smiles.

"Okay, I'll talk to you later?"

"Yes. Because I want to hear all about how the signing went."

I smile.

A crowd is forming. Muffling voices fill the air. Vendors are setting up, displaying their souls on easels. Their life's work in hopes that someone, anyone will support them.

I bite down on the inner wall of my mouth.

Taking a step back from the table, I look with attentive eyes to see if I forgot to place anything on the table.

Some spectators, male and female walk through, stop, lift up one of my books and read the back cover. Couples share their thoughts, but I notice if the man is not feeling it the woman won't buy. Hmm. *Interesting*, I think, as I continue to observe.

Sitting and rearranging my books on the table, two ladies approach my table. One is very obese. The other woman looks in-between sizes. One is wearing a yellow sundress. The other woman a black dress with dark shades hiding her eyes. Why is she wearing shades inside? I wonder.

Interesting.

As the obese woman picks up, *Ev'ry Ho Gotta Daddy* and holds it in her chubby hands. She nudges her friend in the side with her meaty elbow, then scratches her throat.

I lift my head up and give her eye contact.

"Would you like for me to sign the book, ma'am?" I ask in a pleasant tone of voice.

"Ah," she hesitates, then says, "Yes. Can you make it out to: Country Billow?"

"Sho'."

As I reach for the book, the other woman turns her head from left to right as if she is looking over her shoulder. Hmm. Interesting.

"Country Billow," I repeat in my head, then aloud. "That name sounds vaguely familiar."

"Really?" The obese woman says with a burst of excitement in her voice.

I nod. "If I remember correctly I went to Parrington High School and there was this girl that I used to hang with, well, actually there were several of us, but I do remember one named Country. Anyway, is there anything specific you'd like for me to write for her? Or would you prefer just my autograph?"

"If you can, can you have it read:

"To Country Billow,
There are 46 reasons, 4 seasons, 1 you."
Avery ♥

I nod, then sign the copyright page of the book. I then reach for *Kreepin' Wit' the Virus* and give her a *free* copy, just because.

On page 33 I write a little note. Hopefully she'll read it.

"Well, here you go, sistah." I extend my hand out with the book." The obese woman reaches for it, then hands it to the woman in black.

"It was nice meeting you...?" I say.

"Oh, I'm Ursula."

"Ursula," I repeat.

"And you were right about high school." Ursula says, "By the way. This is Country."

"Country?" I say in surprise, "How have you been?"

"Good." She says, still looking over her shoulders.

"We also used to hang together. Yes, now I remember...Country and Ursula. It's really good to see you both."

Country cracks a smile, but I see something—something odd in her. Something off.

"I appreciate you two coming out and showing support." I say to them.

"Well," Ursula says, "I'm all for supporting my sisters. It's a shame more black women can't put their differences aside and just get along, you know?"

"Yeah, I know exactly what you mean, sistah. Black women have a difficult time accepting other black women. Must be something in the coffee we drink. Not everyone likes their coffee black, some like a few cubes of sugar with cream, some like it light and sweet, and some like it extra sweet. If black women could just embrace the differences that we all possess maybe, just maybe we'd stand a good chance of getting along."

"Amen to that," Ursula sings as she tilts her head to the side, then claps her hands together.

Country flinches from the loud sound. She then tries to play it off by opening the book and appear to be reading. Just looking at her in that black dress on this hot summery day, reminds me of someone going to a funeral, not event. And her wearing them shades inside, it is bright as the sun up in here, the jitteriness, nervousness of constantly looking over her shoulder gives me the feeling that something dreadful has happened and/or is happening to her. No. I am not trying to pry, but something doesn't smell right. And when something doesn't smell right, what do most concerned folks do? Look the other way. But I'm not like that or them. Most concerned folks probe as to where the fishy smell is coming from.

I know what you're thinking, *Avery, mind your business*. I am. But listen, when I did my book signing in Teaneck with the tricks, I met some very interesting women. I also met a woman from the Passaic County Women's Center. Her name was Donna Francis.

Donna, a rather doughty, curly-haired brunette. Her mango-colored complexion, caramel-colored eyes, and full-figure frame didn't suggest she was Puerto Rican, until she spoke. I thought she was Italian.

Donna was eager to give me insightful information about volunteering for the Domestic Violence Response Team. She ran down the goals and objectives of this program as well as the minimum standards for volunteers.

The opportunity to help women as a volunteer was something I was seriously considering. I guess Donna had an inkling because she didn't hesitate to pull out an application from her attaché case and hand it to me. For some reason, Donna felt that I would be a great candidate because of me being a motivational speaker. She said that I possess qualities (just from hearing me speak) that would be an asset to the Response Team as well as the victims. Don't get me wrong, I was flattered, but at the time I had a lot on my plate. I had made a commitment to Daisy to get her book out, and that was what I was intending to do. I didn't want to commit to something else I would not be able to complete. One thing about me is, I can't stand to start something and not finish.

When I got home that night and laid the application on my kitchenette counter, I was so tempted to fill it out, but as I looked it over and saw that they needed dang near blood from me with all the information that was being asked of me to provide, like three references. Name, address, and phone numbers of folks that weren't family. Honestly, that was what discouraged me because I didn't have one person I could put down as a reference. Not one. And plus, these days folks aren't as giving with their personal information, not with identity theft and all. And I couldn't well blame them. But then something hit me. I did/do have references. All of my references were business references: Mr. Clyde, Dr.

Fulmore, and Mr. Clausen, ah, Mrs. Jenkins-Rollins. It didn't matter if they weren't all from Paterson, they all played a part in my life. They all knew something about me and my character. So, if the opportunity should present itself again where I have time, can make the time, I'll definitely utilize the folks I do know.

Looking at Country, I think, *I wish I would have found the time because my senses tell me that I am looking at a victim at this very moment.*

After giving Country an once-over and feeling these senses that I am feeling, I think of a way to get closer to her so I conjure up this idea to have a gathering at my house. Call it what you like but I can't just stand here with this feeling swarming in my belly and not at least see if I'm right. No, I may not have the DVRT training under my belt but I have good instincts and my instincts have yet to let up since this woman has been standing in my presence. Like I said before, and I'll say it again, not every woman is doing it for herself.

"Ladies, um, I plan on having a small gathering at my home for women, about women, about me and my book, and I was wondering if you'd like to join in. The more the merrier, you know. I would like to have an open forum of women talking freely about issues that are currently going on in their lives, in their communities, and in their homes. No scripted discussions. Real talk from real women. I want real women with real issues to be a part of this video. If you're camera shy it probably won't be for you, but if you have no problem engaging in conversation with strangers I'd really like for you two to come. The video is going to be called: *Sistahs from the 'Hood of Hard Lovin'* representing women from Paterson. I'm still working out the kinks on paper but I'm pretty optimistic that it will all work itself out. I plan on serving some finger foods and a few bottles of wine. If you're interested I'll give you my number and you can call me and let me know."

"When do you plan on having it because I'm just here visiting? I live in Charlotte, North Carolina." Ursula says.

"Soon. Probably within a couple of days, actually. How often do you come to Paterson?" I ask.

"Not too often. Came up for a funeral. My uncle passed away. But Country might be interested. She lives here."

My eyes shift to Country. "How about it? Think you'd be interested in hanging out for a couple hours with a bunch of catty cats?"

Country scratches her throat, then says dryly, "It sounds like it'll be fun. I'll let you know."

"Okay, well, just in case you do decide to come give me a call on Monday. I'll give you all the details as to where I live and what we plan on discussing." I reach for one of my business cards off the table and hand it to Country. Her hand trembles as she reaches for it. "And ladies, if you happen to know of any other women feel free to invite them. I haven't had much time to promote it because I've been so busy."

"Will do." Ursula says.

Country remains quiet.

"Well, ladies, it sho' was a pleasure seeing you again. Stick around for the reading, eat, drink, and mingle. I have to get to work or this book won't get out."

"Great talking to you, Avery," Ursula says, as they both walk off to check out FAYE'S CATERING.

■■

Lying back on the big throw pillows on the chaise longue, I feel feverish. My body feels sluggish too. *What's wrong with me?*

I was feeling fine a few minutes ago. Feeling lively as I was thinking about Desyre asking me out on a date. Then out of the blue I began to feel weird.

Maybe it's something I ate. I retrace the foods I ate today and nothing was out of the ordinary. Turkey bacon, egg and cheese wrap. Lunch. I had a bowl of homemade broccoli and cheddar cheese soup. And I haven't even eaten dinner yet.

My eyes can barely stay open. I feel so sleepy, lethargic. Possibly I've over exerted myself. These past few weeks have been hectic. Work is fulfilling. But challenging. I don't feel stressed but possibly I am and just don't know it.

"Okay," I say to myself. "You need to take it easy, relax, things will fall into place."

I snuggle on the bed with Ma'am's old chiffon fuchsia throw, and try to relax. Eyelids feel so heavy, so weighty, I can't resist the temptation of falling asleep. My body needs it. My mind needs it too.

Slowly my eyelids close. I'm drifting. Drifting in a peaceful sleep.

I make my way up onstage. Anonymous is cluttered with folks. Some familiar and unfamiliar. I feel so humble to have so many folks come out and support what I have so tirelessly worked for. Having a platform for others to come and vent out their frustrations is cathartic.

As I stand before the mike, this feeling comes over me. Someone is hurting. I can literally feel her agony. Closing my eyes, hearing her voice in my head, I speak into the mike.

Jolting up, face dripping with warm sweat I lean my back against the headboard and gasp for air. What was that all about? Was I hallucinating?

Big, pear-shaped tears stream down my face as I struggle to my feet.

I stand by the bedroom window, peek out eyeing a tall silhouette of a man propped against the brick-faced building of the courtyard, smoking a lit cigarette.

Slowly I remove myself from the window and cower down on the hardwood floor and sit with my knees bent, bare feet planted firmly, trembling.

Breathing heavily. Sweating profusely. Saltwater trickles from the follicles of my scalp, down to the sides and front of my face, down from under my hairless armpits and dissolves in the white wifebeater tee that clings to my clammy skin.

Angered at the thought, I slowly rise to my feet and creep toward the window and peek out through the mini-blinds. The silhouette is gone.

Exhale.

I then sit on the bed. Rest my feet on the soft cotton quilt, bend my knock-knees, rest my chin upon them and wrap my arms around my bare legs, still trembling, but now deep in thought.

I can't seem to shake these thoughts off. *Was I a target? I wonder. Did the person know me, personally? Or was it just something to do?* I turn my face and my cheek grazes the soft skin of my knee. My eyelids close, regretting.

What did that all mean? Am I not supposed to sleep on telling Desyre the truth about me? Dang. Here I go again.

***

With cell phone in my hand, I hear a manly voice say, "Avery, are you there?" Attorney Norman Fest asks.

Flustered. "Yes-Yes, I'm here."

"Did you hear me? The annulment is completed. You're free. A free woman."

Showing no reaction to the news, I hang up the phone, whisper under my breath, "Am I?"

I go back to my bedroom and lie down.

I woke up this morning with a *funky* attitude. For some reason it got under my skin when I looked at my phone and saw that Desyre had texted me at 8:20 AM to say: *Gm.*

I don't want to become his personal computer. I don't want to communicate through technology every single day. Okay. He expressed that he likes to text. That he is always busy. That texting is easier when he is relaxing or running around, but what does that really say, you know?

If he can't or won't take the time out of his busy day to call just to say a simple hello and has to text it just to communicate with me, how are we ever going to get to know each other? Is my voice that annoying that he can't stand the sound of it? Or is there something that he is just not telling me?

Of course my mind is wandering. What do you expect when the man that asked me out on a date hasn't even called since that Saturday? I mean I understand he has a life and a lot going on that I know nothing about, but even I am not too busy to call.

Why haven't I called him? Good question. I think I haven't called because I feel like something is in the way, or possibly someone—someone that he has not mentioned in the conversation we had at my book signing. I don't know but it's something. And it makes me feel uneasy. Like it's too burdensome to just pick up his cellular phone to see how I am doing or feeling or whatever. A simple call expresses so much. Hmm. Maybe he just isn't that interested as I had assumed.

Well, I do respond back to his text:

9:25 AM
   Gm. Not texting today...know u like it. But I can't do it all the time with u. Sorry. It's like talking on my computer. Sooner or later I shut it down too.

We are supposed to do the "lunch thing" today. I wonder if he'll call to say that he is on his way or simply not show up at all. It was his suggestion, not mine.

I glance at my cell phone clock: 10:12 AM. No response. I sigh. This doesn't seem like it's going to go the way I would like. *Get dress*, one of my inner women says. *If he shows up by 11:00, then see where it goes. If he doesn't, then do what you normally do, Avery. Live.*

Don't allow yourself to get sucked in to what someone else wants if it is not comfortable for you. You know the routine by now, men come and men go. This is no different, girl.

I nod on that note, then head upstairs to pick out an outfit to wear. Something colorful, not too short, and not too loose, something that is flattering to marvel at.

In my closet I reach in and pullout my spaghetti strap Minty dress. It's variation of colors: sea-foam green, red, black, beige zigzags seems befitting since my thoughts reflect the same.

I reach atop the bottom shelf and pullout my walnut-colored sandals, walk over to my array of over two hundred earrings and choose a pair of sea foam-green dangling ones. Then I head downstairs to run water for a warm bath. And I think to myself, *Avery, soak. Put your mind at ease and see if you are worth a phone call.*

I undress, but this time I don't look at myself in the mirror. *Nothing has changed since yesterday, girl, you still look the same.*

I raise my right foot to step in the lukewarm water, when I hear my cellular phone ring.

I plant my foot back down on the floor and rush to answer my phone. Okay, I smile, he's calling.

"Hello."

"Hello, Avery," the familiar voice says. "Ah, I know I'm probably the last person you expected to hear from but I wanted to apologize for my actions. Hopefully you'll find forgiveness in your heart to at least be friends."

I blink. "Blu?"

Why is he calling me? Smokie? What happened to his other half?

"Can I come see you one day?" He asks.

I remain silent. I've learned in life to not treat folks as they treat me. I always give that person what they ask for.

I bite down on my bottom lip. "I thought you had a woman. Two women. Why are you calling me? If you didn't want me back then, all you had to do was be honest. I've been through so much that rejection won't kill me. I gave you your space because I'm not hard-up for a man, especially a man that doesn't even know which woman's name to call me. I must admit, that hurt but I said to myself that ain't the first time that that has happened to me." I sigh. "I believe alone time gives a person ample time to see themselves, their good and bad. Sho' I have issues but if I didn't I doubt very seriously if God would've granted me this talent to be a writer. It seems that writing is now my newfound man, life partner. As far as you coming to see me, and as far as you wanting to salvage a 'friendship'," I pause, think of what Johnnie would do. "Friendship is a strong word. I remember the first time I saw you at Garrett Mountain. I couldn't help but stare at you. Admiring your physique, handsomeness. Um, I don't see anything wrong with us being friends."

"Is that a promise?"

"My word should be enough." I say.

"Gotcha. When can I come?"

"What is it that you want, Blu?"

"To see you."

"Whenever you want to?"

"What did you assume I wanted?"

"I didn't assume. I just asked what you want."

"It's not that, I'm a gentleman."

"Why now? Why is it important? I haven't bothered you. I've respected your space. And I carried on with my life. Trying to get back into my groove, pour my soul out to my craft."

"If it's going to be a problem, I'll let it be. You cannot fault me for trying. I do miss your presence." Blu says.

"I don't fault you. But I have a right to ask questions. If you feel to let it be…that's up to you."

"I don't really want to interfere with the thing you love the most. I understand. But we still can hangout, if you like."

"Listen. I accept your apology. Nothing, no one has ever come between me and poetry. I don't think anyone is that powerful, only God. Secondly, I'm okay. Ain't nothing change with me? Still pushing myself. Still striving and determined. Still sassy. So, just be happy. I'm learning how to be with me. Just me. Take care, Blu."

"You are so mean," Blu snaps.

"I'm not mean. I'm just honest. Direct. What I said to you is real. I'm learning how to be happy with self. Appreciate me. And love me. Nothing is mean about that. It is just not what you wanted to hear."

"I just wanted to see if you still had love for a brother. And to see if we can reconnect."

"Listen. As long as I live I'll always have love for you. But I question if I'll always trust you. It is difficult for people to reconnect with no trust."

"Alright, Avery. I still love you, regardless."

"Love? Had you ever really *loved* me?"

"Yes. But I didn't want to get hurt, that's all. I'm able to love again. For the record, you're a sweetheart."

"You have not let your guard down. You haven't been honest. You want what you want. You haven't included me in your life. And you don't wanna get hurt. You hurt me, and left. Declined my phone call instead of telling me the truth. You see other women in front of my face, and smiled. And you don't wanna get hurt. What changed with you?"

"You're wrong! I never seen other women in front of your face when we were dating. I wasn't involved with any woman. That's the truth!"

"Okay. I got one wrong." I smirk. "Okay, what I am trying to understand is...why now? Why? What did you wake up this morning with me on your mind? Or was it last week? I can't keep you happy, I saw that. You assume that nothing you did for me was good enough. I never said that to you. I was surprised. Taken aback of how you reacted when I disclosed myself to you. How you changed. Flipped out on me. Relationships. They're not about money. They're about: compromise, loving one another, respecting one another, acceptance, good and bad. It's about building, sharing, caring, and giving of space and time. It's about communicating and making love."

Blu breathes out, softly, "I always had you on my mind. Just had to get my mind right. To be honest, it shocked me to find out. And I-I freaked out because I was developing feelings for you."

"I understand the shock. I felt the same when I was told."

"Do you think you will have time for me?"

"Time? What do you mean...time?"

"Out of your busy schedule. Quality time."

"I don't have such a busy schedule as you think. I write all times of the day and night. Work. Keep my life as calm as I can. Why do you want this?" I ask, curious.

"I miss those times that we did spend together. Do you?"

This must be a trick question, I think to myself.

"We didn't do much during those times, Blu."

"We did enough."

"Listen. You're a sports guy. Being with me, I don't have cable. I don't even have AC right now. The one I had broke down. And I'm not looking to get either right now. Just trying to get back on my feet."

"I hear you. Hopefully we can work something out."

"Like what, Blu? I want a strong but sensitive man in my corner. Someone that truly wants me and all of my flaws. Accept me 'as is'. Someone that can love just me. Ask yourself, are you that man? Are you that man that will care for me when I'm *sick or just sick and tired*?"

"C'mon. You know I will."

"I don't know that."

"Give a brother a chance."

"Hmm. And what are you going to give me? You want a chance, and if I say, okay, then what?"

"I miss your turkey wings, when you cooking them again."

I sigh, then shake my head, "Blu, I never cooked *you* turkey wings."

Silence.

"We can work on an honest, happy relationship." Blu says.

"I don't know. But what I do know is that this conversation should be discussed in person."

"I want to see your beautiful face anyway."

"Beautiful? Huh?"

"Really, you have to believe me some time."

"Takes time."

"I agree."

"Hmm."

"I'm going to give you time to decide if I'm worth it. I'm willing to be patient."

"Blu, I won't know that just by thinking. I have to see it."

"You'll get that chance to see. I have to work, but I'm taking some vacation time starting Monday."

"Ok."

"By the way, Avery, are you seeing someone?"

"Why?"

"You answered it," says Blu.

"No, I didn't. I asked why."

"I need to know before I pursue you."

I shift the weight from my left leg to my right. "Listen. Your main focus should be reconnecting...friendship...then other. You can't have it your way because you're the one that left. You're the one asking to be reconnected. Obviously you need to think about what you're asking. If you're serious about it or not. Life doesn't stop because of what you realize you want."

Blu sighs. "You're right."

"Ok. And no, I am not trying to be mean...it's just that your demands can't be made. You don't want to pursue me if another man is trying to pursue me, so why reach out after all this time of us not communicating. Just because one pursues one doesn't make him or her the right one. Stay true to your heart."

"I guess you're right."

"You have to know I don't wanna be with someone that is not sho' of himself. There are so many women out and about that you can pursue. Maybe you need to explore, see if you connect with someone. See if you'll be happy. No, I'm not with anyone but I'm open as far as dating goes."

I breathe out a tad bit frustrated. "I was going through a lot at the time of us connecting. Um, I didn't want you to think that I was lazy or a woman that didn't work. I informed you of my situation at the time. But what I failed to tell you was that my being unemployed was a choice. I could've kept my job. But I was going through a lot of emotional stuff. My circumstance took over. And I relinquished my job, a job, might I add, I loved. You once made a comment about women who accept money from a man. You said that you once helped someone and when things went sour, you stopped because it was a way for you to get back at her. I never understood that. You made it about the money, not the person. I felt bad for her. And it made me think of myself. If I was in a relationship with someone who threw what they've done for me in my face, after the fact of doing it.

At the time of you sharing that that made me really look at you a little sideways. I never asked you for anything. If you gave, you gave on your own accord. You have to look at everything as far as how you were with me. You left. You couldn't even look me in my face. Just imagine if we had sex."

"He would've killed you, Avery." Karma says with a deadpan face.

"I apologize for that, Avery. I felt bad about that. Still do. It was just a lot to take in. I'm not like that. I mean, if my lady needs help I give. I never considered you a gold-digger. That never crossed my mind. I've helped plenty of people. Didn't expect anything in return."

"But it really made me think that you really didn't know me. And I tried to deal with it, but it was hard."

"I'm not a cold-hearted person, never have been. I guess you didn't really know me."

Hand sanitizer episode, and you're not cold-hearted. I beg to differ. You damned near pushed me out of your car.

"Blu, we don't know each other. You just know what you've read. But you don't know me. And I don't know you."

"I guess you're right. A lot of stuff I read surprised me."

"And you judged me."

"I never said that. As far as sex, I don't go around screwing everything. Anyway, tell me, did the part about all the men, partners, was that true or not?"

"Like, why do you want to reconnect with me? We don't seem like a good match. I adore you, yes, but I'm tired of hurting. I've lived a lifetime of pain. I'm tired."

"Tell me, the book, *Sleepin' Wit' the Virus* with the character Brick in it."

"What are you asking?"

"Were you that person, that chick, the men, the sex and all…was any of it true?"

"It's a book, Blu. I'm a *writer*."

"If you feel that way as far as us not being a match. I understand. God has a plan for me. As long as I keep doing the right thing. He's going to make sure I'm happy."

Happiness comes from self.

"Why are you so fixated on Brick? What is it? You have to do what is best for you and so do I."

"I'm talking about the *other* guys you had *sex* with that you mentioned in the book. I wasn't talking about Brick per se. I have strong feelings for you, Avery, but it's evident that you don't feel the same. It's okay. I respect that."

"I don't know what you feel for me. You've never told me to my face. You read books that I wrote, now you're questioning me. If I was that person, don't you think it's a little too late to be asking me now? And if I'm not don't you think you've made me feel a certain type of way. Obviously I am not the one for you. I see that."

"Not a problem. I respect your honesty."

"Ok."

Silence.

"I have to say this because I'm not understanding something here. Was this call more of an apology? Or more of wanting to reconnect? I'm baffled. How can you want to reconnect with someone you question? When I was with Brick, we were together as in couple, but Brick and I *never* had sex. After he and I split, I was a single woman for a while."

"I just asked the question to see if it was true about the men. What's done is done. Maybe we can be *friends with benefits*, then?"

I roll my eyes, they well-up. "No, thank you. When the right one enters my life, I'll know. Right now, I'll remain as I am. Please don't call me if you're calling to play head games. And please don't text me again. I'm good as I am."

"You're not what *I* thought you were, Avery. You won't hear from me ever again. I promise!"

273

My forehead crumples. "I'm a woman—a person with feelings. I'm a writer, author, entrepreneur trying to do things to help other women. Whatever your expectations, perceptions of me were that is what *you* created *in your head*. I've been through enough to be judged by someone that cannot be honest. I maybe whatever I am to you but at least I'm honest. I don't play games or on emotions. I'm not stupid. Your heart was never in it but I'm so glad that I have a mind of my own— the gut instincts to know right from wrong—to not fall for everything. Stop judging especially if your shit is not perfect. Start looking at your own life. Your insecurities are visible. Work on self."

Blu cackles. "From where I sit, baby, my life is great! You're the one who needs help. Play someone else as your sucker. I'm not the one."

I feel like I'm drowning in his words, but I manage to swim ashore when I say, "First of all, you contacted me, I didn't call you. Secondly, *sucker*, are you referring to yourself as that, Blu? I'm not going to stoop to your level. I'm just not going to go there with you. Look. Everyone falls in a slump or hits a bump in life. One never knows what to expect from life. Things happen, *unexpectedly*. So I would never say never. I never asked you for anything. If you gave, you gave on your own. But again you're throwing shit in my face as if you've paved the way for me." I shake my head, "At least I'm following my dream. And no, I haven't had anyone helping me financially with it. I'm doing it on my own. I'm working to still pursue my dreams. So I'd rather be *broke* than rich. I'm good. And I'm content for now. I don't play on folks for money. I'm a hard working woman. And that- that is great for me! So it's good that you're where you are in life. I'm not knocking you. You're knocking me. But it is fine because I, too, have come a long way. I'm proud of myself. So go throw rocks at someone else because your words no longer hurt me. Your actions say so much about the man you are. The fact that I pushed myself, no man helped me achieve anything I have. To you I may not have much, but I have a little more than some. Work on self. Stop hating. And stop playing on women. Make up your mind as to whom you want and make it work with that person. First, it was me. Then Narlena. Then Smokie. C'mon. Stop spreading yourself thin, Blu."

After I say my last words, I hang-up. I then block Blu's number. I don't have the time nor the patience for anymore foolishness from him. He can think what he wants. I no longer care to entertain a man that serves *me* no purpose.

My cell phone pings.

I look at the caller ID. It's Desyre.

Smiling from ear to ear, I answer. "Hello."

"Hi, Avery. Just calling to say I'll be there to pick you up at 7:00 o'clock. I know this great restaurant in Montclair that I frequent. You heard of *Green Jubilee?*"

"I'm familiar with *Green Jubilee*. Never ate there before but I was always curious about the food and place."

"Well, you're in for a treat, then."

I remove my mouth from the receiver and crack a smile.

Desyre says, "By the time I get off and freshen up it should be about six. I'll call you when I arrive home, okay."

Where is home, I wonder but don't ask. I'll wait for us to meet up and ease it into the conversation. Hopefully it won't be a big deal as far as him telling me where he lives. I've had my share of men trying to hide their place of residence, mainly because they had something to hide. Or someone.

I don't want to think negatively of Desyre. I want to give him the benefit of the doubt. Just because past relationships didn't work out doesn't mean that all men are the same.

Desyre is different. He expresses himself. He gets angry about important things. He cares. Shows compassion for people. It has been a long time since I've encountered a man like him. Only person that comes to mind that showed concern for others was Johnnie. Good ole Johnnie.

***

Seven o'clock is ten minutes away.

My cell phone rings at six-fifty.

"Hello."

"Are you dressed and ready to go?" Desyre asks.

"Yes."

"Well, I'm in front of your building. I would've parked and buzzed but there is no parking spaces. Don't want to park in the lot across the street because I can't afford to get any more tickets. Paterson police can be brutal."

I chuckle. "I understand. I'll be right down."

"'Kay."

A smile spreads upon my face. A feeling of "special" flutters my heartstrings. *"When will you reveal yourself?"* Avona asks. *"Don't wait too long. He's not like the others. Something different about him. Do the right thing."*

"Shut up, Avona! Just shut up! I haven't even gone on the date with the man and already you're preaching about doing the right thing. Haven't I always done the right thing? Haven't I always revealed myself? Where has it gotten me, huh? Where? Exactly."

The "right" thing. I repeat in my head. The right thing will have me sitting home engrossed in someone else's love story. Why can't I have my own...my own love story?

I sigh.

Shaking my head, no, as I reach for my beaded purse, keys, and turn off the lamp. This evening I will not share. Not on the first date. Nor the second or third. If there should be a second or third. Is it too much to want to have a romantic evening with an attractive man? Laugh. Smile. Enjoy a delicious meal. Drink some expensive wine. Listen to some great music. Dance the night away. Come home. Replay a lovely evening in my head without tainting it with what lives inside me. Can I just have a day without constantly worrying about—?

For once, can I feel sexy and pretty and desirable without all the extra? For once, can I just live in the moment? Deal with my reality tomorrow? Can HIV and I have a day off? Even God rests on Sundays.

Exiting out the lobby door, Desyre jumps out of his idling silver Nissan Altima and opens the passenger side door. I greet him with a smile, then hello, and climb inside. Giving him an once-over. Dang! This man is *fiine*! And he looks extremely good in those black slacks and soft pink button down collar shirt. I'm not feelin' his black leather sandals with dress socks but I can get passed it. He smells soooo good!

Inhaling Desyre as well as the sweetness of coconut-pineapple air freshener, is only making me hungry.

Desyre climbs in the car, and we drive off with the Jamaican tune of Bob Marley's "No Woman, No Cry."

Seeing Bloomfield Ave gives me a melancholy feel. I mean, inside there is a soreness—a missing piece. As we drive pass where Anonymous used to reside, memories of how fulfilled I was seep through. I never knew a place could have such an effect. Anonymous did. Does.

The streets are lively. Couples laughing, loving. Expressing by holding hands, hugging, kissing. The lights and the picturesque scenery really has an emotional attachment to me. I try not to show it, but it's there. Lingering. I hope Desyre isn't able to tell. I don't want him asking me a bunch of questions. Questions I'm not prepared to answer. At least not now. Not before dinner. *Why did I say, yes?* I don't know. Maybe I needed to be reminded of what was. Possibly this evening has significance, meaning.

I can still hear the roar of the crowd. Hands clapping. Muffled voices. Laughter. See the performers onstage reciting their truths. Feeling the vibe. Energy. Hearing the music. Smelling the food. I remember it all. I don't think I've ever been happier. Felt like everything had purpose, a soul.

Now is a different time. Different feel. I'm still reaching out to others, helping, but it's not the same. I spend more time alone in my head.

Then. I was surrounded by people. All kinds of people. Talented people. Worldly people. Dying people. People like Storyteller. So young. So full of great potential. Life cut short by the epidemic of disease.

I inhale to dry the welling in my eyes. Often I think of him. Think about visiting his gravesite at Fairlawn Cemetery, but something always seems to sway me from doing so. Something gives me a visual of him standing onstage with the artistic bandage X underneath his eye, about his neck, and on his right arm— remembering how he gave all, said all, felt all seemingly in one breath.

Smiling inwardly, yes, I remember how slow his mobility was. Those days were the most gratifying of my life. In spite the loss that came, it was moments to treasure. Beautiful moments.

"Penny for your thoughts, Avery," Desyre says breaking me out of my trance. "What are you so deep in thought about over there, huh? Share?"

I hesitate. Not sho' if I should. Not sho' if now is the "right" time. How will I explain *Anonymous*? What it stood for? How it all began? Johnnie? Everything? Me?

I turn my face toward the passenger side window, gape out. Then turn and gape at the side profile of Desyre's gorgeous face. I stick out my tongue and swipe it across my upper and bottom lip.

Breathing out, I tell myself, "I can't do it. Not yet. Not now. Wait."

My conscience speaks, *just see where the evening leads before you leap and fall face down in a puddle of your own tears. See if there is any chemistry before you spill the beans and find yourself eating dinner for one.*

I nod.

"You're awfully quiet over there, Avery. Are you all right?"

I nod my head again, then let out a small, "Uh-huh. Just admiring Montclair. It's been a while since I've been over here."

"Yeah. I love it here. Beats being in Paterson. I think you're gonna enjoy *Green Jubilee*."

"Me, too."

Avona eases in her sisterly advice. "You tell him right now."

"What's gotten into you, Avona? Why are you so aggressive lately?"

Avona replies, "It's difficult enough, Avery. I'm tired. You're tired. Men, they just don't get you or your purpose. They only hear the words, but they never truly hear you or see you or feel you. I'm just tired of seeing you so alone. Aren't you?"

I turn slightly in my seat, face the passenger window, and stare out, wishing Avona would just leave me alone. I'll tell him when I am good and ready. Not today. Not today. I don't want to ruin a perfectly good evening, sink this ship before it sails. I just want to enjoy this man, a delicious meal, and leave my problems where they lie. Inside me.

"Just letting you know I made it up and in safely."

"I would have walked you to your door, Avery, but you insisted that I not. I feel much better now knowing

that you're in safe and sound. Goodnight beautiful."
Desyre says, then yawns loudly.

"Goodnight. Get home safe."

"Trust that I will."

"Ok. Oh, by the way. Um, what time are you getting off tomorrow? I'm cooking, nothing big. Just fettuccine with thin sliced red and yellow onions and some green squash and fresh garlic toppled with a spicy marinara I like. Wondering if you wanted me to put some aside for you for your lunch tomorrow. Or, are you good because I know you did say you cooked earlier?"

"I truly appreciate the gesture, sweetheart. That's so kind of you to think of me. I truly appreciate that immensely. But I get off rather late and you might be asleep by the time I will be able to come by. I finish up at 12:30 a.m. and wouldn't want to disturb you by coming by so late. But I can definitely sample some of your cooking on my day off, if you're not too busy. I really can't wait to see you again. Got me excited."

"Excited, huh? I think I'm taking off tomorrow. I'm a bit tired."

"Sweetness, you can have me every day!"

"You're killing me now." I say.

"Don't want to do that."

"Not use to all the sweet talk, sorry."

"Don't be sorry. Just may take some getting used to, but I can lean back on the verbiage, if you'd like. Don't want to be overzealous. But you make it hard being as lovely as you are."

"Don't change how you are for me, Desyre. Be you. And yes, it will take some getting used to. But, I'm not as lovely as you may perceive me to be. I have my moody days, my just- want-to-be-alone-time-days, my want to snuggle up days, my want to jump your bones days, and my mellow days. Romance is beautiful based on what I've heard. So, please, be you."

"And that I shall be. Just myself. No one else. No fake. No phony. This is the real deal here. I don't know how to be anyone else, but myself. And I see I'm going to enjoy every moment I spend with you. We're human. We have good days and bad days but when you share the day with someone that you want to be around it makes everything much better."

A smile spreads on my face. "True."

"And I really dig that cuddling thing too! I'm kind of big on that. Looks are not everything—they fade away as we get older. Affection. Love. Caring. That will show a person."

I nod my head. "I fully agree."

Where has this man been all of my life? Not only is he conscious of what a woman wants, but he can articulate it so perfectly too.

"Be careful, Miss Lady, don't get all caught up in this Luther-wanna-be just yet. There is still something that needs to be said that has yet to be said. Once you spill the beans then we'll see how articulate he really is."Avona mutters.

"Yeah, yeah." I retort.

"My goodness, Avery, what are you going to do with me?" Desyre asks, then chuckles.

I raise a brow. Oh, I can think of a couple of things.

"I was just sitting on the sofa reading when a question arose in my head as to you and children. You don't have any children, Desyre, but do you want children? Like, what if hypothetically speaking, what if you meet a woman you like, fall in love, but find out that she either doesn't want children or can't have children, would that change things on your part? I mean would you leave her to find that one woman that wanted the same things or similar things as you? It would only be right if you did, don't you think?"

Karma shakes her head from side to side. "You wimp. Just blurt it out and see what this Casanova is going to say. I can't take the suspense any longer. I got a box of Kleenex for you just in case he blacks the hell out."

I ignore her. Try my best to push her out of my thoughts, my head, but that is a difficult task.

"No." says Desyre.

"Why not?" I ask curiously.

"If God wants it or wants to bless me with children He'll let me know. But at this point I very much think that's not going to happen, and I'm okay with it. It will be okay with me if the woman that I am with doesn't want children or can't have any more children. To me love making is a spiritual thing. An emotional thing. Not a quick thing. Something that you would want to last—last forever. Making love is a beautiful thing, but having children is a gift. And I'm okay if I don't have that gift. Thus far I've been blessed."

"Hmm."

Since the conversation seems to be flowing without a hitch I intentionally ease in, "May as well share—"

"Share? Share what, Avery?"

"You know that I'm a writer, but I never divulged the subject matter in which I write about. It often raises a brow. Anyway." Stop babbling and tell the man. "Anyway, I write about women's issues...fic—" I pause myself before I tell a bold-faced lie.

"Like what?"

"Likkkkeeeee..." I sing, "Things women go through: rape, disease, domestic violence, bulimia, prostitution, pregnancy, and abortion... a lot of things. Things that touch the human spirit, my spirit. Things that piss me off. Things that make me wonder and wish I had the power to change pain and hurt and devastation and struggle. I just feel compelled to make a difference, somehow. In one of my books, um, often time's folks assume that the character is me. Thought I'd share that with you now just in case we happen to be out and about and someone approaches me with a slew of questions about one of my books. I mean you might even have questions of your own or not."

I wait for him to respond, but Desyre gets quiet on me.

Oh, shoot! What have I done? I should've kept my mouth shut.

I pause. Listen to him breathe softly into the receiver.

I breathe out.

Damn it, say something!

Before I hang up, Desyre finally breaks his silence. "I was listening to you speak so passionately about what you do. I could literally hear the passion in your voice." His voice cracks, "I wanted your passion to marinate in my spirit. Inspire me to rise above my own obstacles in life."

"Wow. Um, I am left speechless, Desyre. No one has ever said that they wanted my *passion to marinate in their spirit* before. That was beautifully said."

Desyre continues. "Well, I'm not like *other* men. And you're not like *other* women. I think it's great, Avery! You're great. You have a warmth to you. Compassion for others. You're not a selfish person. You give. Probably too much. And you get less-than back. Regardless, you keep striving, keep pushing. I like that about you. I see that in you. It motivates someone who may be lost, you know. You make me want something that I have lost so long ago. You make me yearn for— even make me cry. You make me feel alive. I know I sound a bit, ah, vulnerable. And I am. I am. I find it gratifying to have met a woman like you. And I hope that we can somehow connect in a way that will unite us. You know, bring us closer than just friends. The world awaits to your words, whether you know it or see it or feel it. It awaits. No, I haven't read any of your books, yet, a part of me feels as if every time we are together I'm reading a page at a time. When I look into your eyes, I'm reading chapter by chapter. Word for word. Women need to be reminded of what is out in the world, Avery. Relationships, life, in general, can cause a lot of heartache, pain, agony, and suffering. I find that

283

women take the brunt of abuse, you know. Hmm. You're a very interesting, beautiful, gifted black woman, Avery. Very interesting, beautiful, gifted black woman, indeed."

I scratch my throat, then say, "Thank you for your kind words. It's flattering. But Desyre, I'm just trying to live out my dream. It's not easy, but I'm trying to give something to others that no one ever gave to me."

I can tell that Desyre is smiling over the phone. I can just tell. Dang, this man is beyond my every expectation.

With my free hand I swipe the sweat off of my forehead. Lord knows, I was expecting something else to come out of Desyre's mouth, but he sho' surprised me.

What am I gonna do? How am I gonna tell him? How? And when I do, Lord, please be by my side.

Tossing and turning about the crisp cotton auburn sheets a tingly, burning sensation shoots through to my right shoulder. I stare at the alarm clock that reads 12:36 a.m., as I stretch out my arm and rest it upon the cushiony bamboo pillow, then sigh. Massage my right shoulder with my left hand, kneading my long fingers into the soft tissue, simultaneously squinting my eyes from the shooting pain.

I rise from my bed. As I stand the cottony white Calvin Klein T-shirt drapes about my healthy thighs.

Freshly painted lilac toenails and ashy feet press down upon the hardwood steps as I make my way down twelve, bypass the kitchenette, and walk into the bathroom.

Cold earth-tone tile chills the soles of my feet as I pull open the medicine cabinet and reach for the plastic orange bottle of Cyclobenzaprine muscle spasm pills. God. I hope this works.

The pain feels like a burning sensation.

Pushing down and turning the white cap I empty out one pill. With pill in hand I exit of the bathroom, enter the kitchenette and open the fridge and grab a bottle of spring water. The throb continues, only more intense. It has risen to my neck.

Slowly twirling my neck, I slip the pill in my sodden mouth and then take a few swigs of the cold water. Swallow. Take another swig and another and another as the pill flows down into my stomach.

Oh God, what am I thinking?!

I rush to the bathroom and stick my index finger in my mouth to gag hoping the pill will come back up. I don't want to mix medications. Especially without permission from Dr. Fulmore.

The twinge continues to worsen. Eyes begin to tear-up.

The pain the tingle the burn the throb...tightening of muscle. The pressures of life. The stress. The strife. All I want is for the pain to cease.

Chapter
Thirty-Two

Ursula

White rose petals greet me at the front door. As I open the door, more petals trail the foyer, into our home. Inhaling. The air fills with the familiar aroma of Woolridge's home cooking.

Out of the kitchen comes Woolridge with an apron wrapped around his wide waist, white Hanes crewneck T-shirt and plaid shorts, along with a happy-go-lucky smile on his round face.

He leans in and pecks me on the cheek. Then hands me a glass of red wine, and leads me into the living room, sits me down on the comfy sofa, kneels down on one knee, and removes my flats. He then massages the soles of my sweaty and swollen feet with his warm manly hands.

Tilting my head back, resting it on the soft cushion, I let out a purring moan. I can't tell you how good it feels to have a man like Woolridge. I know I did, but you have no idea how good it truly feels.

Raising my head, I try not to guzzle down the wine, but Lord knows I'm thirsty.

Not thirsty for Woolridge, though.

It sounds bad. Insensitive. Heartless.

"Long day, baby?"

"Pretty much."

"Well, you're home now. Go on up and soak that lovely body in some bubbles. I took the liberty of running your bath. Nightgown is laid out on the bed. I'll bring supper up to you."

Woolridge stands to his feet, humming, as he returns to the kitchen.

With glass in hand I make my way upstairs to our bedroom. The thought of this kind and wonderful, thoughtful man is taking its toll on me. I gotta tell him. I just gotta tell him. Either tell him or leave him.

I really need my girlfriend right about now. I think I'll give Country a call after I soak my tiresome body.

"Baby, wake up." I hear a familiar voice in my ear. Then soft lips pecking my neck. It startles me out of my deep sleep. When I open my eyes Woolridge is on his knees just gazing at me.

"You know you are a beautiful woman. I love you very much. You know, Urs, I get this sick feeling in my belly that you aren't happy. And as much as I don't want to feel it, I do. Are you happy, Ursula? Truly happy with me? With us?"

I am at a loss for words. I wasn't expecting this. What do I do? What do I say, Lord? Tell him. This is your open door to tell him the truth.

I reach for the loofa bath sponge. Squeeze the soapy contraption as I try to find my words.

"Woolridge."

"Yes, baby."

"Woolridge. I feel like I'm changing. Like I'm in the wrong body of sorts. I don't really fully understand what's happening to me. I never felt this way before. But I keep having these strong desires. Desires that don't always require a man. You understand what I'm trying to say? I wanted to tell you sooner but I didn't want to hurt you anymore than I already have."

Woolridge nods his head. "Are you saying that you're attracted to women and men? Do you really think you're bisexual? Or a lesbian? Is that what you're saying? Because if you are it explains a lot."

"What do you mean? I'm confused right now. I don't know what I want anymore." I say with this fluttered look upon my face.

"Well, baby, when we have relations it feels like you're forcing yourself. Like you're not really there. Like you really don't enjoy our intimacy. Honey, I know I'm not as debonair and as handsome as some men, but I thought maybe things would turn around and you would overcome those feelings. I prayed on it. Can't tell yah how many days and nights. Every time we kiss I feel the distance between us. But try to be optimistic. I don't want to lose you, Urs, but I don't want you to be here if this is not where you want to be. I don't want you to be unhappy. That will only make me unhappy. What I can do to help please you? Just tell me and I'll do it. What is it that you want? Do you want a woman? I'll get you a woman? Do you want me and a woman? Baby, just tell me what you want?"

The look of sad eyes on Woolridge face makes me feel horrible.

"Listen, if you need time to think things over. Time to figure things out as to what you really need. Take all the time you need. If I can't have you as my wife, then I'm open to having you as my lover, best friend."

Tears rush down my face. Woolridge wipes them away with his meaty fingers.

Woolridge leans in and kisses my lips so longingly. And when he does, something inside of me melts. I don't feel as tense. If anything, I feel light as a feather. Horny and hot as the devil himself.

I reach for his hand and place it on my left large breast. He gently squeezes it, then leans in and suckles my now hard nipple. A sensation rushes through my voluptuous body. Simultaneously a twinkle sparkles in my eyes.

His hand maneuvers down to my wet meaty thighs. He then stops at the center of my chocolaty stuff. I part my legs giving him permission to caress my clitoris. He does it slow, gently. Rotating his middle finger around and around. My eyes get droopy. Legs tighten up from the fiery arousal.

Woolridge stands and pulls off his shirt and unbuttons his shorts. Drops them, including his boxers to the floor. He steps in the oversized claws foot tub and sinks his hefty body in the water. Facing me, he reaches out and pulls me in to him. He then kisses me so erotically.

The stimulation from his tongue is unimaginative. So sensual. My fingers grip the edge of the tub. Head tilts back and forth experiencing all that he is expressing, professing.

I feel a rumbling in my tummy! Where had he been all these years? I never knew Woolridge had it in him to love me sooooo lovingly. I mean, yes, he knows how to please me on outside of the bedroom, but tonight he gives me all of his manhood. Simply through a kiss. He makes my toes curl, my heart flutter, my eyes tear-up. The man makes me cry. Not because of what I'm feeling— my mixed emotions about my sexuality. But because for the first time in a long time I felt him. His heart. His soul. His spirit. And his rock hard penis.

Somehow he cut through to the heart of me. And I must admit it felt like he punched me right in the stomach. I feel so messed up inside.

Am I a lesbian? Hmm. I don't know. Do I fantasize about being intimate with a woman? All the time. How badly do I want a woman? I don't know. I mean, if I wanted a woman that badly wouldn't I be with one? Wouldn't she have been the one sexing me instead of Woolridge?

I'm so confused.

One minute Woolridge and I have this disconnection. Even when he kissed me I felt yucky. And I never wanted to kiss him back—tongue kiss.

Tonight Woolridge kissed and kissed and kissed every nook and cranny of my body. He made me feel so deliciously sexy in my skin.

We wildly kissed, tongue and all. And I didn't feel yucky. I felt good. I felt special. Special with a special man.

Chapter
Thirty-Three

C ountry has yet to arrive. She returned my call yesterday and I gave her my address and the time of the get together. She said she'd try her best to make it. I don't know what but I heard something strange in her voice. Something. Ursula had already returned to Charlotte, North Carolina. I knew that she wouldn't be able to make it back up north so we agreed to communicate through Skype.

Danell. Well, after she gets off her shift at the hospital she said she'll go home and freshen up, then swing through. As long as I have food I know Danell will be here. That chile loves to eat.

I fill the Pier1 Imports ceramic olive-green tray with thin slices of marble blue cheese, goat cheese, Monterey jack, and sharp and mild cheddar and arrange them like dominions with Ritz crackers. I pour green and black olives in a small bright yellow bowl and place the bowl in the center of the tray. I've already arranged a fruit platter with strawberries, seedless purple and green grapes, kiwi, thick chunks of cantaloupe, honeydew, fresh pineapple, and cut up some lemons and limes for decorations. I meant to pick up a watermelon at the Super SuperMarket but it slipped my mind as I was engaged in conversation with the cashier Inga, while simultaneously placing my less than twelve items on the conveyor belt counter.

Sutter Home Sweet White and Chardonnay, Barefoot Riesling, Sweet Bitch "Shiraz", Pinot, Merlot, Cabernet, and Hennessey are stacked in the oversized ice bucket, chilling. Cans of Pepsi, Coke, and ginger ale are also submerged in the ice bucket too.

A tray full of spicy and mild buffalo wings with ranch, blue cheese, and assortment of other dressings set in the center of the table, along with a large bottle of Red Hot sauce.

Fresh green leaf lettuce, plump and juicy tomatoes that I sliced into small chunks, cucumber, thinly sliced red onions and red cabbage, green and black olives, thin slithers of juicy California orange, Honey Crisp apple, and shredded carrots all combined in a large, shallow white bowl. Tongs are to the right of it with thick chunks of baguette bread stacked high on a bamboo cutting board.

A vase of African roses, yellow carnations, lilies, daffodils and orchids are the centerpiece of the table.

Baked chicken is still basking in its juices. Macaroni and cheese and a pan of homemade cornbread are in the oven. I baked four cakes: carrot, German chocolate, Philadelphia cheese cake toppled with fresh strawberries. And, of course, my sweet potato cheese cake.

Videographer, Rose McFadden, has yet to arrive. She lives in Brooklyn, New York, so I know it may take a while for her to get here and setup. I met her from my Message board. I put for hire ad up on my website and stated that I was looking for a videographer for a project and she corresponded back to me in reference to it. I told her what my plan was and she offered to do it for free. Said it was a way for her to give back to the sistahs. She never went into detail as to what her cause was and I never asked. Figured it was none of my business anyway.

I took Rose up on her offer. Explained in great detail how I planned on getting the documentary out and up on YouTube. She thought it was a great idea. Said she definitely wanted to be a part of it—a part of my cause. I was elated that the sistah was willing to help another sistah out. Simply elated.

Ring, Ring, Rinnnnnngggggg.

I slip my hand inside my apron pocket and pullout my cell phone and answer. "Hello?"

"Well, hello. How's everything there?" Desyre asks.

"Just finishing up, but so far everything is good."

"Good to hear. Good to hear. Just was thinking about you and how great our date went the other night at *Green Jubliee*. Um, I was wondering, um, if possible, if I could see you tonight. A busy woman as yourself still has to have fun once in a while, you know."

Tilting my head back in a flirtatious motion, I chuckle loudly.

All the ladies heads turn in my direction. I don't care. I feel like a young girl meeting a boy for the first time—experiencing her first stomach butterflies.

"You're right. I had a lovely time with you on our date. The food was outstanding. I ate so much I felt like I was going to bust. Thank you for a wonderful evening. The documentary of Nina was so inspiring. You made me feel special. And you're right, all work and no play can put a damper on a single woman's life. What time are you talkin'?"

"Well, I want to give you ample time to finish up what you're doing. Go home and freshen up. You tell me what time is good, babe?"

Babe? He called me "babe". I like the sound of that.

Smiling with my eyes I say, "Ah, say around eight-thirty."

"Eight-thirty it is. Call you later."

"Okay."

293

"When are you going to tell him?" Karma says, hands on hips, tapping her left barefoot on the hardwood floor with a scowl on her face.

"Heffa, don't bother me. Not today. Can't you see I have company? I don't have time to deal with you." I say, with a glare in my eyes.

"Avery! Avery!"

I hear someone calling my name, which breaks me out of my trance.

"Y-Yes."

Claire says, "Someone is buzzing your buzzer."

"Oh." I rush over to answer it. "Who is it?"

"Faye. And a woman named, ah, Rose."

I press down on the button to let them in.

A part of me wants to call Country to see if she's going to come, but then, I decide against it. I don't want to come off as pushy. If she shows she shows. If not—

"When is we gonna eat?! I come fo' the food, chile. You said—" says Mama with her fat bottom lip poked out.

I don't know who dressed Mama but she looks like she is lost from the head down. Her housedress is wrinkled like she balled it up and then put it back on. She smells like she was sprayed by a skunk. And she looks like she slept on one side of her head because her hair is disheveled on the left side and mushed in on the right. Her crazy ass boyfriend, Omar needs to be kicked in his head for allowing her to come out lookin' like this.

"Everyone hasn't arrived as of yet." I tell her.

"Well, that ain't my problem. I'm on time. So, when we's gonna eat 'cause I's hungry. I got sugar and I needs to eat, chile."

I sigh, then remind myself that I did invite her. "Just give me a minute, okay, Mama."

"That's all I'm gonna give you too. A minute." Mama says, then pulls out a Pall Mall cigarette and just before she gets a chance to light it, looks around.

I scratch my throat. "Excuse me, um, Mama, but *you* do know that this is a smoke-free building. You know good and doggone well you can't smoke in here."

Mama smacks her thick lips. "Aiight. I'll go outside across the street. But when I comes back I'll be ready to eat."

Mama struggles to get herself up off the sectional but manages with the help of Wynona giving her a helping hand.

As Mama makes her way to the door she mumbles, "Black folks can't never be on time wit' nothin'.'"

Mama steps out. Faye and Rose step in.

"Hello, everyone," Faye says with such enthusiasm.

"Damn, she's a little too happy for me," Wynona says, sitting on the sectional with her ankles crossed and her nose scrunched up. Her dress looks like a tent on her big butt. She really needs to consider losing some weight. I'm sho' her heart hurts every day. Her hazel eyes look Faye up and down like she got an attitude with her, and she don't even know her. "What she take a happy pill or something. Come over here glowing and shit," says Wynona.

"Don't hate 'cause yo' light bulb don't glow no more. That's yo' man's fault not hers. Take that shit up wit' him not nobody else!" Says Clarice as she breaks into a big smile. She has a very attractive face, but her hair could stand to be combed. I understand she's trying to go natural and all but dang, those peas are crying for some moisturizer. She brushes a piece of lint off her Ashely Stewart black slacks as it lands on the hardwood floor.

Wynona stares Clarice down, then snaps. "Bitch, you don't know what the fuck still glows on me. Yo' big ass probably can't glow neither. Messin' wit' that younglin' like you can't find a man yo' own age. Desperate hoe!"

Clarice quickly jumps into defense mode. Her face contorts. "Don't you be talkin' about my man, you hears me! Keep him outta yo' mouth, fat bitch! You just jealous is all. Jealous 'cause Buster ain't handling his business wit' yo' big ass! I know he need a flashlight to find yo' stank pussy. Next time tell him to sniff. Then he won't have to work so hard."

Wynona puts her hand on her hefty hip and turns her oversized body slightly in Clarice direction.

"You raggedy ass, bitch! Yo' man! Ha! That nigga done fucked so many chicks in this here building alone and you ain't know shit. You walking around here all mighty and proud and shit. Smiling. H-Happy-go-lucky. And he done got finished fucking that chick down the hall from you. What's her name again? The pretty girl..." Wynona takes a moment to think, "That chick in 3J, ah, ah, Tabitha. That's her name. Tabitha."

As soon as Miss Murtha hears the name Tabitha her face turns beet red. She shakes in fury, then blurts out. "That slut! I should've cut that black bitch when I had the chance. She fucked my husband! That crackhead hooker fucked my husband!"

Everyone stops what they are doing when Miss Murtha goes off on her rampage.

Oh, no! I think. *Why, why, why, Miss Murtha?*

Wynona leans her hefty body over and whispers in Gabriella's ear, "Did she just call Tabitha a 'slut and black bitch'? Did she say she should've cut my goddaughter?"

Gabriella's perfectly arch brows knit and her full thick lips hardline as she nods her head.

Both Wynona and Gabriella give Miss Murtha the evil eye.

Lord, if looks could kill Miss Murtha would be dead right now.

Wynona immediately jumps to her wide feet and approaches Miss Murtha still seated on the swivel chair.

With her index finger she points it in Miss Murtha's face. "I ain't wanna put my goddaughter's business out there but— But you confused black bitch! I know you ain't talkin' 'bout my goddaughter. I just know you ain't sayin' what I think you is sayin' 'cause if you is, bitch, I'll fuckin' kill you my damn self. You musta forgotten where the fuck you is. You in the motherfuckin' 'hood. The ghetto. Keep talkin' that dumb shit. My goddaughter ain't nobody's crackhead hooker. She got herself a 'good man'. Talkin' mad shit. Why the fuck you here anyway? Let *you* tell it, you ain't black! Talkin' about cuttin' somebody. You lucky I don't fuck you up right now!"

Gabriella jumps up and grabs Wynona's meaty arm and tries to diffuse the situation, but Wynona is mad as hell.

Miss Murtha stretches her eyes as they bulge out of their sockets. Her thin lips hardline as she jerks her scrawny neck. She then blurts out, "She's a low-class ghetto whore, then! Just like you!"

"Ohhhhh, shittttttt!" Kellie-Wright, JoJo and Glory-Bee sing in unison.

Faye and Rose remain still in the kitchenette with faces of disbelief. I guess they never experienced this kind of drama before. I hope Faye is not offended by Wynona calling Miss Murtha such degrading names. But telling by the scowl on her face...she is.

Rose just looks appalled by Miss Murtha talking about cutting. Her face expresses shock, empathy, execution. Especially her greenish-gray eyes.

I scurry into the living room before it becomes a fighting match or worse a bloodbath. I knew this would happen, I say to myself, but I figured after we all ate. I should've known better than to think that a room full of women could get along.

I try to calm Miss Murtha down but it ain't easy. She is furious. Her face is red as the color, especially her cheeks and neck.

I hand Miss Murtha a glass of Pinot in hopes that she will take it and shut the hell up before she says too much more and starts a fight up in here. I don't need her and Wynona getting into it. They've said enough.

In comes Mama.

Her big eyes look everyone over. "What's going on? Why y'all lookin' evil as aw hell? What I miss?"

No one utters a word.

The tension is already thick enough. I don't need Mama adding lighter fluid to the fire.

Buzz! Buzz!

Saved by the buzzer. I think.

I make my way to the intercom. "Who is it?"

"Nell."

"Hey, girl," I say in a chipper tone of voice. "Come up." I buzz her in, then give her a few to get upstairs by way of the elevator or stairs and tap on the door.

I don't know how but all the ladies find themselves engaging in conversation again.

I look up at the ceiling and whisper, "Thank you, Lord."

Tap. Tap. Tap.

I rush to open the door with a sigh of relief on my face.

"Chile, I never thought you'd ever get here." I say to Danell.

Danell steps in with a perplex look on her face. "Is something wrong?"

I sigh. "Not anymore. It was getting a little crazy in here. Now that you're here I guess this is the best time to eat. Calm these ladies' down."

I take it upon myself to introduce Danell. "Everyone this is my friend, Danell. Danell, seated on the sectional is: Wynona, Clarice, Mama and Gabriella. Over on the throw pillows is: Kellie-Wright, JoJo, and Glory-Bee. And lastly, seated on the swivel chair is Miss Murtha."

"Nice to meet you all," says Danell, as she turns around and is greeted by Faye and Rose.

"Oh, dang," I say aloud, "And this is, Faye. She is a terrific caterer. And this is Rose, the videographer. Sorry ladies, I got sidetracked."

"No problem, Avery," Rose says, then smiles.

Faye extends out her hand to Danell. "Nice to meet you, Danell." Danell extends her hand and they shake.

The buzzer goes off.

I scurry to answer it.

"Who is it?"

The female voice replies, "Us."

"Us" can only be: Minerva Weaver, Wyndow Pain, Burn Bentley, Maxine Stiles, and Soothe-the-Weary Soul. Otherwise known as: *Women as the Faces of Broken Silence.*

Immediately I can feel Miss Murtha's eyes burning in my skin.

I turn in Miss Murtha's direction and nod my head.

There is a tap at the door.

I go to answer it with a huge smile painted on my face.

"We made it, chile." Minerva says, both of her hands planted on her lower back.

"Was it a long ride?" I ask.

"No. Traffic." Maxine says. "We had to keep stopping to find a restroom because *somebody* had to keep going to the bathroom."

"Look!" Burn snorts. "I had to pee."

They all blurt out. "Five times!"

I hang up their purses and invite them to have a seat.

"Everyone this is: Wyndow, Minerva, Burn, Maxine and Soothe. How about you ladies introduce yourselves while I finish getting things ready."

"Hi, I'm Clarice."

"How do you do? I'm Murtha."

"I'm Wynona."

"I'm JoJo."

"I'm Kellie-Wright. Nice to meet you all."

"I'm Mama."

"I'm Glory-Bee."

"I'm Gabriella."

"I'm Rose."

"Danell. Glad you came, ladies."

"Faye. It is a pleasure to meet you all. Please. Make yourselves comfortable. Would you like a drink?"

All the ladies nod their heads.

"What would you like? We have soda, water, cognac, wine: red and white."

"Just show us where it is, Faye," Soothe says, we can get it ourselves. You look pretty busy."

"It's no problem, ladies," Faye says.

"We appreciate it, but we're ok." Maxine insists with a warm smile on her face.

"Ok, well, all the beverages are in the large ice bucket next to the refrigerator, ladies. Help yourself."

"How long have you and Avery been friends, Danell?" Faye asks, as she reaches for some utensils and finishes setting the table.

"Oh, for over a year now. Right, Av?"

Rose takes it upon herself to place the plates and napkins.

"Yep."

"Well, Av, what do you need me to do?" Danell asks.

"Hmm. Nothing but sit and relax. I'm sho' you had a hard day at work dealing with patients all day."

"Sure have. But that has nothing to do with lending a helping hand, girl. Everything looks so lovely. You've been up all night and day preparing this, huh?"

"Yeah. I want everyone to just unwind. Take a load off, you know."

"I hear yah. Well, I'ma go over here and mingle with the ladies to get acquainted." Danell says, as she slips out of her suit jacket, and hangs it on a hanger in the guest closet.

"Would you like a drink?" Faye asks Danell.

"Sure. I'll have a glass of Chardonnay, please?"

"Sure," Faye says, jubilantly.

Danell takes a seat on the sectional next to Gabriella with glass in hand.

After lighting the last Blacker the Berry Sweeter the Juice candle I say, "Ladies, would you please make your way to the bathroom to wash your hands, and then to the long, black wooden dinner table."

Everyone rises to their feet and forms a line toward the bathroom to wash their hands. As the ladies exit one by one I hand them a paper towel to dry their hands, then escort them to their assigned seats as I grab the CD remote and play a rotation of jazz favorites starting with bassist Charles Mingus's, "Moanin'" and "Goodbye Pork Pie Hat" to set the mood during dinner.

Last night I planned the seating arrangement based on personality. I don't know these ladies all that well but the little I do know helped me decide whom to sit next to whom.

At the head of the table seated me, then Danell to my left. Next to Danell is Wynona, then Minerva, then Gabriella, then Kellie-Wright, then Glory-Bee, then JoJo, then Wyndow Pain, and then Burn. To my right seated Faye, then Clarice, then Miss Murtha, then Maxine, then Soothe, then Mama, and then Rose. I have two seats left which is for Country and Blessive but *they* have yet to arrive.

"Faye, would you like to do the honor of saying grace." Faye bows her head and closes her eyes. "Ladies, bow your head, close your eyes, and join hands, please?"

Faye takes Danell and my hand, then continues, "Father. Oh, wonderful Father God, we are here before this beautiful array of food that our friend, Avery, has nurtured over. Let us enjoy this moment, this special day, as we join in sisterhood and feast off of the love and diligence that Avery has so generously placed in this meal. A meal that we are about to partake in. Nourish us, cleanse our minds, and open us up to love one another as You love us all. Amen."

Everyone sings in unison, "Amen."

Looking around at everyone, I don't know *why* but it's something about *food* that brings folks together.

Jazz trumpeter, Chet Baker's chimes in with his "Almost Blue" as we are nearly finished feasting ourselves sick. Saxophonist John Coltrane's "In A Sentimental Mood" followed by Miles Davis's on Tenor saxophone, "I Fall in Love Too Easily" followed by Nina Simone's "Ain't Got No, I Got Life."

As Nina begins to sing the buzzer goes off as we are in the middle of indulging in dessert.

I stand to answer it. "Who is it?"

"Coun—try." She says in a weak breath.

Instead of me buzzing the intercom I rush out the door and down the stairs to meet her. That something odd hit me hard in my chest.

Once on the ground floor, I see Country lent against the lobby wall, gasping for air. Bloody.

Immediately I rush to her aid. Steadily I guide her through the door, onto the elevator, and to my apartment.

The sight of her is beyond words.

As we enter my apartment everyone turns in our direction and gasps.

Country nearly on her last leg hears the voice of Nina Simone and sings along but making the song her own.

Country gently pushes me away. Raises her bruised arms up as if surrendering and blurts out, *"Ain't got no home, ain't got no pride, ain't got no shame, I ain't*

302

got no mo' in me to blame, I ain't got pity, I ain't got no pennies, ain't got no panties just big grandma drawers, I ain't no color, ain't got no mama, ain't got no poppa no mo', ain't got no business, ain't got no heart, 'cause my man tore it apart..."

Country then drops in my arms as if a bloody ragdoll.

The emotion in the room is silent. Not a word, not a peep. Everyone is in complete awe.

Rose takes her position and focuses in on the here and now. She grabs her video camera. Then zooms in on Country. I follow suit as I know this is the moment to share.

All of us ladies help Country to a comfortable chair. I immediately tell Faye to call 911. But Country yells, "Noooo! Not until I do what I came here to do."

I say, "Country you might be bleeding internally. I think you should go to the hospital. This-This can wait."

Country gives me a dead stare. It sends chills up my spine.

"Ms. Love, huh, today is my day to resound. I want women's, all sorts of women's to hear me. See me. See what 'hard lovin' done to me. Don'tchu know, Avery, I am your awakening. Betcha ain't know this, though." Country looks around the apartment. The colorful display of life, art, woman, poetry, ancestry, modern, eclectic style. She looks me in the eyes, I see warmth spilling over. Running down her face like riverbanks. "You sho' has a lovely place. Everything in it tells a story. Sorta like mine. Only difference is yours is much mo' inviting than mine. Each room in my house got memories, bad memories. Each room screams violent screams. Death is splattered on the walls. In the cracks of the floor. On the ceiling. Windows. Doors. I ain't never had a happy home. Calm. Not even as a chile, you know. Internal bleeding. Chile, I've been bleeding damned near all of my existence. I've been a punching bag most of my marriage. I witnessed my mama getting her ass kicked. She dead now. Been dead for some time now. Murdered by my fa—her husband. Can't say it ain't hereditary because my only chile refused to get beaten by a man. Because of fear, low self-esteem, my dependency on him—I allowed this to happen to me. But, no mo'."

Rose nods her head and begins to setup.

Within a couple of minutes Rose has her camera facing Country. The background of the wide window with the Lucky Bamboo plant set in the windowsill, still growing strong and tall.

Country swallows and winces as if the inside of her throat is swollen. She tastes the bloody saliva and makes a wrinkly expression on her face.

"Talk, my sistah." Rose motions her lips to say to Country. And as Rose does fear is written all over Country's face, but she doesn't remove herself from the chair. She doesn't run for cover. Or disguise herself with a wig. Or blacken herself as a silhouette. She reveals her truth.

Country blinks, then squints, and says in a raspy voice, "Sistahs from the 'Hood of Hard Lovin'"…Women's of America…that sistah, that woman that I am talkin' about is… *me*: Country Billow-Martinez. Look at what it *looks* like. Look at me!"

On cue Rose zooms in to give the viewers an eyeful.

Country continues, "Can you see? Can you really see what this has done to me? Look at me! Busted eyes, *broken* jaw, missing teeth, *broken* nose, *broken* ribs, *broken* heart, *broken* marriage, *broken* life, *broken* woman. Do you hear what it sounds like? Listen to me! Listen to how my voice sounds. Shaky, crackling voice. Look at how it looks back at you. Look inside yourself! W-Wondering, w-w-w-w-wishing, and ho-ping to see another day." She pauses, then coughs as her quivering hand reaches for a paper napkin off the coffee table and makes a spitting sound. Ripe blood bleeds through the napkin like watercolors on construction paper.

Everyone remains quiet, still as statues, while Country continues, "This is my testimony.

46 Knows

'I took 46 blows
'For every NO!
'I wailed
'For every fib I told
'For every chokehold!
'Every kick!
'Every punch!
For every: fuck you, black bitch!
For every: you piece of raggedy black shit!
Go cook me somethin' to eat and make it quick.
Now come suck my dick!

'I took 46 blows
'One to the nose
'Then eyes
'One for every lie
'I cried, 45 times
'Like I had committed 44 crimes
'In my lifetime.

'I took 46 blows
'For the lies he told
'Bleached everything pearly white
'Oh, he was a sight
'For sore eyes
'I clenched my might
'Realll tight
"Cause, I began to not know
'43, her became unsure
'What would come of 42?
'41?

'I took 46 blows
'To hear the wind

'The sound of pounds
'T-That did me in
'Time and time again
'40, she was on her way out
'SHOUTING, SCREAMING, WAILING, SWINGING,
'KICKING, BITING, HIDING,
'SOBBING, SLOBBERING, CLAWING,
'CRAWLING HER WAY OUT!
'39, she managed to get away
'Strayed far away from misery
'Met her mate at 38
'Oh, they were very much in love
'But tragedy struck
'37, she was like: what da fuck!!
'And 36, they became chummy
'35, 34, 32, 31...life tasted so dang yummy
'But then 30,
'She took that blow
'Nearly blinded her so
'He was stone-cold to the bone
'Dared her not to leave him alone
'29, she was prone to the bullshit
'When he cracked that whip
'Her jumped sooooo high
'Nearly broke her hip
'When he pulled back that clip
'His intention was to shoot her
'Right between the eyes
'28, she nearly died
'27, 26, 25, they all were chastised, minimized
'It was just a matter of time
'24, she was the whore
'The one who took it as it came
'There was no shame
'In her game
'Till
'Not till, 23
'When she bowed down on her knees

'Praised him with her please
'22, she was undone
'Fit to be tied
'Fit to be tied
'Her vowed to keep her sanity and pride
'21, 20, well, he beat the pride out of 'em
'Over and over and over again
'You'd hear the bed squeak
'Hear the moans and groans
'It was not music to their ears
'Shortly after, 20, she disappeared
'19, 18, 17, they tried to find her
'But 16, 16 knew her was down under
'Sleeping peacefully
'15, 14, 13, they could only dream
'To not live that scene of misery
'But 12, she took it hard
'Nightmares told the tale
'Of how pain took ahold
'Ran cold through 11's soul
'But 10, 9, 8, 7, 6, they knew what to do
'Keep 5's mouth shut
'4, Wake up!
'3, 2, 1, they had 'em run
'Run as far away as they could.

'Yes, I took 46 blows
'Till I couldn't take it no mo'...

'I guess you're wondering what happened to 33
'Well, lemme see
'33, she was the one that convinced me
'To set my soul free
'To not live in fear
'Breathe sistah breathe
'Live sistah live."

307

Chapter
Thirty-Four

Avery

I think to call Desyre. I want to call. I do. Instead I go and open the fridge and grab the pack of Hillshire Farm Cheddar Wurst smoked sausage. Open the cupboard and reach for a small pot, add some cold water in it, place in one sausage, then place the pot on the stove under a low heat to simmer.

Desyre scares me. He's too right. Too on point. I guess I'm wondering if he has flaws. Everyone has flaws. No one person is perfect in this world. Possibly he has dark secrets that he hasn't shared with me. Skeletons in his closet, too.

Would it make a difference if he did? Probably.

I just feel so lost lately. And I don't want to mess things up by falling for this guy. Bottom-line. I don't want to hurt anymore. I don't want to stress over a man. I mean, once I divulge the truth to Desyre I feel like everything may change. He may change. Truthfully I'm beyond terrified. I'm unequivocally scared.

It was different with all the *other* men. Deep down I hoped for the best outcome but a small part of me kind of knew that I would end up alone. I guess that small part of me hoped to be wrong. I hoped for at least one of those men to prove me wrong and make an honest woman out of me by showering me with his love and affection. But all I got back was grief. Heartache and grief and a bad reputation.

Maybe I'm jumping ahead of myself by thinking that Desyre might want more from me—more than I am currently willing to give. Having a man in my life might complicate things. And complications is not something I want right now. I'm just beginning to find love.

Tap. Tap. Tap.

Startled by the tapping on my door. I yell out. "Who is it?"

"Desyre."

I stand still. Not sho' what to do. *Avery, go and open the door, I hear Karma say.* So I do. "What brings you here? How did you—?"

"A nice old lady let me in."

"You should've called first. Look at me, I'm a mess. Give me a minute to change."

"I started to call you, but then my phone died. I forgot and left my charger at home. I was in the area so I figured I'd take a chance and see if you were home. But you're right, next time I will call first. You don't need to change. You look fine in that long T-shirt."

"I'm sorry I snapped at you." I say with a look of mortified on my face. "I've been on edge lately, but it gives me no right or reason to take it out on you."

"We all have our days. Apology accepted."

"Is there something wrong?" I ask.

"I just needed to see you. There is something I need to say to you."

You too, I think to myself, *Well, I guess I might as well take this opportunity to share too.*

I raise up both of my hands. "Before you go any further, Desyre, I need to tell you something."

He gives me this puzzling look. "Avery, um, it's taken me a long time to come to this point in my life, so please, let me say what I've come to say."

Man, does he look good in those sweat pants and T-shirt. With his dreads dangling down the sides of his face—makes me want to leap on top of him. Deep breaths, Avery.

I nod. "Okay. Say what you came to say. I'm all ears."

Desyre's eyes pierce mine. "It was me."

"What do you mean, *it was you*? What are you talking about?"

"I called 911."

"I'm not following you. What are you saying?"

"That evening. I nearly hit you with my car. I called 911, then left the scene."

The contortion on my face stresses skepticism. "It was *you*?"

"It was me."

"Why?" I ask baffled. Instantly my brows knit. "Why did *you* leave me?"

"I saw you that day. And it scared me. I felt helpless. I felt like I didn't want to be considered a suspect. Just because you are doing something right doesn't mean that it will all turn out right, Avery. People get labeled all the time. Black man, dreadlocks, blue jeans and a hoodie. There are enough falsely accused black men in prison based off of one person's words: 'It was him'. I didn't want to take a chance and I find myself in an awkward situation. So I called 911 and left. I'm sorry."

I drop my head and stare at the floor. "Soooo, I take it you already know about me."

Desyre sighs. "Yes, I know. People talk. But I knew you being the woman that you are you'd tell me in your own time. Avery, ever since that day I never forgot about you. I felt a connection with you that day. And I still do. Often I wondered what I would say to you should I ever see you again. Well, I'm looking at you and I came here to say... I want to care for you in a way that you haven't been cared for. I want to love you in a way that you haven't been loved. Protect you with all the might I have in me. I want to give you all of me; mind, body, and soul."

I lift my head up as tears rush down my face. "But I'm—I have—"

"You have, what? Let me tell you what you have, woman."

I remain silent.

Desyre reaches for both of my hands. God, he feels so warm. And when he looks me in my eyes I feel his spirit. Literally. He massages my long fingers, and then he says, "Ms. Avery Love, you have a heart, soul, and a beautiful spirit. I don't have a lot. I'm not one of those Wall Street guys with briefcase and fat wallets and overpriced suits. I'm just an average guy with average money. But I promise you if you will allow me the honor of loving you. I'll love you from your hair follicles to your painted toe nails. I'll love you, woman, *you.*"

Dang! What is a woman to say after a man professes himself in this manner. I think to myself.

Well, this woman—this jacked-up sistah from Paterson, says, "Yes! I'm ready to be loved, but—" I pause, then sniff in the aroma of sausage.

"But what, Avery?"

Quickly I place my hands up to my mouth and dash for the bathroom.

Desyre follows me. "What's wrong, Avery? Talk to me? Tell me?"

With my head leaned over in the toilet bowl and the sound of what is coming out of my mouth—pretty much says what's wrong.

Desyre reaches for the burgundy washcloth off the rack and drenches it with water. He wrings it tightly, then kneels down on both knees and places the cool cloth on the nape of my neck.

I shut my eyes. *God, I am so embarrassed.*

"Get it all out," Desyre says, while gently stroking my back.

311

I think to myself. *God, he is so beautiful—inside and out.*

After puking up what was once breakfast, I remove my head from the toilet bowl, but remain on my knees. I can't seem to face him.

Desyre strokes the back of my head. "Look at me," he asks in a gentle tone.

Slowly I turn in his direction—keep my head bowed.

"Look at me, Avery?" I lift up my head and look him directly in his eyes. He takes me in his arms and holds me so lovingly. He then whispers in my ear. "Do you love him?"

I whisper back. "No. He doesn't even know. Doesn't care to know. I tried numerous times to try to get him to come over so that we could talk but..."

He looks me in my face, then smiles. "So, you're with child. A child needs a father."

My eyes spread. Forehead softens. "What are you saying?"

"I'm saying, I love you. I'm saying I am madly in love with you, Avery. I'm saying that we (you and me) will love this child just as much as we love each other. You do love me, don't you?"

I smile, cry, smile. "You are everything I anticipated you to be. And I pray that I am every bit of the woman you anticipate me to be. I'm so confused. The thought of me being a mother is mind-blowing. Me taking care of someone so dependent on me. I'm scared, Desyre. I guess I need to say the words out loud. Loud enough for you to hear. Not only was I raped. I contracted HIV, too. So you see being in a relationship with me won't be easy. I don't want to disappoint you. Mislead you. Dr. Fulmore and I discussed different ways a pregnant woman can transmit HIV: during pregnancy, during vaginal childbirth, and through breastfeeding. He prescribed me ART, which is supposed to reduce the amount of HIV in my body to an undetectable level. He called it, um, undetectable viral load. It sounds so complex. He said if I take ART during pregnancy, labor, and delivery I should have a healthy baby. But I have to make sho' I continue on my regimen of medications too." I look him in his eyes, "And for the record, yes, Desyre, I do love you. And no, I'm not just saying this because of my situation."

"You have every right to be scared. You have a miracle growing inside of you. I'm not afraid of you, Avery. I want you to believe that I want to be here with you. If that man doesn't want to be a part of this. That's on him. You tried to let him know. Maybe you should give it one last try." Desyre hands me his cell phone. "I'm not going anywhere. I'm here. Right here."

My hands tremble as I take his cell phone. I press the ten digits. He answers five rings in. "Hello?"

"Hi, it's Avery. Um, I just called to tell you that—that I'm pregnant."

"Well, I'm not the father, so don't be calling me." Click!

I hand Desyre back his cell phone, then place my head on his shoulder and sob. "Shhh." Desyre says while caressing my back. "It's okay, baby. We have each other."

"It's not that simple, Desyre. I'm carrying another man's baby. A man that wants nothing to do with me or our child. He won't even take the time to talk to me. Everything is so messed up."

"I disagree. I believe that God reunited us for a reason. Years have gone by and we have never ran into each other. Years, Avery. This moment is a defining moment. If we let it slip away we will never know what will come of it. I don't want to keep dreaming about you. I want to hold you, kiss you, love you now, woman. Now. Let me love you, now?"

In between my sniffling all I can do is look this beautiful man in his eyes and say, "I'm so ready for love, but I'm scared of losing in the end."

"You have no control over what God chooses, Avery. All you can do is live—live and love life while it exists."

"I don't want you to feel obligated because of what happened to me years ago. I don't want guilt to be your reason for wanting to be with me."

"It's not. Believe me. I have seen you in my dreams from that day. And it has haunted me. You and I have been through so much in our lives. I know you don't know my story, but soon you will. I knew that I loved you when you stepped foot in my cab. I felt it. And that feeling has not drifted. It is still here. Here in my heart, Avery." Desyre takes my hand and presses it against his chest. "Feel the power of love."

The End

Jacked-Up Sistah

I woke up this morning with a frown upon my face
Wondered why God didn't just let me
Sleep my high away
Wondered why God breathed life back into me
I was definitely a piece of work
I'd stomp, scream and yell
Scolded my child and wished her to hell
Called my own mama out her name
Told my baby daddy he ain't worth two pennies
Rubbed together
And wondered why he ain't buy me anymore nice things
Told my best friend she ain't nothing but a slut
And her daddy ain't nothing but a fuck-up
And I wondered why she never called me back
Treated my own sister like a stepchild
Said some mean and nasty things to my neighbor
Across the hall
Even told the mailman off… just because
Snapped at the cashier at the grocery store
'Cause she was tryna be slick like she forgot
To give me back my change and shit
Was about to duke it out with a total stranger
'Cause she was all up in my face
Minding my business
After a day like that
I still wasn't done
Something was still gnawing at me
So I cussed this homeless lady out
Because she was getting on my last nerve
Didn't know her from a can of paint
Or her circumstance
Just wanted her to shut the fuck up with all her ranting
and raving like she was fuckin' crazy

315

I sighed, feeling exhausted from my day
Came home and I ain't have nothing to say
Seemed I said it all on the way
Got home about a quarter to eight
But my mind wasn't rested
Couldn't figure out what was going on with me
Just seemed so angry
Day after day
My mood-swings didn't change
My attitude only worsened
Hardly anyone wanted to be around me
Yet for some reason I couldn't understand why
But then, I revisited my steps
Tripped over my right foot instead of my left
I seemed baffled
Couldn't decipher how my life got so messy
*Called my aunt Essie but even she ain't have no time for
me*
*Called my girlfriend Betsy and she just breathed on the
other end of the phone*
*Called my cousin Caroline, she hit the ignore button and
wouldn't accept my call*
Found myself at a dead-end
Felt a bit hopeless, you know
Told myself that I didn't care
Told myself that life was not fair
Told myself that soon death is near
If I don't stop stressing
But I never addressed the truth
Truth
Truth
Truth
Okay, fuck it!
Told myself to chill before I lose my cool
Too late, I've already done that
Back to back to back
Found myself alone for real
Was like, wtf, what's the deal!

Of course I knew I needed to chill
But I was too headstrong
Thought I knew it all
But in actuality I ain't know shit
Just was so use to catchin' a hissy fit
When things didn't go my way
Somehow I'd forgotten that I wasn't holding my own
Huh, my man used to say, "J.S., I like a strong woman.
It takes two to make it nowadays. Don't wanna drag you
around. I like a woman that can walk beside me."
Well, I told that nigga to go to hell
With that sentimental bullshit
And he did
He was gone the next day
But not from drugs
Seemed his heart stopped
When I stopped caring
I had long relinquished my grip
Got caught-up
Said the hell with this muthafuckin' shit!
I needed to get high
And just do me
So that's exactly what I did
But even me, didn't get my drift
Yeah, I was losing it for real
Funny thing is
Salvation opened its door
But by then I'd done some things
Sold my body to support my habit
Got comfortable with it
But Salvation kept calling me back
I said, fuck that bitch!
She told me to just wait and see
See, if I bump into Now-Later
See, how much progress I'd make
If I just surrender
I stuck my middle finger up at her
Said, "Go catch a clue, bitch!

Nobody wanna hear that dumb shit!"
But then a funny thing happened
Not funny as in ha-ha
That bitch Now-Later had relapsed
I was like, "Ohhhh, shitttt!"
How the hell this bitch trip up? Slip up?
Two? That's who...
Two, he did her dirty
I was like, "Dammmmmmmn, that's fucked up!"
'Cause Two was s'posed to be her boo
But she soon found out that that shit wasn't true
Now what she gon' do?
I don't know but it bothered me
I was like, "Damn, girl, you was on your way
And you let that nigga trap you
Whatchu gon' do?"
She looked at me, looked me up and down
She rotated her neck, then said, "Whatchu gonna do?"
I was like, "Whoa, bitch! I came to your rescue!"
She snickered right in my face
That got me pissed
I was like, "Bitch, fuck you!"
She said, "Fuck you, too, dirty bitch!
You ain't no betta than me
You just ain't stopped to see
That we are both strung out.
At least I know ...I'ma hoe
You don't
Walkin' around here like you God's gift
Lookin' like walkin' death
That shit ain't even pretty
Done lost your ass and your titties
Girlllll... bye!
I bet you got that shit!
That shit, that's right that shit!
So don't flatter yourself by coming to my rescue
You need to save yourself
Stop worrying about everybody else

Fuckin' trick!'"
Those were fighting words to me
I wanted to stomp that bitch!
But for some reason I wasn't in the mood to fight
Now-Later, she hit the nail on the head
She was right
Her words bit into me
Deeply
It must've been my lucky day
'Cause maybe six months later I was on my way
My way on this path to recovery
Drugs, they sure had a hold on me
Had me actin' a fool, I must say
But today it is a bright and brand new day
Even with death on its way
I had a full-blown awakening
Yep. AIDS
But, I'm okay
I'm still here to say
Say my right from wrong
Just think of this as a notecard
A notecard that reads:
"J.S., I like a strong woman. It take two to make it
nowadays. Don't wanna drag you around. I like a
woman that can walk beside me."
Yeah, that's what my man used to say
Funny how he knew my fate
I appreciate that fact that he cared
Just wished he was still here
Here to see
Who I've become
That strong woman
That strong one.

—Karla Denise Baker

About the Author

Ms. KARLA DENISE BAKER

Born and raised in Paterson, New Jersey, Karla Denise Baker fell hopelessly in love with poetry at the young age of 10. With a small voice, the novice poet expressed deep views of her own bleak upbringing through the written-word. Her purpose was to heal her inner woes.

It wasn't until April, 2008, that her voice spoke with conviction. Inquiring minds began to listen to what the young woman had to say.

It took nearly two years for the novice writer to complete her first manuscript, *Anonymous*. Birthing her protagonist Avery Love did not take much effort because it all came to her in a vivid dream. Hearing the voice of a woman, feeling her agony, and listening to her tell her story is all that Karla can explain.

A voice roused her out of her sleep and this mid-thirty year old African-American woman told her tale with such delivery that Karla had no recourse but to express empathy.

After submitting *Anonymous* to 30 literary agents and receiving 30 rejection letters of: *Not Interested*.

Karla took a leap of faith and self-published her first novel under her imprint: *The Write Message*.

The story began with Avery residing in Paterson, New Jersey. Was it by coincidence? Others assumed otherwise.

The story goes as follows:

Working as a paralegal for Bruman & Prescott Law firm in lower Manhattan, Avery was returning to Paterson.

It was a nippy evening on January 9, 2000, when Avery arrived back in Paterson. She walked the downtown street of Broadway heading for the parking lot on West Broadway. Suddenly, a predator lurked from a dark alley and dragged her to the back of an Electronics store. She was brutally raped and savagely beaten.

Maybe a year later, Avery makes an appointment to her primary doctor for a routine check-up.

A sunny day in July, Avery revisits Dr. Fulmore. It was then that he revealed her results. HIV-positive.

The whirlwind of Avery's tale put the writer/author under scrutiny. With so much to gain and nothing to lose, Karla penned a sequel, *Sleepin' Wit' the Virus* and continued to write the pages to Avery's life.

"People questioned other people about me. Is this a self-portrait of her true life?" Karla explained. "It was maddening. I felt spotlighted everywhere I went. I had to ask myself: 'Did it really make a difference?' I mean, the damage was already done. Nothing could be changed to undo what had happened.

"I submitted my manuscript *SWtV* to a literary agent in New York and she basically stated that the story was interesting but that she didn't know how to market it. That baffled me. Why? Because the protagonist is HIV-positive? She never elaborated on why, but it really got me to thinking. HIV exists. People have it. People are still having sex with it. People are still in denial of having it and are not always using contraceptives. And people are not being truthful about having it. People are living with it and dying because of it. There is an epidemic for a reason. I don't understand how this subject matter is not marketable? What? Love and HIV don't go hand in hand? Please. People fall in love with HIV. People get married with HIV. People have hardships, drama, and crisis living with HIV. So why can't I (the black chick from the 'hood) write a fictitious story about a woman inflicted with it but not base every aspect of her life on it.

"Before the rape Avery was just an everyday ordinary woman. People labeled her because of the disease. That really got to me. I took it personal, you know.

"If it takes this to get folks to read then it's worth the stigma that is attached to it. Seems people focus more on the HIV than her being raped anyway. That gave me even more of a push to allow her voice to be heard with book after book after book. I guess you could say I became obsessed looking toward Avery for closure of my own inner pain.

"Kreepin' Wit' the Virus, Trickin' Wit' the Virus and *Jacked-Up Sistah* are continuations of Avery Love's life."

The promising author went on to say, "Yes, yes, yesss! I am very proud of what I've created from this mind of mine. I have nothing to hide. Dang, sho' can't hide behind my hair because I'm practically bald," she chuckles. "This is a time for women to care about their well-being. To care about themselves. I cannot voice that enough. Hey, I've made plenty, plenty, plenty of mistakes when it came to men. But in each I've learned something new, something different. Something that told me to care about myself.

"Whether HIV or not, women have to start taking precautions. Women have to stop making excuses and depending on men to provide them with happiness. Women have to step-up to the plate and realize that self-happiness, self-love, self-motivation, self-sufficiency, and self-contentment will provide them with the essentials to have a better quality of life. Women have to learn to put themselves first."